CURSED: BOUND

CURSED: BOUND

BOOK TWO

X. Aratare

RAYTHE REIGN PUBLISHING, INC.

CURSED: BOUND—BOOK 2

Tiger-shifter, Lord Bane Dunsaney, released Nick Fairfax from the deal that bound the young man to his service for a year. Then Bane fled, afraid that the beast inside of him would harm Nick if he stayed. He never thought to see Nick again.

Little did Bane know, Nick has chosen to stay at his estate, Moon Shadow, to await the return of the lord who has his heart.

But can lasting love survive when there are tiger-sized secrets between them?

Book 2 of our modern, M/M retelling of Beauty & The Beast.

Cursed: Bound is the second part of a 3-book series. Part 3 is coming out in 2017.

After fleeing his uncontrollable attraction to Nick, Bane never dreamed that Nick would be in his life again. But when the billionaire returns to his estate, he finds Nick waiting for him with open arms.

Bane realizes he has a second chance with Nick. To be worthy of him, Bane wants to become a better man, but their developing romance is overshadowed by his most dangerous secret: Bane is a cursed tiger-shifter, and the beast stirs every time they start to become intimate.

Bane is disturbed by how the tiger wants Nick as a *mate*, but he finds himself unable to control his possessiveness, especially as Nick ventures out of Moon Shadow and sees the darker aspects of Bane's life.

And, as a man deeply betrayed by his own father, Bane struggles to understand why Nick won't abandon the family who treated him so badly...

Cursed: Bound ends on a cliff-hanger, which will be resolved in Book 3, Cursed: Beloved (2017.)

CHAPTER ONE

CURSED

Over one hundred years ago in India during the British Raj ...

Lord Bane Dunsaney stood over the fallen white Bengal tiger with his rifle slung over his shoulder. The tiger had collapsed on its side by the watering hole. It 2s startlingly blue eyes were closed forever.

Bane sank down onto his haunches beside the beast. He laid his rifle on the damp ground and placed a hand on the beast's side. The fur was so *soft*. He gripped and released it several times, relishing the feel of it sliding through his fingers. He almost wanted to lean down and rub his cheek against it.

"Tarun, it's done," Bane called over his shoulder to his servant. The man had remained where they had taken cover until Bane confirmed the kill. "Not as much sport as I'd hoped, but the beast is magnificent all the same. I will have it turned into a rug and put it in a place of honor. Not even Father can claim it isn't a worthy trophy." When Tarun did not answer him, Bane turned around, frowning. His frown turned to shock. His servant was surrounded by other Indians. "Who are you people?! Release my servant immediately!"

There were over half a dozen of men, all carrying daggers, standing a dozen feet away with Tarun frozen in the center of them. Two of the men held daggers to Tarun's throat. Bane noted that the men were swathed in robes of white with black stripes.

Like the tiger, Bane realized and swallowed. He had a feeling he knew who these people were and why they were here. *These are Jalal's people. I've killed their sacred tiger and they want revenge.*

Jalal had also been his servant. The man had warned him not to hunt this particular tiger claiming the beast housed the spirit of *all* tigers. Bane had scoffed at his words. He had tried to send the man back to his estate, but Jalal had disappeared into the steamy jungle without a trace.

To run back to his people and tell them what I intended to do. Though I do not see him here. Hiding out of sight, perhaps? The coward!

This story about tiger spirits was ridiculous. It was just some scheme to get money out of hunters. He likely needed to have paid these villagers in advance to hunt on their land. Bane's jaw clenched. Now he would have to somehow appease these people without Tarun or himself being harmed.

Bane met Tarun's eyes and tried to calm him with a look. Tarun swallowed nervously. His nostrils flared like that of a horse that wanted to bolt, but his servant held himself very still. The blades of the daggers were so sharp that they had drawn blood simply by being pressed against his skin. A thin trickle of crimson ran down Tarun's neck to pool in the hollow of his throat.

Bane considered going for his rifle. But in the time it would take him to reach it, bring it up and sight one of their attackers, Tarun's throat would be slit and likely one of those daggers would be stuck in Bane's chest. So no fighting them. He had to talk or bribe their way out of this. Again, he cursed his luck.

"I am the son of Lord Richard Dunsaney. My name is Bane. Tarun is my man. You would be wise to release both of us now and this will be forgotten," Bane intoned. He wondered if they even knew English, yet he had no choice but to speak it. He did not know the language of these local tribes. They were so small, so isolated, that it had never mattered enough before to learn.

Until now.

At that moment, a wizened old woman emerged from the jungle. She, too, was swathed in the white and black striped material, but her forearms were bare. They were as thin and brown as old sticks. It seemed to him that a strong wind could snap her in two. Her face was impossibly wizened. The creases were so deep that her features were nearly swallowed by them. Bane guessed that she was the elder of the village. If he could reason with her then she might let them go.

"Madam, we have not been introduced, but I am ..." Bane let the sentence drop as the old woman tottered past him.

He turned to see what she was doing. She grunted with obvious effort as she crouched down by the tiger's body. She had a tiger amulet around her neck. She clutched at that with one bony hand while the other touched the tiger's head. Her eyes, which were as black as the onyx stripes on the tiger's coat, closed as she murmured a prayer. He couldn't understand the language, but it was clear from her tone and attitude that she was praying. He waited for her prayer to be over before he spoke again.

"You have no right to hold my man," Bane said firmly, hoping that someone in the village would translate what he said to her. "I was the one to kill the beast. Not him. Release him and we can discuss this as rational human beings. You ..."

Her eyes opened and his voice failed him. She lifted her head until they were gazing into each other's eyes. Shock flooded him when she spoke to him in perfect English then, "You know what you have done."

"I've killed a beast. An *animal*. I have done nothing wrong. Nor has my man, Tarun," Bane's voice seemed too loud. He noticed that there were no other sounds. No insects whirring. No birds cawing. Nothing at all.

The hand that she had been resting on the tiger's head she placed into the mud by the pool. "The spirit needs a place to dwell. You must provide that place as you have stolen its form."

Bane opened his mouth to laugh and deride this superstitious nonsense, but then he thought that if he agreed to do whatever she wanted then he and Tarun could go. But then he saw the mud around her hand begin to *bubble*. Steam rose up from where her hand was completely submerged in the mud.

"Bloody hell, what—what is going on?" he gasped.

"You must provide the spirit a home. You have stolen a life. You must give yours," she said, which did not answer his question at all.

Bane tried to back away, but, suddenly, he was surrounded by four of the villagers. Though they were scrawny and much smaller than he was they were able to drag him down to his knees and pin his arms behind his back. Two daggers were then held to his throat. He felt the prick of their points against his skin and smelled the coppery scent of his own blood. He heard Tarun shout for them to let Bane go, but his words became a strangled cry.

"Tarun? TARUN?" Bane cried, but he heard *nothing* from his servant. Had they murdered him? Had one of those knives sliced across the man's throat? Rage filled Bane. "You are murderers! You are monsters! Let me go! LET ME GO!"

The old woman took her hand out of the mud. It was completely covered with the steaming, bubbling, superheated sludge. It smoked in the air. It was coming directly for his face.

"No! No! NO!" Bane cried.

He struggled but they held him in place. The old woman with the burning hand came closer and closer.

"You must house the tiger's spirit for all time. Because you have disrupted the natural order of things you will *never* have harmony, you will *never* have peace, you will be a *beast*, until your heart is true to another." Her hand was hovering over the right side of his face. Her black eyes met his Siberian blue ones. "For you, Lord Bane Dunsaney, are now *cursed*."

Bane screamed as the burning hand was pressed against the right side of his face.

CHAPTER TWO

TRANSFORMATION

The present, Moon Shadow, Winter Haven ...

Nick Fairfax put a hand, palm down, a few inches over the coals in the grill. They were not quite hot enough for the steaks. He was always too eager to cook the meat. He knew he needed to wait until the fire was so hot that the outside of the meat would sear the instant he placed the steaks on the grill, trapping the juices inside as it cooked.

"Nick, do not even *think* of putting those steaks on the fire!" Omar Singh's delightful Tamil-accented voice called out.

Nick jumped back from the candy apple red Weber grill like a guilty little boy. He said sheepishly, "I'm sorry, Omar, I just love playing with the fire. Hearing the steaks *sizzle* is the best part."

"They will not *sizzle* with the grill only *warm*." Omar walked down the back porch steps towards Nick carrying a bowl of marinating onions, sweet peppers and tomatoes. He smiled as he set the bowl down on the nearby prep table right by the steaks. "You are incorrigible where fire is concerned."

The Indian man leaned over the grill, assessing the coals critically, and then said, "Five or ten minutes more and the coals will be ready. We must wait until they are white-hot.

Only then can we put the steaks on. Besides, Bane will not be here for a little while and we do not want the food to get cold before he arrives home."

Nick's heart leaped into his throat and seemed to lodge there for a moment, making it impossible to speak at the mention of Bane's arrival, but, finally, he got out, "Are—are you sure? Is he *really* going to be back tonight? I mean I know he told you he was, but he's said that before and stayed away."

"Yes, I am certain. The pilot called me as soon as they landed. Bane is already on his way home from the airport as we speak."

Nick forgot to breathe for a moment. He forced himself to take a deep breath and swallowed. "So he's *really* coming home? He's *really* going to be here in ... what? Ten, fifteen minutes?"

"Yes."

Nick wiped suddenly sweating palms on his shorts. His heart was thumping like a drum. "And he has no idea that Jade and I are here?"

"He has *no* idea."

Omar's smile did not quite reach his eyes even though keeping Nick and Jade's presence at Moon Shadow a secret from Bane had been the Indian man's suggestion. Nick had only reluctantly agreed. But now with Bane actually coming home, Nick's doubts redoubled that keeping his presence here a secret was a good idea.

Maybe we should call Bane and let him know I'm still here and Jade is hanging out for the weekend. He loves his privacy and I don't think he's fond of surprises.

"Are you still sure this is a good idea?" Nick asked as he shifted from foot to foot. "To *surprise* him, I mean, with me being here?"

"Oh, I think it will be just *fine*. Bane needs a little excitement in his life," Omar stirred the marinating vegetables as he spoke. He did not, however, meet Nick's eyes. The Indian man's movements were jerky instead of smooth and controlled like usual, too.

"You're nervous about him coming home and finding me here!" Nick accused.

"No –"

"Omar!"

The Indian man sighed. "Maybe a little. But I know in Bane's heart that he wants you here. I just am not sure that he will *realize* that at first."

"I still don't know why he ran out of here in the first place. And *you* won't tell me though I know you know the reason." Nick gave Omar a pointed look.

"It is for Bane to tell you," Omar gave his usual answer, which was no answer at all.

"But it's been a month and Bane hasn't tried to contact me, let alone explain anything. You've talked to him. He didn't mention me to you." Nick ran one hand through his platinum hair.

"He only took a few of my calls and then only to give a few one word responses. He would answer no questions of mine that did not pertain to domestic duties. So you are not alone in him not explaining things. But, what I do know, is that he needs you Nick" Omar said, sounding quite certain.

Nick started pacing. "If he wanted anything to do with me, Omar, he would have, at least, asked about me."

"No, he wouldn't. When something or *someone* matters to him, and there are ... are *issues*, he will not speak of it at all." Omar answered. "What I will say about why he left is because he felt it was for the *best*."

"For who?"

"For *you*, of course. So calling you would be too painful. Speaking of you would be an agony to him," Omar explained. "So we just have to show Bane that him being away from you is *not* what is best for you or him or anyone involved."

"Right. Sure. Okay. Oh, God, I don't know!" Nick paced again. "Do you think he is going to be madder if we call him now and let him know I'm here or if he just finds me here when he arrives?"

"I think there is little difference at this point. In fact, telling him in the car would give him time to *stew*," Omar pointed out, shaking the tongs as he did.

"Stewing is *not* a good thing for Bane."

"Definitely not. Seeing you will remind Bane of everything good and he will come to his senses." A smile—a *genuine* smile—lit up Omar's face. "You are *eager* for Bane to return, aren't you?"

"I am. Scared shitless, too. I've hardly been able to stop thinking of him since he left," Nick admitted. "I would *never* have believed I'd feel this way when Bane and I first met."

"That was not a good time. Bane behaved very badly," Omar said.

The bad behavior Omar was referring to was the deal. Nick's father, Charles, and his two older brothers, Steven and Jake, had run Fairfax International, which had specialized in taking over vulnerable companies, stripping them of their assets, and loading them up with debt before sending them into bankruptcy. But when Fairfax International had tried going after one of Bane's companies, Bane had turned the tables on his family. Bane loathed all that Fairfax International stood for and he had no mercy when he took over the company. He not only stripped Nick's family of their livelihood, but threatened to ensure that they would be on the street unless they accepted a *deal*.

The deal provided that Nick's father and brothers would work in Bane's companies for a year. They would have to demonstrate by the end of that time that they had learned Bane's business philosophy. But that wasn't the full extent of the deal. Even though Nick had nothing to do with his family's business, Bane required Nick to serve him for that same year in whatever capacity Bane wanted. If after a year, all the terms had been met, Nick's family would be given Fairfax International back. If the terms weren't met ... then Bane would leave his family destitute and hound them wherever they went.

Bane had called Nick's part of the deal an "internship", but what it ended up being was Nick acting as an assistant to

Omar, Bane's longtime manservant, at Bane's country manor, Moon Shadow. But things had not gone the way *anyone* had intended or expected. Within a very short time of being at Moon Shadow, Nick had been seriously burned, one of Bane's business associates had tried to rape him, and a white Bengal tiger had appeared in Nick's bed and attacked him. Bane had saved him from the business associate, but the tiger was a whole other matter. Bane had disappeared after the tiger had appeared.

And then, after releasing me from my part of the deal, Bane left for a whole month in Europe. Left without a word. Even though things between us were starting to become romantic. It makes no sense!

"Nick? A penny for your thoughts?" Omar's head dipped down so that he could see Nick's face, which was lowered and flushing.

"I was just thinking about the things that happened when Bane was last here," Nick laughed weakly. "At least, no matter what Bane's reaction to me being here is now, it can't be as dramatic as everything that happened back then."

"And that is truly a relief! But I do not think you should worry about Bane's reaction to you being here. Before he left he told you that you could stay at Moon Shadow," Omar pointed out as he always did when they talked about this. He spread the white hot coals in the bottom of the grill with a trowel.

"He did." Nick nodded and felt a bit like a bobblehead doll as his head bobbed up and down over and over again. They had said these things to one another so often that they had the feel of a litany.

"He *assumed* you would leave when he did, but he did not *order* you to," Omar said the next part of the litany as he placed the metal grill over the white hot coals to heat up.

"Not that I would have gone if he *had* ordered me to anyways," Nick pointed out as he always did. "Not doing what he asks is sort of my thing."

"Like me, you have *selective* hearing. Any orders he gives which make no sense or are wrong in some way, we *ignore*."

Nick grinned. "Absolutely."

"But even without all of those reasons for it being *acceptable* for you to be here, Bane has always said that I might have *friends* come over and stay as well," Omar pointed out. "And you and Jade are my friends."

"Absolutely!" Nick agreed.

"And you are also working here with room and board as part of your salary so –"

"So I have every right to be here, too, on that basis."

"Exactly!"

"I think we have about a million explanations for why I am *allowed* to be here regardless of what his lordship thinks," Nick said with a smile.

What he added in his head, but did not speak out loud was, *But what about when Bane asks me why I decided to stay after he ran off without a word? What will I tell him then? You haunt me? I dream of you and tigers every night? Despite being an impossibly aggravating man I see the goodness in you? What he'll really think is that I'm here to make sure that my family isn't put out into the street. Can we really have a relationship—even if both of us want one—when my family's fate is in Bane's hands?*

Omar laid the steaks, four juicy t-bones, seasoned with just sea salt and freshly cracked black pepper, on the grill. The *sizzle* they made had Nick's mouth watering. They were high quality meat from a nearby farm. They were *not* from Mr. Brennan's farm though. Mr. Brennan was the farmer who believed that Bane had a "pet" that was eating his livestock. Nick had found out that was actually true when he woke up with a white Bengal tiger beside him.

"Bane has a *pet* tiger?" he'd asked Omar the morning after finding the white Bengal tiger in bed with him.

The Indian man was changing the dressing on Nick's arm. The four deep slashes in his left upper arm were from the tiger's claws. The tiger had appeared in bed beside him and *pawed* him. Not *clawed* him, but *pawed* him, because Nick was certain the tiger had not meant to hurt him.

"Not a pet, no." Omar dabbed on hydrogen peroxide on the wounds, which caused Nick to hiss. "The tiger is a sacred charge of Bane's."

"That's similar to what you said about your job with him," Nick recalled.

"Yes, the two things are connected."

"Why do I have this feeling that you are hiding something from me, Omar? And that it's bigger than the tiger, and that was a huge freaking tiger!" Nick gritted his teeth as Omar gently wrapped his arm with gauze.

"It is not *my* secret to tell, Nick." Omar sighed.

"So there *is* a secret?" Nick would have felt triumphant except for the fact that Omar looked so *pained*.

"Yes, and that is all I can say."

"Does it have to do with where Bane *went* when the tiger showed up to cuddle with me?" Nick asked.

Bane had been the one cuddling with him when he'd fallen asleep. He couldn't quite understand how the tiger had replaced the billionaire. Had Bane gone to the bathroom and the tiger slipped in to take his place? No, because Bane would have returned at Nick's yell. Had Bane left for a night stroll and the tiger decided to curl up somewhere warm? Maybe. Had Bane seen the tiger get out and gone after it while the tiger had hidden in Nick's bedroom? Maybe that was it.

"Bane must be the one to explain all this to you, Nick. I'm sorry –"

"Don't apologize, Omar. If it's Bane's secret you're right not to reveal it to me," Nick responded with a sigh. "Just when is he going to be back to explain? In a couple of days –"

"When he has come to terms with the tiger," Omar answered.

"You sound like he's reasoning with it. But you said he took it away with him. I just don't know why he left without a word to me. He could have explained to me about the tiger. I would have understood!" Nick protested.

Omar's dark brown eyes had met his. "He will come back, Nick, and when he does, I am *certain* he will tell you everything."

Omar had repeated most of these assurances throughout the long month waiting for Bane's return. Now that Bane was coming back, Nick felt tongue-tied. He probably wouldn't be able to remark on the weather let alone ask Bane about his secrets.

Omar placed a hand on Nick's upper arm, breaking him out of his thoughts. "Don't worry, Nick. I was the one that decided we would *not* tell him about you still being here and –"

"You're not taking the blame for this, Omar!"

"My selective hearing will take the blame."

Omar smiled genuinely. He then stroked Nick's bare arm, just below the four scars from the tiger's claws. They were thin white lines now. He thought they looked rather cool. His skin was a deep bronze which made them stand out all the more. He rarely tanned, but due to the terrible sunburn he'd gotten within a few days of coming to Moon Shadow, his skin had finally turned a golden brown.

"I don't want *anyone* to take the blame. I want Bane to be happy I'm here," Nick said, speaking aloud the simple truth. That had him pacing for the third time.

"He will be," Omar assured him. And then with less assurance, "In the end."

Nick tilted back his head and laughed. "Yeah, that's the problem! Getting to that *ending*. I want a happily ever after, damnit."

"You deserve it. Both of you do."

There was a soft squeak of hinges as Nick's best friend, Jade Lessitor, shouldered the screen door open. Nick glanced up just as she stepped out onto the back porch. She was wearing a black tank top, pink shorts along with ruffled pink socks and black tennis shoes. Her black hair was spiked up like a rooster's and she wore frosted pink lipstick and black eye liner. She was carrying three white wine spritzers, which contained chardonnay, fizzy water and fresh squeezed lime juice.

Though they had sounded kind of girly when she first told them what was in them, Nick found he loved them.

"Drinks, boys!" she called as she came down the stairs and sauntered over to them.

Omar took one of the perspiring glasses while Nick took another. The three of them clinked their drinks together.

"Cheers!" they said in unison.

"Go sit down and relax. I have the grill." Omar shooed them towards the shaded porch with the comfortable rattan furniture.

Nick was going to object—wanting to play with the fire *and* help Omar—but Jade hooked an arm through one of his and drew him towards the porch's sofa. They sat down side by side on it. She put her feet up on the footrest, crossed her legs at the ankles, and rested her head against his shoulder as she sipped her drink. He took a large swallow of his. The tartness of the wine was cut by the fizz of the soda water. It was refreshing and he downed half his glass.

"You're nervous," she guessed.

"I'm ... yeah, I'm a little nervous. Or maybe *a lot* nervous. Bane could be here at any moment," Nick admitted.

To calm himself, he looked at the tripod set up in the garden where his Nikon was sitting, waiting for him to take photographs. Photography was his passion and what he wanted to do with his life. He loved photographing ruins and nature most of all.

Moon Shadow was an old manor house with a sprawling garden that had been abandoned for over twenty years before Bane had purchased it. The garden had become overgrown, especially the formal rose garden in the back. Vines had crawled over the mansion's stone facade as well.

When Nick had first seen it, Moon Shadow had looked abandoned, but not any more. Omar had hired gardeners who had worked tirelessly for a month to restore the garden. Nick had also helped to weed and prune, but mostly he had photographed the transformation of Moon Shadow. He hoped to share these photographs with Bane, to show him Moon Shadow's rebirth. He itched to go to his camera now, to fuss with it until Bane came. But he would just muck up any pictures he tried to take considering how anxious he really was.

"Let's say that Bane comes home, sees you here, gives you a huge sappy smile and a kiss. He's *thrilled* you're at Moon Shadow. You're his *true love*," Jade said, punctuating her words by giving him a sloppy kiss on the cheek.

He pushed her off and snorted. "Bane doesn't believe in ordinary, everyday love let alone mythic true love."

Though Omar was notoriously tight-lipped about Bane's other secrets, he had revealed that Bane's belief that love didn't exist came from a disastrous relationship that Bane had had with his father's best friend, Alastair. Alastair had been a handsome, older man that had taken advantage of a teenaged Bane and hurt him so deeply that Bane had retreated from any more emotional entanglements.

Until me. He cares for me. I know it.

Jade continued, "Well, let's just say that he comes home with a new lease on life and new beliefs, he gives you all the love you can want, but ..."

"But?" he asked even as his heart seemed to drop into his feet. He trusted Jade's judgment and he had a feeling he knew what his best friend was going to say.

"*But* he's still keeping your family to the terms of the stupid *deal*. You're free, yes, but are they? No," Jade said. "While some people might rejoice at the idea of Charles and your brothers on the street, you're not one of them. So if *they* aren't free then *you* aren't free either."

"My father and brothers are the type of people that Bane loathes. *You* loathe them. *Everyone* loathes them. Maybe they deserve whatever they've got coming to them," he pointed out. He crossed his arms over his chest, pressing the cool drink against the back of one forearm.

"But, Nick, you *don't* loathe them. I know you. You can't be in a relationship with a man that's going to toss even the *loathsome* Fairfaxes out on their behinds," she said sadly.

"Like I said, maybe they deserve it. I've done my last favor for them. I've done my best to help them. Bane wouldn't have given them the chance to redeem themselves at all, but for me. They rise or fall on their own," he said, his voice neutral yet somehow fragile.

"Maybe they do." She hugged his arm tightly. "But you're my favorite bleeding heart, Nick. So, I think, unless Bane gives up his *revenge* against the Fairfaxes, well, I'm afraid that any relationship between you will lead to *heartbreak*."

"None of them have called me since I started the *internship*," he pointed out even as his own heart tumbled farther into his feet at her words.

"True. They're terrible people. I've never disputed that."

"Not one of them has even visited me to make sure that Bane isn't taking advantage of me!"

"Even though you would *like* him to take advantage of you?" Jade's eyebrows rose.

"That's beyond the point! My family does not know that," he said.

"Again, *true*. They really are *shitty* relations." Jade nodded sagely and sipped her drink.

"So *why* should I care about them?" he asked.

"I don't know." She sighed and kissed his cheek. "But you *do*."

A leaden heaviness filled him even as the scene before him was heart-wrenchingly beautiful. The formal garden used to be a wild tangle, but now it was a picture of pristine order. There was a row of white blooms then a row of pale pink ones followed by a soft red until, finally, the last row of roses in the garden was such a deep crimson that the flowers almost looked black.

Nick had capped every day off by taking a picture of the garden at 6:30 p.m. That was in five minutes. The light from the sun was at its most golden at that hour. It seemed to gild the flowers. It was when he *most* ached for Bane so it was fitting, in a way, that Bane should return just then.

"Time for the picture." He patted her arm.

She didn't let go, instead tugged at him until he looked over at her. Jade's forehead was creased with concern. "I wouldn't say these things lightly. I'm just worried, Nick. I don't want your heart broken by this guy who seems quite capable of shattering it."

"I shouldn't have told you about *everything* he did and said. I should have only let you know about the *good* things so then you could only praise him to me and picture a perfect life for us." He gave her a crooked grin.

Her green eyes sparkled. "I would have wheedled it all out of you. After all, it only took me one month to get every detail from you and we've dissected them from every single angle. I can't wait until I actually meet the man. Bane's more of a myth than a real person to me now."

"Believe me, he's *larger* than life."

They both grinned and he gently disengaged his arm from hers. He downed the rest of his drink and left the empty glass on the table.

"Go create art, Nick! I shall be a lady of leisure!" she called to him as he jogged down the stairs towards his camera.

As soon as he looked through the viewfinder, he felt calmness flow through him. As he prepared for the final picture of the day he thought of Bane. The man had become rather mythic to him, too, as the days had passed by. He had dreamed about their kisses. He had fantasized about those massive hands on his bare back, waist and ass. He had been haunted by Bane's fierce, possessive behavior when he had saved Nick from the odious Dean Kettering. And Nick had also been obsessed with tigers. A white Bengal tiger that had shared his bed for one night.

A tiger with the most soulful eyes ...

CHAPTER THREE
HOMECOMING

B ane leaned back against the headrest in the passenger compartment of the Maybach. The luxury car's leather seat cradled his body and should have relaxed. Under other circumstances, he would have fallen asleep. But he wasn't heading through Winter Haven and every one of his senses was on high alert.

Nick is somewhere in this city and that means I cannot linger. Moon Shadow will be quite close enough. Possibly too close.

The beast let out a mournful snarl more like a wolf's howl as they passed by the Fairfax International building. Not that Nick would be in the tower. He likely would be staying with his best friend, Jade, or perhaps even back at the family home. Bane had been careful not to ask Omar *anything* about Nick. He had feared that once he had started asking questions that he would not have been able to stop.

The beast collapsed into a heap in his chest after that snarl. Neither of them had any energy. The beast had kept him completely free of illness for over one hundred years but ever since they had left Nick a month ago, Bane had been listless. The gloss was gone from his hair. His skin was sallow. His eyes had lost their spark. He had been unable to do anything except sleep and yet no matter how long he slept he was still exhausted. Not even the roses he kept around him seemed to live as long as they once had, withering and dying within a day. He'd finally stopped having any flowers in his rooms, because it depressed even more as he watched them wilt.

When Omar had seen him over Skype, the Indian man had blanched. His right hand had gone up to the tiger amulet around his neck. His voice had been soft, but urgent, "Come home, Bane."

And Bane hadn't had the will to resist that request. The truth was that he hadn't wanted to resist. He wanted to be at Moon Shadow. He wanted Omar's gentle presence to surround him. He wanted his beloved roses to perfume every breath he took. He would be able to remember Nick at Moon Shadow, too. He would be able to recall every moment of Nick's short stay in his life and he would alternately relish each and every memory of Nick and excoriate himself at the same time for squandering those past times. It would truly be a pleasurable torment in some ways.

Self indulgent! Foolish! There should be no pleasure at all for me!

His head thrashed against the headrest. How had he ever thought that forcing Nick to work for him, a virtual prisoner without his cell phone or computer, had been a good idea? He'd even taken the young man's camera! It was true that he feared his curse would be revealed and recorded by the camera, but that wasn't why he had taken away Nick's things. He had wanted to keep control of Nick completely, to cut Nick off from his friends and family, to make Nick utterly dependent upon him.

How had he allowed himself to think that punishing the one person who had nothing to do with Fairfax Industries was right? He had justified what he had wanted to do by painting Nick as a vapid, spoilt beauty. Not that even vapid, spoilt beauties deserved to be treated badly. His actions were eerily similar to what his father would have done. Lord Richard Dunsaney had taken what he wanted no matter the cost. And

Bane had wanted Nick. He could admit that now. Seeing his father in himself so clearly made him realize that he just had to make it all stop.

And then the beast had hurt Nick. Had taken over Bane's body, shifting Bane from man to tiger, and then had *clawed* Nick's shoulder. Would the young man ever be able to look at his reflection in the mirror and not remember his horrific time at Moon Shadow? Nick would, undoubtedly, see those scars and curse Bane's name. But some part inside of him was glad that even if Nick's memories of him were bad at least Nick *would* remember him.

I cannot turn back time and meet Nick under different circumstances. I cannot go back and somehow treat Nick differently. I cannot be a different man altogether. What's past is past. I don't even know what I wanted with him. A friendship? No, not just that. A romantic relationship? But how could I be his lover when I do not believe in love? I wish to believe. I do. But I know better. Love is an illusion.

The crunch of Moon Shadow's gravel drive under the Maybach's tires broke Bane out of his thoughts, and his eyelids fluttered opened. He had not realized that he had closed them. He was so very tired. But when Moon Shadow came into view with its profusion of rose bushes, he felt a sudden rush of energy. He drew down the window and took in a deep breath of the roses' fragrance. The air was drenched with their perfume.

He caught sight of the fountain that Nick had cleared off. His heart clenched as he saw that more work had been done to restore the sculpture. Did the fountain function now? He'd imagined Nick and himself standing arm in arm as the fountain was turned on for the first time. He quickly looked away from it when he had the crashing realization that Nick would *not* be there when that happened.

I should have told Omar to leave it alone! Now it will only torment me as I think of what could have been.

The Maybach glided to a stop just under the portico. Bane didn't wait for Peter Handel, his driver, to open the door for him. He got out himself. He nodded to Peter without having to say anything about his bags. Between Peter and Omar, all his things would be taken care of. His clothes would be washed, pressed, and put back in an organized fashion in his closet without him having to direct any of it. If anyone was spoiled, it was him.

He went over to the front doors and felt another wave of disappointment that Nick was not going to be inside to greet him when he opened them. Even when they had been sparring, there had been an excitement in the air just having Nick nearby. He'd been something to look forward to. Now Bane wondered whether he shouldn't have just stayed away longer. But he was here and he was tired. He needed to reclaim Moon Shadow from Nick's ghostly presence. He pushed open the doors and stepped into the polished foyer. He expected silence, but what he heard instead was laughter. *Nick's laughter.* And a woman's?

"I thought you were going to take pictures of the rose garden, Nick, not of me!" a young woman protested and gave a squeal followed by a laugh. "Get away, get away from me, camera boy! Omar, make him stop!"

"I am sorry, Jade, but you are pretty as a picture. I asked Nick to take me some photos of you and I will have them," Omar chuckled.

Another squeal and an elongated, "noooooooooooo" followed afterwards.

"All right, Jade, *fine.* I won't take pictures of you. Back to the garden, I suppose," Nick's voice feigned disappointment and he let out a long sigh to accompany those words, but then he couldn't hold back the laughter.

Nick ... Nick ... Nick ...

The beast inside of him leaped to life. It was immediately happy. It wanted to race forward, towards the sound of that laughter, and rub up against Nick, claiming him. Bane found himself taking five staggering steps forward, his heart was in his throat, and sweat broke out over his whole body. Bane was shocked at the violent physical reaction he had to the thought of Nick still being there.

But he can't be here! I must be mistaken.

In a daze, Bane walked through the foyer and down the long hallway to the back porch. There was a sizzling sound. The scent of cooking red meat had Bane's stomach rumbling. The beast, too, suddenly had an interest in food. The two of them had gone off eating since leaving Moon Shadow.

Bane caught sight of Omar grilling. The Indian man was dancing in front of the grill, singing under his breath and sipping a drink. He then saw a young woman—*Jade, it must be*—sitting on the porch, also sipping a drink. She picked up a book and began to read. He took all of this in, but his focus was on Nick.

Nick's back was to him. He was looking through the viewfinder of a camera he had set up on a tripod just at the base of the back porch stairs. There was the soft click of the button being depressed as Nick photographed every angle of the now completely restored formal rose garden. But Bane cared nothing for the flowers at that moment. It was Nick who filled his vision.

The young man was wearing a white, sleeveless t-shirt and khaki shorts that showed off his long, tanned legs. The terrible burn Nick had suffered had become a magnificent tan. The white t-shirt practically glowed in contrast to his golden skin. The tan also emphasized the four thin scars from tiger's claws on Nick's left bicep. But even that guilty reminder of what the beast had done could not overcome the joy that filled him at seeing Nick.

When Bane pushed the screen door open there was the familiar squeak of recalcitrant hinges and everyone but Nick turned towards him. Jade let out a small gasp as her green eyes caught sight of him. She kept the book up mostly covering her face as if she thought she could hide her presence from him. Omar had frozen in mid dance step. His mouth open to call to Bane, but Bane held up a hand to silence him. He had to hear Nick's voice first.

He was trembling. He had never trembled before. Somehow nothing meant more than this moment and hearing Nick speak to him.

Nick continued to stare through the camera's viewfinder, but Bane knew that the young man was aware of him. Bane could hear the frantic beating of Nick's heart. Slowly, Nick straightened and turned towards him. The young man's penetrating gray eyes fixed on his and a quirk of a smile appeared on his lips.

"Bane, you're home," Nick said warmly and then in a very different tone, "Oh, my God! Bane! Are you all right?"

Bane had fallen to his knees. Simply collapsed. He had no idea how it had happened. One moment he was standing there and the next he was on his knees. One moment Nick had been at the tripod welcoming him home and now Nick was crouched by his side, holding him up by one arm. Jade was on the other side of him, wrapping one of his large arms over her slender shoulders. Omar raced up the steps and dropped down on his haunches in front of Bane. He cupped Bane's face.

"Oh, Bane, you are so ill! You did not look well on Skype, but it's worse than I thought!" Omar exclaimed.

He felt Nick run a hand through his hair. "He's as pale as a ghost, Omar. Bane, you haven't been taking care of yourself. Why?"

Why? Because I left you and I believed that I would never see you again, Bane thought but could not say.

"I'm sorry I—thank you for helping me. I haven't been eating properly and travel exhausts me. I just had a dizzy turn, that's all," Bane mumbled. Embarrassment had him flushing hotter. To faint was a sign of weakness! "It will pass in a moment and I will be myself again."

But while it was true that he had barely eaten that *wasn't* why he was reacting this way. It was *Nick. Seeing* Nick again, *smelling* Nick's scent and *hearing* Nick's voice saying those words were what caused it.

Home. Home. Home.

"Let's get him to the couch," Jade suggested.

And somehow they lifted him to his feet and got him over to the couch where he collapsed again, but this time into a sitting position. He let his eyelids flutter shut and rested the back of his head against the wall. He was acutely aware of Nick's presence to his right. Nick's sundrenched scent filled his nostrils. His body warmed Bane's side. The urge to turn and bury his face against Nick's chest and just breathe him in was almost overwhelming. But Bane held himself terribly still so he would not be tempted to follow through on this desire. Nick was here. He must do *nothing* to scare him away.

"Let me get you a glass of water," Nick said and moved to go into the house.

"No! Do not leave me!" Bane's eyelids flew open. He had caught Nick's nearest wrist in an iron grip.

Nick's gray eyes were looking into his with concern, tenderness and worry. Everyone went silent and Bane flushed deeper. He was acting like a madman. Hadn't he just promised himself *not* to scare Nick? Yet he'd grabbed the young man and his fingers were wrapped tightly around Nick's wrist. What was he doing? He quickly released his grip and looked away from him. He had to get a hold of himself. He had nearly *fainted*. He had never done that in his entire life. And now he was pleading for Nick to stay near him like a child for its parent.

"Of course, I won't leave. I'm not leaving," Nick's tone was tender. "I'm right here."

But I thought you left. I thought you would never be here again.

"I'll get the water," Jade offered.

She quickly got up and went into the house. It seemed like she was back in an instant, but Bane knew his sense of time was off. Nick took the glass of water from her and held it to Bane's lips as if the billionaire wasn't capable of drinking on his own. Bane was going to object to this, but when he raised one hand up to take the glass it was shaking. He dropped it back into his lap and sipped the water with Nick's help. The water was cold and clean with a bite of minerality.

"Thank you," he said.

"Feeling a little better?" Nick's voice was cast low.

Bane nodded as he seemed unable to speak. Embarrassment again flooded him. If any of them had any idea of the true reason for this state he would have been humiliated.

Omar lingered a moment and then said, "I better keep an eye on the steaks. You need food, Bane."

"I'll help!" Jade jumped to her feet.

There was a meaningful look between the three of them, but Bane felt so lightheaded he couldn't read it. Besides, he didn't dare look at them closely. Jade and Omar walked over to the grill together, talking softly. The scent of roasting vegetables and grilling meat wafted over to him. Bane's stomach grumbled again. The beast licked its lips.

"You *are* hungry," Nick said with a soft snort. "Once we get some food into you, you'll be much better."

Bane nodded. He let his long hair slide across his face, hiding himself from Nick, even as he kept stealing glances at the young man. Nick tucked Bane's hair behind his ear. Bane tried to cover his face again, but Nick caught his wrist and held his hand instead. The tiger let out a pleased huff at the touch.

"Is it really just lack of food and sleep, Bane, that's causing this weakness?" Nick asked, his voice urgent with worry. "Do you need a doctor? We could get Dr. Trevelyan here –"

"No, there's no need to do that. I really will be fine again. My trip was ... *trying*."

From the moment that Bane had left Nick's side he had felt wretched. His head had pounded. He had no energy. He had stopped eating. At times, he had actually felt he was dying. He had told himself that was ridiculous. The curse ensured that he would never die. But every moment he had been away from Nick had been torture.

"I'm sorry that you had to leave so *suddenly*." Nick's gaze was searching his face.

Bane blanched. What explanation had Omar given Nick for his absence? Bane had just assumed that Nick would have left after he did and wouldn't question why Bane had fled Moon Shadow. But Nick had stayed. Omar *must* have told him something. But what?

He chanced a glance at Nick again and saw very serious gray eyes regarding him. He opened his mouth, but nothing came out. He honestly had not prepared a story to explain his behavior. It would have to be a very *good* story, because from an outsider's perspective he had acted like a fool by rushing off in his car without a word of explanation. Nick had been attacked by a *tiger* in his house and he had just taken off without checking if Nick was even all right.

But I could not stay a moment longer not even to check if he was well. It was not safe for him. The beast took over my body. Then a disturbing thought came to him. *It could happen again. Nick isn't safe with me now ...*

"Omar told me about the tiger, Bane," Nick said.

Bane's head jerked up and his eyes flickered between the Indian man and then back to Nick. "He *did*?"

"I could give you that line about tigers being wild animals and not pets, but I have a feeling you already know that." Nick grinned.

Bane stared at him blankly. *Pets?*

"I just really wish that you had told me about the tiger *before* he showed up in bed with us," Nick snickered. "He must have missed you in the night and come looking for you. Saw a nice bed that smelled like you and cuddled down."

Bane's eyes went wider.

"I'm pretty sure that I scared him more than he scared me." Nick barely brushed the scars on his arm. "But I got a few cool souvenirs out of it."

"You're scarred," Bane breathed. "I scarred you."

His fingers hovered over those four raised ridges of flesh and he swallowed bitter bile that rose up in his throat.

"The *tiger* scarred me and I know he didn't mean to hurt me," Nick corrected.

Bane's eyes flickered up to Nick's face. He was so beautiful that it almost hurt to look at him. His platinum hair had been bleached even lighter by the sun. There was a fan of freckles over his nose and cheekbones. His lips were a kissable pink. His gray eyes were clear as the sea. Bane dragged his gaze away. Looking into Nick's eyes when he was this out of control was a mistake.

"The tiger is ... my responsibility. That is why whatever it does is my fault." He lowered his head and his hand curled tighter around Nick's. The young man's hand was engulfed by his, swallowed by it. Bane was so much larger than he was. He could break Nick very easily without meaning to. "You are so ... fragile."

"I'm not fragile." Nick tossed his head back with a touch of masculine pride. "You and the tiger are just *huge*."

"So Omar told you that I have a ... a *pet* tiger that got out of its cage and went to sleep in your bed?" Bane clarified. He had truly thought for a moment that Omar had revealed the curse to Nick. Unlike the "story" he had told the young man a month ago, Nick might have believed Omar after he had seen the beast.

"You make it sound *absurd*, but that's what happened. What other explanation would there be?" From the half grin on Nick's lips he was certain the young man would *never* guess the truth now unless he saw Bane transforming. "Just what did you do with the tiger? You didn't—didn't hurt him, did you? I know that you captured him and took him away. That's why you left, right? You raced off because you had to trap him and take him someplace safe?"

The beast stared at Bane out of baleful eyes. He had taken it away from Nick. That was harm enough. But Bane lied, "No, I—I didn't hurt the tiger. I just took it to a—a private zoo in Europe. Where it can run free and *not* harm anyone. Especially you."

The beast flattened its ears and growled at him. It wanted out to be with Nick. It wanted to sleep again with Nick resting against its chest. It wanted to groom Nick.

The full moon is not for two weeks. You must wait! And when I cede my form to yours, you will NOT be going anywhere near Nick. You hurt him once. You will not do it again.

He had to give over control of his body to the beast at the full moon but at no other time. Except there obviously had been times very recently when he had lost control with Nick and the beast had taken over while he slept. The beast let out a low rumble, but then Nick was stroking the back of Bane's hand. The beast, surprisingly, settled.

Nick shifted beside him. "You didn't have to take the tiger away. I would have loved to have seen him."

Bane noted that Nick called the tiger "him" while he thought of the beast as "it". Nick was in some ways correct as when he transformed he was a *male* tiger, but the beast could inhabit either a female or male form. Calling it "him" somehow made the beast seem less like a *monster* and more like a *person*. He felt uncomfortable with that.

"It would not have been safe, Nick. I was foolish to have it here, especially with you in the house," Bane lied.

"Where did you keep him?" Nick's face shone with curiosity.

There was a cell in the basement where Bane would be locked up during the full moon. So in a way he wasn't completely lying when he said, "Basement."

"You kept him in the *basement* away from the sun?" Nick looked faintly appalled.

"I know that it wasn't right," Bane quickly said though if he had his way the beast would never see the light of day. "But it was the best I could do."

"I'm glad you took him to a zoo then. Being in a basement cell couldn't be good for him no matter how much you cared for him," Nick murmured, still looking concerned.

Cared for him? Oh, Nick, nothing could be further from the truth!

The beast growled at him, but it whapped its tail appreciatively at Nick. Its expression soon became a sleepy eyed one of pleasure. Not that Nick could see it. Not that Nick would *ever* see it again.

"Yes, well, I've learned my lesson." Bane lowered his head. He hated lying to Nick, but he could not tell him the truth.

"So Mr. Brennan was *right* that you were the cause of his lost farm animals," Nick chuckled.

"The beast ... *tiger* sometimes got out and had some *fun* chasing Mr. Brennan's sheep and then eating them," Bane answered. "But let us not talk of it any longer. It makes me unhappy."

"I'm sure talking about the tiger makes you miss him. But letting him go was for the best, Bane."

Nick offered Bane another sip of water. Bane was able to take the glass from him this time and sip from it without spilling liquid down the front of his shirt. Though he was certainly hungry, he no longer felt so weak and out of control. He felt *better* than he had since ...

Since I was with Nick last.

He found himself relaxing, too, for the first time in a long time. The sweet summer breeze brought the scent of roses and barbeque to him. He laced his fingers with Nick's. He found himself smiling as Nick's thumb lightly passed up and down the back of his hand.

Suddenly, Nick asked, "Do you need help with your stuff? Are your bags still in the car?"

"No, Peter will get them." He paused then said, "Nick, you're no longer an *intern*. You don't need to serve me."

Nick's lips quirked into an amused grin. "I wasn't *serving* you. I was just asking to *help*. If you didn't look like death warmed over I would be making you get your own bags."

Bane snorted. "Yes, you *would* have me do that."

Nick's hand tightened on his. "But if you *need* me ..." Nick looked away from him, high color flooding his cheekbones. "But if you *need me* to do anything I'm ... I'm here and happy to help."

Bane felt hope soaring in him, but just as quickly insecurity clamped down on. He cleared his throat and asked, "That is ...

that is good of you. More than good of you. But Nick ... what are you doing here?" Bane finally got out.

"I work here," Nick answered neutrally though there was the slightest stiffening in his posture.

Bane frowned. "But you are no longer bound by the deal—"

"I know I'm not. You don't understand," Nick interrupted him. The young man's hands fidgeted in his lap. "I'm *working* for you as your photographer and all around helpmate for Omar."

"You're *working* for me?" Bane repeated stupidly.

"Yes, I am." Nick nodded. "And may I add that you are quite generous with the salary, not to mention the free room and board. It's a pretty sweet deal all around." Nick grinned at him, but there was uncertainty in his eyes.

"Why would you wish to remain here after—after *every-thing*? I don't understand this at all." Bane frowned.

"Because I *want* to stay." Nick lowered his head and Bane was reminded of a donkey who put its ears back and would not move.

"But—but you were *burned*—"

"I'm fine now. Better than fine. Don't worry. No scars," Nick answered. "And I won't get burned like that again. I only work in the garden during the early morning hours and late afternoon now when the sun isn't that strong."

"And he has plenty of sunscreen!" Omar called from the grill, which meant he had been listening closely to their conversation all along.

"I *do*. Besides I've got a great base tan now. See?" Nick stuck out his arm that was a golden brown. Of course, that arm also had the scars on it from the tiger.

"But what about—about Dean Kettering's attack –"

"You saved me from that," Nick reminded him and shrugged as if the attempted rape were nothing. Bane knew that wasn't true, but Nick was clearly intent on not letting it affect him any longer.

"And what about the deal?" Bane finally asked, unable to meet Nick's eyes as he did.

"That's over. *For me* over anyways," Nick said and cleared his throat.

Quite. I still have control over Nick's family. Bane felt a touch of unease at this. Would Nick have a problem with that? *Nick's family has earned this punishment. And Nick understands that.*

"But, Nick, I don't believe you would stay here simply for a *job*. I mean ... wouldn't you rather be *elsewhere*? Doing something else away from *here*?"

Away from me? But Bane kept those last two words inside. The beast inside whined as it wanted to nose Nick's soft skin, not chance sending him away like Bane was doing with these stupid words.

"No. I want to be *here*." Clearly, sensing that this wasn't enough to satisfy Bane, Nick added, "And, after all, I need to save up for school next year. I will make more working here than I would at any other job and I'm getting to practice my art every day."

Bane's head lifted and his heart stuttered in his chest. "You've been taking pictures of Moon Shadow?"

Nick's hand tightened on his. His eyes were shining with pride. "I didn't want you to miss any part of the transformation. Besides, even though Omar wasn't fond of the old, overgrown Moon Shadow I sort of miss it. But now we have photographs of how it was."

Bane thought of the pictures of the fountain that he had stolen a glimpse of when Nick was asleep with fever. "You'll show them to me?"

Nick smiled that same smile he'd given Bane when he'd first welcomed him home. Nick's voice was filled with that warmth again as he said, "After dinner, I'll show you *everything*. I promise."

CHAPTER FOUR

TRICK OF THE LIGHT

D inner was far quieter than usual. Bane needed quiet to recover. Nick found himself mostly tongue-tied. Luckily, Omar and Jade kept up light-hearted banter. Nick smiled and nodded, but he kept sneaking gazes at Bane.

It was strange to see Bane so tentative and almost *shy*. Nick caught the billionaire gazing back at him through his fall of dark hair as if he didn't really believe Nick was actually there. It was a *hungry* look. Bane seemed to *need* to see him, to gaze upon him, to drink him in as much as he needed the meal he devoured. Nick ended up giving over half of his steak to the billionaire.

Bane hesitated before accepting it. "Are you certain? Aren't you hungry?"

"I'm good. Omar made homemade chips and salsa this afternoon and I pigged out on that," Nick assured him. "Go ahead. Eat it. I think you need it."

"I should have purchased more steak," Omar lamented.

"It's okay, Omar. Really. I've had more than enough. Go on, Bane, finish it," Nick urged.

The billionaire cut up the meat and devoured every piece of it. His Siberian blue eyes were fixed on Nick with every bite. Nick felt both self-conscious and treasured by his regard.

He wished he knew what it meant. They had held hands after Bane had collapsed, but Bane had been careful not to touch him since then. Yet the billionaire seemed starved for his presence. So how was Nick to know whether the romance that had been kindled between them a month ago could be reignited?

Needing to track the tiger down right away makes Bane's quick getaway somewhat reasonable. But I remember his expression in the car. He was desperate to get away from ME. And he never tried to contact me after he fled. He didn't take my calls either.

All in all, Nick had questions about what had happened the night the tiger appeared and Bane left. He wasn't satisfied with Bane's behavior. But then he thought of Bane's reticence about himself and Omar's hints of secrets. If he pressed Bane, would he get answers or would he just push the billionaire away?

Should I let this go? If Bane tells me then he tells me, but if he doesn't then ... well, he doesn't.

After they had finished eating, Omar and Jade had made a quick exit from the porch to give him and Bane privacy. The Indian man claimed to have quite a bit to do with cleaning the dishes and then putting together the menu for the rest of the week now that Bane was back. Jade stated that she was tired even though it was only 9 p.m. She drew Nick aside before going up to bed.

She cast her voice low, "I think I was wrong."

He cocked his head to the side. "About what?"

Her gaze darted towards Bane who stood at the bottom of the porch steps, gazing out at the rose garden. The large blooms nodded under the moonlight like sleepy children. "Him. I thought that this thing between you was just *casual*, you know? But it *isn't*."

Nick felt a rush of pleasure go through him. He trusted her judgment in relationships and she had never said anything like this before with any of the other guys he'd dated. "Why do you say that?"

Jade's gaze went distant. "The way he looks at you. The way he's aware of every move you make."

"He watches everybody. He knows where they are and what they're doing at all times. He's hypervigilant." Nick shrugged even as he hoped that she was right.

"He's only like that with *you*, Nick." Jade gave him a small smile. "Not with anyone else. He has eyes for no one but you. I think he glanced at Omar and me about twice the whole evening. I can only imagine how *intoxicating* it must be to have the attention of a man like that."

A man like that ...

Nick's gaze unwittingly went to Bane's back. His shoulders were broad while his waist was taut. He had these impossibly long legs. His dark hair hung in long ribbons just past those powerful shoulders. Nick imagined what it would be like to wrap his arms around Bane's waist and rest his cheek against the big man's back. His eyes would drift shut as Bane's heart-beat would fill his head. Nick blinked and shook himself out of the fantasy. He turned back to Jade.

"He's just surprised to see me here, that's all," Nick said.

Jade laughed and shook her head. "Don't be blind, Nick! Bane is too dangerous not to see him clearly."

"*Dangerous?*" Nick's eyebrows rose up in surprise.

Jade looked serious again. "Yes, *dangerous*. He's one of the most beautiful men I've ever seen. And he's intelligent, charismatic and *obsessed* with you. That's a lethal combina-tion." Her right hand squeezed his left forearm.

"But there's hardly anything between us! I mean a few kisses and then he ran away, Jade. Yeah, he's back, but who knows if anything is going to happen ..." his voice died off when he saw her disbelieving and rather sad expression. She reserved that look for when he was being overly optimistic about his family. Now, apparently, he was being just as foolish about Bane.

"He stares at you like a man in a desert might an oasis." She shook her head and let out a breath. "This is going to be messier than I thought."

35

"Messier?"

"What I said about him and your family still stands, Nick. He can't have you in his bed and them over a barrel." Her gaze focused on Bane's massive shoulders. The billionaire turned his head to the side and Nick had the clearest impression that he could hear every word they said though it should have been impossible. "Just be prepared for a wild ride. Try to protect your heart. If you can."

"I'm totally going into this with my eyes open. I can handle Bane." Nick scuffed the porch with his bare foot. "I did it before. I can do it again. Things start going the way I don't want them to and I'll ... I'll bail. No harm. No foul."

Jade punched his arm playfully. "You don't bail on anyone. That's why your family isn't on the streets today, because you sacrificed your freedom for them. Bane's got this alpha thing going on, Nick. A wounded alpha, but still an alpha, which is like catnip to you."

He was going to object, but she got up on her tiptoes and kissed his cheek before turning and heading inside, leaving him and Bane alone. He remembered the last time that they had been alone together after Dean Kettering had attacked him. He had lain on Bane's chest. His head had been cradled underneath Bane's chin. It had been the start of something wonderful. The start ...

But then Bane had left.

Yet he's back now. Can we pick up where we left off? That is the question.

Nick slid his hands into the pockets of his shorts and clattered down the porch stairs to Bane. He stepped up along the other man's side. The billionaire did not look at him, but Nick *knew* Bane was keenly aware of him.

"What do you think?" Nick asked. "Omar and I located some photographs in the attic. They showed how the rose garden looked in its heyday. We gave them to the gardeners and they put this together."

Nick chewed his own lower lip after saying that. He remembered all too well the *last* time he had found photographs in the attic. Bane had been incandescent with rage. That time Nick had found them in an old trunk. They were pictures from India of an ancestor of Bane's. This ancestor could have been Bane's doppelganger except for the scar like a handprint on Bane's face that wasn't on his ancestor's. Nick still thought of those photographs, still wondered about Bane's anger and the ancestor he didn't want Nick to know about.

"And this is how it was?" Bane gestured, his voice colorless, showing no heat or anger.

"The gardeners recreated the look the best they could. We didn't want to completely tear down what was already here," Nick explained. "But let me show you how it got this way. I did promise to show you everything. I've got the tablet loaded with the photos."

Bane surprised Nick when he took Nick's arm in his and they walked together to the sofa. Nick relished Bane's strength. Nick was not a small guy, but Bane made him feel almost delicate in comparison. He could have swung on one of those arms and Bane would have hardly been strained by it. Nick remembered wondering how it would feel like to walk arm in arm with Bane just like this after seeing him do the same with Devon Wainwright. He had been jealous of Devon then. But now it was him on Bane's arm and Devon appeared to be just a memory. He looked up at Bane's face. Those Siberian blue eyes flickered down to his. A faint smile lifted the corners of Bane's lips

"What are you thinking about?" Bane asked.

"Devon."

Bane's eyes went large and he let out an uncomfortable laugh. "*Devon*? Why on Earth would you be thinking of him?"

"I was wondering if you called him while you were away. He's your ... *friend* after all," Nick said too casually and cursed himself. Why had he brought this up? Hadn't he decided to let Bane's silence and strangeness while he was gone stay in the past where it belonged?

Evidently not.

Bane's forehead furrowed. "No, I—I didn't. I only spoke to Omar. No one else."

"Oh, well, I'm sure he was disappointed not to hear from you."

They sat on the couch, but almost immediately Bane turned towards him and held both of Nick's hands. The billionaire fixed those Siberian blue eyes on Nick's. The young man could not look away.

"Were *you* disappointed not to hear from me?" Bane asked, his voice a low burr.

"I ... *yes*, yes, I was. I thought that maybe what we'd shared the night before you left was ... well, maybe you *regretted* it or maybe -"

"No," Bane interrupted. His hands tightened on Nick's, but then he consciously lightened his touch so that Nick would know he could pull away if he wanted. "No, I did not—*do not*—regret it. I could *never* do that." Bane's gaze slid to the roses as he continued, "You must believe me that I thought of you every moment I was gone. The only thing I regretted was being apart from you."

Nick was stunned by Bane's feelings and his intensity. He thought of Jade's word: *intoxicating*. It *was* intoxicating to be the focus of this kind of attention. Of Bane's attention.

"I—I don't understand then. If you *feel and* felt so much for me then why didn't you call me? Why didn't you accept my calls? Why ... why did you leave like that?"

Those Siberian blue eyes were upon him again and Nick's breath caught in his throat. His heart fluttered in his chest.

"All I can say is that I *left* to keep you safe. I stayed *away* to keep you safe," Bane murmured.

"*Safe?* I don't understand –"

Bane put two fingers over his mouth. They were so warm. "I know you don't, but I must ask that you don't question me more about it. I am back now. I do not have the strength to leave again." He gave such a sad smile. "But I will continue to keep you safe. I will do *anything* but leave to keep you safe. Do you understand?"

A million questions rose up in Nick's mind. What could Bane mean? What danger was he in from the other man? But Bane had asked that he not question any further. Another secret to add to the pile. If Nick were honest with himself the mystery drew him more to Bane rather than less. But could he stand not to know the answers to those secrets? He hoped so. But he wasn't sure. Finally though, Nick nodded and Bane took those fingers from his lips. Nick resisted the urge to lick them and capture Bane's taste.

"Bane, I ..." Nick swallowed. "All right. I won't ask you anything more about why you left or—or any of that."

Bane's fingers were under his chin then, lifting his head up so that they were eye to eye. "Thank you, Nick. Just be assured that my actions were not because I felt too little for you, but quite the opposite."

Nick felt himself flushing. "So you're telling me that you *like* me?"

Bane's sculpted lips quirked up into a smile. "More than *like*."

"*More* than like? Well, I *more* than like you, too," Nick admitted. He was grinning so hard that his face hurt from it. He shifted until his bare knees were touching Bane's cloth-covered ones. "So ... if we *both* more than like one another then ... then ..."

"You seem at a loss for words, Nick," Bane chuckled as his fingers slid along Nick's jaw and then feathered them in his hair.

"You have that effect on me ... sometimes ..."

"Oh? Only *sometimes*? I must work harder then."

Bane leaned in. Nick felt the hot puff of his breath. He smelled Bane's scent of cinnamon and sandalwood. Nick's eyelids fluttered shut as Bane's mouth descended on his. The kiss started out as close-mouthed, almost chaste. A soft press of lips. Skin against skin. But it quickly deepened.

Nick opened his mouth in a moan as heat built between his legs. Bane's tongue slipped between his lips. Nick's hands fisted in the front of Bane's jacket as that tongue twined with his, explored every inch of his mouth and claimed it as his own. Bane let out a low guttural growl in the back of his throat that had pleasure cork-screwing up Nick's spine. The primal sound had Nick surging forward against the bigger man. Then, inexplicably, Bane was pulling back. Nick whined and chased after that teasing, wonderful mouth. But Bane grasped his shoulders and held him back.

"W-what? What's wrong? Why are we stopping?" Nick asked, breathless and needy.

"I—It's too much. I need to ... need to ..."

For one moment when he looked up into Bane's eyes he thought he saw *animal nightshine* in them. They glowed this volcanic blue. It took Nick's breath away. He reached up and touched Bane's cheek.

"Your *eyes*. Bane, they're ... *glowing*," Nick gasped out.

"It's nothing. A trick of the light." Bane quickly looked away from him.

"No, I –"

Bane had turned back and there was no glow. "See? Nothing. Just a trick of the light."

Nick opened his mouth to object, but then he closed it. What was he going to say? Human eyes did not glow. It *must* be a trick of the light. What else could it be? Nick frowned. He swore he could almost see Bane's secrets settling between them, blocking them from one another.

Nick looked away. "Why did you stop the kiss? I mean we can talk about *that*, can't we?"

"Of course." Bane's hands tightened on Nick's shoulders. "I felt weak again for a moment and needed to breathe."

Guilt pricked at Nick then and his anger fled just as fast as it had flooded him. His head jerked around so that he was looking directly at Bane again. "Oh, God, are you all right? Do you need to lay down? Maybe we really should call Dr. Trevelyan –"

"No, no, Nick. I just need ... *time* in your presence." Bane smiled wanly.

"Without kissing?"

Bane let out a faint laugh. "I don't think it will be possible to be near you and not kiss you. But just ... we must go slow. I must keep control of myself."

Control? Why is he worrying about that?

"So I make you lose control? That sounds like a good thing in my book." Nick ran his hands up and down Bane's magnificent chest. Even over the clothes he could feel the hard muscle beneath the fine cotton.

Bane grunted. "I am ... *strong*, Nick. Stronger than you might realize. I need to be careful with you."

"You're not like Dean," Nick said, his voice flat even as his eyes flashed with emotion. "I know that day in the shower I made you feel like you were taking advantage of me, but I was wrong to do that. You're nothing like him."

"Those are kind words and I will hold them to me and cherish them."

"Bane." Nick turned and brought his knees beneath him so that he was kneeling on the sofa. He grasped Bane's hands in his. "I'm not a fragile flower. I know the sunburn and the thing with Dean might have made you think I am, but I'm *not*. I'm a man who knows his mind. And I've a mind to have you. So if you're backing off, because you believe that I can't handle you –"

Bane brought Nick's hands up to his lips and kissed them. There was a fond smile on his face. "Not in the least." Bane gritted his teeth. "You're not Devon."

"Ah, *no*, no, I'm not Mr. Perfect -"

"Mr. Perfect?" Bane's voice lilted with amusement.

Nick scowled. "He has perfect hair. A perfect body. A perfect smile and -"

Bane silenced him with a kiss. "Devon might be perfect for someone, but not for me."

"Oh."

"I've made you speechless again. I'm getting better at this." Bane gave him one of those tigerish smiles that Nick missed.

"Yeah, well ..." Nick cleared his throat. "Tell me how *not* being Devon—and *perfect*—is a good thing?"

"I took Devon to bed the first night we met. That is my normal *modus operandi* with beautiful young men." Bane trailed the fingers of his right hand down Nick's cheeks.

Heat built between Nick's thighs again at the almost predatory look that Bane gave him.

"Oh, and I'm not worthy of –"

"You're worthy. So *worthy.*" Bane leaned in and *sniffed* his throat which had Nick swallowing hard. "You're worthy of waiting for." That last sentence was spoken directly into the cusp of Nick's ear. "You're worthy of *courting.*"

Nick shivered with pleasure. He knew that he was moving too quickly. It was because he had dreamed of Bane every night for over a month. Every night the man had haunted his dreams. During the day, he had gone over and over every caress and kiss between them until the need for Bane seemed overwhelming. But the idea of being courted—such an old-fashioned term—appealed to him even more.

"You want to court me? You want to take things slow?" Nick clarified.

"I want to seduce you with sunlight, wine and good food. I want to dance with you under the moon and stars. I want to ache with the need of you and miss you even when you are there," Bane murmured, his hot breath gushing over Nick's throat.

"O-okay," Nick stammered.

"So I have your *permission* to court you?" Bane's eyes glittered.

"Yes, yes, you do."

Bane's large hands framed Nick's face. His expression went from teasing to serious. "I want so much *more* with you than with Devon or any of those others." Bane looked down at their joined hands. "Can you be patient with me?"

"Of course."

Bane moistened his lips. "There's something else."

Nick narrowed his eyes at the bigger man. "You're going to make some of your famous *rules* again, aren't you? Let me check to see where my phone is just to be sure it's safe and in *my* possession."

Bane chuckled and lowered his head. "No, nothing like that. Actually, I'm asking you to trust me again to an extent that I probably do not deserve yet."

"How do you mean?"

"There will be times, Nick, when I ask things of you that you might not understand and I will not be able to explain them. Like my leaving. But I will still need you to ... to trust me and let it go. Can you do that?" Bane looked up at him through that fall of dark hair.

"That's a tall order." Nick looked at Bane carefully. "How many secrets exactly do you have, Bane?"

Bane averted his gaze. "Perhaps too many for you to ignore, but -"

"I trust you," Nick said quickly. "Maybe one day you'll trust me."

Bane grimaced, but said nothing. He certainly didn't deny the truth of it. Nick's heart fell into his feet. Without trust there could be no lasting love.

I need to give it time. Bane will come to trust me. I'm sure of it. I have to show him not only that I'm not Devon, but I'm also not Alastair either.

Bane picked up the tablet that was sitting on the table and handed it to Nick. "You said you would show me your photographs."

"Of course." Nick took the tablet and turned to the slideshow.

One of Bane's arms slid around Nick's shoulders. His face pressed into Nick's hair and Nick heard him taking deep breaths of his scent. He leaned into Bane's side. He felt so safe. So *treasured*. Bane kissed his temple.

"Show me Moon Shadow through your eyes, Nick," Bane murmured. "Let me see everything I've missed."

CHAPTER FIVE

HOPE

T*he next day ...*
"Bane, what are you doing down here?" Omar's voice
floated through the bars of the cell in Moon Shadow's basement.

Bane's eyelids opened. He was lying on a thin mattress on
the basement's floor behind steel bars. He was pleased to see
that the beast had not shredded the mattress this time. Normally, it ripped the mattresses he kept in the cell apart in
protest for being locked up. Bane yawned. The clank of the
chain that bound him to the wall accompanied his stretching.
He met Omar's quizzical gaze.

"What made *you* look for *me* down here?" Bane asked back
instead of answering his servant's question.

Bane only locked himself in the basement during the full
moon. Omar also avoided the basement unless it was the full
moon and then he was only there in order to try to soothe the
beast and help Bane after the shift had ended. So it was as
perplexing to find the Indian man down here as himself. Bane
sat up and cracked his back, letting out a soft sound of pleasure at the soft pops.

Omar's left hand drifted up to the tiger amulet around his
neck. "I sensed the spirit down here and I came looking." He

then shook his head in confusion. "But it is not the full moon! Why have you locked yourself away?"

"I am well aware that it is *not* the full moon, but the beast apparently can cause me to shift when Nick is near and we are—are *intimate*," Bane answered him, a faint blush alighting his features.

Omar's brown eyes widened. "It happened *again*? The spirit caused the shift to occur on its own?"

"Yes. When I was out with Nick on the porch last night I nearly shifted into the beast and harmed him," Bane answered dryly as he clambered to his feet. The concrete floor was cool. He removed the collar from his neck, setting it to the side. The incident had happened *after* he had asked the young man to take it slow. But Bane couldn't heed his own warnings. Nick was so desirable, more desirable than any of his other partners had ever been.

"Did—did Nick *witness* you shift?" Omar breathed out.

"No, I was able to control it ... barely," Bane answered. "But it was such a near thing ..."

Nick had been cuddled against his side. The smell of the young man had filled his nostrils as he leaned over to look at the tablet Nick was holding. Nick was scrolling through the photographs that showed the transition of Moon Shadow's garden, explaining each one to him. Bane ran a finger along the line of the fountain in one of the photographs as Nick paused on it for him to see all the progress that had been made.

"I remember the day you cleaned the fountain off," Bane said, his voice a quiet huff.

"Yeah, me, too. I said some things to you then ..." Nick broke off. The young man's hands tightened on the tablet and his mouth flattened with regret.

"Things that were richly *deserved*, I assure you." Bane grimaced as he remembered his own behavior that day.

"But they *hurt* you. I've never wanted to hurt you, Bane. Not for long anyways." Nick sighed.

"What you said made me *think*. It made me *question* my prejudices. I thought I was judging you from a purely objective standpoint, but no. I wasn't seeing you at all. Yet I *sensed* who you really were. I wanted to be with you after all," Bane confessed.

Nick turned his head so that they were nearly nose to nose. "Wait, you *liked* me then? I thought you hated me."

"I *more than liked* you then. The first moment I saw you I liked you."

Nick's forehead furrowed as he asked dubiously, "In my father's office?"

"No, on the street. I saw you the day that I found out that Fairfax International was trying to take over one of my companies." Bane felt so aware of the closeness of Nick's lips as he spoke. The feelings he'd experienced upon seeing Nick that first time washed over him, but no longer was it tinged with regret.

"That's miserable timing." Nick looked aghast.

"I'd just received the email that confirmed the attack when I saw you. But one look at you and I forget about everything. My anger just melted away."

"But why? I'm a Fairfax!"

"I did not know that then. All I saw was—God, this sounds ridiculous when I think of saying it out loud ..."

"Oh, now you *have* to tell me!" Nick tugged on his arm like an eager child.

An unaccustomed flush heated Bane's cheeks and he raked a hand through his long black locks. Ironically, the nervous movement uncovered his scar. He was about to re-cover the mark, but decided against it. Nick didn't seem to mind the scar so he wouldn't. For the moment, anyways.

"You looked like ... an *angel*," Bane mumbled, reddening even more and looking away.

There was a long silent moment and then he felt Nick's hand on his chin, turning his head so that they were looking at one another again. Nick's expression was a mixture of impish amusement—which seemed to be his usual state—and genuine amazement. "An *angel*?"

"You were *gilded* by sunlight. You were looking up at the sky and just drinking in the sun. You were smiling. Your beauty struck me dumb." He ran a finger down Nick's cheek. "That's never happened to me before. I ... I actually walked towards you, intending to ask you to coffee or lunch or dinner or all three."

Nick's gray eyes widened. "Why didn't you?"

"Your father came out of his office, swung one arm around your shoulders and called you *son*." Bane's lips compressed with the remembered disappointment.

Nick though seemed not to notice. His gaze was distant as he remarked, "This is so strange, but I dreamed you telling me about this."

It was Bane's turn to widen his eyes. "What do you mean?"

Nick bit his lower lip and even under the soft light of candles and the moon, Bane saw a faint flush cross his cheekbones. "I dreamed a lot about you when I first got here and ... and after." He cleared his throat at that, but didn't let Bane ask him more about that by going on, "I dreamed we were on the couch here. Sort of just like this. And you told me about seeing me in the street and being disappointed that I was a Fairfax. You told me that your disappointment back then was part of the reason you were so mean to me. Because you thought you could never have me."

Bane blinked in shock. "Perhaps it is deja vu where you only *think* you dreamed this moment."

But Nick shook his head. "No, I'm certain I dreamed it, because the dream ended with a giant white Bengal tiger jumping up onto the porch."

Bane's breath caught. Nick dreamed of their meeting *and* the beast. He knew that this was portentous, but it was as if his mind couldn't quite accept it. "How—how strange! I was very disappointed when I realized who you were, because of that and well ... because I thought you were be a certain way."

"A spoiled brat, right?" The shadow of a smile curled the corners of Nick's mouth.

Bane sighed. "I will never live that down, will I?"

"No, never." Nick shook his head and laughed. Evidently, the insult no longer stung as much as it once had.

"You know that I regret every base and cruel word that exited my mouth with you, don't you?"

"I know. But I can be spoiled. I can be a brat. So you weren't altogether wrong." Nick shrugged.

"I imagine it must be quite the rare occurrence for I have never seen it," Bane disagreed.

His fingers carded through Nick's fine, platinum hair. The silky locks curled around his fingers. He leaned down and ran his cheek against that softness. Nick let out a pleased sound.

"You know, there was another weird aspect to that dream. The tiger part. You see, I *keep* dreaming of *you* and *tigers*," Nick said the last with a faint laugh.

"After the revelation of a tiger in your bed, I would think so," Bane murmured into his hair. He tried to hide his stiffening at the realization that Nick had dreamt of tigers *more* than once.

"This dream happened *before* the tiger was in my bed." Nick's hands fidgeted in his lap. Bane stilled them by covering them with his own much larger hand. "In fact, the first night I was here I dreamed about—about you and tigers." Nick laughed uncomfortably. "I don't know if I should tell you what the dream was about though!"

"Why not?"

Nick had not been alone in dreaming that first night. Bane could remember the dream he had of Nick. It had involved fellating the young man when he was a tiger before he transformed and finished Nick off in his human form. He was unlikely ever to forget that dream. The beast's blue eyes hooded in pleasure at the memory of the encounter.

Nick shifted against him uncomfortably, but then said, "Oh, fine! You can think I'm a kink if you want!"

"Now I'm *very* intrigued!"

"I dreamed of a tiger *licking* my—well, ah, well, my *cock*," Nick gave out another nervous laugh. "But thankfully the tiger turned into *you* and then you went down on me."

Bane froze. *We have been sharing dreams from the very beginning.*

"Bane, are you okay? Or are you really weirded out that I imagined you as a tiger shifter from the first moment I met you?" Nick looked up at him with faintly worried eyes.

Tiger shifter. My God, he has no idea how right he is. And he can never know.

Bane cupped his cheek, still feeling rattled, but trying not to show it. "Not in the least. The tiger is my spirit animal, remember?"

"Oh, right! That's what you told Mr. Fioretti! Yeah, well, you are tigerish." Nick grinned at him. "In a really *good* way."

"So long as you think it's good, I'm happy," Bane replied faintly. "And you were the mighty eagle as I recall."

"Not really. I couldn't think of anything, but I didn't want to be a *bunny*, which you claimed I was." Nick scowled at him, but he was grinning again. "You don't *really* think I'm bunnyish, do you?"

Bane still felt rocked back on his heels by all the revelations of shared dreaming, but he managed to say, "You are *soft* and *sweet*."

Nick gave him a doubtful look. "I don't think bunnies are sweet. Jade had a bunny as a pet when she was a little girl and it was *mean*. It would poop on the carpet for revenge. It wouldn't let her hold it. It would make this high-pitched scream when angry."

Bane let out a chuckle. "Oh, Nick, then you are most certainly *not* a bunny then."

"And it bit her when she fed it," Nick continued.

Bane was startled into laughter by this description of the evil pet bunny. He pulled Nick closer to him. "My poor Nick. You are not a biter, I take it?"

Nick twisted around to face him and with an impish look in his eyes said, "I *could* be."

Bane's eyebrows rose. "Oh?"

Nick fingers traced the line of Bane's jaw. "You look good enough to eat."

Nick leaned in then and kissed the left side of Bane's jaw. His soft lips opened and his teeth lightly *grazed* Bane's skin. Heat bloomed between Bane's thighs. His cock was immediately and painfully erect as Nick continued to drag his teeth and tongue along his jawline to his ear. Nick nipped Bane's earlobe. His hot breath gushed over Bane's skin.

Bane's hands framed Nick's waist, drawing the young man onto his lap once more. The tablet clattered onto the ground, forgotten. Nick's legs straddled him and their cloth-covered cocks were pressed against one another. Bane's mouth found Nick's and *devoured* it. His tongue slid between Nick's pink lips. He explored every inch of that hot cavern. Nick's tongue *fluttered* against his.

Bane slid his hands around to Nick's ass and pressed the young man's groin against his own. Nick let out a hiccupping moan into their kiss. The young man ground down on top of Bane. Heat blossomed and unfolded from Bane's groin and spread out to the rest of his body. Even his fingertips seemed *hot* with his arousal. He hands skated beneath Nick's light t-shirt and he ran them up and down Nick's spine.

The young man moaned again. His breathing became staccato. He gripped the front of Bane's shirt, holding the bigger man to him like he thought Bane wanted to escape. Then Nick's mouth left his and moved up his face. Light butterfly kisses were placed along his jaw.

And then Nick so *tenderly*, so *gently* kissed his *scar*.

The moment that Nick did that Bane felt the beginnings of the shift. His bones began to tingle. His skin itched. His muscles ached. And terror gripped him.

He surged up while at the same time twisting and dropping Nick gently onto the couch. Bane was then across the porch, gripping one of the columns as if he needed it to stand. He'd moved preternaturally fast and he could tell from the confused gasp that Nick wasn't sure what had just happened.

"Bane? Bane, are you all right?" Nick finally asked.

Bane knew that he should move farther away from Nick. The beast *roiled* within him, just beneath the skin, wanting to get out. Wanting to supplant him, replace him, take control from him. If he shifted right then and there the beast could *kill* Nick.

He heard the light creak of floorboards as Nick got up from the couch and approached him. His head jerked towards the young man again and he saw that Nick had one hand outstretched towards him. The beast *surged* forward, wanting to get to Nick. Bane's fingernails dug into the pillar, splintering the wood.

"Stay back, Nick," he gritted out and the beast's growl was in his voice, trying to steal his ability to communicate, too.

Nick stopped. His face was pale and his eyes were wide with alarm. "Okay, just—just tell me that you're all right. Please."

"I am ..." Bane cleared his throat as the growl threatened to overcome his voice. "You should go inside."

"I'm not leaving you! I don't know what's wrong, but it's clear that *something* is. Let me help you! Let me get Omar!" Nick protested.

"You *must* leave, Nick. Please ... please ..." Bane felt his teeth starting to *elongate* and become sharp. Panic fluttered in his chest like a humming bird.

"But why? Did I hurt you? I hurt you, didn't I? Touching the scar? God, I'm such an idiot!" Nick raked a hand through his hair, looking stricken.

"No, not your fault. I'm just ..." Bane could not explain.

I cannot tell him that I'm going to shift into a tiger!

"Please let me help you." Nick's hands clenched together in front of his chest. His eyes were luminous with concern. "I promise I won't touch the scar again. I swear I—"

Bane closed his eyes tightly as the beast tried to surge to the surface and push him into darkness once more. Ironically, it wanted to soothe Nick. It believed that if it licked him and nosed him that all would be well. It didn't seem to understand that Nick would scream and run from it. And if Nick ran then the beast would chase after him and do what the beast did to all *prey*. It would not remember what Nick was to them both at that moment. It would only know the *chase*.

Don't you understand that Nick will be afraid of you? Of us? He'll scream and run and you'll hurt him. You won't mean to. But you will!

The beast regarded him out of those inscrutable blue eyes. He sensed that it didn't altogether believe him about how this would go down. The beast seemed to think that Nick was *different*. Nick would *understand*. Nick would *accept* them.

Or Nick will flee. You will chase. And you will kill him. Would you take that chance of us losing him again?

The beast settled down. But only slightly. His skin still *prickled* with the chance of imminent shift. Bane opened his eyes. He let go of the pillar, though he kept well away from Nick. Sweat coated his skin from the internal battle to stay in his human form. Nick's yearning for him was almost a physical thing though. He could feel the young man wanting to touch him, comfort him, undo whatever wrong he had committed.

"Nick, you are not to blame for my—my condition," Bane got out. "This is one of those times when I need you not to question, but to—to *accept* what I'm telling you. You are not at fault in any way."

"I shouldn't have touched the scar," Nick whispered, unconvinced.

"At other times it would be fine, but I ..." Bane gave out a helpless laugh. "Tonight I am hanging on with just my fingernails. Being away from you was so impossibly hard. Coming back and finding you here." Bane shut his eyes tightly again. "It is a dream come true. That you *want* me is beyond anything I could have hoped for."

"I shouldn't have pushed things. You asked me not to earlier, but I just kept on—"

"You did what any *normal* young man would do and if I was ... *normal*, too, we could have that, but I'm *not*."

I'm not.

"I'm not interested in normal," Nick said with a pained laugh. "I'm interested in *you*. Whatever that entails. Just tell me what to do and I will do it."

Bane mustered up a soft smile. "First ... stop worrying. Tomorrow, I will be well. Just go in and—and rest."

He didn't know if any of what he was saying was true. Could he contain the beast tomorrow? Would this happen any time he was romantic with Nick? Despair welled up inside of him. But he wouldn't let it conquer him. He couldn't believe that there wasn't some way for him to have Nick. The young man hadn't left him. That was a miracle in and of itself. It must mean something. And they had been dreaming of one another from the start. Didn't that mean they were fated in some way? He couldn't believe it would lead to tragedy.

Nick didn't move. "What about you?"

"I will be going in shortly," Bane assured him. "And I will see you in the morning. Everything will be fine."

What must he think of all this? Kissing my scar has me fleeing from him? Will Nick want a man that's so broken?

Nick hesitated for a long moment. "Bane ..."

"It's all right, Nick. Go on in."

Nick stared at him so long. His expression was unreadable, but finally, he nodded and said, "See you in the morning, Bane."

He then walked inside and Bane had to bite down on a roar of loss.

You are the cause of everything bad in my life! Bane yelled at the beast. *Because of you, we will be alone!*

The beast lowered its head down onto its paws. Its ears flattened. Bane trembled with anger and the need to shift. Once he was sure that Nick was safe in his bedroom, he pushed off of the pillar and stormed into the house. He went immediately to the basement where he had fashioned a prison cell. Bane wrenched the door open.

He locked the door behind him, but left the key in the lock as the beast could not manipulate it. He then stripped off of his clothes in angry movements, scattering them around the concrete prison like fallen leaves. He picked up the metal collar that was attached to the wall by a heavy chain and put it around his neck. The chain was sunk deep into the concrete wall of Moon Shadow. It hung loosely around his own neck as a human, but it would fit firmly around the beast's once he shifted.

Then he had given the beast what it wanted or, at least, *partially* what it wanted. The shift was agonizing. He felt his bones *melt* inside of him and reform in *wrong* ways for a human body. His skin *flowed* around the new skeleton. His own hair sloughed off, but then soft white and black fur sprouted in its place. Every piece of fur was like a tiny dagger as it pushed through his skin. The only thing that stayed the same when the beast took its form were the eyes. Both of them had the same eyes.

The beast curled down in a tight ball on the mattress and mourned Nick. It was then in that mourning that he and the beast had made a decision. A decision that would allow them both what they wanted.

"So you were able to make it to the cell before you shifted?" Omar leaned against the cell's bars in relief.

"Yes, thankfully, but I think that I shall not have this problem again. The beast and I have made an agreement."

Bane picked up his pants and slid them on. The beast hadn't shredded his clothes either which was one of its other favorite pastimes when it was angry with him. But the beast hadn't been angry last night. It had almost seemed forlorn. His allegation that it was the cause of all the unhappiness in their life had struck home. It had just accepted the cage as punishment.

What I said is true, Bane thought viciously even as a stab of guilt went through him.

The beast was curled into a tight ball in his chest and seemed more despondent than before. Perhaps its understanding of the burden it was to him and the threat it posed to Nick was what had caused it to agree to his terms.

"What agreement?" Omar asked suspiciously.

"I have agreed to cede control of my body to it for three days around the full moon," Bane explained as he picked up the rest of his clothes. "I will not chain it in the basement so long as it does not go after Nick."

"Won't Nick see it—"

"Every month, Nick will have to leave Moon Shadow during this time. I'll make up some excuse. Maybe he and Jade can stay in my apartment in the city, use the spa, go have fun in the clubs." Bane shrugged. "I will think of something."

He stepped out of the cage and closed the door behind him. He and Omar walked to the stairs that led to Moon Shadow's first floor. The Indian man had his hands behind his back and a thoughtful expression on his face.

"What is it, Omar? I can *feel* you disapproving from here," Bane remarked dryly.

Omar let out a sigh and gave him a slight smile. "I believe you should tell Nick the truth."

"Omar, that's not going to happen." Bane shook his head at the insanity of what Omar was saying.

"A relationship built upon *lies* is not one that will last!" the Indian man protested.

"Our relationship is *not* built on lies. It has *nothing* to do with the beast or the curse or any of it. Nick is separate from all of that." Bane made a sweeping motion through the air with his right arm.

"You really think that you can separate yourself and the beast? You think there is some bright line between the two of you?" When Bane didn't respond, Omar asked, "And, even if there were such a line, think how the spirit is reacting to Nick's touch! Never has this happened before with any other lover, Bane!"

Bane pushed the door to the first floor open and they emerged into the hallway directly beneath the stair to the second floor. "It has not."

"And you are dreaming of each other," Omar said quietly. He tentatively touched Bane's arm. "Nick could be the *one*."

"My *true love*?" Bane's voice was mocking. "I think not."

"Is he not worthy of—"

"Nick is *completely* worthy, but true love is *fiction*. There is no way to end this curse. None. My only hope is that the beast does not harm Nick." Bane gritted his teeth. "I have to ensure that the curse *never* touches him."

Omar rubbed the tiger amulet. "I think you are wrong about this, Bane. It is foolish to go against nature. Nature always wins."

Bane clasped Omar's shoulder, not liking to see the distress on Omar's face. "I know you only want the best for me and for Nick. I do, too. But you must trust me in this. Nick can never know of the beast. And that's that."

Omar still did not look convinced. But Bane squeezed his shoulder and breezed past the Indian man and went up the stairs. He wanted to see Nick. He wanted to be with Nick when the young man woke. He wanted Nick's gaze to alight upon him and know that everything was all right. He would prove to Nick that last night was an aberration, never to be repeated again. He had conquered the beast. He could have a life with Nick.

Bane felt something stirring in his chest that he had not felt in a long time. It was *hope*.

CHAPTER SIX

ONE CARELESS KISS?

Nick did not dream that night of Bane or tigers. He hardly slept at all, which left little time for dreams in any case. The scene on the porch with Bane—the way the billionaire had *clutched* at the pillar as if he needed it to keep from fleeing from Nick altogether—haunted him.

I should never have touched his scar, but, other than being self-conscious about it, I had no idea it would cause that reaction!

It was a strange reaction to be sure. If Nick's lips on it had *hurt*, wouldn't Bane have simply winced and withdrawn? Not raced across the porch and looked at him out of those glowing eyes that were filled with *wildness*. Bane had seemed like he was the verge of *losing control* of himself. Nick had always sensed that was an untamed side of Bane that was in direct opposition to his outer façade of the English lord, the brilliant billionaire, and the sensual sophisticate. That wild side appeared to be unleashed by Nick's kiss of his scar.

Yet at the same time, he seemed frightened not of me, but of himself. Why?

The night that had begun so brilliantly had ended in Nick going up to his room *alone* to ruminate on these questions and others. He had tossed and turned as he tried to find answers. Finally, his exhausted body had dragged his mind down into sleep, but his last thought before finally succumbing to unconsciousness was that he might have destroyed any chance of him and Bane having a relationship with one careless kiss.

So though Nick had not dreamed of Bane or tigers, he thought he *must* be dreaming when he felt the delicate caress of fingertips skating across his cheek and into his hair. Those fingertips slipped down the side of his neck. They played along his collarbone and rounded his shoulder before drifting back up to his cheek once more.

Nick slept on his side, legs curled up in a half-fetal position. But the kisses had him stretching his legs out and pointing his toes. One of his hands slid out from under the pillow beneath his head and slipped along the silky sheets until it met an obstruction. That obstruction was warm and breathing. That was when Nick realized the caresses were *real*.

He opened his eyes and saw Bane lying on the bed beside him. Bane was on his side, too, facing Nick. His hand cupped Nick's cheek and he drew his thumb along Nick's jaw. The billionaire was smiling softly and his Siberian blue eyes were filled with a quiet happiness. Nick had another moment of uncertainty as to whether he was asleep or awake, because this look was *the look* that he had once imagined on Bane's face as they sat in the chairs in his bedroom, curled up, reading books together. Nick had thought that such a look would never appear on Bane's face—let alone be turned towards *him*—but there it was.

"I must be dreaming," Nick murmured.

Bane's sculpted lips had already been lifted at the corners into a small smile now broadened. "Am I a dream of yours?"

"You are," Nick breathed. "I don't dare move or you'll disappear like *smoke*."

"I'm *real*, Nick, and I'm not going anywhere."

Bane leaned in and kissed him. It was just a soft press of lips, but heat bloomed inside of Nick as if Bane had cupped him and stroked him. His immediate desire though could not make him move an inch. Bane was here. He would not risk ruining it and sending the man fleeing for a *third* time.

Bane's Siberian blue eyes sparkled so unlike the day before when they had seemed dull and exhausted. This Bane seemed refreshed and restored.

"You look really good. Far healthier than you did yesterday," Nick said.

"I feel quite well. I am certain in a few days I will be fully restored, perhaps even better than I was before because *you* will be with me," Bane murmured. His hand was back stroking Nick's cheek as if he couldn't stop himself from touching the young man.

Nick hummed a little in pleasure at the touch. "That feels good."

"You are very touchable. Every inch of you seems to call to my senses. I *must* caress you. I *need* to feel the softness of your skin, the brush of your hair, the sound of your voice. All of you is necessary to me," Bane murmured.

Nick flushed. "After last night I thought that I moved too fast—"

"You are not responsible for what happened last night," Bane interrupted him.

"But if I'm not to blame ..." Nick let the sentence hang.

"It is one of those things I must beg of you not to ask me to explain. Just suffice it to say that it should not happen again, but even if it were to do so, again, it would *not* be your fault and it would in *no way* reflect how much," Bane paused and licked his lips, "how much I want you near me."

It was hard to argue with Bane that he needed more information when the man was saying things like *that*. Things that made Nick's heart beat faster and his skin to flush.

"You need to tell me the rules regarding touching you," Nick said.

"There are no rules." Bane's thumb traced the line of Nick's lower lip, which had the young man's arousal burning brighter.

"But last night when I kissed your scar—"

"Kiss it now."

"What? No, clearly you don't like it so—"

"Kiss me, Nick," Bane commanded then added that magic word, "*Please.*"

Nick's gaze flickered over Bane's face, trying to make sure that this was truly okay. It clearly was yet would Bane just be *enduring* his touch or would he like it? But those Siberian blue eyes were giving him no choice but to lean in and lightly brush his lips against the marred flesh.

It was surprising how soft the scar was. Bane let out a breath as Nick pressed a single kiss to that long-ago wounded cheek. When he pulled back, Nick saw that Bane's eyelids had closed. He had long dark lashes that fanned beautifully against his high cheekbones. Nick's hands framed Bane's face as the billionaire's eyelids slowly opened. They remained hooded as they stared into one another's eyes.

Bane's voice was a soft burr as he said, "My mother told me that to look into another person's eyes is to see their soul."

With an impish smile, even as his heart whipped up its beat again, Nick murmured, "And I bet you thought that was nonsense."

Bane grinned. "I did."

"Has something changed?"

The grin died. Something serious took its place. "Yes, I met you."

Nick swallowed. "The things you say."

"You inspire me." The grin was back and Bane broke eye contact.

Nick let his hands drift down to the front of Bane's magnificent bare chest. He felt the rise and fall of it with every breath Bane took. His nipples, a dark peach, were peaked in the cool air of the room, but his skin was so warm. Nick wanted to rub his cheek against that chest, he wanted to trace every hill and valley of muscle with his tongue.

We're just starting this. Whatever this is. Calm down.

But Nick's pulse fluttered wildly in his throat. Bane's hand had slipped to Nick's shoulder again and he traced the line of

Nick's arm until he reached the hand that was still framing his face. He took it and linked their fingers together.

"You must think me so presumptuous to be in your bed like this," Bane said. "But I wanted to see you the first moment you woke to apologize for last evening and to—to simply see you."

"I don't mind that you're here, Bane." Nick could get used to being woken every day like this. Bane's touch. Bane's kiss. Bane. Bane. Bane.

I don't mind at all.

"I haven't *earned* my place here yet, but I intend to. I would like to start to earn it today." A pleased yet almost uncertain smile lit Bane's face. "Would you join me in a picnic?"

Nick's heart skipped a beat. A picnic where they fed each other small bites of food and exchanged wine-soaked kisses sounded perfect. "I think I could be convinced."

Bane brought their clasped hands up to his mouth and kissed Nick's fingers. "Thank you." He then let out a regretful sigh. "I need to do some work this morning so I must leave you."

"Actually, I need to do some work, too. Jade has some dresses she wants to sell and she needs her photographer," Nick said even as he felt a stab of regret that each of them would have to leave this cool, shadowed room.

"She is a wise woman to have chosen you."

They leaned into each other at the same time, coming together in a mutual kiss. It stayed chaste but they kept their hands tightly locked together. Finally though, Bane got up from the bed, holding onto Nick's hand as long as possible, but soon he was out of reach. His gaze lingered on Nick for even longer moments.

"I shall see you later," Bane said as if he had to assure *himself* that Nick would not vanish from his life.

"Definitely."

Bane turned and walked out. It was only then that Nick realized that Bane had still been wearing the pants he'd had on last night. Nick frowned. He supposed that Bane had likely just pulled them on as soon as he'd woken up. But as Nick listened to the floor creaking as Bane made his way to his own bedroom he was almost certain that the man hadn't come up here last night.

Where else would he sleep? Outside on the porch? On a couch somewhere? I must have just slept through his coming upstairs.

But Nick had this nagging feeling that where Bane had been last night might be another one of the secrets surrounding the billionaire. The fact that Bane had secrets did not annoy him. He hadn't *earned* to know the billionaire's every thought.

Not yet. But I am interested. It is intriguing. And it would help me know what to do and what not to do with him. For someone so strong, he's fragile, too.

Nick's cell phone suddenly buzzed. He frowned again as he wondered who would be calling him this early. He grabbed it from the nightstand and looked at the caller ID. It was his father.

Bane's gone a month and I hear nothing from him. Bane's back less than 24 hours and Dad suddenly has to talk to me? Not a coincidence.

Nick sighed. He answered with a suspicious, "What do you want, Dad?"

There was a pause and then Charles Fairfax's amused response was, "No hello, Nickie?"

"You're not calling for me, are you?" Nick pointed out.

"Of course I am! I called *your* number, didn't I?"

"It's been over a month since we've talked so—"

"Can't believe it's been that long. Been very busy making Bane money. But even so, Nickie, it would be quite hypocritical of you to be cross with me for not calling when you haven't called either," Charles' pointed out, but without any bite to his voice. He didn't, after all, really care whether Nick called him or not.

Nick considered saying that he'd had nothing to report that would have interested Charles, but that wasn't true. His father did not know about Nick's part of the deal being abrogated or that he and Bane were dating. Those were pieces of information that his father would give his eyeteeth for. So why hadn't he told Charles? Because of all the questions about him and Bane that he couldn't answer. At least, Nick hadn't known how to answer them when Bane was away and the status of their relationship was uncertain. But while Bane might still have secrets that he was keeping from Nick, it was pretty damned clear that they were in a relationship.

Nick couldn't keep these things from his father any longer. Bane would be talking to his family sooner or later. If he found out that Nick hadn't told his father and brothers about their relationship, Bane might think he was ashamed of it.

But how am I going to tell Dad this without him freaking out? Is that even possible? Likely, no. So just better get it over with.

While Nick contemplated what to say, Charles barreled ahead, "So how are you doing?"

Nick considered actually telling his father how he was doing, but instead stuck to the neutral and expected, "Just fine, Dad. How are you?"

"Better than ever!" He imagined his father looking out the window of his corner office, surveying his domain, even if it was really Bane's domain. But his father was ever an optimist. "Bane got back from Europe yesterday, didn't he?"

Nick rolled his eyes. He was right about why his father had called, "Yep, he did."

Charles' voice was cautiously casual as he said, "People were surprised that he just took off and cut off all contact except for a few terse emails. Thought he was sick or something, which *never* happens to him, according to the gossips around here anyways."

Nick frowned. Bane had said he was exhausted from working. But maybe it had been dealing with the tiger that had taken so much time. That seemed unlikely, but he had no idea what was required to get a tiger into a private zoo. "Maybe he was working on something for one of his other business-es, Dad."

"Was he *upset* when he left, Nickie?" Charles questioned.

Nick shifted uncomfortably as he remembered Bane's strained expression through the window of the Mercedes. "He had some things on his mind, but he's fine now."

"Oh, well, that's definitely good to know," Charles said, his voice sounding speculative. Nick imagined his father rubbing his jaw as he pondered just how to use this information to his advantage. But there wasn't enough there for even his father to go on. "Does he have you working hard? You're doing a good job for him? Hope he isn't getting too handsy with you!"

Nick gritted his teeth. This was the opportunity he needed to tell his father what was going on between him and Bane and the ending of the deal. "Yeah, about that ... Bane's re-leased me from the deal."

Silence fell on the line. This news had evidently shocked his father.

"Why, Nickie? Did you upset him in some way?" Charles' voice was much less friendly.

Nick found his shoulders curling forward as they usually did when he made an error and his father called him on it, but then, realizing what he was doing, Nick straightened. He had done nothing wrong and his father had no right to make him feel otherwise.

"No, Dad. Things between Bane and I are really good actu-ally," Nick snapped back and immediately wished he hadn't.

Another silence fell then Charles asked, "Are you and Bane ... are you and Bane *dating*?"

Nick's cheeks burned. The last—and only—time that his father had seen Bane and him interacting was when Nick was shouting at Bane about how he was *never* going to sleep with him. He looked a little foolish now considering everything. But then he shook himself. His father didn't judge people on stuff like that. Besides he had said what he had said and now he and Bane were dating. It was what it was.

So Nick said simply, "Yes."

His father started laughing, loud and boisterously. "Oh, Nickie! You really surprise me. I think you must have a bit of me in you."

Nick's brow furrowed in confusion. "Dad, what are you talking about?"

His father evaluated relationships by how well they served him. Nick tried to imagine his father falling for a guy like Bane, but that would never happen.

"You're a clever, clever boy. I give you credit for that. Being Bane's boyfriend must be far more pleasant than cleaning his toilets!" Charles chuckled.

Ice skated down Nick's spine as he realized his father thought he was using Bane to get out of working. "Dad, I'm not—"

"You just have to deal with him for one year. I'm sure you can pull that off with help. Nickie, we should talk," Charles chortled. "Because a man like Bane is *different* than the boys you've dated. And I use the term *boys* on purpose. He's a *man* and a man of very refined tastes—"

"Dad!" Nick shouted, which stopped Charles' speech and had his father quiet for a moment. He went on in a more subdued tone, "Dad, I'm *not* dating Bane to get out of working for him. I'm still helping out here and photographing the restoration of his mansion. I'm also not with him so that you guys will get the business back. That's all on you, Jake and Steven."

Charles stayed silent for long moments and Nick couldn't imagine what his feelings were. When his father did speak, his voice was icy, which shocked Nick. "Son, you *better* be thinking about the family. As Bane's servant you could only mess up his house. He'd likely ignore your mistakes or even not notice them. But as his *lover* you are front and fucking center, Nickie. You have his *full* attention. So if you mess up in that role, he'll *see* and there will be consequences."

Nick was too stunned to speak. He wanted to shoot back that Bane would never hold his mistakes against his family! Nothing that happened between Bane and him would affect the deal!

But I don't know that. I don't know that at all. Even when I think I'm done with my family and the deal there it is again.

Charles talked into his silence, his voice friendlier, "I'm sorry that I was a little stern there, but I need you to understand how *precarious* this makes things for us if you don't *please* Bane. This could go gangbusters or it could become a total shit sandwich. We can't afford the latter. Do you understand?"

Nick couldn't get any words out around the lump in his throat.

"So, we need to meet up. How about you meet me downtown tomorrow? Do you think Bane could spare you?" Charles asked.

Nick licked his dry as dust lips as he answered, "I can't right now, Dad. Bane just came back and –"

"Nickie, we *are* going to talk," his father's tone brooked no argument.

"Maybe the end of the week? I'll call you."

"If you don't, I will call *you*," his father said and hung up without another word.

Nick suddenly felt a headache coming on.

CHAPTER SEVEN
SECRETS, LIES
AND PHOTOGRAPHS

B ane's phone beeped quietly, telling him that it was time
to get Nick and go on their picnic. His heart beat faster in
anticipation. He logged off of his computer and got up from
his chair. He stretched his arms above his head. There was a
soft pop as his spine realigned and he let out a pleased sigh.
He was going to *see* Nick. He was going to *talk* to Nick. He
was going to *kiss* Nick. He left the office with the proverbial
spring in his step.

The morning had raced by as he had flown through all the
work he had been avoiding for the past month. Now that he
was back in Moon Shadow and Nick was in his life again, he
was filled with energy and focus. He felt healthy. There was
none of the weakness that had been plaguing him for the past
month. The only thing disturbing him was how quiet the beast
was being. It was lying down in his chest. Its head was facing away from him. Its tail was still. He thought the beast was
sulking, but, at times, he had this strange idea that the beast
was *plotting*. It had never done that before.

*But Nick has changed things. The beast is different just as
I am different.*

But that thought was lost as he passed by the foot of the stairs and heard the tap of high-heels coming down them. He turned his head to see Jade descending the stairs towards him. Unlike the night before where Jade's hair and clothes had been black as a crow's wing with pink highlights, the young woman was transformed into angelic silver and white now.

She wore an evening dress made of a shimmering silver material that swept down to her knees in metallic folds. Her black spiky hair was covered by a blonde wig that had a profusion of curls spilling down her shoulders and back. Her black makeup had been replaced by stunning red lipstick, glittery black eyeliner and silver eyeshadow. She wore silver high heels. She struck a pose the moment she saw him.

"What do you think?" she asked.

A smile twitched his lips even as tension drew his shoulders together. Normally, he would never have allowed strangers in his home, but this was Nick's best friend. He had to make an exception. So he had a choice about how to deal with the situation. He could be growly with her or he could be a *gentleman*. In truth, there really was no choice. The gentleman it was to be. Besides, he was in too good a mood to be bothered by most anything. So he regarded her with a faux critical gaze. She looked back at him. He stroked his chin, not letting his amusement show.

"Very attractive, but a *bit* overdressed for noontime, don't you think?" he remarked finally.

She sighed. "Can't a girl dream of going to some swanky party where she would be *required* to dress like this even at noon?"

He tilted his head to the side. "If you *really* wish to go to such parties I'm certain that Omar can arrange that. I get piles of invitations."

"That you politely decline in all your English lordship way?" She grinned.

"Indeed, I do. I'm not interested in most parties."

"Because you're not interested in most *people*, right?" Jade's green eyes sparkled with mischief. It was clear that Nick had told her quite a bit about him.

"Very true." He nodded his head in agreement.

"Well, that's something we share then," she said. "I'm not interested in most people either."

"But you like parties?"

"No, I like dressing up." She bit her lower lip. "Actually the reason I'm dressed like this is because I am acting as a model for the clothes. I'm selling this outfit on eBay. Nick's waiting to photograph me in your very beautiful front room. The light in there is just perfect, according to Nick that is."

"Ah, well, Moon Shadow could enhance even your beauty, not by much, but a little."

Jade tossed her now blonde hair and wagged a finger at him. "You're a flatterer."

"You sound surprised about that."

She gave him a rather rueful look. "I guess I *am* surprised. You don't seem like the type that lies *lightly*."

For a moment, the secrets and lies he had told to Nick rose up in him like a tidal wave. Bane looked down at the polished floor. "I have been known to *bend* the truth. But you *do* look lovely. I'm not lying about that."

She let out a faint laugh. "I can see why Nick is so fond of you."

He glanced up at her through his lashes. "I am merely grateful he is."

"I know all his likes and dislikes, you see." She shrugged. "We know the good, the bad and the ugly about each other and about each other's lives."

"And there has much bad and ugly to be heard about recently in Nick's life," Bane said with a press of his lips. He had been the cause of most of it.

"But the *good* overwhelmed all of that. Surely you know that from the way Nick looks at you. And I knew it by how he was glowing this morning."

His head lifted. "Does he seem ... that happy to you?"

Jade laughed. "I mentioned *glowing*."

"Nick *glowed* before me," Bane said, thinking of that first time he saw Nick in the sunlight.

Jade looked at him thoughtfully. "He did. But it's a ... *deeper* glow now with you. Speaking of him, he's waiting for me." She came down the stairs carefully with one hand gliding along the bannister. She nearly stumbled, but caught herself at the last moment. "Damn high heels. They look good, but are hell to walk in. Give me combat boots any day."

Bane took her free hand and helped her down the final step. "I'm glad you were here. For Nick. Not that he ... well, not that he needed –"

"He was a little wobbly there for awhile after you left. But there's one thing you have to know about Nick and that's that he doesn't let on when he's wounded easily," she said with a sigh as they began walking towards the front room. Her arm hooked through his lightly.

The fact that Nick was *wounded* by his absence was both pleasing and guilt-inducing. But he managed to say, "I've noticed that about him. He kept quite silent about how bad his sunburn was."

"Yes. Exactly. I was coming to Moon Shadow the day you left to make sure he was okay. I mean I didn't know about you taking off but –"

"You wanted to see if he was locked up in a love pit perhaps?" Bane gave her a smile.

"Exactly." She gave him a cool look that had him wanting to squirm. He *had* used the deal to keep Nick close to him even though there hadn't been a love pit. Jade continued on, "But instead of finding Nick bound to a bed, I discovered my best friend *anguished* that you had let him out of the deal and decided to leave his life. In a very dramatic fashion, I might add. I saw you driving out of here like a bat out of hell."

He nodded. "That is an accurate description."

She lowered her head so that she could not catch sight of her face. "I highly doubt that you would tell me the *real* reason that you left considering you're not telling Nick, but I really hope it's a good one."

His eyes widened in surprise and alarm. "Did Nick not tell you about my—my *pet* tiger?"

"He did." She let out a breath. "But that's not why you left like that."

More alarm raced through him. He hoped he hid it from her, but she seemed too observant not to notice. "Oh?"

"I'm glad that you aren't insulting my intelligence by saying I'm mistaken." She patted his arm.

"Normally, I would be quite cross about being called a *liar* in my own home," he pointed out gruffly.

A faint flicker of nervousness went through her eyes, but she gave him a smile. "And *normally* I wouldn't say something like this. But Nick really likes you and I'm his best friend." She stopped walking. They were near the partially closed pocket doors that led into the front room. He could hear Nick singing along with the music that issued out of the room. Jade looked up at him with determination. "You have secrets. Nick says he's good with that. He says that he's good with loads of things that ... well, I just love him. A lot. He's the only family I have. I don't care about what your secrets are. Just ... just don't let them hurt Nick. Can we agree on that?"

Bane stared at her. He should have been angry or offended or taken aback. But he wasn't. He knew that she spoke out of a deep affection and loyalty she felt for Nick. Plus, she was right. He was lying to the young man. His secrets were potentially dangerous to Nick, too. So could he blame her for the truth that she had just spoken? No. And anyone who was good to Nick, he could not be angry at. He tentatively laid one hand on her shoulder.

"We can agree on that. Nick is very important to me, too. I will endeavor with all of my power to keep him happy and safe," Bane promised formally.

Jade nodded after a brief moment. "I guess that's all I can ask of you." She let out a breath and smoothed her hands down the front of her dress. She put a smile on her face. "We should get in. I know Nick wants to take a few last pictures before your picnic."

She then turned and fully slid open the pocket doors to the front room. It was filled with sunlight and yellow and white roses. Nick was looking through the viewfinder of his camera with his back to them. Bane felt his pulse in his throat as he looked at the graceful sweep of Nick's spine. His eyes lingered on that pert ass and those long, muscular legs. He watched as the muscles of Nick's forearms flexed as he adjusted the camera's lens.

Without looking over at them, Nick said, "Jade, you're just in time! Get in your place before we lose the light."

The light was gushing in through the bow window. With a swish of her dress, Jade positioned herself between two large vases of roses. Bane leaned against the wall behind Nick. He crossed one ankle over the other and observed the young man that had his breath catching. The beast even turned to look at Nick. Its tail immediately began to whap against the ground.

"Oh, you look great!" Nick enthused and started to shoot. "Put your hands on the edges of the vases. Pick up one of the roses and hold it against your chest. Yeah, perfect!"

He finally looked up from the camera and grinned at Jade. Bane started to clap. Startled, Nick spun around to face him. His lips parted in surprise and beautiful color flooded his cheeks.

"Bane!" he cried. "I didn't realize you were here!"

Nick moved towards him. Bane pushed off of the wall and stepped into the young man's personal space. Bane's nerves tingled as they neared one another. The beast had gone very still.

"I enjoyed watching you work, Nick. I can see your passion for it," Bane said.

Nick ducked his head and rubbed the back of his neck. "Oh, I ... thanks. How long were you there? I didn't hear you come in."

"I didn't want to distract you until your work was done." Bane ran a single finger down Nick's cheek.

Nick bounced up and down on his toes, a contagious grin on his face. "You *are* distracting." He shot a narrow-eyed glance at Jade then who was busying herself rearranging the flowers. "But that doesn't explain why *you* didn't mention Bane sneaking in, Jade."

She shrugged her shoulders. "Maybe I didn't want you distracted either." She went over and took Nick's camera. "I'll download the pics, shall I? And narrow down my favorites."

Nick nodded. "There are a ton of great shots. You won't have any trouble selling that outfit."

Jade scrolled through the pictures and let out a theatrical sigh. "Why do all of my absolute favorite outfits have to be the ones that will fetch us the most money? I'd love to be able to keep this one."

"Yeah, but the problem is that you say that about *every* outfit," Nick shook his head with amusement as he said it.

Jade stuck her tongue out at him.

"All right, *children*, I am hungry. Are we done here for now?" Bane asked with an arched eyebrow at both of them.

"I'm more than ready for a picnic, I'm starving." Nick grinned. His warm gaze showed he was perhaps hungry for *Bane*, too. But then, seemingly guiltily, he turned to Jade. It was clear that he didn't want to just shoot and leave, but it was just as clear that he also really wanted time alone with Bane. "Jade, if you'd like to join us—"

He got no farther as Jade held up a hand and said, "On your *romantic* picnic? Hmmm, let's see if that would be any *fun* for me." She then regarded them both very intently. "Though you *are* very cute together, *no*, I think not. I have things to do. So be gone with you, romantic couple! Leave us singletons alone!"

With a flick of her fingers, Bane and Nick were dismissed. Nick looked up into Bane's face and Bane gave him a quirked grin in response.

"Shall we go have our *romantic* picnic?" Bane asked.

Nick beamed up at him. "Absolutely."

CHAPTER EIGHT

FIRES BANKED

Nick looped his right arm through Bane's left and steered the billionaire towards the kitchen where he knew Omar had put together a picnic basket for them full of goodies. He'd snuck a peek earlier in the day. Omar had shooed him away—saying the contents were to be a surprise—but Nick had seen enough to know that their picnic would be spectacular. His mouth watered just thinking about it.

"Jade is quite ... *unique*," Bane said with only the slightest note of amusement in his voice.

"On a scale of one to ten, how much does having her here bother you?"

Bane gave him a curious look. "It does not bother me. I am a *private* person, but that does not mean I wouldn't like to get to know her as she is your best friend."

Nick fiddled with a stray string hanging from his t-shirt, not quite able to meet Bane's gaze. He knew how much the billionaire valued his privacy and Jade wasn't known for being quiet or unobtrusive. Not that he wanted her to leave or change her personality in any way, not even for Bane. He loved having her at Moon Shadow, but this was Bane's home.

"She's been staying here on the weekends since you left," Nick explained. "It's company for Omar and me. Plus, she and I get a lot of work done while she's here."

"I'm glad. I'm happy that she's here."

Nick let out a huff of unbelieving laughter. "*Really?*"

"*Really.* You clearly enjoy her and that's enough for me," Bane answered simply.

"Oh. Well ... cool. I mean she's my best friend. I, ah, could have her *limit* her visits to when you're most comfortable or I could go to her place—"

"I see no reason to change anything."

Nick's heart felt like it did a leap in his chest. The thought that Jade wouldn't be leaving was a relief to him. But he clarified, "If you're *sure.*"

"I am quite certain."

Nick studied Bane's face, but he could not read any lie in those beautiful features. He noted that the scar seemed less prominent today than it had when Bane arrived. Yesterday, it had been red, raw and painful looking, but now it was a pale pink.

"This is your—your *home*, Nick," Bane said suddenly and he stumbled a little over the word 'home'. "You are welcome to bring anyone you like to stay over."

"My—my *home*?" Nick's felt his throat tighten. He *had* been thinking of Moon Shadow as home unconsciously, perhaps *hopefully*, but he hadn't really thought that Bane would think so, too. He'd grown to love the place, not to mention Omar. He couldn't imagine living anywhere else. Somehow in a very short time, Moon Shadow had sunk into his very bones.

Bane took in a deep breath. "Yes. Your home. If you wish it to be."

Nick's throat went tight with emotion, but he managed to get out, "I—I *do* wish it to be."

"Then it's settled." Bane squeezed Nick's hand.

Settled. God, that sounds so good. I should be freaked out. He just came back. But it's like everything's slotting into place. Just as it should be and I'm happy with it.

"What are you thinking, Nick? You have the most *interesting* expression on your face," Bane chuckled but there was a slight note of concern there.

Nick flushed. He found himself too unsure of his own thoughts to share them so he said instead, "I was just thinking that you look pretty damned stunning today."

Bane did. He was wearing a pair of lightweight linen pants, a shirt with thin lavender and green stripes and a linen sport coat, but no tie. Nick had never understood how a suit could be comfortable, even without a tie, but especially in the summer. Yet Bane made them look as light and airy as Nick's shorts and t-shirt.

"And you are also beautiful." Bane touched Nick's chin affectionately.

"In my ratty shorts and holey t-shirt?" Nick guffawed.

"You could wear a sack and be transcendent." Bane's eyes shone with affection.

Nick was about to make a joke about love being blind, but caught himself. Bane didn't believe in love and, surely, what was between them was too new to be called that. Yet Nick's heart beat faster in his chest as if disputing his logical thoughts.

The heart wants what it wants, Nick recalled his mother saying to him. She had been looking at his father when she'd said it as if loving Charles Fairfax was something completely out of her control. Not that his father had ever been unkind to her a moment in his life. Unlike how he was with Nick, Charles had doted on his wife until her last day. *He changed after that. He buried himself in the business then. Suddenly, nothing else mattered other than making money. Maybe it's not a coincidence.*

They reached the kitchen. From inside the room, Omar's voice suddenly burst forth into song. Something about flowers and sunshine that had Nick and Bane both laughing. They found the Indian man dancing and singing at the sink. He did not stop when they entered but instead shifted a hip towards the rattan picnic basket that looked to be filled to the brim with food and drink. The neck of a champagne bottle stuck up under one of the lids while a crusty loaf of French bread poked out of the other.

"There is silverware and glasses inside the basket," Omar sang with another hip shake.

"You're in a good mood today, Omar," Bane remarked dryly. His eyes narrowed slightly at the Indian man as if suspicious of something.

"I am indeed! It is a *beautiful* day," Omar answered and shot a meaningful look at Bane, which Nick could not interpret. Again, he got the sense of secrets that the two men shared.

I don't care about Bane's secrets. They don't matter so long as he is mine, Nick thought, but even his mind voice didn't sound all that convincing. He shook himself. Today was not going to be ruined by baseless dissatisfaction. It *was* a beautiful day and he was going to enjoy every second of it.

Bane picked up the overflowing picnic basket with his free arm, keeping a firm hold on Nick with the other. "This looks fantastic, Omar. Thank you."

"You are most welcome, Bane." Omar did another hip-shake.

"Do you need me to come back at any certain time to help with the house or dinner?" Nick asked the Indian man.

"Oh, no, all is taken care of. You are free as a bird!" Omar cried.

Nick wondered if Bane weren't here whether Omar would disclaim there being any work he could use a hand with, but he knew better than to try and get the Indian man to admit it now. Omar clearly wanted Bane and him to have a wonderful day together and Nick really wanted that, too, so he didn't press too hard. He would make it up to Omar another time.

"We will see you later, Omar," Bane said and Nick waved goodbye to the Indian man.

The two of them went out the back door. The scent of roses washed over them. Their gorgeous, sweet smell filled Nick's nose as they made their way down the steps and sauntered through the bursting blooms on the new gravel path. Their stones crunched beneath their feet. That and the whirr of insects were the only sounds for a companionable while.

"I love how quiet it is out here. You can almost believe we're the only people around," Nick remarked. "I used to think I was a city person, but I've felt so at peace here. My photography has never been better."

"I cannot wait to see more of your work."

"Oh, you will! I intend to *bore* you to death with it and demand many compliments." Nick grinned at him. He was rewarded with an "imp" which he was beginning to love as a nickname. Then he said, "But, in all seriousness, Bane, I want to hear your *true* thoughts on my work. I want to improve."

"I shall endeavor to give an educated opinion, but, in the end, Nick, art is in the eye of the beholder," Bane answered him.

"Yes, true, but *you* have a good eye." Nick gestured back to the house. "You picked Moon Shadow."

Bane dipped his head in acknowledgement. "The first time I saw Moon Shadow was in high summer. It was just going on dusk and I came out here. When all I heard were the call of night birds and the rustle of the wind through the roses, I *knew* I had come home. Moon Shadow told me how she wished to be decorated. I serve her."

"I can believe that. Is Moon Shadow like your estate in England?"

Bane nodded. His gaze went dark though. "Yes, but that house, like the one in India, offers me no peace. Too many bad memories."

"I'm sorry." Nick squeezed Bane's hand. He wondered if that darkness came from memories of Alastair or of Bane's abusive father or of his mother's suicide. There was so much in Bane's past that was terrible that Nick felt he was trying to avoid icebergs in stormy seas.

"You need not be." Bane smiled fondly down at him. "I am afraid that I think life is mostly a hard slog with brief moments of happiness."

Nick thought that sounded grim and said so, "I've always liked to think that while it's inevitable that life throws bad things at you, it's how you decide to react to them that determines whether you're happy or not. How you act is the *only* thing you can control."

"With that positive attitude, I can see how you have always made the best of things."

Nick flushed with the praise. "I don't know if I *always* have. But I just know my life has been really good compared to most people's. I try to keep it all in perspective." He realized then that his words might make it seem he was saying that Bane was not acting gratefully, too, so he quickly added, "Not to say you haven't! I mean –"

"Oh, no, I often forget the blessings in my life. I am a gloomy creature by nature. I think it is because I was raised on a romantic view of the world. It encourages dwelling as much on the darkness as on the light in life," Bane admitted.

"Well, there's not much darkness right now, is there?"

Bane slid his thumb over the back of Nick's hand that he clasped. "No, there is not."

It seemed to Nick that their good fortune at this moment was like the high noon of life. He worried that it would not last. He normally wasn't one to fear change, but now he did. Now he wanted to hold onto every golden moment and hug it to him.

To distract himself, Nick asked, "Where are we going to picnic?"

They had walked through the rose garden and were heading towards the tall grass field beyond. Nick really had no idea where their final destination was.

Bane gestured towards a path that cut through the grass and headed towards the forest. "There is a clearing in the forest not far from here where the air is sweet and it is wonderfully shady."

Nick already longed for the shade under the thickly canopied trees. The sun was brilliant and hot. Despite wearing far more clothing than Nick, Bane looked impeccably cool. Nick plucked at the front of his sweaty t-shirt.

"Do you own the forest, too?" Nick asked.

"No, Alric Koenig owns it. I tried to buy it from him, but he—*politely*—refused. In fact, he wished to buy *my* land. I was *not* as polite when I refused him," Bane remarked with a tigerish grin.

Nick's eyes widened. Alric Koenig was the richest person in Winter Haven. He had a fantastic estate at the very top of the Hill, which was literally a hill in the middle of the city. His father would have given his eyeteeth to live on the Hill, but people who lived there rarely sold their properties and then only to people who were *approved*. His father had never been approved. It was also said that wherever one saw more than one tree together in Winter Haven that Alric owned the land. He was supposedly fanatical about keeping the forests surrounding Winter Haven free of construction, but allowed people to wander his woods as much as they liked so long as they caused no harm.

Bane confirmed that they were not trespassing when he added, "Alric, of course, still *sweetly* told me that I was allowed to use the woods as much as I liked."

There was something in Bane's voice—though irritated at clearly what he saw as high handed behavior—that indicated that he was still honored to be invited to use Alric's land. That had Nick chuckling.

"So even *you* are a little in awe of Alric Koenig!"

Bane snorted. "Not in the least. Did I not just tell you how I withstood his attempts to gain Moon Shadow? And I purchased the property on the other side of here so his expansion is cut off for now at least in this direction."

Nick bit his lower lip, but couldn't hide his smile at Bane's affront. "I think you doth protest too much. C'mon, you were just *a little* intimidated by him. Even my father is awestruck in his presence."

Bane's Siberian blue eyes darted down to him, even as he pretended to adjust his grip on the picnic basket. "You mean was I awed by Alric's looks? Alric is quite beautiful in an almost *otherworldly* way. He strikes mere mortals dumb, or at least some of us."

"My guess is that your temper kept you from being fully under his spell." Nick shook his head in amusement.

"Have *you* met Alric?"

"Only once and being a *mere mortal*, I admit I was dumbstruck by him. I think I tried to speak in his presence but only got out a few monosyllables and drooled on myself. But that was *before* I met you. Now I would be quite *immune* to his charms." Nick threaded his fingers though Bane's.

Bane kissed his temple again and Nick beamed. "I am glad of that. I am a very *jealous* creature."

"I wouldn't have thought that considering you had an *open* relationship with Devon." Nick wanted to bite the words back as soon as he said them. Anytime he spoke of the "perfect man" his jealousy just screamed out.

If he'd worried that Bane would be upset by it, he needn't have. Bane tipped his head back and laugh. "Oh, Nick, you are quite silly about him."

Nick gave Bane a rueful smile. "I guess it's hard for me to believe that you choose me over Devon. I mean he would never wear a ratty t-shirt or have messy hair." Nick gestured to himself.

Bane glanced down at Nick's outfit and hair with an indulgent smile. "You defeated Devon on the field of battle. You don't need to worry about him any longer."

"On the *field of battle*? Was that what the dining room was then when I was serving your guests? Because I'm pretty sure that's when I won you over. I fainted in your arms. Very manly of me and all, but it worked somehow."

"Considering your fever and how much pain you must have been in I'm amazed you were standing at all." Bane almost sounded stern like Jade in a way. Nick flooded with pleasure at the caring that indicated.

They passed under the protective cover of the trees and the temperature lowered a good ten degrees. It was still warm, but not scorching. The scent of the forest, of green growing things, and moist earth flowed around them. Bane picked out a nearly invisible path between the trunks and soon Nick saw their destination. It was a circular clearing in the woods. There was a wide swath of grass to sit or lay down upon, but enough shadows from the tree's overarching limbs that they could escape the sun if they wished to.

Without having to say anything, the two of them worked together to spread out the blanket and arrange the food. Inside the basket there was a bottle of chilled champagne, perspiring bottles of water, a loaf of French bread, oozing brie cheese, a sharp cheddar, a variety of cold cuts from salami to smoked turkey, nuts, grapes and finally two dense-looking brownies for dessert.

"Omar made sure that we wouldn't starve even if we get lost in the woods for a week," Nick laughed as he spread his hands at the massive amount of food.

"He wants to fatten us up," Bane said.

"I'm good with that!"

Bane merely snorted and shook his head. The billionaire took off his suit coat and neatly laid it down on the blanket before rolling the sleeves of his shirt up to the elbows. Nick marveled at the flex of muscles in Bane's forearms. He'd always had a thing for forearms and Bane had these perfect ones ending in almost slender though substantial wrists and elegant hands.

Bane caught him staring avidly at his revealed skin and lifted one eyebrow as a smile twitched his lips. "What fascinates you so?"

"Ah, nothing! I mean it's just you're always so covered and the forearms ... well, forget it."

Bane leaned towards him. His smile widening and becoming almost tigerish. "Now, you know, when you say things like that you just *intrigue* me more. So *what* interests you about my forearms?"

Nick flushed, but he leaned in towards Bane and lowered his voice, "You don't show a lot of skin, Bane, so when you do I take notice."

Both eyebrows rose. "I see. Well, when I was brought up one had to be modest. A revealed ankle was cause for alarm."

"When you grew up?!" Nick repeated. "Turn of the century, right? Because you're totally *ancient*. What are you? Like thirty-five? Yep, you *are* a Methuselah. It's good for you that I like older men."

Bane only smiled at him and said nothing. To distract himself from Bane's forearms, Nick grabbed the champagne and ripped off the foil before undoing the cap and drawing out the cork. Unlike how they showed in movies and television where the cork shot out of the bottle with a loud pop, Nick performed the uncorking the *proper* way. That was to slowly ease the cork out, allowing nothing but a breath of air to escape at the end.

Bane's eyebrows rose. "You did that correctly."

"Don't act so surprised! When I was brought up, I was taught how to properly open champagne." Nick then stuck out his tongue to show how adult he was, which had Bane chuckling. In a more serious tone, he explained, "Champagne is my *favorite* so I learned the appropriate way it should be opened."

"I will remember that you love champagne from now on."

From the intent look on Bane's face, Nick guessed that the billionaire would *always* remember his favorite things and surprise him with them. A warm glow suffused him again. He'd dated a lot in high school and college, but it had always been casual. But what he felt for Bane was *anything* but casual. He tried to tell himself that it was just that first flush of infatuation that made him feel as if the stars were aligning to bring them together. This couldn't be as *magical* as it felt.

As if we're meant. Nick shook himself. *I hated him just a month ago. Now it hurts not to see him for an hour.*

Nick then thought of his father's warning that he couldn't mess this up with Bane, because it would mean more than just a broken heart. It would mean that his family would be out on the street.

Surely Bane wouldn't do that! I couldn't care for him if he would do that!

But though he told himself this with fierce certainty, he did not ask Bane to confirm it. In fact, he kept his mouth tightly shut as if in fear that he would say something—*any-thing*—that might bring that issue to the fore. That included the lunch he was supposed to have with his father at some point.

I'll tell him later about that. I don't want to ruin this moment.

Nick picked up the two delicate flutes that Omar had included in the basket and filled them both with the bubbling alcohol. Bane was already gracefully sprawled on his side on the blanket. Nick handed him a glass. The big man took it almost absently. His hair was not hanging in his face, a truly rare occurrence and, more importantly, Bane didn't seem to notice. His Siberian blue gaze was taking in the greenery around them and the splashes of sunlight on the grass. Normally, Bane seemed filled with tightly coiled energy as if ready to pounce. He was restless as a rule. But now, he looked like a cat lying in the sun, contented to stay still forever.

He looks peaceful. This is how he should look. This is how things should be.

Nick blinked at the *rightness* he felt with those thoughts. He took a deep drink of his champagne. The straw colored liquid was icy cold and tickled on its way down Nick's esophagus. He lay down beside Bane, facing the big man. His gaze swept from the top of Bane's head to his feet. His eyes lingered on the 'V' of flesh revealed at his throat and, of course, those exquisite forearms.

"I imagined this," Nick said.

Bane's gaze immediately snapped to him. "Imagined or dreamed?"

Nick ducked his head. "With all these crazy dreams I told you about, I'm sure you must think I constantly dream about you—and *maybe* I do—but I just imagined this."

Bane reached out and ran one hand slowly down Nick's arm. "I imagined you at Moon Shadow, too."

"Scrubbing toilets?" Nick raised an eyebrow.

"No, imp, though –" Bane gave him a speculative look and then laughed when Nick hit his arm. "No, of course not I did not fantasize you scrubbing my toilets. One of the things I imagined was you and I standing by the fountain when it was turned on for the first time in twenty years."

Nick bit down on his lower lip to stop himself from blurting out that this could happen. Omar had called a service that was to come in the next few days to fix the fountain.

Bane continued, "That imagined moment had an incredible impact on me, because ..." He paused and lowered his head, not able to quite meet Nick's eyes. "Because it meant so much *more* than just the simple excitement of seeing part of Moon Shadow come alive again. We were *in* this together. I cannot explain it. I'm sure I sound like a fool."

I can make that vision a reality Bane, Nick thought fiercely.

Out loud, he simply said, "You don't sound like a fool. You never could. And I like that idea a lot."

Bane's hand paused in its travels up and down Nick's arm. He squeezed Nick's bicep and sat up. "I'm sure you're hungry. Let me prepare you a plate."

Nick watched avidly as Bane neatly cut wedges of cheese for him and made little sandwiches with the French bread and cold cuts. Everything he did for Nick he did with exquisite care. Bane topped Nick's champagne glass off first before refilling his own. He gave Nick the best of the fruit and the choicest bits of meat and cheese. He watched attentively and made sure that the moment Nick's plate emptied he would be ready to prepare more little sandwiches for him. Nick felt this sense of unreality enfolding him. He had *never* been this happy or content.

Thankfully, they talked of inconsequential things like Nick's schooling and Bane's travels while they ate, because Nick's throat felt too tight with unspoken emotions to actually concentrate on any deep topics. Instead, the conversation was as light and sparkling as the champagne that fizzed in Nick's veins. It was only when Nick reached over to feed Bane a piece of fudgy brownie that things turned from light to *heat.*

"Something sweet?" Nick offered and pressed the brownie to Bane's lips.

The billionaire's blue eyes hooded as he opened that sensual mouth for Nick to pop the brownie inside. Just as Nick did, Bane's mouth closed around the sweet treat *and* Nick's fingers. Sweat broke out on Nick's upper lip when he tried to draw his hand back, but Bane caught him by the wrist. Bane ate the brownie bite with a sensual smile on his lips.

"Are you going to eat me, too, Bane?" Nick sounded breathless though he had been going for teasing.

"Let's see if you're sweeter."

Bane drew Nick's fingers to his mouth again. His tongue slithered out and lapped at the sensitive digits. Nick had never thought that finger licking or sucking could be sexy, but it felt like there was a direct connection between his fingers and his cock now, especially when Bane moved that agile tongue up and down the length of his pointer finger.

He said he wanted to move slowly. This doesn't feel slow. Maybe he's changed his mind.

The billionaire's eyes glittered with desire and possessiveness as if when he looked upon Nick, he looked upon the greatest treasure that he could ever have. Nick shivered as Bane kissed the palm of his captive hand.

"Are you finished with the food?" Bane asked, his voice a husky whisper.

"H-huh? Oh! Yeah, couldn't eat another bite," Nick got out, his brain short-circuiting from the arousal.

Bane moved the plates and cutlery off the blanket so that every inch of the soft material was open for them to lie down upon.

"Nick, would you let me ... see your back." Bane's head lowered and his black hair hung over his face.

"What? Why?" Nick asked suspiciously.

"I need to see ..."

"If I'm scarred?"

Bane nodded.

"I'd rather go back to the finger sucking. How about we do that instead?" Nick teased rather desperately.

"I'll give you a massage."

"Bribing me with those magnificent hands of yours, are you?" Nick asked, with a catch in his voice at the thought of one of Bane's massages. This one wouldn't be chaste. They were together now.

The billionaire nodded again, his hair still like a curtain over his face, hiding his expression. "It has been bothering me since I returned. I need to see you in the sunlight. Please, Nick. It will make me feel better."

Nick knew there was *some* damage from the blisters on his upper shoulders and lower back, but he didn't care about that. He worried though that Bane would though. Not in the sense that Bane wouldn't be attracted to him any longer or anything like that, but the billionaire would blame himself for the damage.

"Please," Bane repeated and, like always, Nick found that he couldn't refuse the man when he asked politely.

In Bane's mouth 'please' is a super power.

He pulled his t-shirt over his head and laid down on his front, pillowing his head on his hands. He felt Bane straddle him, sitting lightly on the backs of his thighs. A thrill of desire went though Nick at having Bane's weight atop him. The billionaire's fingertips lightly stroked the tops of Nick's shoulders and then slowly drifted down his back, inspecting every inch of him by touch. Bane paused over those areas where Nick was pretty sure there were faint scars.

Wanting to fill the silence, Nick quickly said, "No great damage done, see?"

"There is some," Bane's voice was low and slightly hollow.

Nick bit his lower lip, but said nothing. He felt Bane lower-ing his head. Coils of his hair brushed along Nick's skin before he felt Bane's tongue lightly lap one of the scars. He let out a shuddering breath. Nothing had ever felt *this* erotic. There was something almost *animalistic* about it.

Bane paused for a long moment as if trying to read Nick's reaction to the lick. When Nick didn't object or jump up and push him off, Nick felt another soft cat-like lick over his scars. His cock, which was already hard just being in Bane's pres-ence, filled more as that licking continued until Bane had lapped at every single scar.

"I would do anything to undo the damage to your back," Bane whispered. His pressed his forehead against the top of Nick's spine. His hot breath gushed over along Nick's skin.

"Not your fault, Bane."

"You were only out there because of *me*. Because I was *cru-el* to you. I made you feel *terrible* about yourself when all the while ..." Bane let out a harsh huff of breath. "I don't deserve you. I don't know why you're still here, let alone with *me*."

Nick tried to twist around to see Bane's face, to tell him with words and looks that it wasn't the billionaire's fault. But Bane held him in place. Nick felt the *effortlessness* of that hold. Bane was so much stronger than he was. He flashed back on the time that Bane had him pinned to the wall in that attic. Just like back then, Nick felt arousal build up deep in his belly. He wasn't afraid. Not even back then when Bane had seemed so out of control.

"I know you wish to tell me that I'm not to blame. That you forgive me. But I don't want you to," Bane murmured. His breath seemed to dance down Nick's spine. Nick's cock hard-ened more in his pants. "I want to *earn* this joy. I want to *earn* you. Let me?"

Don't say please, Bane. Don't say please, because I can't resist you.

"*Please*, Nick."

Nick let out a soft laugh. "Magical powers. That word on your lips has magical fucking powers, Bane."

Bane chuckled into the cusp of his ear. It was a rich, rolling sound. "You've always been so susceptible to politeness."

"No, Bane, I'm just susceptible to *you*."

Bane drew in a sharp breath and then those lips that had been hovering by his ear kissed him. Nick shivered and arched up against Bane's solid body above him. He felt the heavy, hard line of Bane's erect cock press against his ass. The big man grunted and then pressed down against Nick's buttocks. Nick twisted his head around and Bane's lips slid along his jaw and kissed the side of his mouth.

Their bodies writhed together. Nick pushing up. Bane pressing down. Bane's lips kissed every inch of skin he could find, but he did not let Nick get up. Nick's cock was an iron bar in his pants. He was going to cum without Bane even touching his cock. That had never happened to him before.

Bane bit down on the top of Nick's spine as he snugged his cock in the crevice of Nick's ass. Nick bucked as his own cock jerked and a gush of precums wet the front of his shorts. He wanted out of his shorts altogether. He wanted to feel the slide of Bane's velvety organ across his anus. Another gush of precum exited his cock at just thinking about it. Bane bit down harder and Nick gave out a soft cry of pain. He wasn't hurt and the pain had felt good, taking some of the edge off. Bane, though, immediately reacted to the pained cry and Nick felt him withdrawing.

"I—I'm sorry, Nick. Did I—did I hurt you?" Bane asked, his back rigid.

"No, never. That felt so good!" Nick twisted underneath the man so that he was facing up Bane. The billionaire's eyes were glowing again in that impossible way. It was like they were filled with blue witchfire. But as strange as this was, as different as Bane was, Nick found himself eager to experience more. He breathed, "Don't stop."

"I—I *bit* you, didn't I? I seem to remember doing that and then *rutting* against you like –"

"Hey! I was *rutting* right back," Nick laughed. "I'm into what we're doing."

"I'm like an *animal* with you. I'm –"

"No! Bane, I *liked* what we are doing." Nick held him tighter. "There is nothing *wrong* about what we did."

What happened to him that he thinks this? Something must have happened to him in the past. Maybe with Alastair? Can I ask? Or will that make it worse?

Bane sagged forward. "I'm sorry, Nick. I don't know what's wrong with me. I should be normal. The beast—I mean, I am ... *myself.* Or I was myself."

Beast? What is he going on about?

"You were a perfect gentleman. Well, I think you know what I mean." He lightly kissed the side of Bane's neck. "Except that you left me wanting here."

Bane let out a huff of laughter but some of the tension left him. "I suppose I left us both that way. Now I am *more* sorry if that is possible."

Nick bussed his lips against Bane's cheek. "Yes, but you also wanted to go *slow* and we weren't heading that way."

Bane's expression was all serious again. "I seem to be unable to do anything as I plan with you."

"Then stop planning. Just enjoy the day with me, Bane. That's the only plan we need."

"I will try." Bane peppered his face with kisses. He pressed their foreheads together. "I will leave all the planning to *you.*"

"Can we finish what we started? Or would it be too much?" Nick asked. His cock was pressing painfully against the zipper of his shorts.

"I don't know if I trust myself, Nick."

"I know you're struggling with control, Bane. I don't claim to understand why, but ... let's try something different," Nick suggested.

"What?"

Nick gently urged Bane up so that they were both sitting on the picnic blanket. Bane looked beautifully rumpled. His eyes still burned with blue light, but the fires were slightly banked. Bane's hands lay on top of his thighs. Nick noted that the fingers were slightly curled as if Bane was holding onto himself so that he wouldn't touch Nick. The place where Bane had bitten him throbbed pleasantly. Nick forced himself though not to touch it. He sensed that any reminder of the biting would cause Bane to retreat. How the big man didn't know what a turn on his possessive, animal side was, Nick couldn't guess. But, obviously, they would have to work towards Bane letting that side of him out. So, instead, Nick had a completely different idea. Instead of Bane getting to be the Alpha and controlling things, Nick would be the one in charge.

"I want you to lay down on your back," Nick requested.

Bane frowned. "Why?"

"Suspicious, aren't you?" Nick laughed. "I want to be the one in control, Bane. You don't have to do anything."

Bane's frown deepened. "I do not give up control easily, Nick. I like being in charge."

"I know you do, and I like it, too, but you need to *relax* and you can't do that when you're the one directing things. You'll have to *trust* me." Nick ran a hand down Bane's cheek. He decided to use the magic word himself, "*Please*?"

The big man hesitated for just a moment, but then Bane sprawled onto the blanket in that graceful yet powerful way. Nick felt like cheering, but didn't. Evidently, politeness worked on Bane, too.

Bane watched him out of hooded eyes as Nick straddled him. Nick pulled out the tails of Bane's shirt from his pants. The big man's eyes widened slightly, but he left his hands at his sides. Nick then undid the shirt's buttons, revealing that magnificent chest inch by inch. He ran his fingers lightly up and down the center of it, enjoying how Bane's stomach muscles jumped with every fluttering pass. When he went to undo Bane's belt, however, those muscles *really* jumped and Bane let out a hiss of breath.

"What are you doing?" Bane asked as Nick unzipped him.

"Making sure we don't get messy." Nick grinned then added, "I think the way for you to gain control is to take some of the edge off first. We've been wanting one another for over a month. Both of us just need to *indulge* a little and then we can go as slow as you want."

The pulse of Nick's incredibly hard cock was proof of that. He felt like the zipper might break from the force his cock was putting on it.

Nick reached inside Bane's pants and took out the billionaire's cock, which was as big as the rest of him. Bane's cock was warm and alive in his hands. He stroked the velvety organ and Bane shivered. His Siberian blue eyes were glowing again. Nick didn't care that human eyes shouldn't have been able to do that. Bane's did.

"Just relax, Bane. Let me be in charge," Nick repeated soothingly.

Bane's eyelids slid shut and he let out a shuddery breath before his head fell back completely on the blanket as Nick slowly stroked him. Nick unbuttoned and unzipped his own pants and took out his cock. He let out a soft breath of relief as his cock sprang free of its cloth and zippered prison.

He pressed their shafts together and let out a low hiss. The feeling of his shaft against Bane's was heavenly. Both of their cocks surged upwards in his hands as if with intentions of their own. His balls almost immediately drew tight against his body. Nick breathed deep to regain control before he began to stroke them both up and down. Bane's hips lifted beneath him and Nick realized his weight was not going to keep the big man down.

It's going to be a wild ride.

Nick grinned and swiped his thumb over the the head of Bane's cock. It was flushed an almost ruby red and as large as a plum. He shivered in pleasure at the thought of that being inside of him. It would take some doing.

But not yet. Bane wants to go slow and we're already going faster than he planned, but I need give us both release. He's not like anyone I've ever been with, but I think this will help him.

Nick was acting purely on instinct. He didn't know Bane's likes and dislikes yet, but the big man responded beautifully.

He massaged Bane's balls. The billionaire's breathing hitched and his hips rose. Nick rode the movement fluidly, holding onto Bane's waist with one hand while he stroked their cocks with the other. Heat bloomed in his balls and precum gushed from the head of his cock and Bane's. The earthy, musky smell was pure sex. His cock quivered. Bane's plumped further and Nick let out a soft huff of laughter as he imagined that happening when Bane was *inside* of him. He would really have to be stretched to have sex with this beautiful, wild man.

He slicked his hands with precum and formed a tight tunnel around both their cocks. Bane's eyelids cracked open and through the long, dark lashes he could see what looked like blue flames burning in Bane's eyes. The big man made a low, almost animalistic sound like a purr of a massive cat. That sound corkscrewed up Nick's spine and he nearly came right there and then.

"*Mate*," Bane whispered in a voice that was almost a growl.

That was the word he had used in the dream and it hit Nick with the force of a ton of bricks. His hands jerked and closed tightly on their two cocks. He found himself leaning down over Bane and kissing him rather frantically. Bane's large hands wrapped around Nick, one behind his neck and the other around his waist. Their cocks were pressed tight against their bellies and Nick rocked forward. Bane let out a hiss of pleasure. Nick's hips jerked forward again as the need to have friction against his shaft became more intense. He tried to sit up again and stroke them both, but Bane would not release him and that turned Nick on more. So instead he thrust his cock against the big man's stomach muscles that were as defined as a washboard.

Bane's one hand on Nick's waist held their groins tightly against one another. His other hand feathered through the back of Nick's hair, keeping their mouths fused upon one another. Nick breathed through his nose as Bane would not release his mouth for anything. Tongues, teeth, hot, wet, the surge of arousal building in his so strong that Nick felt like his cock was on fire. He thrust frantically forward again and again. Then his back of arching as his balls drew impossibly tight against his body and he was cumming. The first spray of his semen triggered Bane's orgasm, too.

The hot stream of semen against Nick's bare chest had his cock quivering, wanting to expend more cum, but he was empty. Sweat slicked his back, streaming down his spine, as he collapsed bonelessly on top of Bane. Their cum and perspiration sealed them together, but he didn't care. It had been a primal coupling and both of them had needed it. Bane especially.

Nick's eyelids were fluttering shut when Bane gently kissed his forehead. He could feel the big body beneath him was completely at peace. There was no tension, no strain, just calm. Nick was able to barely open his own eyelids one last time to look at Bane's face. The blue fires were gone from his eyes. Those flames were banked. Nick grinned and let his head flop back down on Bane's chest. The big man was all right now. Whatever had ailed him was exhausted for the moment.

"Thank you, Nick," Bane whispered or so Nick thought as the words were said just as he drifted into sleep, safe in the billionaire's arms.

CHAPTER NINE
STARGAZING

"**O**mar," Bane paused and leaned his hip against the kitchen counter. "Is there ... is there ... do you know ..."

"What are you trying to ask, Bane?" the Indian man inquired.

Omar had just finished washing off one of the dinner plates. He handed it to Bane to place it into the dishwasher. They had all eaten under the stars again on the porch. Jade and Nick were still outside talking and having a glass of port. Bane had retreated into the house the moment he saw Omar do so. He needed to ask the Indian man about the beast, about what had happened just that afternoon with him and Nick. It had been wonderful, but parts, like where he had started acting like an animal, had been also mortifying and mystifying.

"Something *happened* today that *shouldn't* have been possible," Bane began hesitatingly.

"Oh?" Omar paused in his dishwashing and turned his full attention to Bane. His expression was alert though not alarmed.

Not yet.

"The beast —"

"Spirit," Omar corrected.

"*Beast*," Bane insisted peevishly. Currently, the beast was sitting in his chest again with its back to him. It's tail was not even moving. He flushed as he explained, "Nick and I were being ... *intimate*. The beast was *contained*, but suddenly *I* started acting like—like an *animal*. Biting the top of his spine and growling and behaving like the beast might. Yet the beast was *not* in control."

"And you did not *wish* to do this?" Omar asked carefully.

Had he *wished* to do it? He had *enjoyed* doing it. It had seemed almost *natural* to do it. But it was *not* how he had ever behaved with a lover before. For a moment, it had been like there was no separation between the beast and himself. He wanted to claim his *mate*.

Not mate! Nick is my lover. I am not some base creature!

He finally said to Omar, haltingly, "It is not—not how I *usually* am. This is not the way I would treat someone I care for in bed."

"Was Nick afraid or harmed in any way?" It was only in this question that Omar sounded at all alarmed.

"No, he seemed—and *seems*—fine." Bane raked his hands through his hair. "He thought I was so overcome being with him finally that I simply lost control. Too much pent up desire."

"Could that have been the case?" Again, Omar was very careful in how he phrased his words. "You were devastated when you thought the two of you could not be together."

Bane shifted uncomfortably. He could not deny that the word "devastated" was correct. When he had left Nick and Moon Shadow he had felt like he was dying.

"Perhaps I am very eager to be with him. Maybe ... maybe that is the cause of it," Bane finally said, but he didn't like that explanation. It didn't seem true to him. And the beast was facing very much away from him so he could not see if it was hiding knowledge from him. "I was just wondering if there is anything in the lore about this."

Omar shook his head. "No, Bane, you are the *only* human that the tiger spirit has ever shared a form with. There is no *lore* for what you are." A wave of panic went through Bane. No lore? No answers? Omar must have seen something in his face, because the Indian man quickly added, "But if you wish to know what I think –"

"I do," Bane assured him.

"I do not think that there is a *bright line* between the spirit and yourself. You share a body, but perhaps—perhaps you share *more* than that." Omar looked at him almost beseechingly as if he was *asking* something of Bane in this statement.

"You think that the beast and I are ... what? The *same* somehow? Becoming *one*?" That thought terrified him more than anything. It was also the thing that he had thought himself earlier. But he rejected it now with full force. The beast was *separate* from him! They were not the same! They could not become one person!

Omar held out his hands as if to calm him. Bane began to pace.

"Bane, *integration* is not a bad thing –
"You don't understand! If we *integrate* then I'll *never* be free! Your family will *never* be free! Don't you understand that?" Bane threw his arms up in the air.

"Bane, I do not consider myself imprisoned. My family is *honored* to take care of you and the spirit," Omar answered mildly.

Bane's head lowered. "I do not know what I would do without you, Omar, but I want a life with *Nick*, too, and if the beast makes that impossible ..." His hands fisted at his sides. "Then damn it to *Hell*."

He strode out of the kitchen and into the hallway. He only paused to collect himself when he reached the back door. He looked out at Nick and Jade. The two of them were leaning on the railing. Nick stared down at his glass of port thoughtfully.

"So your dad wants to have lunch this week?" Jade was asking.

Charles asked Nick for lunch? Nick didn't mention it to me. I wonder why.

Bane paused, his hand on the handle to the door, but he didn't turn it to go out. He knew he should announce himself, but he had a feeling that Nick might be more forthcoming about this lunch believing that just Jade was present.

"I told him about Bane and me, that we're dating," Nick said with a sigh. "He doesn't want to see me to catch up, see how I am or even to congratulate me on finding a great guy. Oh, no, he wants to *coach* me about how I should behave with Bane."

Bane's mouth flattened into a thin line. Charles had no idea how to please him! Even in business, Charles was clueless about his likes and dislikes. Already, he was having to veto Charles' "efficiency measures" which involved laying off productive employees and increasing pay for senior management. He could only imagine the bad advice that Charles would give Nick in regards to their relationship.

Jade let out a bitter laugh, which encapsulated exactly how Bane felt about the whole situation. "You've got to be kidding me!"

"No, I wish I were," Nick sighed. He took a sip of the port.

Bane's nostrils flared at Charles' presumptuousness. The man *would* think he could "coach" his son so that everything between Nick and Bane worked perfectly. But he couldn't manipulate Bane. Not even through Nick.

"What a surprise! Not." Jade shook her head in exasperation. "Nick, I don't think you should go. Screw him. It's not like he can give you any *good* advice about Bane."

Bane was all for that and his good feelings towards Jade grew.

"I know that. Believe me, I'm not going to actually *listen* to anything he has to say. I'm just going to let him talk *at* me. He'll feel better and we'll be done with it," Nick said with a shrug.

Bane felt a deep sense of satisfaction at Nick's dismissal of his father. Yet that satisfaction felt wrong. He should *hope* Charles would be a man that Nick could love and respect. But he doubted Charles could ever be that person.

"So you're just going to go and suffer through lunch?" Jade bumped her shoulder against Nick's.

"Pretty much." Nick bumped her back. "I've got to tell Bane about it."

"You're not going to suggest that he go on this lunch with you, are you?"

"God, no! I can imagine that scene. If I wanted to *end* my relationship with Bane as quickly as it's begun that's the route I'd take." Nick let out a slightly hysterical laugh. "Besides, Dad wants me alone so we can talk *about* Bane. Can't exactly do that in front of the man now can he?"

"And what *exactly* will you tell Bane about this lunch?"

Nick, don't lie to me. You don't have to, Bane willed as he stared at the graceful line of Nick's back.

"The truth. That I told Dad about him and me and that Dad wants to talk things out," Nick said with a shrug.

Bane let out a breath that he didn't know he'd been holding. Nick wouldn't lie to him. He felt a prick of his own conscience. He expected Nick to tell him the truth about everything, but here he was lying to the young man about the very core of himself.

He would never believe me if I told him I am possessed by a tiger spirit. And showing him the shift is out of the question. Even if I were behind bars, it might be safe. And ... and I couldn't take the chance he would reject me.

"I'm sure that truth is the best policy," Jade said. She turned her head and looked at Nick with an indecisive expression on her face. "Nick ... I'm sure what I'm about to say is probably crossing a million lines but –"

"Say it."

"You're not responsible for your family. You can't live your life considering them all the time," she said, her expression taut. "They don't appreciate it and—and they aren't doing the same for you. Hell, if they hadn't messed up with Bane in the first place none of this would have happened."

"I know." Nick stared hard into his port again. "But it's just *hard*." He let out a shuddery breath. "I want to do both, you know? Live my life and take care of them, too."

Jade gave Nick a kiss on the cheek. "You have the biggest heart. I just hope no one breaks it."

The two of them went quiet as they looked out at the rose garden. Lightning bugs lifted off from the grass and their soft glow gave the scene an utterly peaceful look. Bane felt a sudden sense of unworthiness for the lovely young man outside. Only through Nick's big heart were they together now.

I will be worthy of him. I will be the gentleman.

Bane stepped outside to join them. The squeak of the screen door caused Nick's head to swing around. As soon as Nick caught sight of him a wide smile appeared on the young man's face. He set his wineglass on the railing and moved eagerly into Bane's arms.

"Bane, I wondered where you went to!" he cried and pressed a kiss to Bane's cheek.

"Just bothering Omar. Attempting to help clean up and getting in the way," Bane lied and felt a twinge of guilt. He hugged Nick tighter to him. He needed to tell the young man something of the truth of himself. He needed to share something real with him so he didn't feel like a complete fraud. But what?

"Let me go see if I can bother Omar any better," Jade said as she took in the two of them embracing.

"Jade, you don't have to go –"

"Oh, yes, Nick, I think I do." She patted his arm and headed in, calling out Omar's name gaily as she did.

"I hope I didn't cause her to flee," Bane said as he smoothed his hands down Nick's back.

"No, she's just giving us time alone together," he said.

"She's a good soul."

He felt Nick grin against his shoulder. "Yeah, she is. She likes you by the way."

"I like her, too." Bane pressed a kiss to Nick's forehead. "There was no need for her to leave the porch though. I actually want us to go up into the tower. I have something to show you there."

"The tower? Cool! I remember when I first came to Moon Shadow I imagined that people stargazed from up there," Nick said, his eyes shining with enthusiasm.

"It's funny you say that, because I have a telescope," Bane told him.

Nick's eyes grew huge with pleasure. "Race you!"

The young man was already turning and running. Bane felt the beast *freeze* then turn its head. Nick was *running*. Nick was running *away* from him. The predator's need to chase flooded him. He dug his fingernails into his palms.

He is playing. He is not really running from us. He is playing.

Even as his heart galloped in his chest, Bane took the time to grab the bottle of port along with glasses for him and Nick. Then he was racing after the young man with preternatural speed. Nick had a headstart on him, but it was nothing. He flew after Nick, his upper lip drawn back from his sharp white teeth.

The young man cast a look back over his shoulder on the stairs. Nick's face was alight with laughter and smiles. It didn't even falter at the tigerish grin on Bane's face. The beast urged him to grab Nick, to pin him to the wall, to grind their bodies together until Nick gave up and promised never to run again. Sweat broke out on Bane's upper lip and not from the exertion of running. He pushed the beast back.

"First one to the tower gets a kiss!" Nick called, completely oblivious to the internal struggle Bane was having.

"Nick, do not run!" he called. "I will chase!"

"That's the idea!" Nick laughed and put on some extra speed.

Bane forced himself to lope so that he was just a hair's breadth away from Nick. The young man let out a shout of surprise when he realized how close Bane was. Nick put a touch more speed into his run. For Bane, running like this was effortless. Nick did not have the benefit of the beast's endurance and speed though and began to tire on the tower's staircase.It wound up three stories in a tight corkscrew. The two of them dashed up the stairs. Bane could have easily beaten Nick to the top, but he let the young man stay just out of reach. The beast's tail was whapping the ground eagerly.

Catch him, catch him, catch him and pin him. Make him ours, the beast murmured. It was like a thrum in Bane's blood. It took all his control not to simply drop the port and glasses and leap on Nick's back.

When they made it to the top, Nick doubled over to catch his breath. Bane, of course, was breathing normally. The urge to pin Nick to the wall or, better yet, to the floor clawed at Bane's insides, but he held himself still. Nick hadn't been truly running from him. Nick was his. This was just playing. He repeated that over and over again.

"I get a kiss as soon as I can breathe without pain," Nick gasped out, completely unaware of Bane's internal conflict. "So not fair that you're not even breathing hard!"

"Oh, I am," Bane lied. He swiped at the sweat on his forehead that came from simply hanging onto control and not exertion.

Nick thumped Bane's arm, still gasping. "You so are not! But that's okay. I like that you're so strong and fit."

"You do?" Bane's voice lowered to a husky growl. It was good to be admired by one's mate.

Mate ... that is ... that word is ... not correct. Nick is my lover.

But a voice inside of him whispered, *Mate. Mate. Mate.*

"How could I not?" Nick straightened, his breathing normal again. "How could *anyone* not? Your body is a work of art, Bane, and your mind is even better."

Bane realized that his hands were shaking from the effort of holding back. He set down the port and glasses on a side table and curled his fingers against his palms. He took in long deep breaths before turning back to Nick. The beast was watching Nick out of narrowed eyes. If their mate tried to run again, it *would* do what was necessary.

He was playing, Bane told it.

The beast ignored him.

Nick had recovered his breath and was checking out the space. The tower was octagonal. Besides the stool there was an old yet comfortable loveseat in crimson damask against one wall. The wooden floorboards creaked beneath Bane's feet as he went to the pulley system that allowed a portion of the ceiling to slide back and for the telescope to have an unimpeded view of the sky. He felt Nick's body heat against his back. The young man was so *close*. Again, the thought of pinning him to the wall, thrusting a thigh between his legs, and smashing their lips together ran through him.

I am a man. Not a beast. I will be a gentleman.

He turned around and Nick stepped even closer so that there was barely an inch between them. Nick's pupils were large and dark like pools. "I'd like my kiss now."

A shiver of pleasure went through Bane. "You did *win*."

"I hope you think that we *both* won."

Bane cupped Nick's face, careful to keep his movements gentle. His fingers feathered in the young man's platinum hair before he leaned down and pressed his lips against Nick's. The young man's mouth opened beneath his like a flower blossoming. Their tongues tangled together languidly. He could taste a trace of the port, sweet and rich with undercurrents of raisins. When they broke apart, Bane's heart was thumping hard in his chest and his breathing, which hadn't been affected by the run, was now fast and short. The beast was absolutely still within him.

You're planning something. I know it. But we have our deal. If you break it …

Bane let the sentence hang. He wasn't sure what he would do if the beast broke their accords. Sending Nick away would only hurt them both. There was nothing he could do to the beast that wouldn't also hurt himself. He hoped that the beast understood that this was simply how things had to be if Nick was going to be with them.

Nick, who knew nothing of his internal torment, turned to the telescope and asked, "That was better than any trophy though I think you *let* me win."

"Perhaps I did. But as you said, we both won in the end."

Nick, reluctantly, pushed away from him. "We won't do any stargazing if I stay that close to you. You're really irresistible, Bane."

"That word is not strong enough to express what you are," Bane replied. His hands seemed to move of their own accord towards Nick again, but he forced them down at his sides.

Nick smiled at him, genuinely pleased. "So ... show me how to set the telescope up to see something?"

"Of course."

Bane moved past Nick, acutely aware of the young man's warmth and citrusy scent. He leaned down and adjusted the telescope to focus in on the moon. The moon was the most impressive object in the night sky and it seemed fitting that Bane should show it to Nick as it had so much power over him and his shift. At 350x magnification, he was able to focus in on some spectacular craters, rills and mountains. He stepped back and gestured for Nick to look. The young man eagerly placed his right eye against the eyepiece and let out a gasp of pleasure.

"It's incredible! I had no idea you could see so much with just a small telescope!" Nick cried. "I admit that I always forget the moon is a so much more than this white disc in the night."

"The moon is a wonder in many ways." Bane poured port for both of them. He was thankful to see that his hands were steady now. No more shaking. "In the past, people worshipped the moon even more than the sun. They believed that the phases of the moon were related to the life cycle of all things on Earth."

Considering that his own curse seemed tied to the moon, Bane couldn't help but think those ancient people had gotten things right in some ways. He had studied the moon and the myths, trying to understand the connection between the spirit and that cold, dark hunk of rock that circled Earth. But he had never found any answers.

"That totally makes sense," Nick said. "The way the moon waxes and wanes is like life and death."

"The moon was also equated with wisdom and justice." Bane took a sip of the sweet, thick port as he recalled his useless studies. "Conversely, the moon is also associated with madness. For example, the term 'lunatic' is derived from the word luna, which is the term for moon."

When he had first turned into the beast he had felt like a lunatic himself. The moon had been bone white and huge that night. A moonbeam had hit him and his skin had *shivered*. His mother had seen it. His father had missed it. But in the end, neither of them missed him transforming into a massive Bengal tiger. He remembered the bone white moon had gone red after that ...

"People were said to be moonstruck, right?" Nick's voice snapped him out of his thoughts and he was utterly grateful for that.

"Yes, you are correct." He did not want to think of that first shift or what had happened after. His eyes went to Nick who still was staring through the telescope at the moon. He felt a wave of affection run through him. Nick was the opposite of his dark past. He was a shining future.

"And, of course, there are all those tales of werewolves who turned from men to beasts on the full moon," Nick reminded him.

Bane's heart thudded heavily. *It is not only werewolves, Nick.*

The moon's light sifted through the opening above them and touched the back of Bane's hand. He jerked it out of the light and brought it up against his chest. He rubbed at the spot as if he could feel his skin *shivering* again. But it wasn't. The beast was quiescent in his chest.

I am in control. Not the beast. I am human. I am a man.

Nick looked for a moment longer through the telescope before turning to Bane. Bane offered him the second glass of port. Nick took it and, with a teasing smile, asked, "So are you a moon worshipper?"

It was, of course, a joking question, but it hit closer to the mark than Nick could ever know. Bane was quiet for a moment as he stared up at the night sky through the sliding roof. Instead of answering, he asked, "Did you know that the full moon has different names depending on the month?"

"No."

"In July, it is known as the Hay Moon, which does not quite sound so impressive, but in February it is called the Ice Moon and in October, the Blood Moon," Bane explained. "And a second full moon in a month is called a Blue Moon."

He hated those months when there was a second full moon, when he lost himself to the beast twice. He was always especially irritable during that time as the moon's pull seemed to tug at his control the whole month rather than for just a few days preceding the full moon. But then he thought of his behavior that afternoon. The full moon was still far away. The beast was silent yet he was *still* affected. Was the moon gaining more power over him?

"Blood Moon sounds creepy!" Nick's head was tilted to the side and he was regarding Bane intently.

"What is it?" Bane asked.

Nick rested a hip against the wall and said, "You just surprise me all the time. There are so many layers to you and I feel like I learn something new every time we talk."

"Do I seem like a cypher to you, Nick?" His heart tumbled a bit, because he didn't think his secrets defined him.

"No, just ... *complex. Interesting.* I *want* to know more about you," Nick admitted.

Bane licked his lips. An idea had come to him. One that would perhaps give Nick his wish to know more of him. He didn't know if this was a good idea or if it would just cause him to have to tell more lies or lick more wounds, but he said, "Ask me anything."

Nick blinked and took a sip of port as if to give himself time to think. "*Anything*? Are you sure?"

"No, but I am not taking it back, Nick. Ask me a question. Whatever you like," Bane said, desperately wanting to give Nick something of himself.

"All right." Nick tapped the edge of his glass against his lower lip. "But only if you ask me one, too. Basically, we take turns."

"That sounds more than fair." Bane found himself grinning and almost eager to hear Nick's questions and ask his own. "You go first."

"I'll go easy on you. At first, anyways." Nick flashed a grin. "Favorite color?"

"Bah, Nick, too easy. *Crimson*," he said.

Nick's eyebrows rose up. "Crimson? Not just red, but *crimson*?"

"Yes, crimson is a *deep* red with touches of almost black within it." He held up the crimson port. "There's something very primal about it."

Nick nodded after a moment. "Crimson it is! Okay, now it's your turn."

Bane took a swallow of port and found his gaze sliding down Nick's front to his long, tanned legs. He *felt* Nick grinning at his admiration. He looked up at Nick's face. "When did you know you liked men?"

Nick rubbed the back of his neck. "Oh, well, I think it was when I was ten."

"Ten?!"

"Don't sound so *scandalized*!" Nick chuckled. "A lot of ten year old boys have crushes on their gym teachers. His name was Matt and he had the best frigging forearms you've ever seen. Tanned and muscled and –"

Bane held up a hand. "No more about this Matt's forearms! I believe I shall be jealous beyond measure if I hear more about them!"

"Aw, you don't have to be jealous. Your forearms are *far sexier*." Nick grasped Bane's right forearm and kissed it. Another shiver of pleasure ran through Bane as Nick's hot breath gushed over his wrist.

"That you liked men's forearms at ten ... is surprising to me," Bane admitted.

"Why?" Nick grinned.

Bane shrugged. "I suppose I imagine you innocent at that age."

"I was innocent!"

Bane grasped Nick around the waist. "Maybe I *still* think you are."

"Anyone ever tell you that you're *sweet*?" Nick leaned forward and their fronts were pressed together. A thrill of pleasure went through Bane.

"*Sweet*? No." Bane shook his head. He tilted his head to the side. "*Powerful*? Yes. *Sexy*? Yes. But *sweet*? Oh, no, no, no."

Bane kissed Nick deeply. The young man seemed to melt against him, wrapping his arms around Bane's neck. When they broke apart, Nick's gray eyes were shining in the moonlight.

"You're powerful, sexy and *sweet*." Nick kissed Bane's nose. "What about you? When did you know that you desired male forearms?"

Bane swallowed. "When I ... when I met Alastair."

Nick's eyes went huge. "Alastair? So he introduced you to love and then ... took it away?"

"There was never love to begin with." Bane grimaced when he saw Nick's face fall. "I do not mean ... I ..."

Suddenly, Nick smiled though it was a little forced. "I don't expect you to change your mind in a few days or a month or ... okay, the thing is that I think I can convince you that love is real. But it's going to take some time."

Bane didn't feel the usual disdain towards such a declaration. In truth, he *hoped* that Nick could make him believe again.

"I believe if anyone could prove me wrong, it's you."

"So ... Alastair was your first lover and the first man you ever lusted after?" Nick said after a quiet moment.

"More than that. When I met him I didn't even know I *could* feel such a thing for a man," Bane confessed. His skin prickled. Sweat suddenly broke out across his upper lip. Just thinking of Alastair had him becoming edgy, but he forced it down. He would tell Nick what he wanted to know.

Nick ran his hands up and down Bane's arms. "Don't think about him. I can tell that even saying Alastair's name makes you tense."

Bane considered this. It was the perfect excuse to change to another topic. Nick would not press him about Alastair. Yet ...

"I want to tell you about Alastair," Bane found himself saying.

"You don't *want* to. You don't *have* to either." Nick put his hands on Bane's chest, petting him.

"Perhaps *want* is the wrong word, but maybe *need* is," Bane's mouth formed the words without him consciously willing it. But he did not take those words back. He *meant* them.

Nick looked uncertain, but said, "O-okay. What do you want—*need*—to tell me?"

"I do not know." Bane let out an uncomfortable laugh and ran a hand through his hair.

"Maybe we start with what is he like?" Nick suggested.

"*Was.*"

"Was?" Nick's eyes widened.

"He's dead, Nick. Dead and gone a long time ago," Bane answered and saw Nick's confused expression. Bane only appeared thirty-five to Nick's eyes. The young man couldn't know that over half a century had passed since Alastair's death. Instead of letting Nick ask questions for which he would have to lie, Bane found himself launching into the story of Alastair.

"I was just eighteen when I met my father's best friend, Alastair Hillingham," Bane began as he settled his back against the wall opposite Nick. He found himself telling the story as if this had happened to someone else. Clear and matter of fact. He wondered how long this tone would last. "Alastair was nobility, but all of his family's money had been lost by the prior generation. He was handsome, charming and *broke.* He'd come to India to rebuild his family's fortunes. When I first met him, he seemed to me everything a man *should* be, and my own desire for men, which I had suppressed all my life up until that point, could be suppressed no longer. Especially when *he* pursued *me*."

CHAPTER TEN

ONCE UPON A TIME IN INDIA

***

"**B**ane, do you remember Alastair Hillingham? He's an old school mate of mine from Eton," Bane's father Lord Richard Dunsaney asked.

Richard was still a handsome man. Large boned, muscular and athletic. Having just turned forty, he was starting to take on that patrician look that so many of their ancestors had. It was said that Dunsaney men aged into their looks. His father's cheeks were ruddy and broken veins appeared along the sides of his nose from drinking too much, which was aging him quicker than nature would have. Yet he still had a raw, animal magnetism.

Bane looked less like his father than his mother with softer, less aquiline, more sensual lines. Sometimes Bane thought that it was the fact that they didn't look much alike that made his father hate him. So he was surprised that his father would introduce him to the friend who made him smile so sincerely.

Since Alastair had arrived at the house that morning, he and Richard had immediately gone into his father's study and stayed there. Bane had heard raucous male laughter, an unfamiliar sound in their home, coming through the sturdy teak door. Only when dinner was about to be served had his father emerged with their guest and introduced him for the first time to Bane.

"I can't say I do remember you, sir," Bane said, turning towards his father's school mate.

Alastair was six feet tall with pale blonde hair and laughing blue eyes. He had that fair English skin that was like cream, which would soon burn in India's tropical climate unless he was very careful. He wore a pair of off-white pants tucked into leather boots and a pale gray shirt flared open at the throat showing a hint of a muscled chest and some fine blond hair that matched his head. His blue eyes were fixed on Bane with surprising intensity. It made the eighteen-year old Bane suddenly feel very shy as if Alastair could see right through him. Alastair shot out a hand towards Bane for him to shake, which Bane took. It was warm and strong. A strange electric tingle flowed up his arm.

"Well, you were only five or six years old when I visited," Alastair remarked, large shoulders shrugging. "You can't be expected to remember."

"I am sorry that I do not, sir," Bane said softly. He wanted to hold onto that hand longer, but though Alastair allowed the touch to linger, the older man was the first one to let go. There was something in his eyes then like a question had been asked and Bane had answered it, though Bane wasn't sure what the question or answer actually were.

"I can't believe that this is little Bane!" Alastair shook his head as he turned to Richard. "My God, last I saw him he didn't come up to my waist and now, look at him! He's nearly taller than I am. Now he's a man, Richard."

Bane's father gave them both a smile that didn't reach his eyes. "Not quite a man yet, Alastair. He still goes about with his head in the clouds. I blame his mother for that."

"How is Mary? I haven't seen her yet." Alastair actually glanced around the dining room as if Mary was hiding behind some of the furniture, but Bane's mother was not there.

"She's not feeling well," Bane explained quickly. He hadn't yet had a chance to tell his father that she would not be joining them for dinner. "She asked me to pass along her regrets. She hopes to see you tomorrow, Alastair."

His mother loved India, but the climate had not been kind to her health. She was often feverish. Mostly, she pushed through her illnesses, especially when company came, but this time she had not done so. In fact, when Bane had come to see her that afternoon, telling her that Alastair had arrived, she had actually looked displeased.

Bane had, at first, thought that her dismay was likely because his father was apt to drink even more than usual with company over. Drinking always increased Richard's already volatile temper. He had nearly beaten a servant to death with his horse whip just last month after a particular long bout of drinking. Only his mother's attempts to distract his father while Bane had hustled the grievously wounded servant away had saved the man's life. The man, Nadal, had thanked Bane profusely.

Nadal had grasped Bane's hands in his bloody ones. "I swear, sahib, that my family shall always serve you and yours. From this day forward, I pledge my life to you and the lives of my children and grandchildren."

"Please, Nadal, you must rest. Do not worry yourself about thanking me." Bane had felt sick that the man should thank him. His father had done this terrible thing. His actions were nothing in comparison.

But Nadal had not been dissuaded. The intensity of his grip increased. "No, sahib, I swear it. We shall serve you."

"I am at your service, Nadal," Bane answered.

Considering what had happened to Nadal, it was understandable that she was worried about Richard's drinking, but that did not completely explain her unease about Alastair. She seemed to dislike the man though Bane could not imagine why. Bane found him quite *fascinating*. And his father appeared to be in a better mood than Bane had seen him in ages with Alastair there.

"Bah! Mary spent too much time today in the heat with those paints of hers! The fumes alone would make anyone sick. I should have them thrown out and then she cannot poison herself anymore with them!" Richard waved a hand through the air as if he could sweep all of her paints and paintings into the trash.

"Father, surely you don't mean that!" Bane cried. He feared that his father *did* mean exactly that. This made him speak up. Normally, he kept silent when his father was cruel. It was the only way to avoid the man's blows. But he absolutely would not about his mother and her painting.. "It would *destroy* her if you forbid her to paint."

Bane's father rolled his dark gray eyes even as he slapped Alastair on the back and led him to a seat at the table by his side. "That's my son for you. Always defending his mother."

Bane refused to flinch at the insult intended in his father's words. He stood straight even though inside he quailed at rousing his father's temper. Richard never looked at him but to see fault even when Bane did something his father considered manly like hunting. Bane was the best shot in the area, but his father had taken it as a slight to his own skills with a gun when Bane out-shot him. Bane remembered all too well the backhand he had received after a hunting party where he had killed the water buffalo when his father's shot had gone wide. He had tasted blood in his mouth and had a large, dark purple bruise on his cheek for days afterwards

"Being protective of one's mother is a *good* trait, Richard, and you make it sound like a failing," Alastair said with a touch of gentleness in his tone.

Bane's father's mouth twisted in distaste. "Bane doesn't understand a *man's* values, Alastair. He only understands a *woman's*. I suppose it's my fault. I allowed Mary to be in charge of his education. Should have sent him back to England, but too late now, I suppose."

Bane said nothing and tried to ignore the pain those words caused. He held himself very still. Alastair cast a glance over his shoulder at Bane. For one moment, there was a look of sympathy in his eyes. Bane smiled at him weakly. But then

Alastair was back completely in his father's orbit and any private communication between them seemed impossible.

Dinner had Alastair and his father talking of old times, of long forgotten friends and wild adventures, which mostly involved too much alcohol and horses. Bane listened avidly, but did not participate. His father would not have liked him to speak and he was too overwhelmed with Alastair's voice, the way he moved and how his eyes sparkled in the candlelight to add to the conversation anyways.

Dinner was a far more pleasant affair than it had ever been before. There were no tense silences. The air was filled with laughter. And then there were the looks between him and Alastair. Looks that had heat building between Bane's thighs. As much as Bane looked at Alastair, Alastair looked at Bane. It was like a game. They would only look at each other when Bane's father wouldn't notice. Their eyes caught many times. There were the secret smiles, too, smiles that had Bane's stomach doing flips.

Alastair told them that he staying at a local hotel, but Bane's father wouldn't hear of it and soon Alastair was living with them. He had a room on the second floor of their house that overlooked the garden. His room was right next to Bane's and they shared a balcony. But even so, Bane saw him little in the beginning as Richard was constantly taking Alastair with him all over the city.

Bane tried not to be disappointed about this. He knew that Alastair needed the business contacts to get his fresh start going in India. Bane's family had always been wealthy and now Alastair needed that wealth and Richard's connections to restore his own fortune. But finally a day came when Richard had to check on one of the mines he had an interest in and hadn't asked Alastair to go. This trip would take him away from the house for a week. Bane's heart had hammered and his stomach twisted in excitement at the thought. Since his mother mostly kept to her studio and rested in her rooms, he would have ample time *alone* with Alastair.

"You are very jumpy today, my son," his mother said from her stool in front of her easel. Her dark hair was drawn up into a bun and though she wore a light muslin dress there was still a sheen of sweat on her skin.

"I'm just glad that Father is gone," Bane admitted. "Though he has been in fine fettle since Alastair arrived."

"Yes, he has," she replied colorlessly.

He had joined her that morning as she had painted and Alastair had slept. He feared he would drive himself mad by constantly drifting out onto the shared balcony and listening to the other man's soft breathing. Alastair and Richard had been out late the night before at the local British club, drinking, smoking and playing cards. Alastair likely wouldn't be up for hours so Bane had forced himself to leave the second floor and sought out his mother.

"Alastair keeps him ... occupied," Bane continued lamely.

"And kept him out of the house so that helps, too, doesn't it?" she responded dryly. She wasn't exactly rebuking him as she sometimes did about speaking ill of his father. Merely pointing out what was true. "And when he is here, he and Alastair are wrapped up together. They have hardly paid either one of us any mind. I suppose that does make things *better* in a way."

"I'm sorry, Mother. I know I shouldn't speak like this about Father."

"I understand why, my son. I feel oftentimes the same, but Alastair ... he brings his own problems."

Bane could not imagine what those were, but he found himself loath to ask her. "That painting is rather good."

It was a landscape that seemed to capture some of the light of India. His mother blushed and shrugged.

"It is potentially *acceptable*."

No, it's brilliant! Do not downplay your skills!" Bane jiggled one leg and then got up from where he was sitting to pace.

"If you are going to pace about, Bane, I would ask you do so *outside* so that I am not distracted," she laughed. "What little skills I have easily fly away."

Bane stopped and sighed. "I don't know why I am so restless."

She took one of his hands in both of hers. He was struck how thin her fingers looked. So frail and light like a bird's. There were daubs of dried paint along the sides of some of them. "You have been playing the dutiful son and avid listener when your father is here, trying to be a good host to Alastair. Now you are playing supportive son to me. You need to enjoy yourself."

Again, Bane noted the strange tenseness in her tone and affect when she spoke of him. Alastair was nothing but courtly to her so Bane did not understand her reluctance to enjoy his company.

"Why don't you like Alastair, Mother?" The words were out of his mouth before he could think better of them.

Her blue eyes widened. "I like Alastair!"

"No, Mother, you do not. You dislike him intensely. Why?" Bane pressed.

Her gaze darted away from him towards her canvas. "Dislike is too strong a word really. I—I don't know what I feel about Alastair. He and your father were great friends at school. Nearly inseparable. But then it came time for both to settle down and have families. Your father and I were introduced and ... well, we married."

"And?" Bane was not connecting his mother's dislike of Alastair with her marriage.

"Your father was—was very *attentive* when we were courting. I did not even know Alastair existed then, but after we married, Alastair came around more and more." Her eyes grew distant as she remembered. "And suddenly, it seemed that the Richard I had known, fallen in love with and married wasn't ... wasn't *real*."

"Wasn't *real*?" Bane frowned. But then he thought of how his father had been with Alastair as opposed to how he normally was. His father's temper had surprisingly cooled and he seemed *happy*. The moroseness that typically chased him hadn't appeared. His drinking hadn't improved, but the violent bouts of anger hadn't followed it as often. He had even spoken with more civility to Bane.

"When Alastair came into our lives, I saw *another* Richard. A very different Richard. And I realized then that ..." her voice drifted off. She shook her head. "Well, I suppose it is normal for a wife to be jealous of her husband's best friend. After all, men can do so many things together, share things, that a man and wife cannot. Perhaps it is just jealousy that clouds my feelings about Alastair."

"They are very special friends," Bane said uncertainly. He felt that he was missing something, a hidden meaning beneath his mother's words. If he knew the right questions to ask he felt he would understood what she meant.

"Yes." Her expression went bleak. "Very *special*." She shook herself once more. "Now I need to paint and you need to go use some of that energy. So off with you!"

Bane smiled. He could see his mother was fighting to be lighthearted. He would not press her further and have that illusion break. "I will see you for tea then later."

"Yes, yes, but go have fun, my son," she urged.

He nodded, but already she was deeply involved in her painting and did not see it. He turned and left her. His feet took him to the second floor. Perhaps he would have the courage to ask Alastair to spend some time together. He wasn't sure what they would do, but something. He went into his own room and out onto the balcony, intending to check if the other man was still asleep before going to his door to knock. But he didn't have to go far to find Alastair.

The man was on the balcony, his elbows resting on the railing as he cradled a cup of tea in his hands. His hair was still tousled from sleep. He only had on a pair of white, flowy pants. Bane's gaze fixated on that lean muscular chest. Alastair's nipples were a sweet pink that had Bane's lips parting as his mind offered him the unbidden image of fastening his mouth onto those tight nubs and *sucking*. Forbidden heat built up in his groin and his cock twitched. Bane gasped in dismay and Alastair turned his head at the sound.

"Oh, I'm sorry, I didn't realize you were—I'll just go." Bane hurriedly spun on his heel to leave, but Alastair seemed to move inhumanly fast and grasped Bane's left wrist. That light hold froze Bane in place.

"Don't go. Please. I'm so glad you're here," Alastair said.

His voice was soft, but Bane could hear him clearly even over the crying of the birds and the rush of the wind. Alastair's mouth was directly against the cusp of Bane's left ear. His breath skated along Bane's throat and under the collar of his shirt. Bane's nipples beaded almost painfully in response.

"You're glad I'm here?" Bane's voice sounded deeper than normal in his own ears.

Alastair let out a soft huff of laughter. "Of course, I'm glad, Bane. I've been wanting to spend some time with you *alone* since I first saw you." His thumb moved lightly over the sensitive skin of Bane's wrist. "Haven't you wanted the same thing?"

Another trill of heat ran through Bane. Again, he knew that there were undercurrents of meaning in Alastair's words and actions just like there had been in his mother's. But Bane couldn't fully grasp that hidden meaning. All he could do was *feel*. His body seemed to know something. His mouth was suddenly dry as dust and his cock again twitched. He tried to answer Alastair with a 'yes', but he couldn't form the word so he just nodded.

"Good, I'm so glad," Alastair said. "I truly wish to get to know you, Bane. I want that to begin *now*."

"I want that, too," Bane answered, his voice rough with unfamiliar desire.

Alastair covered Bane's hand with his. "Tell me about the India *you* love, Bane. Your father seems to have only disdain for this place, how it differs from England, but I think you see it quite differently."

"I do." Bane's heart seemed to surge up into his throat at Alastair's words. His passion for this country knew no bounds. He felt like it was a part of him. He could never imagine leaving it. Even the things he hated about it he still loved in some ways. "India is ... magic."

Alastair's eyes widened. "*Magic*?"

Bane let out a self-conscious laugh even as he was *acutely* aware that Alastair's hand was still covering his. Heat bloomed between his legs again and sweat suddenly covered his upper lip. "I think one feels *closer* here to the meaning of things."

"What things?"

"*Everything*." Bane struggled to explain it, but then realized words would never suffice. "Let me show you. That's the best way and then you'll see what I mean."

"Lead me where you will." Alastair squeezed Bane's hand.

Bane had taken Alastair into the market in town. The sellers sat on the dusty ground with their wares out in front of them or displayed in their tents. They inhaled exotic spices and handled the brightly colored fabrics that glowed with such vibrancy that they almost looked unreal. He then took Alastair into a courtyard where a Rangoli—a design created with dry flour to which natural colors were added—was being created on the ground. The three women who were working on it gave them shy smiles and bows before returning to their work of creating flower and petal shapes with the colored flour. He and Alastair watched the women create the design with their careful almost graceful movements for almost an hour.

Finally, Alastair shook his head in wonder. "Such intricacy! Such beauty! And made of something that will soon disappear. All this work will be washed away."

"Yes, but there is something more precious about it, because it won't last," Bane pointed out.

"Perhaps that's true. In a way, this represents life, does it not?" Alastair remarked. "Our efforts compared to the power of time are nothing really. We think we are creating lasting impressions on this world, but, in reality, our lives are but flickers of a candle flame and our accomplishments less than that especially when one has no capital. Then we truly are forgotten."

"That sounds so grim!" Bane said with surprise.

Alastair shook himself and one of his brilliant smiles returned that had Bane's heart beating faster. "Forgive me. I'm just feeling a little glum. I think it is because I fear that I will never accomplish anything."

"That's not possible! You're bursting with ideas."

"I am, but I do not have the funds to proceed with any of them." He gave Bane a lopsided smile. "It seems that Fate gives some men all the ideas, but other men all the money."

"But, surely, Father will help you!" Bane protested, not believing for a moment that Richard wouldn't support his best friend.

There was a dark look in Alastair's eyes, but it quickly passed away as he said, "Your father is considering it. Now show me more of this India that you love."

"It's getting too hot. We need to rest for today. I promise I'll show you more tomorrow. Perhaps we could go hunting," Bane suggested.

"Rest, huh?" Alastair got this speculative gleam in his eyes. A rather predatory smile lit his lips as he stepped into Bane's personal space. "I could definitely see myself *resting* with you beside me."

Bane's heart threatened to hammer out of his chest. "But that's—that's –"

"We'll just *sleep* beside one another. If that's *all* you want to do." His breath glided over Bane's cheek.

"I ... I don't know what you mean." Bane's mind didn't know what he meant, but his cock seemed to as it pulsed and stood up at attention.

Alastair touched his cheek. It was a brief brush of fingertips and then it was gone. "You have time to think about it."

The two of them walked back to the house. Alastair touched Bane the entire way home. Just the barest of touches on his shoulders, forearms, throat, cheek and hips. He slid a hand on Bane's waist. His fingers brushed along the base of Bane's spine. His fingers lingered against Bane's neck. By the time they returned to the house, Bane's head was filled with Alastair.

Alastair threw himself down on one of the couches in the high-ceiling living room. His booted feet rested on the top of a low table. He poured himself a few fingers of whisky and lit a cigar. The smoke curled around his head as he stared at Bane through hooded eyes. He was so handsome with his platinum hair and pink mouth, strong jaw and aquiline nose.

"Sit down beside me, Bane," Alastair said with a laugh. "You have this vinegary expression on your face as you stare at my boots. I feel like I'm about to hear a woman's voice nagging me not to muss the furniture."

"That *is* one of Mother's favorite tables," Bane said. He knew he was hovering and he wanted quite desperately to sit beside Alastair, but he knew that something would happen between them if he did and he wasn't sure if he was ready for it yet. Or perhaps he was *too* ready for it.

Alastair drew his feet off the table and put them firmly on the ground. He spread his arms wide as if to show his good will. "I would never want to *damage* anything that Mary cares about." For one moment, Bane wondered if there was a mocking tone in Alastair's voice, but then the older man was patting the couch beside him. "Sit with me, Bane. *Please.*"

Bane slowly walked over to Alastair. The older man watched the movement of Bane's long legs as if mesmerized. His gaze slowly swept up Bane's entire body until they were staring into one another's eyes. Bane felt lost in Alastair's blue stare. He found himself sitting down on the couch in the very corner so that there was as much space between them as possible. That was when he noticed the arousal that tented Alastair's pants and his cheeks flamed. He quickly looked away, staring, unseeing forward. Alastair laughed.

"You're the cause of this, you know. Since the first moment I saw you, I have been forced to wear my loosest trousers," Alastair said.

"I—I do not know what I would have to do with—with *that*," Bane stammered out, gesturing blindly towards Alastair's crotch.

"How can you not know? How can you be so unaware of how incredibly *beautiful* you are?" Alastair whispered as he touched a stray lock of Bane's hair.

Bane stilled at the touch. "Women are beautiful. Men are—"

"*Beautiful*." Alastair turned so that he was facing Bane. "It's rare, but some men are just far more lovely than any woman could be. And you are one of them."

"I am *not* a woman," Bane said stiffly. He admired his mother and other women greatly, but his father had always used "being like a woman" as the ultimate insult.

"No, no, you are not, which is why I cannot get enough of you." Alastair's fingers continued to curl in Bane's hair.

The rich smell of tobacco and whiskey—masculine smells—smells that had Bane normally cringing in fear of being struck by his father, rolled off of Alastair and Bane was afraid again. But not of being struck, but of wanting what he should not, of desiring what was forbidden by the laws of men and God. Yet he did not get up from that couch. He did not move away from Alastair even though it was clear that the older man was acting on lust for him.

"What do you want with me?" Bane whispered. He both desperately wanted to know and not know at the same time. He knew he should turn their conversation to other things. He should stand and get one of the servants so that nothing could happen between them. But he continued to stay where he was.

"To take you into my arms. To kiss you. To hear you moan." Alastair finished off his cigar, stubbing it out in the glass ashtray. The whiskey was also gone and the heavy, cut crystal glass was on the table, leaving Alastair's hands completely free. Free to touch.

"Men do not—men do not do that with other men." Bane pressed himself against the arm of the couch. His breathing came in staccato gasps. His own cock painfully pressed against the front of his trousers and was easily observable.

"They don't?" Alastair was suddenly against Bane. Their bodies pressed together. His breath ghosted across Bane's face. More whiskey fumes. Bane almost felt drunk from the scent alone.

"No, it is immoral. It is *unnatural,*" Bane protested weakly even as his whole body *burned* with desire.

This must be sin. This is how the Devil gets into men's hearts by making it seem like they are on the verge of Heaven when they are on the verge of Hell.

"Men have been loving each other like this since the beginning of time. There is nothing more *natural* than seeing beauty such as yours and being *inspired* by it. Being *drawn* to it. Wanting to *touch* and *taste* it," Alastair said.

"It is against all laws that we—that we—I cannot think with you so near! Alastair, we mustn't!" Bane cried.

"You do not need to *think,* Bane. You just need to *feel.*"

Alastair touched Bane's nearest thigh. His fingers slid up to just barely brush Bane's cloth-covered cock. Trills of heat raced up through Bane's shaft and deep into his belly. His heart was beating so hard, Bane thought it might break through his chest wall. He was frozen in place and all his strength seemed to have left him. Alastair's mouth pressed against Bane's ear. His breath tickled and aroused.

"Alastair, this is—this is ..."

"Do not worry, Bane. If we must *burn* in Hell for such activities, I will burn for the both of us. That is how much I want you. Do not deny me." Alastair kissed Bane's earlobe, drawing it into his mouth and sucking lightly before raking his teeth across the sensitive skin.

Bane arched up, his mouth opened and moans spilled from his parted lips. Alastair's mouth glided along Bane's jaw before he covered Bane's mouth with his own. He tasted of whiskey and smoke. His tongue was liquid and hot. Arousal, like a wave, crashed through Bane's young form. Alastair was on top of him, straddling him. Bane pressed up against that hard, masculine body. His cock surged in his pants. He had never felt this with another person. His arousal had never been so wild and raw.

This is a sin! This is wrong! This is Heaven and Hell and I ... I do not care. I cannot stop this. I do not wish to stop this!

Bane's hands reached up, almost of their own accord, and feathered through Alastair's hair then gripped it and held the older man against him as if to stop Alastair from escaping. The older man laughed into their kiss and then Bane was kissing him back and laughter turned to moans. The older man ground the base of his palm against Bane's erection. Bane nearly screamed with the pleasure of it.

Alastair began to massage his cock through his pants. Suddenly, his fingers were at the fastenings of Bane's pants, undoing them, and reaching in to take out Bane's cock. Bane nearly came right then and there, but Alastair squeezed the base of his cock and the urge faded. Then Alastair was breaking their kiss and Bane whined, trying to follow after his lips.

"Why are you stopping?" Bane gasped. He didn't want to stop. He didn't even want to pause. Because he feared he would start thinking and doubting that this was right if they did.

"Not stopping," Alastair chuckled. "Just doing this properly so we can both enjoy it fully."

Alastair undid his own pants and suddenly his cock was revealed. It was thick and long. It was a dusky rose in color. The head was slick with precum. Musk wafted up from it and Bane's own cock twitched painfully. He had never allowed himself the pleasure of looking at another man's penis. Now he stared at it and wished he could devour it.

Then Alastair was fisting both his and Bane's cock in both of his hands and began to stroke them at the same time. Bane let out an almost animalistic cry as lightning strikes of pleasure shot through him. The feel of his cock against Alastair's was phenomenal. It was like having a hot, velvety bar press against his own. Alastair's masterful caresses had Bane helplessly flopping back against the couch. His cock throbbed and jerked. Alastair's thumb ran along the top of Bane's cock, smearing the shiny precum across the broad head.

"So beautiful, Bane. God! So beautiful. I can't wait to be inside of you. Having you clench around me."

Alastair's eyes were dark with desire. He leaned forward and captured Bane's open mouth. His tongue slipped inside of Bane's mouth. His tongue flickered against Bane's as his hand squeezed their cocks together as he stroked up and down. Bane's hips rose and fell. His balls tightened against his body. He was going to cum.

"I am going to—my release –"

"Let go, Bane."

"But our clothes!" Bane cried nonsensically.

"Let go. Paint me with your cum," Alastair whispered into his right ear and then lightly bit it.

That last bite had Bane arching up one final time. His cock strained skyward. The first gush of semen almost surprised him. His semen sprayed over Alastair's shirt and coated his fingers. Alastair's orgasm came then as well and more semen rained down on both of their clothes. Alastair continued to stroke them both, slowly, as if milking every bit of semen from their bodies. Alastair then got off of him, finally releasing their cocks when the touch became almost painful.

Bane sprawled bonelessly on the couch. His eyes were almost shut. His breathing slowed. Alastair's arm was around his shoulders and he leaned in, kissing Bane lazily. Bane turned his head so that Alastair could kiss his mouth. The older man obliged. Their tongues tangled together. Bane already felt a new stirring in his loins.

Alastair rested their foreheads together. "You are a revelation, Bane."

"I did not know—I had no idea—that it could be this way," Bane murmured.

"This is *nothing*. I will show you everything, Bane. All the forbidden pleasures between men," Alastair promised.

Bane stilled. "You said *forbidden* so you think –"

"Forbidden by *society*, Bane. But society forbids anything that is too pleasurable," Alastair said. He continued to kiss Bane's lips. "But I've never cared what society has to say."

"Except, of course, Alastair was lying," Bane said to Nick.

The young man stared at him. Nick had hardly seemed to blink as Bane had painted those early days with Alastair.

"There's more," Nick finally said. His grey eyes were bleak and filled with pain for Bane. "I *know* there's more and it's all *bad*, isn't it?"

Bane drained his glass of port and poured himself another. His hands were shaking slightly. The scent of whiskey and cigars rose up in his mind and he could almost smell them in this room. They were the twin scents of Alastair and his father. Love and hate. Desire and disgust. Nick stared up at him with such concern. His good heart was clearly breaking already, knowing that something terrible was to come, something that would wipe love out of existence for him.

"Yes, there's more to the story of Alastair and me, Nick," Bane admitted as he drained that second glass of port. "And it *is* bad. But I think I knew from the beginning that it was going to be a *tragedy*."

CHAPTER ELEVEN

WHISKEY AND SMOKE

Tension had built up in Bane's shoulders and back as he continued to speak of Alastair. He was practically hunched over now. His large frame was curled in on itself.

"You don't have to tell me anything more, Bane. Really, you can stop," Nick said. He was petting Bane's back. His face was a mask of pain.

"I wish to continue," Bane got out. He had to tell it. This story would explain so much to Nick about who and what he was while he kept the rest of himself in shadows.

"I don't want to cause you pain. This is causing you pain and I want to stop it." Nick's hands gripped Bane's shoulder.

Bane lifted haunted eyes to him and tried to explain. "I have started this and I must finish it. I want you to know and I want to ... *rid* myself of it."

It was the last part that seemed to have Nick understanding and reluctantly nodding. Bane needed to purge himself of the memories of Alastair. If he told this story in full then perhaps it would no longer have the power over him that it currently had. He wanted to be free of the memories and start fresh with Nick.

Nick gripped Bane's shoulders. "Don't do this for me though, Bane. I didn't realize ... I don't know why I didn't think how telling all this would affect you before."

"*You* are not causing me pain," Bane assured him. "It already happened, Nick. It can't be stopped. I want to remember this."

He drew Nick against him, feeling the thump of Nick's heart, the warmth of Nick's body, and the rush of Nick's breath. He would hold onto Nick as he conjured up the past.

Bane's voice became softer as he continued the story, "That week with Alastair was like a dream. It wasn't the sex, but it was the *tenderness* and the way he spoke to me as if I was something *precious* that truly enthralled me to him. I felt like a plant that had been starved for sunlight that had suddenly been placed in the sunniest spot on the sill."

Bane leaned back into Alastair's arms and the warm, soapy water of the bath sloshed over his chest. He loved bathing with the older man. Not only because it meant being naked and rubbing against acres of Alastair's pale, kissable skin, but it also meant simply being held and caressed. And they *talked* in the bath. They talked of the *future*. A future that included the two of them being together.

"I've got an eye on a mine. Everyone thinks there's nothing of value in it, tapped out. Even your father doesn't see it as worth a damn, but I think everyone is *wrong*," Alastair said.

"Why do you think they're wrong?" Bane rested his head against Alastair's shoulder.

The older man ran his wet hands down Bane's arms and then laced their fingers together, before he answered, "I've seen some geology reports that indicate ... well, I am telling *you* this, but *only* you and you can't repeat it. Especially not to your father."

"Surely you've noticed, Alastair, that my father and I do *not* talk *at all* if I can help it," Bane said bitterly.

His anger at his father had increased over the week as Alastair had pointed out, sometimes subtly, sometimes not, how *cruel* his father was to him, not to mention how *unfair*. He had never allowed himself to think that his family wasn't normal, that his father's coldness and anger wasn't what everyone experienced. But now he realized that it wasn't natural, it certainly wasn't right and maybe, he didn't have to accept it anymore.

"I know, but this is crucial. I need your word, Bane," Alastair said sternly.

"You have my word! I swear I would never do anything to harm you!" Bane twisted around in Alastair's arms. It shifted the older man's cock away from his ass, but he wanted Alastair to see in his eyes that it was true.

"I know. Thank you. I've just been ... well, I've had so much bad luck in this world," Alastair sighed. "This might be my last chance to set things right. I don't have two pence to my name. Being poor is quite miserable."

"I'm sorry. I want –"

Alastair put a finger over Bane's mouth. "I know you want to help me and the fact that if you *could* you *would* is enough for me. I just wish ..."

"Wish what?"

"With wealth comes *privilege*," Alastair said.

Bane cocked his head to the side. He could think of many things being rich gave one as opposed to being poor, but he sensed that Alastair meant something quite different than what he was considering. "What kind of privilege?"

Alastair gave him a slow, sensual smile before leaning in and kissing him. The slide of tongues had Bane's stomach muscles fluttering with desire. The kiss ended, leaving both men breathless for a time.

"The kind of privilege where no one questions you if you have a beautiful young man come over and spend the night again and again and again. The kind of privilege where you need not marry a woman for her money," Alastair said.

Bane's heart twisted slightly as he thought of the fact that the wealth in his family had all come from his mother's side. Had that played a role in why his father had married her? His heart also twisted harder at the thought of Alastair with someone else.

"Could you marry for money, Alastair? Could you marry without love?" Bane asked.

"I certainly hope it won't come to that!"

"But could you do it?" Bane asked out loud, but thought, *You would leave me, us, this, for money?*

"I'm looking a bit too threadbare to attract the fairer sex. And I don't think I could even *fake* arousal for a woman." His face screwed up. "But if it's that or destitution, I might be so inclined."

"That will never happen!" Bane cried. "The mine will work out and you'll be rich and we'll be ... well, you'll be rich."

Alastair immediately kissed Bane's temple and held him close. "You are a treasure, Bane. As rare and wonderful as any I will find in that mine."

Bane's heart beat faster at those words. "You make me feel so *different* than anyone else ever has. Not even my mother's love has ever made me feel so treasured and hers is unconditional."

Alastair's hands trailed down Bane's spine and rested just on the swell of his buttocks. "Because you've been locked away by your father. God knows, I can see why. You would have been devoured by our friends at Eton."

Bane frowned. "I don't understand. Why would they have devoured me?"

"Bane, your father and I were lovers for a long time. We often traded partners at school for variety, but all of us were interested in lovely young men. It was rather a sport to see how many virgins we could acquire during term." Alastair squeezed Bane's ass.

Bane's breathing sped up from the illicit touch, but he struggled to keep his mind clear as what Alastair was saying was hugely important. "You mean my father and you—*did this* together?"

"Oh, yes, this and a lot more." Alastair kissed down Bane's throat. "And he was ranked *second* below me in seductions!"

Things started to slot into place: his mother's dislike of Alastair, her cryptic comments about his father changing after their marriage when he had secured her fortune, and his father's reaction to Alastair's visit. "And now? Are you still—still *with him*?"

"You need not be jealous," Alastair laughed. "He made his choice. He married your mother for her fortune and moved to India."

Bane though was sitting up in the bath. "You do not understand! My father has talked with such *venom* about sodomites. Why do you think he loathes me? He understood before I did what my nature was. How could he be a homosexual and feel those things about others like himself?"

Alastair let out an exhale of breath and his expression became serious. He stopped the teasing touches. "Because your father hated—*hates*—that part of himself. He is a great believer in society, but, at the same time, he knows that if society knew the truth about him, it would throw him out. It is a contradiction that has eaten at him."

"A few years ago, there had been a young man here that was—was *openly* a sodomite and Father physically *attacked* him," Bane said softly. "Father had to be dragged off of him. The young man went back to England. He suffered a broken nose, ribs and left arm. Father would have *killed* him if he hadn't been dragged away."

Alastair ran a wet hand through his damp hair. "I'm sure your father was interested in him and the frustration of not having him caused him to lash out."

"This young man never did anything to Father! No flirting! No spurning! Nothing!" Bane protested.

Alastair's lips flattened together. "Your father told me that he has not pursued male love since coming here. But I highly doubt he's stopped *wanting* it. He couldn't help himself at college. He couldn't keep his hands off of me the moment I arrived here. Marrying your mother did not curb his desire. Why should coming to India do so when there are so many more opportunities to do what his nature demands?"

Bane lowered his head. "Speaking of my mother ... does he—he enjoy women at all?"

Alastair's blue eyes hooded slightly. "You were conceived Bane, but as we all know, respectable women have no interest in sexual gratification. It is all about procreation. So she probably wasn't pressed very hard to fill their marriage bed."

"Once Father comes home, what happens?" Bane asked Alastair.

Alastair stilled in his stroking of Bane's hair. "We must be very careful. Exquisitely careful."

"We already are. I mean we have hidden this from Mother and the servants—what? Why are you laughing, Alastair?"

"You think your mother and your servants do not know about us?" Alastair shook his head and sighed.

"They don't!"

"That one servant—Nadal, I think his name is—he knows. He is in the corridor right now, keeping others away so that we have privacy," Alastair said.

"What?" Bane's eyes grew large. He began to get out of the tub, but Alastair grabbed a hold of him and pulled him back down.

"He is your friend. Your ally. Loyal to you. That is a good thing." Alastair stroked Bane's chest until Bane settled down.

"This past week has felt like we were in our own private world. I had no idea that anyone else even *guessed*," Bane confessed, curling against Alastair's chest.

"But we were *not* in another world. *You* may not have noticed other people, but other people noticed you—or I should say *us*," Alastair corrected.

"Even my—my mother?" Bane's mouth went dry at that.

"Have you not realized that she has retreated more and more into painting? She stopped joining us for dinner some nights ago," Alastair pointed out.

"But I thought it was her *health* that was keeping her away!"

"Seeing you and I together makes her *ill*, I'm sure," Alastair said airily. "Deja vu, I imagine."

Bane's head lifted from Alastair's chest. "She disapproves. She doesn't want her son to be—be a sodomite."

For the first time, Bane felt a quelling of the unadulterated happiness Alastair had brought to him. If anyone outside of those loyal to them were to find out what they were to one another, it wouldn't just mean public censure, it could result in them being jailed or worse.

And if Father found out ...

Bane closed his eyes tightly and shuddered. Alastair was stroking him again, kissing him tenderly.

"What evil thoughts are you thinking?" Alastair asked between kisses.

"I was thinking that Father must never find out about us. He would—I am certain he would hurt both of us and I could not bear you being injured for loving me," Bane whispered.

Alastair's expression went blank for a moment. It was clear that he was thinking furiously. But then he kissed Bane's forehead as if he had made a decision. "We must make sure that he doesn't, but if he does, I will protect you, Bane."

Bane stilled at those words. "You would protect me?"

"I won't let him hurt you anymore, especially not over me. I'd take you away from here. We'd be poor together, but dammit, we would be together and he would never get his hands on either of us."

Bane had no desire to leave his mother, but the thought of escaping his father? Of being free of his rages and sneers? Of being with Alastair with the world at their feet? His heart soared in a way that he had never allowed it to in the past. He had always been so careful to have only small wants and no plans. Now he could see a light at the end of the tunnel, a way out.

And maybe, if we succeed with this mine, we could rescue Mother from Father as well.

"I want to do it, Alastair," Bane said suddenly, surging up against the other man.

"Do what?" Alastair asked, clearly unsure what Bane was talking about and perhaps that should have clued him in as to what would come later, but it didn't.

Bane knew his eyes were shining. "Build a life together. Buy that mine! Show everyone it's full of treasure! Have a life together!"

Alastair laughed. He cupped Bane's face and kissed him. Bane responded back eagerly. It was then that they both heard raised voices in the hall. One of them was Nadal's.

"Sahib! Where are you going, sahib? That room is occupied! You mustn't go in there!" Nadal cried.

"GET OUT OF MY WAY!" Bane's father cried.

There was the thunderous sound of Nadal's body hitting the wall. Bane knew that sound, because his father had done the same to him one night. Slammed him against the wall with such force that his head spun.

"My God," Alastair whispered.

They were both frozen in the tub when the door burst open and nearly split in two from Richard using his foot to kick it in. His father stood there, his face beet red, sweat pouring down his forehead, and his eyes twin pools of hate. He was *seeing* them. He was seeing them *naked*, in each other arms, and there was no mistaking what they were doing. He knew everything. Bane couldn't quite believe this was happening. It was like every nightmare he'd ever had was coming true.

"Did you think I wouldn't know, Alastair?" Richard's voice was surprisingly low. He ground his teeth though after every sentence. "Did you think it would escape my notice that you were *sodomizing* my filthy, ungrateful son?"

Alastair was pale as milk, but he somehow managed to speak and even sound jaunty, "Why are you so upset about it?

You never said he was off-limits. Are you angry because we can't *share* this time?"

Something in Bane's chest curdled. The thought of his father touching him *like that* was horrifying. The thought of Richard touching him *at all* brought out a cold sweat.

"Share? SHARE? He's *my* son! He's *mine*, Alastair! Not *yours*!" Richard advanced upon them. "Just like it's *my* fortune and not yours!"

Bane struggled to get up. His hands slipped on the sides of the tub as he desperately tried to stand. His legs felt weak underneath him, but then he saw that upraised hand. "Father, don't! Stop!"

He bodily threw himself over Alastair, but he needn't have bothered. The blow wasn't meant for Alastair, but for him. His father punched him and Bane saw stars. Richard grabbed the back of his head, tangling his fingers painfully in Bane's hair before striking him again and again. Bane felt the bruises bloom like poisonous flowers on his cheeks, forehead and chin.

"Stop, Richard! Stop! What the Hell are you doing, man?" Alastair cried. He used one arm to shield Bane from the blows.

"Filthy little sodomite! Filthy cur! You would do this to me! You would dishonor me! You would try to steal from me, too!" Richard howled his contradictory claims.

"Richard, enough!" Alastair shouted.

Richard froze. His eyes were glittering with what looked like madness. His teeth were exposed like an animal's. "You think you can tell *me* what to do? Who are you, Alastair?"

"Your friend," Alastair responded weakly.

"Father, please …" Bane whispered as his head spun.

"My friend? No, you're *not* my friend any longer. You're a *supplicant*, Alastair, because you're a pauper! You *need* me. I don't need *you*. We aren't equals!" Richard said with a vicious laugh. "It's not like it was back in school where your pedigree *mattered*. Out here, *money matters*. And you haven't got any! But I do and you need it!"

"He doesn't need it. He's more of a man than you," Bane cried.

"Oh, is he?" Richard guffawed acidly. "Has he convinced you that you'll have a life together? That he can protect you and give you all you need?"

Bane looked up at his father balefully. "So what if he has?"

Richard grinned, but it looked more like a death's head grin. "So what if he has? Well, it's *nothing* to me what he's promised you, because I know it's all *lies*."

Alastair shook his head. "I've seen what you're doing to this boy and it has to stop, Richard. You're abusing him and –"

"I'll give you the money for the mine," Richard interrupted.

Alastair stilled. "What does that have to do with this?"

"You know very well what it has to do with this!" Richard snapped. "Give Bane up and you'll have a life again. Don't and I'll *ruin* you, Alastair."

"Alastair won't abandon me to you, Father. Your money can't buy everything!" Bane snapped. His gaze didn't even flicker over to Alastair's face, because he was so sure that it was true.

"Financial prosperity or total ruin, Alastair. Your choice," Richard offered.

"You won't ruin him, Father! You can't!" Bane cried. "Alastair, don't listen to him! He may have money, but he has few allies! There are many who would see him destroyed!"

"Such a loyal son I have!" Richard's eyes smoldered with anger.

"It's the truth! You've always said that it is better to be feared than loved!" Bane shot back.

There was a stare down between Richard and Alastair. Richard won as Alastair's gaze dropped away.

"I won't let you hurt Bane any longer, Richard. That has to stop," Alastair said softly, still looking down.

It wasn't exactly the rousing speech that Bane had expected, but in his mind, he added the indignation and outrage that wasn't actually there. He wanted to hear Alastair say that it was an insult that Richard thought, if even for a second, that he would take the money and leave Bane to Richard's mercies. His mind added those lines in, too.

Richard though must have seen and heard something very different in Alastair's voice and demeanor, because suddenly, he calmed down. Bane had only seen him look this way right before he closed a lucrative deal.

"Let's talk about this like civilized people. Get out of the bath, Alastair, and meet me in my study. Bane, you will go to your room and stay there!" Richard's eyes flashed as he looked at Bane then he turned on his heel and left.

The silence that fell afterwards felt supercharged and surreal at the same time. Bane realized that he was trembling, badly. Alastair was so white he looked like a marble statue, yet he urged Bane up.

"Come on, Bane. Let's get dressed," Alastair said. "Maybe I can have a conversation with him —"

"No!" Bane clutched Alastair's shoulders. "Let's not talk with him. Let's just leave! I mean, he'll only offer you money to abandon me and you won't do that!"

Alastair's expression shuttered for a moment. "Let's just see what he has to say."

"But I won't be there! I'm to stay in my room! I —"

"Let *me* try and convince him to let his anger go about us, Bane. You'd be surprised at how convincing I can be," Alastair said. "Now come on."

None of Bane's pleas seemed to get through. Instead, Alastair had them both out of the tub and into their respective rooms. Nadal's unconscious body was not in the hallway as Bane had feared. Perhaps the servant had not been too gravely injured and had gotten away.

"Alastair, please rethink this! There's no reasoning with Father! It's his way or no way! You must believe me!"

"I know your father in a different way than you do. I can reach him. Just let's dress, Bane. Let go of me and let's … let's just dress," Alastair said, not meeting Bane's eyes.

Bane felt like something had been ripped out of him when Alastair left his bedroom to go into his own to dress. Alastair hadn't even kissed him. He had leaned in as if about to do so but then had pulled back at the last minute. It seemed like mere moments later that Bane heard Alastair walking down the hall, intent on meeting with Richard, alone. At first, Bane had sat there, wet and nude on the bed. But with the fading of those footsteps, he had sprung into action.

Alastair will see that Father cannot be reasoned with. And then we will be forced to leave here. I will pack my things and his.

With that resolution, Bane dressed quickly then dragged his suitcase out from the closet. He threw in clothing, not even seeing what he was stuffing inside. He then raced out onto the balcony and into Alastair's room. The bed was made and the closet was open. There was nothing inside of it. There were no clothes. No suitcase to hold them. The room felt abandoned.

Did he take his suitcase with him to speak with Father? He must have. He must know he can't reason with Father and intends on us leaving. Yet he did not tell me to pack.

Bane lingered upstairs for a long time, waiting for Alastair to come get him. He strained to hear any yelling from his father's study. But all he heard was silence. Finally, he was unable to bear the suspense any longer and he had begun to fear that Alastair had come to harm. Bane jumped up, grabbed his suitcase and ran downstairs. His father's study door was cracked open. There were no voices coming from within though he smelled tobacco and heard the click of one of the heavy crystal glasses being set on top of the desk.

Bane found himself reaching forward and pushing the door open. He had visions of seeing Alastair dead on the floor with a widening pool of blood around his body. His father was capable of that and he could think of no other reason for the silence in that room.

The door swung open and he saw his father sitting behind his desk, feet up, head wreathed in cigar smoke and the amber glow of whiskey in a tumbler to his right. He smiled at Bane. There was no one else in the room. Richard's eyes dropped down to the suitcase that Bane held absently now in one hand.

"Going somewhere, Bane?"

"Where's Alastair? What have you done to him?" Bane whispered.

"I've made him a very rich man. Well, that is if he doesn't piss it away as he is wont to do," Richard said.

"No, that's a lie! You've hurt him! You've –"

"He's *left*, Bane. He's left *you*. He brought down his suit-case, too. Right to business. A deal," Richard chuckled. He puffed on his cigar. The cherry burned red hot. "He did make me promise not to hurt you. Wasn't that good of him?"

"No, you're lying! That's not possible –"

"But then, of course, he didn't actually *stay* long enough to find out if I would keep my promise." His father leaned down and picked something up. Bane didn't long have to wonder what it was. His father put it on the desk with a thump that seemed to reverberate throughout the house. It was a bull-whip.

"No." Bane's voice had lost all power. His bladder felt weak. He thought he might vomit right then and there. He didn't believe that Alastair had left him. He was certain that his lover was dead somewhere in the house or grounds. Just like Bane would be very soon if his father had his way.

Richard swung his legs off the desk to the floor and stood up. He fingered the handle of the whip and there was almost a dreamy expression on his face, which hardened into fierce anger. "You let him *soil* you, Bane. You let him open up that *weakness* in you. I can almost *smell* him on you from here. You –"

Bane didn't wait to hear anything more. He dropped the suitcase and then he was running towards the front door. He heard his father pounding after him. He reached the door and grasped the handle. It wouldn't turn in his hands. They never locked their doors during the day and Bane dumbly kept try-ing to turn the handle that wouldn't turn. In the few seconds it took him to realize he had to *unlock* the door, his father was upon him.

"Come back here, Bane! COME HERE!"

Bane sprinted into the morning room, but his father caught him there. Richard lunged and grasped him around the waist. Both men went down with a thunderous shaking of the floor. But then Richard was crawling up Bane's prone body until he had his hands around Bane's throat and he *squeezed*.

Bane tried to rip his father's hands away, but he wasn't strong enough to do it. Richard in a rage was almost unstoppable. Bane began to see stars and was making a gagging sound as he struggled for air. The world went gray and dim. His hands fell down as Richard continued to squeeze.

"I'll teach you to *soil* yourself and our family name. I'll *teach* you," Richard spat against the side of his cheek.

Just as Bane thought he was going to die, the squeezing stopped. Bane tried to take in a deep breath, but he couldn't. His throat felt crushed. Everything was dim and blurry. His father had him by the ankles now and was dragging him towards the front door. One of the runners bunched up beneath Bane's lower back as he was pulled.

"I will teach you. I will *leave my mark* on you so you never forget this lesson!" Richard swore.

Bane struggled weakly, but he couldn't break his father's hold or get up. He heard the front door being unlocked and then was being dragged outside onto the porch and then onto the gravel. He felt it cutting into his back as the sharp stones ripped through his shirt. His father was taking him to the stables where there was a post.

Like what he did to Nadal. Hitched him to the post and whipped him down to the bone.

Bane dug his fingers into the gravel, but his hands would hardly form fists and there was nothing to hold onto. They were at the stables. Bane thought he caught sight of a frightened stable boy, but it was just a flash of a face and then gone. He hoped his father hadn't noticed. There was no need for yet another death.

Richard dropped Bane's feet, but, immediately, had his wrists, tying them securely to the post. Bane let out a cry that earned him another cuff to the head that had his world spinning and graying out again. Bane slumped down as he felt his shirt ripped from his body. He knew what was coming. He had seen it done to Nadal. But his mind was on Alastair.

Oh, Alastair, I'm so sorry! So sorry! I caused your death!

Then he heard the slither of the bullwhip as his father uncoiled it.

"He thought you were beautiful," Richard's voice was rough. "I'll make sure that no one ever thinks *that* again."

The first blow caused all the grayness to disappear. Pain, bright and shining like a million stars, rushed through Bane and brought him to full and terrible consciousness. He screamed.

"You killed Alastair!" he shrieked.

Another blow. This one sliced across the entirety of his back and bit into his hip. Bane felt the skin part and blood *gush* from his wounds.

"He's *gone*, Bane! As good as dead to you, but still alive! Gone to find another boy to debauch! To soil! Left you here! LEFT YOU! For money!"

"NO! I don't believe you! I'll never believe you!"

Another blow that licked up his neck and caused blood to stream down his front. And another that sliced deep into his ribs. And another. And another. And another. Bane couldn't yell out his claims of murder after the third. He stopped even being able to scream as his vocal chords just gave out as the blows kept coming down like the monsoon rains. The grayness was returning, almost like an old friend, when the blows suddenly stopped as a gunshot rang out.

Alastair! Alastair has come back to save me! But no, he's dead! He's never coming back again!

"RICHARD, TOUCH HIM ONCE MORE AND I'LL KILL YOU!" his mother's voice rang out in the still air.

Bane's head slowly lifted up to look for his mother. His eyelids would hardly open. Everything was fading in and out. But he saw her. She was standing a few feet away. She had a hunting rifle. She was holding the rifle expertly, just like Bane had taught her. She had his father in her sights.

"Mary, put that —"

She fired again. The bullet send dirt and rocks spraying over his father's front. "Get away from him, Richard. So help me God, I will send you to Hell where you belong."

"He deserves —"

"NO! Don't you dare! Don't you DARE!" Mary shouted. "There is NOTHING on this Earth that could make him earn this. NOTHING! Now get away from him. Goddamn you, Richard, get away! I will not miss next time!"

Bane heard the whip fall to the ground like a serpent that had been felled then there was the crunch of gravel as his father stepped away from him.

"Nadal," his mother said.

"Yes, Mrs. Sahib?" Nadal was at her side. He was walking with a decided limp, a limp he would have the rest of his life, but despite the agony he must have been in, he had gone to her to help Bane.

"Help Bane. Oh, God, his back! Oh, God, help him!" That was the only time he heard his mother's voice break that day.

Nadal was suddenly crouched beside Bane, undoing his bonds. "It will be all right, sahib. I promise. I will take care of you."

Bane couldn't even speak to thank him. He couldn't even beg his mother to look for Alastair's body. The world went black.

CHAPTER TWELVE
LOVE DOES NOT EXIST

One year later, still in India, during the British Raj ...
Bane drew the finely woven tuxedo shirt on over his shoulders. The wounds on his back had healed long ago, but had left long ropy scars that were still sensitive to the touch. He thought he would bear them to the end of his days. He didn't know then that when he received a far more virulent scar on his face that the ones on his back would fade to nothing as the spirit healed them. But now, his back felt tight and tender. He buttoned the shirt slowly. It wasn't the pain that had him hesitating though. There was a knock on the door and Tarun stuck his head into Bane's bedroom.

"Do you need help dressing, sahib?" the Indian man asked.

"No, thank you, Tarun. My back is just a little sore today," Bane answered with a faint smile.

"Oh, you will feel much better at the party." Tarun picked up the waistcoat for him.

Bane took it and slipped it on, but he didn't agree with the other man's sentiment. Other than to hunt, Bane had hardly been in society since the incident with his father. He had spoken to few except his mother, Tarun and Nadal. His father had seen fit to be away at their tea plantation since the beating and Bane hoped that he would never return. That was, undoubtedly, a vain hope. Richard would come back and the violence would resume once more against his mother and himself.

Maybe next time I won't survive it just like Alastair didn't survive it.

Though he had looked every day for evidence that his lover had left the estate alive no one had seen him exiting it. There was no word of him in town. Alastair would never have stayed away from Bane if he were alive anyways. He would not have left Bane to Richard's tender mercies. He would have made contact, but there had been none. So despite his father's protestations to the contrary, Bane knew his father had killed his lover.

Alastair loved me. And when you love someone you would never abandon them. He wouldn't have left me to my father and his whip.

Bane dreamed of Alastair every night and woke up biting back the scream of his name. He still felt the whisper of Alastair's hands on his skin and mouth on his lips. He remembered the murmured words in his ears of love and caring. He remembered Alastair holding him and feeling safe.

His father would never pay for what he had done, because he was Lord Dunsaney. there was no body so they had no proof other than Bane's words against his father's in any case. He knew who would be believed. Even in the infrequent letters to his mother, his father wrote that Alastair was alive and that he had betrayed Bane. But Bane knew his father to be a liar as well as a monster.

Realizing that he had stayed silent too long to Tarun's inquiry, he finally said, "I am not in a party mood, but Lady Dunsaney would like me to accompany her, Tarun."

He stepped over to Tarun and the Indian man helped him into the tailored tuxedo coat. He buttoned the final three buttons and turned to face his Indian servant.

"Do I look presentable?" he asked.

"Oh yes! Most certainly you do! I hope you will have a wonderful time, sahib," Tarun said kindly and gave him a small bow.

"Thank you. Start planning a hunting party at the end of the week. After tonight's gathering, I will need the jungle's embrace."

"Of course, sahib."

Bane met his mother downstairs. She was wearing a white dress threaded with pearls and a diamond tiara on her head. Her long white silk gloves felt cool against his skin as she looped her arm through his.

"You look beautiful, Mother," he told her.

A faint blush colored her cheeks. She beamed at him. His father's absence had done wonders for her. "I *feel* beautiful. And you look handsome as ever, Bane."

She pressed a gloved hand to his cheek. He turned his head into the touch.

"The carriage awaits," he told her and led her outside.

Tarun was already seated in the driver's seat of the open-air carriage. The two lovely dark brown mares tossed their glossy heads under the starry sky. He helped his mother up into the carriage. When they were both seated, Tarun lightly moved the reins and the clip-clop of the horses' hooves filled the air.

The party they were going to was only a mile away at Lord Lithgow's. There would be mountains of food, fountains of champagne and endless dancing. Lord Lithgow was known for his extravagant parties and Bane was sure that tonight would be no different. But that brought him no delight.

He imagined what it would be like if Alastair were going with him to this party. They wouldn't have been able to dance together. They wouldn't have been able to kiss in corners, no matter how dark. They would have even had to watch how much they looked at one another and how many times they "accidentally" brushed the backs of each other's hands. But Alastair would have been in the same room with him, breathing the same air as him and Bane would have been able to hear his voice and smell his scent. Alastair would have been alive and that would have been more than enough.

"You know that Cecilia Lithgow expressed a great interest in seeing you tonight," his mother said, breaking him out of his thoughts.

"Which one is Cecilia? There are so many giggling girls that I cannot tell them apart," he responded dismissively even as his heart clenched. Why would his mother speak to him of this young woman? She knew what his preference truly was.

His mother tittered. "Well, when you have as many pretty girls as you do fluttering about I think you're quite excused from remembering which is which. But with choice comes opportunity." She took his hand. "Have you thought about your next opportunity?"

"You mean ... marriage, do you not?" His voice was hardly louder than the clip clop of the horses' hooves.

"I do," she said with a gentle smile. "Cecilia is a sweet girl and her fortune and family are equal to our own. She would be a fine match."

The desire to please his mother, to make nice, nearly overcame him then, but the memory of Alastair silenced that and he said carefully, but firmly, "Mother, would you condemn Cecilia or another one of those young women to the life you've had?"

She jerked back as if struck. "You would never hurt them! I know you are not like your father –"

"Not in *that* way." Bane took in a deep breath. "I *am* like him though ... in my *preferences*."

His mother looked rigidly forward. Her lips opened and shut. Finally, she said, "What happened ... that was Alastair's doing. You would *never* have done those things –"

"That's not true," he interrupted her. "Alastair merely opened the door. I stepped through it willingly and now ... I cannot step back. I *will not* step back."

"Bane, you cannot live this way. It will *never* be accepted. *You* will never be accepted."

"So I should induce a poor girl into a loveless marriage? I do not think so, Mother. I will remain alone," he said.

"Bane —"

"That is my choice, Mother."

They rode the rest of the way in silence to Lord Lithgow's estate. He saw her looking at him with concern in her eyes, but he would not meet her gaze. He stared straight ahead, feeling the smallest modicum of peace that he had chosen to remain true to who he really was.

Tarun pulled up in front of the blazing mansion of Lord Lithgow. There were a dozen carriages ahead of them dispersing their occupants into the steamy air. They were all drenched in silks and furs despite the hot and humid weather. Diamonds, rubies, emeralds and countless other precious stones hung from the guests' earlobes and layered their necks and wrists. They were like the glittering stars come to Earth.

The steps to their carriage were extended and Bane went down them first before handing his mother out of the carriage. They walked arm in arm up the white stone steps to the Lithgow estate's front doors that were flanked by two servants. He and his mother glided inside the house and to the ballroom beyond. There before them were swirling dancers like dervishes in silks and jewels. He caught sight of a champagne fountain. Elegantly attired servants moved about the rooms with more drinks and bites of food. There would be a formal dinner as well, but not for several hours yet.

A servant announced them, "Lord Bane Dunsaney and Lady Mary Dunsaney!"

A few heads turned towards them. Friends of his mother's waved for them to come over. Others looked at them curiously over the tops of feathered fans. Others still gave them cold stares. His father was not well liked inside or out of his family circle. Bane ignored all of them, coolly staring forward without acknowledging anyone. But that was when he caught sight of someone out of the corner of eye who should not be there, who should not be *able* to be there.

Alastair ...

For a moment, Bane could only hear the wild thumping of his own heart and the rush of blood in his ears. He thought he might have gone mad. The grief that had plagued him for a year must have finally taken over his mind, because not fifty feet away was his dead lover. But Alastair was not dead. He was alive! Wonderfully and gloriously alive and Bane could not believe it.

"I would like to speak to the Roths, Bane," his mother requested, a slightly concerned look on her face stemming from the fact that he had seemingly frozen in one spot.

Blinking, he turned to her, dazed with a sense of unreality flooding him, but somehow he managed to sound almost normal as he said, "Of—of course, Mother. I'll escort you to them."

As soon as he took her to her friends, he quickly excused himself with only a few muttered words that likely made sense to no one. He felt his mother's eyes on his back, but she had not spotted Alastair so she had no idea why he was behaving as he was Besides, perhaps the man was actually a ghost that only he could see. But he immediately knew that wasn't true. Others could see his lover. Alastair was surrounded by a gaggle of women. His lover looked like a black raven in his tuxedo amidst all the white, rustling silk gowns. The nearest person to Alastair was Cecilia Lithgow who was fluttering her fan *and* her eyelashes.

Alastair was in fine form. His rich, booming voice rang out as he told some story to the ladies who tittered in appreciation. Alastair spoke about the trials and tribulations of the jungle, making them sound amusing while at the same time painting himself as brave. All Bane could think was that Alastair was alive! Alive! And glowing with health and beauty. But even as Bane inched his way around the edge of the crowded ballroom towards the other man the fact that Alastair was alive started to take on *dark* tones.

If Alastair was alive then did that mean his father had been telling the truth all along? Had Alastair taken money in exchange for leaving him behind? That couldn't be it. Alastair loved him! He knew it!

Had his father somehow convinced Alastair that he would be ruining both their lives if the two of them stayed together? No, that was not something Richard Dunsaney would say. It was too caring. And it wouldn't have been true. Alastair, above all people could have found a way for them to be together without public censure. Bane was sure of it!

Could Alastair have had doubts about the depth of Bane's feelings for him? Could his father have convinced Alastair that Bane's affection was paper thin and wouldn't last? Bane's heart beat dully in his chest. He loved Alastair with his whole being.

But Alastair would have come and spoken to me if he had such doubts! He wouldn't have just left the house without another word to me!

Watching Alastair bewitch the crowd of women reminded Bane that the other man had a fairly unshakeable ego. He would never believe that Bane did not love him absolutely and completely unless he had full proof of it. So no, that, too, could not have been the reason Alastair left as he had.

That, of course, left the issue of money. Did Alastair take money from Bane's father in exchange for abandoning him? The scars on Bane's back *burned*.

Bane was only fifteen feet away from Alastair now. He could hear the other man's voice clearly. It skated down his spine. His heart galloped. His breathing went ragged.

Alastair will have an explanation, a good one, for leaving and not contacting me. I might not be able to think of it myself at the moment, but there will be one.

As if Alastair had heard his thoughts, the man's blonde head turned and his eyes fixed on Bane's face. The expression that was there for only a fleeting second had Bane skidding to a halt. It was *guilt*. Bane's chest felt so tight that he couldn't take in another breath. He knew then and there that his father had not been lying. Alastair had taken the money and left him to his father's *tender* mercies.

He would not have known that Father would beat me!

But that thought died almost as fast as it had come. Alastair had *seen* Richard strike him in the bath. Alastair *knew* his father's temper. And, even if he hadn't, he'd left Bane without another word for *money*.

Bane felt bitterness start to bubble up in his chest like an unending fountain, painting everything inside of him black. A small part of him was crying out: no, no, no! It wanted to cling to the idea that he was reading too much into that look. That he must give the other man a chance to explain. The look, after all, had gone as fast as it had come. On someone else whose face Bane did not know as well he would have thought he imagined that guilt-filled flash. But he *knew* he had seen it and he *knew* what it meant. Yet hope still struggled in his chest.

Before he could make up his own mind about what to do—to stay or walk away—Alastair plastered a smile on his face and warmly waved Bane over.

"Bane! How good to see you, my friend." Alastair actually briefly touched Bane's back as he joined the group. Bane could feel the touch through his clothes and his scars ached. Alastair continued, "Ladies, do you know Lord Bane Dunsaney? If not, please let me have the privilege of introducing him to you."

Bane nodded woodenly to the group. Cecilia Lithgow sauntered over to him and offered her gloved hand to be kissed. There was a pearl bracelet on her wrist and a flashing diamond and ruby ring on her finger. He took her hand and kissed it perfunctorily.

"Bane, it is so good to see you," she purred. "I should have known that the two most handsome men in our little corner of the world would know one another."

Bane felt the dull thud of his heart and the whoosh of his blood in his ears again. It nearly blocked out all sound. He wondered what Cecilia would think if she realized that the two most handsome men in town were lovers.

Had been lovers. Not anymore. Alastair left me. For money.

"It's a pleasure as always to see you," Bane murmured, the words automatically falling from his lips.

"Mother didn't think you would come," Cecilia said with a flick of her fan towards her blond curls. "She said you've been a practical hermit this past year."

Bane's eyes darted to Alastair. Did he recognize the significance of that time frame? Did he question *why* Bane would be out of society for a year? Alastair's gaze though was on Cecilia only as if there was no one else in the room. Bane's stomach suddenly felt full of ice.

Alastair burbled, "Who could miss your mother's parties, Cecilia? A dead man would rise from his grave to come."

"And where did you *rise* from to get here, Alastair? I did not know you were in town," Bane found himself saying, his voice different, deeper, colder than it had ever been.

"Oh, I just got back into town. Working my mine, you know," he said without meeting Bane's gaze.

"*Your* mine?" Bane's voice was brittle.

Alastair's eyes flickered about the room as if looking for an exit. "Yes, I, ah, *purchased* a mine. I'm sure I told you—"

"So you obtained *investors* for this mine? You didn't have any money of your *own* when we last talked," Bane interrupted, knowing it was rude to do so and even ruder to discuss business like this among strangers. But he found he did not care.

Again, that flickering gaze. "No, no, I came into some money. Ladies, would you excuse us for a moment?"

The women fluttered their fans and eyelashes again. Only Cecilia's speculative gaze followed them. Alastair's hand was suddenly gripping Bane's elbow. Bane ripped his arm away from Alastair, but the man grabbed him again, more firmly this time.

"Bane, don't make a scene!" he hissed, his eyes pleading.

A scene? As if I care about his reputation or my own! People think the worst anyways, because they DO the worst!

This was something his father would have thought, but Bane found that perhaps he didn't believe it altogether wrong any longer.

Alastair steered him toward the back garden. When they were away from the house and screened by a rose bush, Bane yanked away from Alastair even as it hurt to not have the other man's touch.

"Bane, what has gotten into you? Why –"

"I thought you were dead," the words spilled out like blood on the ground.

Whatever Alastair had been about to say the words quickly died. "W-what? D-dead? Why would you think—"

"I thought Father *killed* you," Bane interrupted him. His hands clenched and released at his sides. "Because, you see, he told me that you had left because he'd paid you off. But I didn't believe that. I could *never* believe that of you. So I thought he killed you. Buried you on the property somewhere in an unmarked grave. I've been searching for that grave for a year."

Alastair stared at him, still and unblinking, before he ran a nervous hand through his hair. "Richard would *never* kill me—"

"Why not? He's killed men for less." Bane let out a hopeless laugh.

"Not his friends!" Alastair retorted.

Friends? You consider yourself his friend? But you do not know yet what he did to me. I still cling to the idea that you would feel differently about my father if you knew. But maybe that is a vain hope.

"So what happened exactly between you and him?" Bane asked. He had to know the truth. He would know if Alastair was lying to him.

"What did your father tell you?" Alastair's eyes flickered over Bane's face, trying to read what he already knew.

"Just tell me your side," Bane demanded.

The man paced with his arms crossed over his broad chest. Even now as Bane looked at him his heart ached. Alastair was as beautiful and masculine as he remembered. Even the scent of him on the air drew Bane like a moth to a flame. But Bane did not move, holding his ground against the almost irresistible pull.

"You must understand that without funds, without a way to make back my fortune, that we had no future, Bane," Alastair said with a shake of his head.

"But you said that even if we were poor we'd figure out a way –"

"That was romantic nonsense! *Money* is what gives a man freedom. So when your father found us, I realized that there was really only one way forward." He stopped pacing and faced Bane. "I took the money and left. We'd had a good time."

"*A good time?*" The words tasted like ashes on Bane's tongue.

Alastair grimaced. "That's not what I meant! You—you were *wonderful*, Bane. I was happier with you than I've ever been with anyone else, but you *must* understand that it was all a pipe dream without a fortune! So when your father offered the money for me to leave—which I would have had to do anyways—I … I, well, I cut our time *short*. That's *all* I did! So stop looking at me like I betrayed you! That's naive nonsense!"

Bane found himself strangely calm as he said, "So you walked out, unharmed, and with the money?"

"You make me sound like a cad, but, Bane, there was no future between us without a fortune and … look, I thought a clean break would be better than a long drawn-out goodbye," Alastair explained. He wouldn't quite meet Bane's eyes. "I had no idea that you thought I was dead."

"No, clearly, you did not," Bane remarked simply, his heart feeling dead in his chest. "And you used Father's money to buy the mine you told me about?"

Alastair winced almost as if the mine itself was a sore subject. His voice was rather sorrowful as he said, "Yes."

"And has it made you your fortune?" Again, Bane's voice so calm even as inside of him he felt like a hole had opened that threatened to swallow him entirely.

Another wince and Alastair laughed bitterly. "The mine was a bust and all your father's money is gone."

"I see," Bane remarked tonelessly.

"So I had to return to civilization and ... and, well, *do* what I had hoped to never have to do." Alastair's shoulders bunched.

"And what is that?"

Alastair let out a bark of laughter. "Marry! God help me, but I'm here to sell myself to the highest bidder." He gave Bane a rueful look. "It's the only chance I have left not to be in the gutter. So here I am! Flirting with the likes of Cecilia Lithgow! Though she's got a mind, at least, even if her body leaves me cold. Though." Alastair's eyes hooded as he regarded Bane. "I'll be in town if she and I marry, Bane. We'll have opportunities to meet ..."

"We could just take up where we left off, you mean?" Bane's voice was neutral, so neutral, as he reached up and undid his bowtie.

Alastair looked around them, nervously, but there was a smile on his lips. "Bane, I do not think we should start *here* though it is intriguing. We should perhaps go deeper into the garden. More private and all that."

"No, here's fine. There's light," Bane answered.

Bane undid the buttons of his tuxedo jacket, then the vest and then the shirt. Alastair tried to help him with those fastenings, but Bane stepped out of his reach. Bane shucked off the jacket and the vest. He untucked his shirt and it hung loose at his sides. Again, Alastair tried to move towards him, a hungry, lust-filled look in his eyes. But Bane held up a hand.

"That last day we had together," Bane said quietly. "When you spoke of what we could do if we had enough money—that no one could touch us if we were just rich enough –"

"Yes, I remember," Alastair said, his gaze practically feasting on Bane's bare chest.

"After you left, my mother told me something—something she thought would give me heart. She wanted to give me a reason to *live*, to know that I would not always be under my father's thumb," Bane said, licking his dry lips. His mouth felt dry as dust. "You see, I *have* that kind of fortune."

"What are you talking about? Your father —"

"The real money comes from my mother's side and her father left the money in trust for me when I turn twenty-one," Bane told him. "My father was given some funds, but they are *nothing* compared to what will be mine in just two short years."

Understanding bloomed in Alastair's eyes and a wild light as well. It reminded Bane of the look in a gambler's eye when he was certain that the big win was coming on the next hand of cards. "Then ..."

"With that money, we could have been free *together*," Bane said.

"Bane, you act like that is something that cannot happen now! But it *can*. I'm here. You're here. We're both still *mad* about each other —"

"No, you were never *mad* about me. You'd never have left me to my father if you were. If your *love* was worth anything at all you would *never* have left. And I ... I am no longer mad about you. That was *beaten* out of me." Bane turned his back to Alastair and dropped the shirt to reveal the terrible scars.

Alastair drew in a sharp breath. "My God, he really did it."

"He told you what he was going to do to me, didn't he?" Bane flinched as he felt the lightest brush of Alastair's finger-tips against his skin. But it was the terrible knowledge that Alastair had left him even after hearing his father's threats that hurt the most. It was another lash across his back.

"He was in a foul temper, but I told him to leave you alone," Alastair said lamely. "I didn't really think —"

"But you knew his *temper*. You *knew*, but your cowardly, craven soul just *hoped* that you were wrong, that leaving me didn't matter, that I would be all right, but, in your heart, your black and shriveled heart, you *knew* what he was going to do to me. But you had to have *your money!*" Bane pulled his shirt back on and turned to face Alastair.

Alastair blanched. "Bane, I did not know –"

"You did not *wish* to know!" Bane picked up his tuxedo coat. "You left me. And now ... it is *my* turn to leave you."

Bane knew he had stripped Alastair of words for now, of his feeble excuses. Bane told himself that he was *glad* that he'd hurt the other man. Alastair *deserved* to be hurt.

He said he loved me. Maybe he did. Maybe this is all that love is: an illusion, a falsity, a tissue thin covering for lust. Yes, that's the truth of love. It does not really exist.

He turned away from Alastair and began to walk around the side of the house. He could not go back inside even if he dressed. He would stay outside and wait for his mother to be done with this party. He had no taste for anyone's company other than Tarun's.

He heard Alastair call his name, trying to get him to come back to the darkness beyond the rose bushes. But Bane kept walking and Alastair did not chase after him. He found Tarun by the carriage. The Indian man straightened up and stepped towards him.

"Sahib, is everything all right?" Tarun asked.

"Yes, yes, I'm fine," Bane lied. "That hunt I asked you to arrange at the end of the week, Tarun."

"Yes?"

"Let's make it tomorrow. I feel the *need* to kill something."

CHAPTER THIRTEEN

MATE

B ane had watched as Nick's expression went *bleak* as he told his story. The young man's face had transformed from its pretty tan color to pale and drawn as he'd talked. Faint tremors had started running through Nick when he'd reached the part about the horsewhipping. Bane should have stopped then, but once the spigot of his past was opened he found that he couldn't shut it off. He *had* to tell the rest. He *had* to confess it all. Well, *most* of it. But when the last dregs of what he could say spilled out, Bane immediately regretted telling Nick *any* of it.

He's sensitive and gentle. He will never understand men like my father or Alastair. I should not have exposed him to this ugliness. My guilt over lying to him has caused me to make another mistake. I've told him so much.

Nick's gaze suddenly focused on him again with a laser-like intensity. When he finally spoke, the young man's voice was low and rough with anger, "Tell me again that Alastair and your father are dead, Bane. You did say that before, didn't you? That they're dead?"

"Yes, they have been gone for a long time," Bane assured him and swallowed. His throat felt raw from speaking so long.

Nick nodded. "Good. *Good.*" He lifted his chin. "Because if they weren't, *I* would kill them."

"Nick, my sweet, beautiful boy, I would not have you within a thousand miles of those men for all the *world.*"

Bane embraced the young man. He dropped his head down so that his face was buried in Nick's soft hair and the silky skin of his neck. He breathed in and Nick's scent calmed him. He pushed away the memories that clung to him. Nick clutched Bane back as if he were afraid the big man would be taken from him.

Nick's voice was muffled as he spoke against Bane's chest, "I thought you were going to tell me that Alastair had cheated on you or done something else bad, but *nothing* like that. God, I'm sorry. So sorry. I know that's not enough!"

Bane could hear Nick's horror at what had happened to him. He'd lived with it for so long now that it didn't have the same power to shock him any longer. It just made him angry and distrustful. Yet now he realized how *upsetting* the story would be to an outsider. He should have *prepared* Nick at least. Yet another mistake—and he was desperate *not* to make them with the young man, but they seemed to be piling up around his feet.

Bane murmured, "I did not mean to distress *you.*"

"Distress *me?*" Nick grasped his shoulders and looked up at Bane with such tenderness. "Bane, I'm worried about *you.* This happened to *you.* Those men—your own father and your lover—they hurt *you!* I can't—can't even *imagine* what you must have felt and *feel.*" Nick shook his head as if he had no words. "I should *never* have asked you about it."

Bane let out a breath. "You helped me *purge* it."

"Just by talking about it?" Nick sounded disbelieving.

"Yes, that, but also ..." Bane struggled for the words. "Alastair was a *boy's* idea of a relationship. "You are a *man's.* I can see that now."

Nick flushed, evidently pleased by his statement. "I don't know about *that.*"

"You *are*. Trust me on this. As I told you the story, I could see how Alastair had always been a cad. There were practically red neon signs alerting to me that he was bad. But I didn't see them. Or maybe it is fairer to say that I *ignored* them. I was a romantic fool and he wasn't worth the *angst*."

"You weren't a fool. You were just *innocent*."

"Innocent? I suppose. It's hard to remember being that way. It's been so long," Bane admitted.

"I know I can't make up for what your father and Alastair did, I can't undo it, I can't stop it as it's already happened, but I swear, Bane, I will find a way to make you forget it," Nick promised.

Bane closed his eyes. Nick wanted to erase Alastair and his father from his life. But that really wasn't possible. Alastair's betrayal had set a chain of events in motion that had led Bane to go on that fateful hunt, which had led to the curse. He could even say that the death of his father and his mother's subsequent institutionalization was also caused by the revelation that Alastair's "love" had not even been skin deep. Indeed, what had happened between him, Alastair and his father had set him on the course that had led him *here,* too.

But here is hardly bad. Here is wonderful.

He thought the last as he looked down at the top of Nick's platinum head. Nick was the ultimate gift he could have ever been given. Terrible things had happened because of Alastair's cowardice and his own naiveté, but wonderful things had happened, too. Nick and Omar were just two of those wonderful things. But they were *magnificently* wonderful, more than most got in a lifetime. Maybe it was time to let the anger and hatred he felt toward Alastair—and even his father—*fade*. He wished he could tell Nick the whole story and share with the young man the revelations that flooded him now. But he couldn't. He just couldn't.

So Bane held Nick tighter and said simply, "Just stay with me, Nick."

"I'm not going anywhere. I promise."

After a few moments, Nick pulled back from his chest again so that they could be face to face. He was so beautiful in the moonlight. His platinum blond hair was silvered. His gray eyes were the color of liquid mercury. His skin was a golden cream again. Bane's heart lurched when he looked down at that face, that face that was starting to feel as *needful* to him as food and drink.

"Tell me what you need," Nick pleaded. "I sense you need something. I will give it to you if it is within my power."

Bane framed Nick's face. There were so many answers he could give to that request, but he found himself saying *exactly* what he needed, "*You.* I just need you."

Understanding and love flooded Nick's face. "You have me."

"I want to lose myself in your body tonight. May I?"

"Yes, God, *yes.*"

Bane lifted Nick up in his arms and carried him to his bedroom. Nick's eyes never left his and Bane could tell from the young man's utterly accepting expression that Nick wanted to be with him that night. He wasn't sure of his control enough for them to fully make love yet, but he needed to kiss, caress and adore every part of Nick. The beast seemed quiet so perhaps it was safe.

The room was moon-shadowed, matching the mansion's name, with the only light coming from the slightly parted curtains. The silvery light slashed across the center of the bed. When Bane laid Nick down upon it only the young man's torso was illuminated while his face and limbs were in darkness.

Bane immediately toed off his shoes and socks. The wood of the floor felt cool beneath his bare soles. Nick pulled off his t-shirt and shimmied out of his shorts and underwear before lying down again. Bane's mouth went dry as he looked at Nick's defined stomach muscles and the cut lines of his hips. Nick's cock was already half hard and rising up from its nest of tight curls. Bane reached down and stroked the young man once, which had a gasp exiting Nick's mouth.

"You are gorgeous," Bane breathed.

"You have too many clothes on. Though you look luscious in those suits, you look even *better* out of them."

Nick sat up and got onto his knees. His hands went to the lapels of Bane's jacket. He slipped it off. It fell to the floor with a rustle. Nick began undoing the buttons of his shirt, kissing the skin that was bared after undoing each one. Bane drew in a sharp breath when Nick pulled the tails of his shirt from his pants. The fine cotton *rushed* over his engorged cock. He groaned and leaned down to kiss Nick. The young man clung to him and the kiss lasted until they both needed to breathe. Breathing still quick, Nick then slid the shirt off of Bane's massive shoulders, running his hands just under the cotton so that he was touching Bane's skin.

"I used to imagine touching you. Having the *right* to just run my hands all over you," Nick murmured as those hands dropped to the button of Bane's pants.

"Really?" Bane rumbled, letting one eyebrow lift up. He tried to remember if he had caught Nick looking at him lasciviously. "I never caught you admiring me. You seemed to have a frown more often than not when you looked at me."

Though there were those moments in the shower and when I spread cream on his back when he wanted me. But the body reacts to touch. The mind is what causes people to look.

"I was *clever* and *quick* with my lustful glances. You've got this body to die for." Nick's clever fingers unbuttoned and unzipped his pants and cool air circulated around Bane's hard, hot cock.

"I am acceptable to you then?"

Nick chuckled. "No need to be humble. You're incredible. Every time I saw Devon running his hands over you I wanted those hands to be *mine*."

"Your jealousy is so ... *sweet*."

"I'm not sweet!" Nick laughed. "You make me feel like some kind angel or something when you say that."

"You are truly good." Bane cupped his face and drew it up so that they were looking at one another. He put all the seriousness he could into his voice as he said, "Nick, you make me a better man."

Nick blinked. His hands stilled on the zipper to Bane's pants. His expression suddenly softened and he gave Bane a brilliant smile. "I think that is the best compliment I've ever gotten."

His thumb ran along Nick's jaw. "You do not think it's true though?"

"I'm not going to say that. I'm going to take the compliment, because—"

"It's *true*."

"Because I *want* it to be true," Nick corrected. He turned his head into Bane's left palm and kissed it.

"And that just proves my point about you," Bane rasped.

Desire flowed through him like warm honey. Nick's mouth on his palm felt more erotic than a blow job at that moment. Tingles of arousal had Bane's cock pulsing behind the still closed zipper. He heard the brief hiss of his zipper being undone. Nick kissed his palm once more before he turned to look back up at Bane's face. His hands went to the waistband of Bane's pants and he slowly tugged them down Bane's thighs until they dropped to the floor. Bane stepped out of them and kicked them out of the way. Mr. Fioretti made clothes that could take abuse though he was sure the Italian tailor would be tutting over the crumpled suit.

Nick's hands were suddenly on Bane's cock and a serious look entered his eyes. "You need to tell me what you want. I seem to overstep so often."

"It's not that. I have a hard time keeping control with you," Bane confessed.

"You don't need to keep control, Bane. I'm not a fragile flower. You won't crush me if you let go."

Bane so wished that was true. "You are precious to me."

"So you're still worried you'll harm me? I guess that's another mystery about you, but I'm okay with that. You don't have to reveal any more secrets," Nick continued. There was a flash of regret on that lovely face as Nick, undoubtedly, remembered how asking about Alastair had seemed to hurt Bane though it had truly freed him.

"All you need to know is that I ..." Bane's throat seemed to close up then as he realized what he *wanted* to say: *All you need to know is that I love you.* Love. Love. LOVE. He didn't believe in love. He was careful never to use that word even though people were careless with it all the time. But for him he gave that word all the *power* that it was imbued with from all the tales and poetry that tried to capture it. Yet he *felt* it right at that moment. The word that had nearly tripped off his tongue had *never* been there for anyone since Alastair and, this time, he knew Nick was deserving of it. But the word stuck there, unsaid and aggravating. He swallowed hard and said lamely instead, "All you need to know is that I care for you. Deeply."

Nick seemed unaware of what he had almost said—or was it *confessed?*—and just responded with simple directness, "I love you, Bane."

Bane's mouth opened in shock. Was Nick saying it casually as one would say: I like you, too? But he realized there was a hint of color crawling from Nick's cheeks down his neck and the young man was not meeting his eyes.

He means it.

Bane's mind seemed to stutter-step. He should say something. He should acknowledge this confession. But he stood there stupidly. Nick did not seem crestfallen. In fact, he almost seemed relieved that Bane was silent.

He likely feared that I would lecture him about how love is a fantasy for the foolish.

Bane caressed Nick's cheek and the young man tilted his head into it. Teasing gray eyes rose to his.

"You said I was *sweet*," Nick remarked, his smile growing with every word. "Are you? Sweet or salty or a little spicy?"

"I—I don't know."

"I think I need to find out.

Nick *pulled* on Bane's cock, making him crawl up onto the bed and then the young man pushed him onto his back while *still* holding onto his cock with one hand. Nick lowered his head down and took Bane's cock into his mouth. Bane's hips lifted of their own accord and he let out a gasp. The heat and suction had him wanting to thrust his cock all the way down Nick's throat. But he was large and Nick was precious. It took all his self-control to lower his hips to the bed. He gripped the bedclothes instead of Nick's hair and held on as the young man drew more of his cock into that lush mouth.

The moonlight from the windows highlighted Nick swallowing his shaft inch by inch. Heat built in Bane's core and pulsed upwards. Nick's tongue pressed against the vein on the underside of his cock and Bane shut his eyes, trying to find more control, as his cock trembled under the hot, tight assault from Nick's mouth and throat.

One of Nick's hands wrapped around the last few inches of his cock that the young man could not devour. Nick began to move up and down on his shaft. His mouth and his hand were completely aligned so that Bane was constantly feeling the pressure he needed on his member. He heard a ripping sound and knew that the sheets had just shredded in his hands.

Mate. Mate will taste our seed, the beast said with an eagerness that was almost dizzying.

It was so shocking to actually hear the beast speak that Bane lost all sense of Nick's mouth and hand on him for a second. His eyelids flew open and he stayed very still, listening with all his might for the beast to say more. The beast was turned around for the first time since he had blamed it for their unhappiness, looking outwards. It was kneading his chest and watching Nick eagerly go down on them.

You mustn't hurt him. You need to remember our deal, Bane pleaded for he felt the prick of fur just underneath his skin. The thought of changing into the beast right then and there as Nick was sucking him off was beyond terrifying. Sweat broke out over his upper lip.

"Bane?" Nick had drawn off and was looking up at him, confusion written large on his face. "Is something wrong? Do you not like what I'm doing?"

Bane realized that he had rocketed up in bed without realizing it. He blinked and released the ruined sheets to frame
Nick's face with his hands.

"Nick ..." Bane swallowed. What could he say? Not the
truth! Nick likely thought he was so strange about sex already
though. He forced a smile on his lips and said, "You're perfect,
but you've been taking care of me all day and I *really* want to
take care of you. I need to take care of you."

It wasn't a lie exactly. He did want to take care of Nick,
but more importantly, he had to keep control of himself. It
would be much easier to keep that control if he were sucking
Nick off.

"Are you sure?" Nick's brows were drawn together in uncertainty. "We don't have to do anything—"

"I want to. I want *you*. You've no idea," Bane rattled
out desperately.

The beast had stilled in his chest when Nick had stilled. It
was angry at Bane *again* for interrupting what it thought to
be a sacred act.

Let's taste his seed in real life this time, Bane told it. *Won't
that be sacred, too? Don't you want to have his taste on
our tongue?*

This last line was dangerous. What if the beast *liked* how
Nick tasted? What if it liked it *too much* and wanted a bite?
But the beast looked out at him with Siberian blue eyes that
were hooded and he felt only desire but no hunger for food.

Nick caught the wrist of the hand Bane had against his
cheek and the young man gave him one of those tender, brilliant smiles. "I'm good with whatever you want."

If only I could just tell him the truth!

But that was impossible. Nick might very well run from
him. Nick was not frightened off by a man with "issues" about
sex, but could Bane truly expect the young man to accept what
he was? A tiger shifter? A monster? A dangerous beast?

"I know," Bane's voice cracked when he finally spoke. "I—I
need to do things my way. Is that all right?"

"Yes, whatever you need."

"Thank you, Nick."

Bane was intent now on making the young man once more forget his oddities and lose himself in passion instead. He easily flipped Nick onto his back and settled himself between those long, lean legs. He held himself up on his forearms, positioning his mouth over the head of Nick's engorged, rose-colored cock.

He let out a hot breath which stirred the pearlescent pre-cum that coated Nick's slit. The young man let out a strangled cry. Nick was sensitive. He remembered doing this in their dream that first night together. He couldn't wait for the taste of Nick's seed on his tongue again and experience the fullness from it in his belly.

Nick's cock was long and lean like the rest of him. It was pretty. Bane lapped the tip of it and was rewarded with Nick's hands in his hair. Unlike himself, Nick had no compunctions about ripping bedclothes—or Bane's head sheer off—from pleasure. The slight pull and sting on his scalp was erotic.

Bane lazily let his tongue linger over the sensitive slit. Nick gasped and his hips shifted. Another lick and Nick moaned. Another and the young man pulled his hair like one would the reins of a horse, but he didn't want Bane to stop. He wanted Bane to *go* and go *fast*. At least that's what Nick murmured. This just caused Bane to grin and take even more time to enjoy the earthy, citrusy taste of Nick's cum.

Bane drew one finger down the length of Nick's cock, loving the slight hiss from the young man as he reached Nick's balls and rolled them in his fingers. They felt hot and full. He mouthed down the shaft and then drew the right ball into his mouth entirely. Nick's hips tried to jerk up, but Bane had anticipated that, and was holding him down with one hand. His preternatural strength far surpassed Nick's. Nick let out an almost pained cry as Bane sucked and sucked and sucked on that ball, but wouldn't let Nick move. When he pulled off and looked up at Nick's face, resting his chin on Nick's lower belly, he saw baleful gray eyes looking back down at him.

"I thought you wanted to take care of me. It seems you're just teasing," Nick murmured hoarsely.

Bane rubbed his cheek against the side of Nick's cock and grinned. "I *am* taking care of you. I'm just doing it *slowly*."

Then with Nick's eyes full on him, Bane licked the pointer and middle fingers of his right hand until they were slick and gleaming. Nick's eyes widened as Bane then *slipped* that hand between Nick's parted thighs and moved it *back*. Bane did let Nick's hips lift then as he drew his wet fingers over Nick's opening. The young man's head fell back on the pillows and his breathing grew fast and frantic.

Bane pressed up into Nick's body as his opened his mouth and sank down onto the young man's hard cock. Nick's shaft easily slid down his throat and he only stopped when he felt his lower lip press against the top of Nick's balls. Nick uttered a low moan that stretched out for half a minute. Bane *swallowed* and that moan became a keening whine.

Bane's fingers sank up to his knuckles in Nick's ass. He spread them apart and slowly drew them out again. Nick's heels beat a tattoo against the bed. Bane swallowed again around that hot, hard cock, feeling it *tremble* inside of him. Nick thrust up then pushed back down, not sure what he wanted more: Bane's mouth or his fingers. Bane would give him both.

Bane began to thrust and suck in unison so that Nick was a helpless babe in his hands. The young man's stomach muscles rippled as he fought to control his orgasm. But Bane was relentless. He added a third finger and thrust them all *deep* inside. He found Nick's prostate and the young man practically levitated off of the bed. Bane grinned around Nick's shaft. He already felt it plumping, filling his mouth and throat more as Nick's balls tightened against his body. The young man was going to cum in moments.

Bane plunged his fingers all the way to the hilt inside of Nick's pliant, willing body. Nick gasped and arched until his heels and top of his head were the only things still touching the bed. Bane sank down fully onto Nick's cock and sucked hard and long. Nick's hands pulled and strained in his hair.

The young man practically howled, "Cum! I'm going to cum!"

Bane knew that Nick was giving him the opportunity to pull off if he didn't want to swallow, but he did want to. The beast was salivating as Nick's cock went even more rigid in his mouth and throat before the first hot gush of semen left Nick's body and entered his.

Bane had given countless blow jobs in his long life. But never had it felt like *this*. Like a kind of *joining*. It was as if Nick's cells were somehow combining with his, not to create a child, but instead to cement a connection on a cellular level. His eyes closed in ecstasy as he drank down every last bit of seed that Nick released.

The young man collapsed back onto the bed. His eyes were closed. Sweat caused some of his hair to curl around his face. Bane slowly slipped his fingers from Nick's still-spasming ass as he withdrew his mouth off of Nick's cock. He couldn't help but give the now soft organ a few more licks. Nick's taste was on his tongue and he didn't want to lose it.

His own cock was still hard. He got up on his knees and began to stroke himself as he watched Nick out of hooded eyes. The young man was a picture of erotic repose. Nick's hands lay limp at his sides. His cock was still glistening with saliva. His legs were drawn far apart and he had some of the attitude of being well-fucked even though Bane had only had his fingers and not his cock inside Nick.

Not yet.

The beast had collapsed after taking Nick's seed with him, but it roused as Bane masturbated. It knew what he wanted to do, what he almost *needed* to do. The beast approved. Bane's breathing grew ragged as his orgasm crested over him and creamy white ribbons of cum landed on Nick's belly and chest. He was still rock hard even though he had just cum. For it wasn't the release of his orgasm that he needed. It was something far more intimate. The young man's eyes opened sleepily.

"Oh, Bane, you should have let me do it," Nick bleated.

"No, I wanted to and I want—*need*—to do this."

Bane started to *massage* his cum into Nick's skin. His fingers tweaking Nick's nipples as he moved the creamy seed over Nick's body. The young man moaned.

"Fuck, this is so hot," Nick admitted with a faint laugh. "It's like you're—you're *claiming* me."

"Yes, yes, I am. You're mine, Nick. No one can have you but me. You're *mine*." Bane's hands almost paused in their frantic rhythm to make Nick smell like him. What he was saying was animalistic. He could hear the beast's growl in his voice, but he couldn't stop. Didn't want to stop.

Nick didn't seem perturbed by this at all. "Yes, I am yours. I want to be yours."

He drew Bane down in a long, deep kiss even as he let Bane paint his body with cum. The beast was pleased. This was *natural*. This was *right*. This was what one did with a *mate*. For once, Bane did not even try to argue for he felt the same way.

An hour later, after a shower and more kissing and petting and, finally, with Nick slumbering peacefully in his arms, Bane went over one part of the story that he had not—and *could not*—tell Nick for it would reveal his immortality, the curse and so much more.

Almost thirty years to the day after he had last saw Alastair at Lord Lithgow's party, Bane had traveled to London on business. Even though decades had past, Bane had still kept up with what was happening in Alastair's life.

His former lover had married Cecilia, and, from what he heard, Alastair had not made her happy. They were one of those couples who led completely separate lives. Bane knew Alastair took many male lovers on the side, but he and Cecilia had conceived a daughter. Alastair had doted on the little girl, but she had died young from a disease. Alastair and Cecilia had then proceeded to have even *less* to do with one another. Bane had then heard that the couple had returned to England and Cecilia had died.

Bane had never thought to meet Alastair again. He kept his activities in London to a minimum in order to avoid seeing those who might remember him or his family from their India days. Soon he wouldn't have to worry about that though as all his old acquaintances would be dead. Though Bane had been cursed at only twenty-one, he had *matured* fully, only stopping aging when he looked about thirty-five. The curse had allowed him to reach his peak strength and beauty. Then it had kept him there.

Like an insect in amber.

Yet Bane's mind was not on Alastair nor did he fear being discovered at all though he was out and about. In between business meetings, he had gone to walk in Regent's Park to enjoy England's lush greenery even in the heart of London.

It was a brilliant spring day. The green of the grass and leaves of the trees had been mesmerizing. They were a vivid green that almost looked unreal. These were not the exotic colors of India, but England had a beauty all its own. He tilted his head towards the sun that streamed down the branches of one of the trees and allowed his eyelids to fall shut, but then he heard his name.

"*Bane*?! Bane, is that you?" The voice was that of a man, but with the whispery, shaky quality of old age.

Bane's eyelids fluttered open and he turned towards the voice. The speaker was an elderly man with a shock of white hair. The old man was sitting on a park bench just opposite him. It took only a moment before Bane recognized Alastair's blue eyes, though they were now rheumy rather than clear as they had once been. Alastair also sported a mustache that he had not had before.

Alastair blinked at Bane as if he was seeing a ghost. He staggered to his feet and reached out towards him. "Bane?

How can this be? You look ... *the same*. I mean ... you look ... it *is you* though, isn't it?"

Bane stared at the upraised hand that was drifting towards him. Memories of the many times that hand had caressed him or carded through his hair flashed through his mind right then. But instead of the strong confident grip, Alastair's hand now trembled. Liver spots dotted the back of it. He could see the ropey veins beneath the thin skin.

Bane felt no panic at being recognized. No one believed in immortality. It was surprising that Alastair had jumped to the conclusion that it was him. Normally, one would think Bane was a relative of the remembered person. But Bane saw the beginnings of the end in Alastair's eyes and understood that, like a child, the world was no longer certain, but full of wonder and terror again as death approached for his former lover. The beast inside of him smelled illness. Alastair had cancer. It riddled his bones and organs.

"You think you know me?" Bane finally asked when Alastair was a few feet away.

"Yes, it *is* you. It *has* to be you," Alastair said. His hand hovered over Bane's cheek. "I would never forget your face. No matter if a hundred years had passed. It is *you*."

"You have a good memory, do you?" Bane asked. Anger coursed through him at Alastair's statement that he had never forgotten him. Alastair had forgotten Bane *thoroughly* when it had actually counted.

Alastair shook his head. "Not so much anymore. But you ... *you* I cannot forget. It is you, isn't it, Bane?"

"This person you think I am, why do you remember him so well?" Bane asked.

"Because he was—*you*—were—are *still*—very special to me," Alastair said.

Bane allowed a sharp smile to cross his lips. "*Special*? How special? A *lover*?"

A flustered look crossed Alastair's face and his hand quickly dropped to his side. He looked around them to see if anyone was watching or listening. Homosexuality was no more accepted at that time than it had been thirty years earlier.

"*Not* a lover then," Bane said airily.

"No ... I mean, *yes*, yes, a lover," Alastair admitted. His sallow cheeks flushed, but he stared directly at Bane. "Tell me it is you. Tell me that, by some miracle, it is you, Bane."

"This person you remember," Bane said. "When was the last time you spoke to him?"

Alastair's head lowered. "It was a long time ago."

"What were the last words you spoke to him?" Bane pushed.

"I—I don't—"

"Don't remember? Don't *care* to remember?" Bane mocked coldly. The beast growled. "He made such an impression on you that you accost a man on the street thirty years after—"

"Thirty years! It *is* you, Bane!" Alastair's head jerked up. "Only *you* would know the date."

Bane leaned in. He used his huge size to intimidate often, but Alastair did not quail before him. Even though he was elderly and frail and dying, he still was brave after a fashion. Bane whispered icily, "I am *not* the young man you knew."

"But—but you—you *must* be."

Bane's eyes smoldered with anger. Again, he wasn't afraid of Alastair knowing it was him. No one believed what old men said about real and true things that could actually be verified. They surely wouldn't believe an old man ranting about someone who hadn't aged in thirty years. So Bane decided to have a little more revenge.

"The young man you knew *died* after being *left* by the man he loved. He died after being *traded* for money to a monster. A monster that *whipped* the life right out of him. Or don't you *remember* those parts of the past?" Bane snarled.

Alastair shrank in on himself in shame even as his eyes widened in horror. "Richard promised not to hurt you."

"Some men's promises are not worth the air used to make them." Bane's smile was still rigidly in place. "Do you know any men like that? Perhaps if you looked in a *mirror* ..."

Alastair's shoulders sagged and he passed a shaky hand over his brow. "I never thought—I *believed* you would be all right. I was desperate, but—"

"Why are you explaining yourself to me?" Bane asked. "Like I said, I'm not the young man you remember. *Your betrayal killed him.*"

He had walked away from Alastair then for a second time, leaving the old man staring after him with tears of grief in his rheumy eyes. Just like the first time he had walked away from Alastair, Bane had hoped to feel some form of retribution or even triumph that he had caused Alastair to feel a fraction of the pain that Bane had over the years. But he had not. Instead, it had left a hollow feeling in his stomach and the sense that he had lowered himself by attempting to hurt a dying man.

Bane looked down at Nick in his arms and vowed he would do better. He would be better than his past. Better than Alastair and his father. He would be the man that Nick deserved. He would be worthy of the title of "mate".

CHAPTER FOURTEEN

THE FOUNTAIN

"**A**re you *sure* that the fountain will work?" Nick cast his voice low even though Bane was nowhere in sight.

Omar was keeping Bane occupied in the kitchen while Nick and the plumber were outside by the fountain. Surely, not even Bane's super-hearing could catch what they were saying! But still Nick kept his voice low and glanced nervously at the closed doors to Moon Shadow. He didn't want Bane to come out and discover his plan for the fountain. He wanted it to be a surprise.

The plumber—Dave, as the embroidered patch over his heart proclaimed him—was clearly trying not to roll his eyes. Nick had asked this question a dozen times and counting since he had come that morning to finish the fountain's plumbing.

It had been a struggle to keep Bane out of the loop with Dave insisting on speaking loudly and rattling his tools. When Dave had asked to use the washroom, Nick had blanched before rushing inside Moon Shadow to distract Bane from the strange man entering the house. Nick had told the billionaire that Dave was the florist. But then Bane had wanted to go talk to him about next week's order and so Nick had to add to the lie that it wasn't the *normal* florist and it would be *pointless* talking to Dave. The billionaire had looked at Nick strangely, but finally relented, especially when Nick had started kissing him.

Nick didn't need an excuse to kiss Bane. Waking up in Bane's arms that morning had made him want to stay in them the rest of the day. They had been spooned together with Nick's back against Bane's front. The silky slide of one of Bane's legs across the top of his had caused Nick to become achingly hard. Bane's soft breaths against his spine and the sleepy kisses the billionaire had placed on his shoulders and the back of his neck had caused Nick to bite his pillow. In between the soft press of lips, Bane had whispered words of adoration that had warmed spaces in Nick that he hadn't known were cold.

Nick had turned around and Bane had shifted on top of him. Bane's eyes had been heavy lidded and a frisson of desire went through Nick as Bane seemed only half tamed at that moment. Half a highly civilized man and half a wild beast seemed to lurk beneath those tailored clothes and sexy British accent.

Nick wound his arms around Bane's muscled neck and brought the big man down for slow, languid kisses that seemed to burn his skin. Bane settled himself between Nick's thighs and started rocking their groins together. With their lips fused and the steady slide of their cocks against one another, they had both cum, swallowing each other's moans of completion.

Bane clearly had issues with losing control during sex. He seemed to fear to let go as if he would hurt Nick when he did. But Nick was willing to work with him, because those times that Bane *did* let go—just a little—were magical.

And then there had been Bane's words as the sunlight peeked between the curtains. As their cum was drying on their bellies, Bane murmured, "I want to wake up with you every day."

Every day ...

"Me, too." Nick grinned up at the ceiling and then Bane was on top of him again, kissing him, and they made even more of a glorious mess of each other.

"You could let me *test* the fountain fully and then we could *truly* be sure," Dave suggested, interrupting Nick's thoughts.

Nick blinked and focused back on the moment, "N-no, it has to be the *first* time only when Bane's here."

Dave gave him a curious look. "What's this all about?"

Nick slowly smiled as happiness and excitement filled him. "I'm trying to make someone's dream come true."

Dave let out a huff of a laugh. "Well, I think this is as good as I can make it for you. All you need to do is turn that valve there and it should work."

"Right." Nick looked where Dave pointed to a valve at the base of the fountain.

Dave clapped his shoulder. "Good luck. If it doesn't work, come get me. I'll be by my van."

"Thanks for parking outside the gates and for everything else," Nick said, his heart beat speeding up as he contemplated bringing Bane out there. He really hoped the fountain would work. It was superstitious nonsense that if the fountain worked that their relationship was *meant* or something like that and if it didn't ... well, that didn't bear contemplating. But he felt it nonetheless.

"No problem."

Dave hefted up his tool box and walked off down the gravel drive. Nick wiped his suddenly sweaty hands against the tops of his shorts. He should go get Bane and Omar now, but he hesitated and just stared at the doors into Moon Shadow.

He remembered the first time that he had crossed that threshold. He'd had no idea what to expect. One year of service to Bane in exchange for his family having the opportunity to get their fortune back had sounded absurd. He'd been convinced that Bane simply wanted a sex slave or something. He knew now that the last thought was the absurd part. Though Bane *had* been deeply attracted to him and the plan *had* been to get Nick as near to him as possible no slavery was intended. But what neither of them could have anticipated was that Nick would come to love Bane.

He'd told Bane he'd loved him last night. He'd somehow managed to make his voice sound almost casual when he said it. Like it was no big deal.

Right, no big deal. Like my heart wasn't threatening to beat out of my chest when I said it.

Bane hadn't said he loved Nick back. He'd said he cared deeply for Nick. But that was enough ... for now. After hearing what had happened to Bane in the past, he completely understood why the billionaire believed love was an illusion and shied away from even expressing the sentiment. The very word "love" had to be associated for Bane with betrayal and pain. And while Alastair and Bane's father were dead and they could no longer physically hurt the billionaire, they still *haunted* him.

I'll make so many good memories for him that the sheer weight of them will crush the ones of Alastair and his father.

This was going to be one of those memories.

Nick drew in a deep breath and smoothed his hands down the front of his pale green t-shirt before walking towards the mansion. When he pushed open the doors, it seemed that Moon Shadow reached out and embraced him. There was another massive vase of roses in the foyer, a mixture of white and the deepest purple that they were almost black. As he walked past them and into the hall beyond, he heard Bane and Omar's voices wafting out from the kitchen. Omar had induced Bane to cook a bolognese sauce that the billionaire was famous for. Nick hadn't tasted Bane's cooking yet, but if the smell of the rich, red sauce was any indication, he was in for a treat.

He stepped into the kitchen. Bane standing at the kitchen island before a cutting board. He had an eight-inch chef's knife in one hand and was slicing garlic into paper thin slices. He looked incredibly handsome and masculine in linen pants and an airy white shirt with his sleeves rolled up revealing beautifully muscled forearms. His elegant fingers held the stub of garlic as he expertly shaved off see-thru pieces of the pungent plant. The billionaire immediately looked up when Nick entered the room. His face was alight with happiness. Nick's face hurt from how hard he was smiling in response.

You make my heart sing, Bane.

"What have you been doing with yourself, Nick? I thought you were with Jade, but Omar tells me that she has returned to the city," Bane said as he cleaned off the knife and went to wash his hands in the sink.

"She had to source some more dresses," Nick said.

"I am already missing her," Omar said from his post by the stove. He was stirring the deep red sauce. Nick could see bits of meat, carrot, onion and celery bobbing to the surface as Omar drew the spoon through the bolognese.

"Me, too. But it's necessary. She goes to second-hand shops, estate sales and even paws through what people put out by the side of the road," Nick explained, resting a hip against the island, admiring Bane's graceful movements. "That's where she gets her stock. It's amazing what people throw away. Especially rich people." He grinned at Bane.

The billionaire chuckled. "I've been known to be wasteful myself. Jade is quite resourceful to take advantage of that. Will she be back for dinner?" Bane wiped his hands off on a blue and white striped kitchen towel.

"Depends on her finds, but not likely. She's planning to stay away a few days." Nick shrugged and he found himself focusing on the flex of muscles in Bane's forearms.

"She will be missed." Bane tossed the towel onto the countertop.

Nick gave him a lopsided smile. "I think she'll be happy to know that. So ..." He pressed his hands together in front of him.

"So?" Bane came near and cupped Nick's face. Nick's skin tingled as Bane ran his thumbs along his cheeks.

"So ..." Nick repeated, his mouth suddenly dry.

"It's clear that you want to tell me something." Bane cocked his head to the side in amusement. "What is it?"

Nick opened his mouth and shut it. He opened it again, but no words came out. He shouldn't be nervous. It was only in his head that this fountain was a big deal. Even if it totally didn't work, if the water started spraying everywhere, Bane would likely laugh and still appreciate the thought he put behind it. Then they'd get Dave back and it would be fixed. But Nick wanted it to be *perfect* the first time. He wanted to give Bane something that went as it should. Nick met Omar's eyes over Bane's right shoulder. Omar knew all about the plan with the fountain and he, clearly, also saw how Nick's nerves were causing him to be tongue-tied.

"Nick has something to show you," Omar said helpfully.

Bane's eyebrows rose. "Oh? What?"

"It's out front," Nick managed to speak finally.

He took Bane's hands in his and started to lead the big man out of the kitchen and into the hall. His heart felt like it was doing a rumba in his chest. Omar hurried after them.

"Your nervousness is really intriguing me," Bane laughed.

"I hope you'll like what I have to show you," Nick confessed. "I hope it *works*."

"Works? Now I'm *certain* I have no idea what you're about to show me." Bane's Siberian blue eyes sparkled with delight.

Nick smiled back, but found he couldn't speak again because he was just too nervous. He led Bane out of the house to the circular gravel drive where the fountain took pride of place in the very center. The fountain had been cleaned of plants and debris. The muck of ages had been washed off of it. It didn't look new by any means. In fact, it looked like it had been there *forever* just like the rest of Moon Shadow did, which always gave Nick a sense of permanence that no other home he'd had did.

"What am I supposed to see, Nick?" Bane's confusion had grown and his eyes were flitting over the drive and the flowers, looking for something *new*.

Nick pulled Bane by the arm over to the far side of the fountain so that Moon Shadow itself was part of the view. Bane's arm snaked around his waist.

"Omar, would you do the honors?" Nick asked, gesturing to the valve.

"Oh, yes, it is my pleasure!" The Indian man crouched down and turned the valve.

For one heart stopping moment, nothing happened. Then there was a gurgling sound and water sprayed from the nymph's horn and spattered onto the seashell below. At first, the water came in awkward gushes and then in a continuous, almost musical stream. It sounded *right* as if Moon Shadow had been waiting to have the sound of the fountain introducing it to the world. Nick let out a yell of triumph and clapped his hands together. Omar joined in.

"It is beautiful! Just like I thought it would be," Omar cheered. "Now Moon Shadow is complete."

"It is," Nick agreed.

It was then that he realized that Bane had been completely silent. Nick's heart was in his throat as he turned his head to see the billionaire's expression. Bane looked stunned. It was the sort of expression one got when one saw a ghost or deja vu or woke from a dream and didn't know what was real and what wasn't.

Slowly, Bane turned his head towards Nick, leaned down and kissed him. Nick eagerly kissed Bane back. His hands feathered in Bane's hair. They kissed until he was seeing black dots for lack of air. Those Siberian blue eyes were fixed upon him and there was *awe* in them.

"You remembered what I said about—about *this*." Bane gestured towards the fountain while still keeping a hold of Nick with his other hand.

"Yeah. Actually, I had it all planned beforehand, but not as a surprise exactly," Nick confessed. "But knowing how much it meant to you for us to see it start flowing *together* I wanted to make sure that happened. I even have the poor plumber standing by his van outside of the gate."

"Ah, so the florist was really a plumber!" Bane laughed.

"Yes," Nick agreed with a blush. "I thought you were going to figure it out."

"You were very clever, Nick!" Omar grinned.

"I admit I noticed you were acting a tad strange, Nick, but I knew there was no harm in it and you seemed happy, which is all that matters to me." Bane kissed Nick's right temple.

"Was this how you thought it would be?" Nick asked hopefully.

Bane's smile was like the sun. "Oh, yes, this was *perfect*, Nick."

Nick beamed. The butterflies in his stomach were now circling happily. Bane kissed his temple and held him tight.

"I wouldn't let the plumber test the fountain fully. I wanted us to be the *first* people who saw it work," Nick explained.

Bane's eyebrows rose. "You were quite intent on making my vision come true."

"I was." He gave Bane a wicked smile. "Probably makes you worry where I'll put all my energy next."

Bane laughed. "Actually, I cannot *wait* to see what you do."

"I don't have a plan yet. But something will come to me."

Nick was rewarded with yet a third kiss then Bane said, "Now, let me meet this plumber and thank him for his good work."

"Absolutely. Omar, you want to come?" Nick asked.

"I must get back to the sauce! It might burn. But send along my thanks." Omar gave the nymph a pat on the head before heading back into Moon Shadow.

"Looks like it's just us." Bane's eyes hooded and Nick squirmed. "Until we reach the plumber."

"I can handle that."

Bane laced his fingers through Nick's. They headed to the mansion's gates where the plumber waited. The soft purr of Bane's cell phone broke their companionable silence. Bane pulled it out and his face scrunched as if he'd bitten into something sour.

"Who is it?" Nick asked curiously.

"Your father," Bane answered, again making that sour look. "He's called me half a dozen times since I returned, leaves ridiculous, avuncular voicemails. He has not gotten the hint that I am not returning them. I will only speak to him at the required meetings. Nothing more. We are *not* friends. We are *nothing* to one another."

Bane firmly hit the Dismiss button and slipped the phone back into his pocket. Nick's stomach did an uneasy flip. His dad knew about him and Bane. He didn't *want* his father to speak to Bane. He'd say or do something that would really piss the billionaire off. But, at the same time, his heart fell into his feet at Bane's last words. Charles *was* his father. Did Bane expect Nick to ignore his family? Maybe even disown them? Couldn't Bane be at least *civil* to his dad for Nick's sake?

Yet these questions somehow couldn't get past the lump in his throat so he asked none of them. He told himself that he didn't want to ruin this moment with Bane. He'd just made one of Bane's dreams come true. He'd created a good memory. He shouldn't spoil it.

CHAPTER FIFTEEN

GOLDEN DAYS AND
SILVER NIGHTS

Time flowed in an unending stream of golden days and silver nights. Being with Nick felt effortless, felt *right*. Bane had never been so happy, not even in those first giddy days with Alastair, because Nick was *real* and *good* and Bane was so lucky to have him.

He had walked with Nick through Alric's forest with the leaves rustling above them and the chirp of bird adding song to the air. They had picnicked and gardened. They had read books to one another on the porch by candlelight. Often Nick's head would be in his lap and Bane's fingers would be carding through the young man's hair as he read out loud. Nick claimed his accent made *everything* sound better.

They'd gone to nearby farms and picked strawberries, raspberries, blueberries and blackberries until Moon Shadow seemed overrun with bowls of sweet fruit, pies bursting their lattice tops and luscious cakes studded with the bright reds and dark purples of the berries. They'd chased each other around the garden with the hose to relieve the summer heat. Bane had decided that they would put in a pool for next year. He wanted to see Nick in a swimsuit and *without* one, swimming in blue, blue water. Omar and Jade were often there, too, joining them for long dinners where they laughed, talked and sparred about every subject imaginable. Wine had flowed like water. Mixed drinks heated their skin. Champagne sparkled in their veins.

Bane had never felt so alive. He had never felt so incredibly *blessed*. And that, of course, sometimes filled him with fear. Because he was *cursed*. The moment he forgot that something terrible was *sure* to happen.

Yet, right now, at this moment, he wanted to enjoy it all.

The wind rushed through Bane's hair as he drove the Mercedes hardtop convertible with the top down through the twilight, winding roads that surrounded Winter Haven. The city itself was a sparkling jewel in the distance. It glowed on the horizon. The Mercedes' sleek silver form with night black leather interior and walnut accents swept over the asphalt like a night bird. Bane looked in the rearview mirror and saw that the scar on his face wasn't as visible as it had been before he and Nick had gotten together.

But it's still there. I cannot forget that. As is the beast ...

Nick shifted against him. Bane spared a quick glance down at the sleeping young man snuggled against his side. The seatbelt was holding Nick farther away from him than he would have liked, but safety was paramount. Bane grinned as Nick had somehow found a way to make himself comfortable in the car using Bane as his pillow. Nick had been exhausted after the long morning and afternoon in the sun and sand.

They had gone out sailing on his friend's, Marco Ardan's, fifty-four foot sailboat. Marco had wanted to talk business, which Bane had done while sipping champagne and looking out at water that had been this spectacular amethyst blue. While he and Marco had talked and sailed, Nick had perched at the front of the boat, his legs thrust through the railing, riding the waves. Business done, Bane had joined him, sitting behind him on the deck. He'd felt the heat of Nick's sun-warmed body against his own. They'd fit together perfectly.

Now, even in the car's low light, he could see a greater smattering of freckles across Nick's nose and cheeks than had been there before the sail, despite the liberal use of sunscreen. Bane had applied the creamy liquid all over his beautiful lover. Now they were driving back home to Moon Shadow where they would share a bed that was more *theirs* than *his*. They would go to sleep in one another's arms and wake up in the morning to long, lingering kisses.

They had yet to make love fully as Bane's skin always started to prickle the moment he even considered penetrating Nick. The beast seemed to fully come alive at those moments, too. Terror had him shutting down. Terror that he would shift. Terror that the scars from the beast's claws on Nick's arm would be the *least* injury that he would inflict on the young man that meant the world to him. Every time he shut down, Bane cursed himself. Nick, however, soothed him and acted like it was not a problem. But Bane knew it was.

Perhaps after the shift, after the beast has its freedom, then I will be able to fully possess Nick. The full moon is not that far away after all.

In fact, the full moon was only four days away. Bane chewed his inner cheek. He hadn't yet told Nick he would need the young man to vacate Moon Shadow for a few days. He had no idea what excuse he could possible come up with for Nick to do this *every* month. For a moment, Omar's face flashed in his mind's eye. While the Indian man had not repeated his advice of telling Nick the truth, Bane saw it in his eyes as every day passed and his shift grew nearer.

I will figure something out. Everything will be all right. This thing between Nick and I feels meant.

At that moment, a bent female figure appeared in the Mercedes' headlamps. Bane slammed on the brakes and swerved around her. He heard the screech of his tires and smelled the acrid scent of burnt rubber. The Mercedes rocked to a halt.

For a moment, Bane just sat there: heart in his throat, bitter taste of fear and adrenaline on his tongue, breathing coming in ragged gasps. He looked over at Nick, expecting the young man to be bolt upright, woken by the near crash. The seatbelt he had just been lamenting now was the most precious thing ever. Nick could have gone through the windshield without it.

"Nick? Are you all right?" Bane asked.

Nick was fine. *Very fine.* He was *still asleep.* The seatbelt had jerked taut as Nick's body had flown forward, but then it had drawn him right back against the Mercedes' buttery leather seat. Nick's head lolled to the side and the young man let out a sleepy sigh.

"Nick?" Bane cried, but it did no good. The young man was asleep, not unconscious.

"He is fine," an elderly female voice said.

He jerked his head around towards the old woman who had chosen to simply stand in the road like a fool! Bane snapped his head around, furious at her and himself. But he managed to grate out, "Madam, are you all right?"

The half-light was causing his usually sharp vision to fail him. He could only see the outline of her, but not her features.

"I am beyond such things," she said. "Leave the young one. Come."

Bane looked back at Nick. He should take him to the hospital. He shouldn't be considering listening to her. But he *was.*

"Leave him, Bane. He is fine."

The use of his name had Bane snapping his head around towards her again. This was not *normal.* He still could not see her face. Who was she? He had to find out. He checked Nick one last time. The young man made a sleepy, contented sound.

He is all right.

With that last thought, Bane viciously pushed the release of his seatbelt and got out of the car. His legs shook slightly from the adrenaline. He approached her, knowing he likely seemed a hulking beast as his movements were not graceful, but jerky, angry. He normally tried to be far more tentative with people due to his size, but his body still wasn't fully under his control. And he was angry.

He stepped over to her until there was only a few feet apart. She had not spoken since he left the car and his sense of alarm at all of this grew larger and larger, yet Bane would not back down. He would not retreat to the car. This was just an elderly woman, not a foe. She might need help. How had she gotten all the way out here on her own? She, undoubtedly, was in shock. But a voice at the back of his mind reminded him about *another* old woman who he had underestimated. And she knew his name.

"Madam, are you hurt? Lost? You should not be out here in the middle of the road. It is not safe ..." His voice dropped off.

He should have been able to see her face at this distance, but he still could not make out one of her features. It was as if she was a black cutout. He swallowed and reached towards her.

"Madam, please say something ... *anything* ..."

His fingers touched her darkness and he felt a blast of wet heat. It was the steam of the jungle. Instead of being on a country road in the United States, he was in the middle of the Indian jungle and the priestess who had cursed him was before him.

They were in a small clearing with a fire crackling to his right in a fire pit. He smelled the raw earth and flowers of the jungle. The firelight did not extend beyond the ring of cleared ground. The night-shrouded jungle around them was alive with the sounds of animals. He heard the padding of predator paws.

Tigers. Many tigers.

When Bane looked into the trees he saw the jewel-like shine of dozens of animal eyes. The tigers were circling them, coming closer and closer. His hands curled into fists at his sides as a wash of sweat coated his face. He wanted to leap away from that place. For once, he wanted to shift into the beast and run through the forest faster than his human legs could take him. But he was rooted to the spot. He could not move, let alone shift.

He turned back to the old woman. She was leaning on a staff that was the same nut brown color as she was. Her features were almost lost in the profusion of wrinkles. He wondered how old she had been when she'd died. For this was the woman that had cursed him over 100 years ago and she was surely dead now.

"What is this? Why have you brought me here?" Bane demanded to know. Rage built in him and he added, "What are you going to torture me with *now*?"

He had killed the beast's form, but he hadn't understood the repercussions. He'd killed plenty of game that was thought "sacred" but none of it actually had been. Though he could almost hear Omar telling him at that moment that *all* of that game had been. Simply because he hadn't been *punished* for it didn't mean that the animals weren't sacred. But he thrust those thoughts away from him.

"Tell me!" he demanded.

She stared at him silently in response. Her dark eyes were like onyx chips. She did not even blink.

"I made a mistake!" he continued, his voice going raw. "Haven't I paid for it yet? What more do you want me to do?"

She seemed like a statue to him. For one wild moment, he wondered if she actually *was* a statue. But then there was a slight creak as she adjusted the staff and the illusion of immobility was broken.

He licked his lips and said, "I've found someone, someone very special. He is—is beyond precious to me. I want a life with him! But the beast won't allow it. It will come between us! Even now it stops me from being with him as a lover should."

The woman pointed to the ground between them and where there had been nothing but packed earth before now lay a magnificent dead white Bengal tiger. Blood pooled around its body like a black lake. Bane jerked back, but his feet were still frozen in place. He raised a hand up to block out the view of the destruction of life.

"I *know* I did wrong! I should never—*never* have shot the beast, but I did! Yet must I pay for it forever?" he wailed.

That was when she spoke, "*Still*, you do not understand."

"What don't I understand? Tell me and I will do or be whatever it is you ask of me!"

Her head crooked to the side. "Yours is not the only life you must consider."

"I don't understand!" He shook his head in confusion. "Who's life am I forgetting? Nick's? I know he wants to be with me and, somehow, I will become worthy of him—where are you going? You cannot leave me here!"

But she was already turning away from him, dismissing his frantic words. He called out to her to stop, to come back, to tell him what he needed to do. As she disappeared into the jungle, he thought he heard her say, "You must live the life you stole. Not just your own."

And then she was gone.

And that's when he thought he knew what she meant and rage burned in him.

"I give the beast whatever it wants! But I won't give up Nick for it! I won't!" he shouted at the jungle, but only the echo of his voice rang back at him mockingly. He knew she was gone. He was alone in this place. He used to love India, love being away from civilization, but not now.

I have to get out of here. I have to get back to Nick! I left him in the car. He's asleep. Helpless. Anything could happen –

The snap of a twig stopped Bane's thoughts cold. He straightened. The hair on the back of his neck stood straight up on end. The jewel-like eyes were staring at him. The tigers were standing just outside of the fire light's edges. He knew that the tigers were about to attack. They would leap upon him and tear him limb from limb. They would carry parts of him off into the jungle and feast upon his flesh, blood and organs. He would become a part of them and then a part of the jungle itself. Poetic in a way. But Bane had everything to live for now. He had Nick.

Bane's own breathing filled his ears as he reached down and *tugged* at his right leg. His plan was to *wrench* his foot physically off the ground. But it didn't move. The sole of his shoe didn't even shift a little bit. Sweat poured down his face as he tried to *shuffle* towards the fire, at least. If he could grab one of the tree limbs that were on fire then maybe, just *maybe*, he could use it to keep the beasts at bay. But he could not shuffle. He was stuck.

And then he heard a *crack* and saw the head of a massive white Bengal tiger emerging from the treeline. Then another. And another. And another. Bane stood up straight. He would die on his feet.

Nick, forgive me.

Bane closed his eyes as the tigers all leaped towards him. He couldn't help the shout he gave as he felt their claws brush his face ...

"Bane!? What's wrong? Did you have a bad dream?" Nick asked.

Bane was sitting bolt upright in bed. His shout still echoed in the room. Sweat soaked the sheets around them. His hair was plastered to his forehead and his heart was practically beating out of his chest. Warm hands were suddenly on his shoulders and back. Nick was touching him, petting him, *soothing* him.

"Bane, it's okay. I'm here. You're here. We're both safe," Nick murmured.

Bane looked around the dim room and realized from the soft gray light coming from the chink between the curtains that it was still early. They were in his bedroom. They had been sleeping. He'd had a nightmare. His mind ordered itself like dominos falling one after another.

Yesterday, they had gone sailing just like he had dreamed. He had driven them home, again, just like he'd dreamed. Nick had laid his head against his shoulder and slept the whole way home, again, just like in the dream. But there had been no elderly woman in the road. There had been no jungle. There had been no tigers. He let out a breath of relief. It was indeed a dream. A frightening one that had felt real, but was just a dream nonetheless. Thankfully, it had not been one that Nick had shared with him.

"I—I'm sorry, Nick. I had a nightmare," he croaked out, his mouth dry as dust. Nick reached over him and grabbed a glass of water that he lifted to Bane's lips. Bane drained it off gratefully.

"It's okay—oh, shit, Bane! I must have scratched you in my sleep!" Nick cried and Bane felt the press of a tissue again his cheek.

"W-what?" A solid lump of ice formed in Bane's stomach.

"There are just a few shallow scratches on your face, but still ... I hope I didn't hurt you," Nick sounded so guilty.

"I'm sure you did not." Bane took the tissue from Nick's hand and stared down at the streaks of crimson on the white material. "Perhaps I did it myself. You mustn't blame yourself."

Just a dream. It was just a dream.

He felt the beast looking at him out of hooded, glowing eyes. His heart thudded heavily in his chest. Nick's arms were suddenly around his neck.

"I hope that nightmare wasn't spurred by my lunch with Dad later today. Though I think that I should be having nightmares about that. Not you. Considering I'm the only one going," Nick teased.

Bane remembered then that Nick had told him last night as they were preparing for bed that he was meeting Charles for lunch. The tatters of the dream scattered as he thought of Nick with his father. He didn't like it. But it wasn't like he could object, though he hoped that Nick would give up Charles and his odious brothers eventually. A part of him—that sounded suspiciously like Omar—tutted that it was not right for Bane to want Nick to lose his family, but Bane couldn't help but feel it would be for the best. Then they wouldn't have to be bothered by the Fairfaxes ever again. The beast made a surprising growl at that and Bane blinked.

What? He asked it. *What do you care about the Fairfaxes?*

Though he was not sure, he thought he heard the beast respond, *When have you cared about any but yourself? So do not speak for me.*

But then Nick was kissing him and he was distracted from the beast. Besides what would the beast know about family and love and caring about others? Nothing, nothing at all.

CHAPTER SIXTEEN

LUNCH DATE

Nick tugged at the collar of his Fioretti-original shirt as he walked down a crowded noon-time street in Winter Haven. He was headed towards Mangino's, one of his father's favorite lunch spots. Mangino's had a beautiful outdoor seating area with comfortable lounge-like seating and broad umbrellas to keep the sun off. The attractive wait staff, an excellent wine menu and fantastic northern Italian food just added to the restaurant's allure. He normally *liked* going there, but all he felt now was strangled at the prospect.

It wasn't the shirt that was causing him to feel this way. It was the upcoming meal and his father's *unwanted* advice that would be dispensed at said meal. Of course, that advice would be all based on his father getting things to go *his* way not on Nick or Bane's happiness.

Maybe I can just cut him off. No, that won't work. It'll just make it worse. Better to let him talk and just nod and smile. Nod and smile. I can do that.

He tried smiling as practice and a woman, who happened to glance up at him at that moment, winced as if in empathetic pain. Maybe he *shouldn't* smile. Maybe just nodding would be enough.

He decided to concentrate instead on the memories of his skin sliding against Bane's from just that morning. But the other memory of Bane waking up, screaming, intruded. He'd asked the billionaire about it, but Bane had been evasive. Nick had ended up sharing his own dream with Bane instead, hoping to encourage quid pro quo.

Resting his chin on Bane's broad shoulder, Nick had said, "I dreamed of tigers again."

He thought that would interest Bane, but he hadn't thought it would *alarm* him. Bane stiffened and turned to face him. His Siberian blue eyes glowed in the low light of dawn.

"What did you dream?"

Nick's gaze went distant as he remembered, the room around them falling away, just the sense of Bane's skin under his hands. "I was in the rose garden out back. I'm not sure if it was dawn or dusk –"

"The shift," Bane whispered. When Nick looked at him curiously, he added, "The shift from night to day, day to night."

"That's a cool way of thinking about it."

"Please continue. I did not mean to interrupt."

"So I'm in the garden and the light is just so ... *beautiful.* The roses were damp with dew and they sparkled like diamonds. I was leaning down to sniff this red rose—so deeply red that it's like *blood* fresh from a vein—and I saw *movement* in the corner of my eye."

In his dream, the rose bushes had been more like rose *hedges*, making a maze of the back yard. The roses were thickly clustered together, leaving hardly any room for the green of their leaves to be seen, yet he had caught a glimpse of pure white fur and black stripes through them. The low growl had told him that he wasn't mistaken in thinking the tiger was there.

The hair on Nick's arms and back of his neck rose. He knew he had to get back into the house. But when he turned towards Moon Shadow, the rose garden had truly become a maze. There was no straight path between himself and the back door.

He ran. He dashed down flower lined paths, only to find himself hitting dead end after dead end and having to retrace his steps, losing precious seconds and his lead on the four-footed beast. Sweat plastered his t-shirt to his chest from the exertion, but also the fear. The tiger was coming for him!

He ran down one last path and found himself facing a wall of roses. It stretched above his head, blocking out his view. And that was when he heard the growl behind him. Nick spun around, breath coming in gasps, heart slamming against his chest, and there was the white Bengal tiger at the end of the path.

It was huge, almost the length of a car and its shoulders were mid-way up Nick's chest. Its paws were as big as his head. It was looking at him out of these incredible eyes that looked just like Bane's.

Nick held out his hands in front of him as if he could physically fend it off. The tiger sauntered, unconcerned and taking its own sweet time, down the path until it was inches from his palms.

"What did it do?" Bane's voice was barely above a whisper. The line of his body was rigid.

Nick squeezed his shoulders. "Don't worry. I said *dream*, not *nightmare*. It actually rubbed its head against my hands. It wanted to be petted."

Bane's Siberian blue eyes opened in shock. "P-petted?"

"Yeah! It actually laid down and rolled over on its side to give me full access to its tummy. It was so soft and it kept licking me like it was petting me back!" Nick laughed at the memory. "And then I started to get tired and ... I don't know how to explain it, but I knew the tiger wanted me to lay down with it. It would keep me safe while I slept. The sun had set at some point and the moon—this huge full moon—was hanging over us and I curled down beside it. It put this big paw around me and licked my cheek. Then I fell asleep in the dream, peaceful, safe. I actually felt *loved*."

Nick looked up at Bane's face as he said the last. The dream hadn't been sexual exactly. But there had been this sense to Nick that he and the tiger were connected in some way. The sense of being loved was absolutely real.

Bane stared at him for a long time. His expression was unreadable. His right hand reached up and he ran his fingers over the scars on Nick's shoulder. The touch was so soft, so barely there, yet Nick felt it scarred him just like the claws had done.

"The tiger *does* love you, Nick, but it's *still* a tiger. Still a *beast*. Still dangerous," Bane murmured.

And that was the last Bane would speak of it. He did not tell Nick of his own dream, just looked at him as if the billionaire wanted him to understand something that he could not say. Nick kept catching the billionaire looking at him with that same unreadable expression throughout the morning, especially on the drive into the city. Though Bane was not coming to lunch, he had been determined to drive Nick downtown.

"You really don't have to drive me to lunch. It's probably better if you don't. Dad will undoubtedly say something that will make us both want to punch him," Nick had said when Bane had offered to drive him instead of Nick riding his motorcycle into the city.

Bane had grinned. "I have no doubt that Charles will be *himself*, but I have business in town today, too."

"Okay then maybe let me off a block away so my father doesn't see you?" Nick suggested.

"I feel like a parent whose child doesn't want them to drop them off at school, because they won't be seen as cool any longer." Bane chuckled.

Nick ran his fingers down Bane's front, resting the palms of his hands on the big man's pectoral muscles. He could feel the steady thump of Bane's heart. "Trust me, if you were my dad I'd be *so* into incest. So *very* into it."

Bane gave him a smoky look. "I think I would be there with you. But, in all seriousness, I will drop you off a block away or however far you wish. Then after lunch I'll rescue you—I *mean* pick you up to take you home."

"You *will* be rescuing me." Nick groaned.

Bane gave him another smoldering look before kissing him. "I want to be your knight in white shining armor."

"You already are. This will just add to your tally of brave deeds."

Nick tried to keep the good feeling of Bane's arms being around him as he approached the restaurant and saw not just his father, but his two brothers awaiting him at the "best" table. They looked like three crows in their black suits.

Like carrion eaters.

Nick's chest seized as he realized what this would be: an inquisition. His father had told his brothers about him and Bane. Now all three of them would pepper him with questions he would never answer and give him advice he would never follow. And they would consider it *their right* to do so because *his* dating life affected *their* lives.

Nick smoothed down the front of his crisp white shirt and buttoned the lightweight gray suit coat. This was one of the suits that Mr. Fioretti, the renowned tailor of Winter Haven, had made for him. Bane had insisted on him being properly dressed when they had first met, even going so far as buying thousands of dollars of suits for Nick. It was ironic that Bane no longer minded if Nick wore cut off shorts and a ratty t-shirt even during the formal dinners. He hadn't actually dressed up until today since Bane had gotten back. Nick was glad though that he was wearing the suit. It felt like *armor* against his family.

"Nickie!" his father called and waved a hand to further attract Nick's attention.

Nick plastered on a smile and put a spring in his step as he went over to the table. His father stood up and actually gave him a back slap. His brothers gave him anemic waves, but remained seated at the table. Jake had dark sunglasses on and was staring at the menu like he would murder it. Steven polished his wire-rimmed glasses with one of the pristine napkins. Charles' gaze slipped from Nick's face to the suit.

"Nice suit, Nickie. Is this ... it *is* a Fioretti original, isn't it?" Charles grasped the lapels of the coat and practically took it off Nick to see the tailor's tag in the back.

"Yeah, Dad, it is." He shrugged the older man's hands off of him and sat down, cheeks burning with embarrassment. He cast a quick glance around, but it didn't appear as if anyone noticed.

"Bane bought this for you?" Charles stated more than asked.

Nick thought about lying, saying he had used his own money for this suit, but none of them would believe him. So he answered crisply, "Yeah, he likes people to be dressed for dinner."

"How *many* of these did he buy you?" Charles' shrewd brown eyes narrowed at him.

"I don't know," Nick tried to be vague, but that just made it worse.

Steven's eyebrows rose. "He brought you so many you *don't* know the exact number?"

Nick flushed and that alone confirmed what Steven thought. Like always, every time he tried to parry with them things went wrong so maybe nonchalance would work. "Like I said he likes to dress for dinner and I didn't exactly have a wardrobe for that so he had Mr. Fioretti outfit me for the year."

"You do know that like *one* of Fioretti's cheapest suits is like $10k minimally, right?" Jake snorted.

Nick flushed hotter. He *hadn't* known that and considering his closet was stuffed full of the suits he could only imagine how much money Bane had spent on him even when he had "hated" Nick.

I'll have to make sure that I wear them now. Can't let all that money and hard work go to waste!

His father saved him from having to utter some inanity by slapping his back again and saying, "That's good. Shows Bane takes care of what's his."

Nick's stomach did a strange flip that was both a queasy reaction at being referred to as *Bane's*, but at the same time *liking* the idea of belonging to the billionaire. Nick quickly grabbed the embossed paper menu and hid behind it, hoping that would end this part of the conversation.

The menu held only a few items. Mangino's was known for high end Italian food that was so fresh and fine that every meal was a work of art. Already, the crusty Italian bread was on the table ready to be dipped into a plate of green-gold olive oil mixed with inky, thick balsamic vinegar and topped with shavings of parmigiano reggiano. His father broke off a few slices for himself and handed the still warm loaf to Nick who did the same.

"I took the liberty of ordering us a nice barolo," his father said, referring to the wine.

"I really shouldn't drink before going back to the office," Steven said stiffly.

"Take the stick out of your ass, Steven. It isn't going to matter how hard we work anymore," Jake said coldly. "It's only going to matter how Nick fucks—"

"Jake!" Charles snapped and sent a sulphurous look at his oldest son before Nick had a chance to get angry.

"But it's *true*! Jesus, Nick, did you *have* to date *Bane*? I mean of all the guys you could have put out for—"

"How many times do I have to tell you that this isn't a *bad* thing, Jake?" Charles hissed.

Jake slumped down into his chair. Nick wondered if the sunglasses were on because his older brother had been drinking his sorrows away the night before. His sorrows being Nick's dating decisions. Nick swallowed down the bile that rose in his throat.

"Nothing bad is going to happen because I'm dating Bane," Nick got out. He sounded defensive. That wasn't good. He took in a deep breath. "You guys are still being judged on how well you follow Bane's business practices, okay?"

"Nick," Steven said, his voice measured and cool as it always was, which was a relief. At least Steven wasn't treating him differently now that he was dating Bane. That thought died on the vine as Steven continued, "You can't be that naïve. Of course your relationship with Bane will play a role in whether we get the business back or not. If he's *with* you and *happy* at the end of the year then, even if we've made mistakes, it won't matter. He'll look upon us favorably. But if you and he are *not* together or things are *not* good between you then I am *certain* that he will take it out on us."

It was said so simply, so precisely, that Nick couldn't deny it. Besides, it was exactly what he had been thinking himself, but ignoring since Bane returned. Yet he hadn't—and *wouldn't*—discuss it with Bane. It wasn't just cowardice. It was practicality. No matter what Bane said now, if at the end of the year Bane and he weren't happy together then his family *was* likely to pay. Nick suddenly felt cold.

If I believe that then ... He couldn't finish the thought. He wished he'd never come to this lunch.

"I'm sure Nick knows that." His father sopped up some of the oil, balsamic and cheese with the bread and chewed it thoughtfully. "But I'm thinking that we can turn this to our advantage—"

"Dad, I'm *not* going to do anything—"

"Do anything *what*? To help your family out? No, you're too *good* and *pure* for that! Why couldn't you just keep cleaning Bane's goddamned toilets instead of warming his bed?" Jake burst out again.

"I *did* clean his toilets. He let me out of the deal, Jake. He released me before ..." Nick shook his head. "I can't believe this! I had *no* duty to help you guys out before. And now? I *really* don't!"

"Nickie, we're family." His father placed a hand on Nick's nearest forearm. "We know that you sacrificed for us. You're, undoubtedly, the only reason that Bane gave us the deal at all." Jake opened his mouth to dispute that, but Charles sent him one of his famous quelling looks and Jake's mouth slammed shut with an audible click. "It's obvious to anyone with two brain cells that Bane was attracted to you *before* he made us the deal. Am I right, Nickie, or am I right?"

Nick thought about not answering him. He didn't want to reveal anything to his family about himself or Bane. But he realized that this was unreasonable and his father had figured it out anyways so he nodded.

"And you had the *good sense* to accept his advances." His father smiled at him genially.

"It's not like that, Dad! I *really* care for him. I'm not doing this so he'll give you Fairfax International back," Nick gritted out.

His father's astute gaze regarded him for long moments. "God, you are so like your mother! And that is a *good* thing, too, so long as you have her common sense as well."

"What do you mean?" Steven was the one to ask, putting his glasses back on his face.

"Though Bane likes to pretend that he and I are a different species, the truth is that we are quite alike," Charles explained and an actual fond expression graced his face. "I'm ruthless, never pretended otherwise, and married to my work. I thought I had no room for a woman in my life, but then I met your mother and the things that used to matter to me suddenly didn't so much any longer. I had other concerns. I had you boys." Charles spread his arms wide and smiled at the three of them. "The thing is that I believe that while Bane is like me, I also think that Nick is just like your mother."

"You think Nick and Bane are going to get married?" Jake crossed his arms over his chest.

Charles looked at his eldest son with a touch of weariness. "I *think* that if Nick means as much to Bane as your mother meant to me that we won't just be getting Fairfax International back—"

"Dad! I'm not dating Bane so you can make more money or get into his businesses or—"

"Of course not, Nickie, but things might go a certain *course* if you keep it together." Charles patted his hand.

"Bane and I have just started dating! I have no idea where this is going to go. I know you're worried, but I'm sure that things will be fine for you guys. I won't let you down, but I'm not dating Bane to restore the family business or anything like that," Nick insisted again, feeling as if no matter how many times or how many different ways he said this that his father wasn't listening to him.

Charles patted his hand again to placate him. "I understand, son. Now let's have some lunch and you and I should talk alone afterwards."

Nick thought he was going to be miserable during the meal, but he had forgotten the *other* side to his father, the charming side, the side that had them all laughing at his stories. And that was the side that Charles employed the entire time they ate.

The meal started with a salad of fresh greens and bright, bursting cherry tomatoes. Then they were served delicious ravioli stuffed with veal and ricotta in a sage and butter sauce. There was a delicate fish course that followed. The fish was so fresh that it melted in Nick's mouth. Finally, they finished with hunks of rich taleggio cheese for dessert.

His father was sipping a cappuccino when his brothers took their leave, muttering that they had to return to work. Charles leaned back in his chair, looking satisfied and happy as he stared out at the passersby. Nick was tense, because he expected his father to return to the subject of him and Bane at any second. He wasn't disappointed.

"A man like Bane needs taking care of, Nick. Do you know how to do that?" Charles asked.

Nick agreed with his father that Bane needed caring for. Omar though was quite a bit better at it than he was. "I'm learning."

Charles nodded as if that was the expected—and *right*—answer. "Have you started sleeping together?"

"DAD!" Nick's cheeks flushed a nuclear red. He leaned forward and whispered, "I'm *not* going to tell you about what we do in bed."

"Keep him interested, Nickie. Be adventurous and eager to explore. Be giving," Charles advocated, ignoring Nick's squawk of protest and didn't lower his voice at all.

Nick crossed his arms over his chest even as he wished he could disappear. "I'm already like that, Dad. I don't need *you* to tell me."

"And make sure you look *nice*. Wear those suits he had got for you. Don't go around in shorts and t-shirts like you always do," Charles said, which had Nick groaning.

"Bane *likes* me in shorts!" Then hearing what he had just said, he dropped his head against the back of the chair. "I cannot believe we're having this conversation."

"There's an *art* to being in a real relationship, Nickie. I'm betting that Bane likes to dote on you. Accept it, but don't get spoilt. Act surprised *especially* when he does something nice that you expect. Your mother always acted like the roses I got her every Friday were a surprise," Charles said and an unfamiliar soft smile was on his face.

"You miss her." Nick suddenly realized that it was sadness in his father's tone that he was hearing.

"I do. Every single day." Charles reached and patted Nick's nearest forearm. This patting thing was getting out of hand. "You really are so like her."

Nick wanted to ask his father why, if he was so like the wife he loved and lost, that Charles didn't treat him better? Why was he the outsider in the family? Why was he made to feel like everything he cared about was wrong or stupid? But he didn't ask those questions. He sat there, silent, staring into his own coffee cup at the remains of the rich cream.

"Bane likes my photography," Nick said suddenly. He had his phone with him and could show Charles his work if his father wanted to see it.

"Oh, Nick, don't show him your art. Men like that only *claim* to like what you're doing when they really don't care,"

Charles said with a dismissive wave of his hand. "They're happy that you're happy and *occupied*. But running a business empire and taking your little pictures are *hardly* of the same importance."

Nick's cheeks flamed for a very different reason this time: anger. A hard, cold ball appeared in his stomach. "Bane doesn't think that way. His mother was an artist. He's insisting that I concentrate on my photography. Makes sure that I have everything I need and as much time as I want to work. Bane's very sensitive to art and—"

"All right, son, but just don't *bore* him with it. Be careful you're not just seeing what you *want* to see instead of what's actually *there*." Charles finished his coffee. "Just remember that when it comes down to it, it's *Bane* who matters the *most* in the relationship. Forget that and you might lose him and we might ... well, we won't talk about that."

Nick felt that hard, cold lump in his stomach grow larger. He watched as his father paid the bill, signing the receipt with his typical flourish and winking at the cute waitress who had served them. Nick stood up when his father did, feeling numb and sick. Charles was looking at him avuncularly. He did the customary hug-pat.

"We need to keep closer in touch, Nickie. If you have any questions about what to do with Bane—"

"Yeah, sure, Dad, I'll call you," Nick interrupted. He had *no* intention of calling his father about *anything* ever.

His father didn't seem to notice his coldness. Charles just nodded and smiled before joining the crowd and disappearing into Winter Haven's streets. Nick stood there for long moments. He didn't know what he felt. Rage? Despair? Dread? His father had made him afraid, he realized. Afraid that Bane didn't really care about him. Afraid that he really didn't matter. Afraid that he'd picked a man *just like his father* to love.

Nick shook himself.

That's such crap! My father doesn't know anything about Bane. And they are NOT alike!

Nick left Mangino's with his head held high. He was to meet Bane back in front of the DeClare Building in about ten minutes. He knew he would be there a little early, but he hoped the billionaire would be there early, too. He really needed to see Bane, hear Bane's voice, feel Bane's touch. That would erase every doubt and baseless fear the lunch had raised.

Nick turned the corner. The DeClare Building was directly ahead of him. He smiled. He was going to see Bane in moments!

And then he did see Bane.

Bane and Devon Wainwright exited the DeClare Building, arm in arm. Both of them were laughing and couldn't have looked happier.

CHAPTER SEVENTEEN

UNEXPECTED MEETING?

E*arlier ...*
Bane had doubts about leaving Nick alone with Charles for lunch. As he watched Nick walk to the restaurant, he told himself that it was *just lunch*. What could Charles possibly do to Nick at lunch? Yet his own father could do quite a bit of damage during a single meal.

Charles is not like Richard though. For all of Charles' faults, he is not a monster.

Yet hadn't Charles hurt Nick in the past? Hadn't he thrown Nick to Bane to do whatever he wished for a whole year? That had him amending his thoughts. Charles could *not* be trusted with his Nick. He should be kept as far away from Nick as possible. Bane would like nothing more than to ensure that they never saw one another again. Again, that little voice that sounded a lot like Omar, pointed out that it wasn't right for Bane to *hope* Nick was cut off from his family.

How Charles Fairfax ever had such a son is one of the mysteries of the universe!

Yet he knew that disentangling Nick from his family would likely be a slow process and he had to move carefully about it. So he didn't object to the lunch and, after dropping Nick off, Bane had forced himself to go to Sloan Wu's law office in the

DeClare Building even as he felt the beast's attention scanning the city for Nick's spiritual signature. The full moon was approaching and the beast wasn't sulking like it usually was. It was far more alert, far more aware of Nick.

That dream that Nick had, that was your doing, wasn't it? He asked the beast.

The beast's tail thumped like a metronome, but said nothing. Bane tried not to be angry or frustrated by that. He'd lived a long time without the beast speaking to him. The fact that it had started to intermittently shouldn't matter. He shouldn't *hope* to hear its voice. Or so he told himself.

You will keep our bargain, won't you? You won't try to take over from me until the full moon? And you won't harm Nick?

The beast regarded him through hooded eyes, tail still thumping, ears still pricked for Nick's voice.

If you betray me ... he stopped. If the beast did then both their lives were ruined. *Nick only stays with us because he does not know about you. And it has to stay that way.*

The tail paused in its movements and he thought that was agreement. But then he thought of how the beast had appeared in Nick's dream without him, encouraged Nick to pet it and even lay down beside it! There was no harm, he supposed, if the beast kept its visits to Nick solely in dreams. But he feared the beast would forget that a tiger in *dreams* was far different than a tiger in *life*.

Bane stepped into the elevator that took him to the top floor where Sloan had her office. The receptionist, a man in his early twenties, practically jumped up from the glass and steel desk to greet him. He immediately took Bane into Sloan's office. She stood up and was about to come around her desk to greet him when he waved her down. She was on the phone, speaking through her bluetooth to another client. The receptionist departed quickly after Bane refused an offer of water or coffee. He sat down opposite Sloan and crossed his long legs casually one over the other.

Sloan signed off with her other client and took the earpiece from her ear. She regarded him over the black, onyx desk. He regarded her back. Her long hair was drawn back in a sleek ponytail tied at the base of her skull. She wore a charcoal-colored shirt suit with white silk shirt and a strand of pearls around her throat. Like the rest of her deceptively simple, minimalistic office, she appeared neat and spare, but it all cost the earth.

"So, Bane, you look well," she said in that quiet, purring way of hers.

He couldn't help but smile, because the cause of the glow about him was Nick and thinking of Nick always made him smile. "I *am* well."

"You have news to share with me?" she asked, her head tilting slightly to the side in a birdlike manner.

A trickle of alarm went through him. He guarded his privacy jealousy yet it seemed that she already knew of Nick. Sloan had her ways of finding things out, but he and Nick had just begun a relationship. They hadn't even left Moon Shadow together until today. Yet he was *certain* she knew all about it.

"What news would that be?" he hedged.

She held herself very still and looked at him out of dark eyes. "You left for Europe the day after that unpleasantness with Dean. You sent me a text letting me know that the deal regarding the Fairfaxes as to Nick was void yet Nick continued—and *continues*—to stay at Moon Shadow. During your time in Europe, you returned no phone calls or emails. Henri, who caught sight of you over there, reported to me that you looked ghastly. You returned just last week and you're now glowing and ready to work. Hence, *something* has changed. Therefore, what is your news?"

Bane recalled vaguely seeing Henri LeBlanc in the street in Paris. They had spoken briefly. Bane had been desperate to get away. He had little recollection of what he or Henri had said. Henri reporting this to Sloan could be viewed as concern or interference. He didn't know which he thought it was.

"Why don't you tell me what you *think* that news is, Sloan," he suggested.

She sighed and shifted in her seat. "Anyone with half a brain could see your feelings for Nick during that disastrous weekend."

"Disastrous for *Nick*. Hardly for you," he pointed out, annoyed somehow that she would find it disastrous when nothing happened to her at all.

She waved that away. "I felt for the young man. He seemed quite nice and ... innocent."

"He is more than nice," Bane said loyally.

She tipped her head. "I'm not surprised to hear it. So you *are* dating him?"

Dating sounded so juvenile and there was nothing teenagerish in what he felt about Nick. His relationship, if one could really call it that, with Alastair had been teenagerish. He was amazed at how telling Nick what had happened with Alastair had truly freed him of it.

If only I could tell him of the beast ...

Realizing that Sloan was still waiting for his answer and fearing she would think his delay was a reflection on his feelings for Nick, he quickly said, "Yes, we're together."

Again, she stared at him a long time and when he said nothing more, she said, "On the phone you said wanted to talk about the other Fairfaxes."

"Yes, I want to know what trouble Charles and his other sons have tried to get into," Bane said.

There was the smallest of hesitations from Sloan as if that was *not* what she had expected him to say, but then she was all business. She brought up a document on her Mac iBook and scanned it. Her voice was cool and professional as she said, "The Fairfaxes are actually doing *well*. We've caught most of their excesses such as eliminating positions and ending charitable contributions. The other things they are suggesting *would* increase profits, but are skirting very close to the edge of the law though not passing over it."

"You know I'm not comfortable with playing fast and loose," he told her.

She nodded. "I'll have the questionable plans vetoed. They *are* very good businessmen—especially, Charles—even if they have the morals of raptors," she smiled as she said the last. "They're keeping within the deal though one wonders if they are truly within the *spirit* of it. Though does that really matter *now*?"

He blinked at her in confusion. "What do you mean 'does it matter'? Of course it matters!"

She tilted her head to the side and regarded him for long silent moments. "You are with Nick."

"Yes."

"And that's not changing the deal with the Fairfaxes?" She folded her hands before her on the desk as if expecting him to say something or order her to do something. He had no idea what she was getting at.

"I'm not sure I understand," he said.

Again, she stared at him and then lowered her gaze. "Bane, I'm not one to interfere in your personal life ..."

"Say what you have to say, Sloan," he ordered.

She lifted her gaze again. "Don't you think that keeping the Fairfax family's fortunes beholden to the deal will adversely impact your relationship with Nick?"

He stared at her back for long moments, no thoughts in his head, before saying, "No, Nick is ... is *separate* from his family. He dislikes them as much as ... as anyone."

Sloan regarded him again in that intense way, but he could not read her thoughts. "I see. Well, if that changes, please let me know."

He wanted to tell her that, of course, it wouldn't change. He'd released Nick from the deal and he would provide for the young man, but his family? Again the surety flowed through him that Nick would be better off without them in his life. If Bane could he would banish Charles, Steven and Jake from Winter Haven so that Nick never had to see them again. Nick, undoubtedly, saw things the same way.

He and Sloan spent the rest of the hour discussing his other business ventures. When that was done, he gratefully rose from the spindly metal and leather chair that barely contained his massive frame, knowing that she had another client. Not that she would ever be the first one to say anything about his going. If he wished to stay there all day, her other clients would wait. This made Bane more assiduous about checking her schedule and watching the time so that he did not run over their appointed hour.

"Continue to monitor the Fairfaxes for me, Sloan. I appreciate the hard work," he said.

She gave his hand a firm shake and he left her sleek office, still wondering what she had been getting at about Nick's family. Nick was separate from his father and brothers. Nick hated his family's business. Nick wouldn't even call his father except under duress. There was no real fondness whatsoever between Nick and his older brothers either. There was only familial duty, which Bane thought proper ... *in its place*. But with time and distance from them, Nick, surely, would be content to let his family rise or fall on their own merits.

Bane was so deep in thought as he waited for the elevators to take him down to the lobby to await Nick that he barely noticed when someone stepped up beside him. The scent was familiar, but the beast did not alert him as it normally did of Devon's presence.

"Bane?" Devon's smiling face suddenly appeared in his line of vision.

Bane jerked upright in surprise. "D-Devon! I—I didn't hear you approach."

"I was being *stealthy*," Devon laughed.

"Ah, well ... it is nice to see you," Bane said awkwardly. The truth was that it wasn't *nice* to see Devon. He had rather hoped to never see the other man again, but that was unworthy of him and impractical considering the amount of charitable work he did with the young man. His affections had turned to Nick and he had treated Devon rather badly over it. He had not even considered calling Devon to see if he was all right after driving Dean home in the middle of the night. He had not been a gentleman with Devon. He had Nick now. He was fully happy. He didn't need to be petty with Devon. He should be kind. With that in mind, he said, "I'm actually glad to see you. I've been thinking about the last time we were together at Moon Shadow with Dean."

Darkness passed through Devon's eyes for a moment, but then he was smiling and his face was placid once more. "Ah, yes, Dean."

"I wanted to—to thank you for taking him *away*," Bane said, the word "away" sticking on his tongue. He would rather have tossed Dean out on the street and had the bastard walk back to Winter Haven.

"No need to thank me. The whole situation was a mess and … well, if I helped clean it up in any small way, I'm glad," Devon replied evenly.

The elevator doors whispered open and Bane allowed Devon to enter first. Devon pressed the button for the lobby as soon as Bane stepped in.

"I don't know if you've heard, but Hermitage Pharmaceuticals' financial difficulties went public and the stock tanked," Devon said, his voice deceptively neutral.

Bane's jaw clenched. He couldn't care less that the attempted rapist's company was cratering. He felt for the people who worked there, but not Dean. "Yes, but that wasn't really unforeseen, was it?"

"No, like I told you, Dean's reaching out to the Fairfaxes was his Hail Mary pass," Devon said. "Since that night with Nick, he's stopped drinking and –"

"I don't care, Devon," Bane's voice was clipped. "I can see that you want to excuse his actions—for some reason—but there *is* no excuse. When you get drunk do you try to rape young men?"

"No, of course not."

"Then why would you try to excuse Dean's actions by claiming *alcohol* is the culprit? Being drunk didn't make him do that. It's a part of who he is."

The elevator announced their arrival at the lobby. This time Bane didn't allow Devon to go first. Instead, he stepped out into the cool, marble lobby, intent on getting away from the other man.

"Bane, wait!" Devon plucked at the sleeve of his shirt.

Bane turned to look at the other man, a scowl on his face. "What?"

Devon looked stricken. "I'm sorry. I didn't mean ... what Dean did to Nick was unforgivable."

"And?" Bane's eyebrows rose, waiting for Devon's inevitable and inexplicable defense of the man.

"And *nothing*. I was wrong to defend him. It was just ..." Devon ran a hand through his hair and sighed. "You know he was a family friend for years and I—I have good memories of him. It's hard sometimes to let those go."

Bane's gaze slid from Devon to the bright, sunlit streets beyond the doors. He thought of what he himself had done to Nick with the deal. Many would consider that unforgivable, too. But Nick had forgiven him. Perhaps he could accept—if not understand—that Devon might still have a softness for the man?

"I understand, Devon, but I must ask that you not bring up Dean again with me. We see him differently," Bane said.

"Of course. I was stupid to—to do it this time. I don't know what I was thinking," Devon confessed.

"You were trying to reconnect," Bane said, recognizing it.

"Yes." Devon gave him a wry smile. He put his hands on his hips and looked towards the doors. "I was. Things changed between us so quickly, Bane, and I'm not sure what happened."

I fell in love with Nick, Bane thought and his mind stuttered on the word "love". It had come to him so naturally.

Devon glanced up at him through his lashes. "I heard you went to Europe."

"I did. I needed to ... do some business there," Bane lied.

"And Nick stayed at Moon Shadow?"

"Yes."

"Well, of course, he did. He's working for you," Devon quickly clarified.

"No, he's not," Bane answered and for some reason felt his cheeks burn. He had no reason to feel guilty. The thing between him and Devon had been casual and non-exclusive. He had every right to be with Nick. Yet this conversation was not one he was keen to have.

Devon's brown eyes widened for a moment and then another quick flash of knowledge crossed his features. "So you *did* decide to pursue him after all and you released him from the deal?"

"I did," Bane answered curtly. "We are together now."

"Yes, I can see that in your expression. So it's going well?"

"Very well." Bane remembered Devon's expressed intention to continue to pursue him even after he had revealed his feelings for Nick to Devon during the ill-considered weekend. He had a sudden strange thought: had Devon been in Sloan's office to reconnect with him? Had Henri called Sloan or had Henri called *Devon* and had Devon told Sloan about his appearance? He was, undoubtedly, being paranoid. Why would either Sloan or Devon lie to him? "Devon, what brought you here?"

"Oh, I had charity business with one of Sloan's partners," Devon said with a blythe wave of his hand as if it was no concern. Somehow that made Bane *less* easy in his thinking.

"Well, it was a happy coincidence then that we met up." Bane gave him a tight smile.

The beast was very still in his chest. Its ears flickered. It felt like it was being stalked. It didn't like that.

"Very happy. I'd love to get coffee or a drink and catch up if you have the time," Devon said just as Bane turned his feet towards the exit, ready to go outside to meet with Nick. "There are a few events that your companies are hosting for me that we should get some details on."

"I'm meeting Nick –"

"That's no problem. The three of us should talk. The next event is on Friday and we haven't confirmed some of the key details. I'm sure Nick wouldn't mind sharing you for a few glasses of whisky, would he?" Devon gave him his most winning smile.

Bane didn't answer as he sought an excuse to break away, but he'd forgotten about the Friday event. It was often easier to get the details worked out in person than through emails and texts. Yet he didn't wish to continue spending time in Devon's presence. He wanted Nick rather desperately. He wanted Nick and him to be *alone* rather desperately.

"Let's walk and talk. I want to get out of this air conditioning." Bane started walking to the revolving doors. He stepped inside one and exited out onto the street. The warmth of the summer sun embraced him and his shoulders immediately eased. The beast told him that Nick was near and a huge smile crossed his face at the anticipation of seeing him.

Devon stepped out onto the street beside him. "Nick's a photographer –"

"An excellent one. His work is exquisite," Bane quickly said.

"Good. Maybe we can work in some of Nick's art with the next event," Devon suggested.

Bane's first instinct was to say 'no' because he did not wish to have Devon and Nick in the same room, let alone having to interact with one another. He knew that Nick was jealous of Devon, though there was no reason to be.

But this would be good exposure for Nick's work and it would be for a good cause.

"I think that would be an interesting idea," Bane said carefully. He started smiling and the beast's tail was wagging as suddenly he smelled Nick's scent on the wind.

"That's great!" Devon took his arm companionably. "We can turn this chance encounter into the beginning of something wonderful."

"Yes." Bane turned his head towards where the scent was coming from and he saw Nick approaching. He grinned wider until he saw Nick's expression.

The young man's steps had slowed. He had clearly seen Bane and Devon. The look on his face was stricken.

CHAPTER EIGHTEEN

UP IN SMOKE

N ick felt like he was in Hell.
How else would one describe being at the exclusive whisky and cigar club, Smoke, with your lover and his former "perfect" boyfriend?

They were seated in a soft-as-butter leather u-shaped booth with a wide mahogany table between them. Bane was in the middle with Nick on one side and Devon on the other. The seating arrangement made it feel like they were *sharing* the billionaire instead of Bane being all Nick's. It also allowed Devon to keep touching Bane's arm. A pat. A stroke. A squeeze. A lingering brush of fingers of Bane's elegant wrist. Nick's blood boiled so he took another sip of whisky and grimaced.

I hate whisky. But Bane and Devon seem to love it. All part of the ambiance of this place. He glanced over at Bane who was leaning back in the booth, looking relaxed and rather debonair as he sipped the amber liquid. *And I wanted to show Bane that I could be cool with whatever he and Devon did. I'd rather be any place else than here.* Then he remembered the lunch with his family and amended that to, *Any place else, but with Dad and my brothers.*

Nick had never been to Smoke before himself, but he'd heard it was a place where young men hooked up with older

227

men for a *fee*. Certainly not a place that he would ever think of going, though he knew of a few guys in his year at school who had supposedly done it to pay for tuition. How much sex was a whole year's worth of tuition? Nick didn't want to know.

The club looked like the library of a wealthy man with all the mahogany, leather and fine whisky on display. The smoking of cigars was restricted to an air controlled room with a glass fronted door. Nick could see through the door. Curls of smoke reached for the room's ceiling as men puffed and laughed. He wondered if his father had ever come here. Not for the young men—Charles was straight—but for the sort of jocular companionship that a place restricted to the masculine sex seemed to produce in some men. Besides, his father would like to rub elbows with all the wealthy men here. Make friends or rather make *deals*.

"More business is done during a game of golf than ever in the boardroom," Charles had told him and his brothers every chance he could. For that reason alone, Nick had avoided golf like the plague. If only he had done the same with Smoke.

No matter where he looked, he *saw* the secret side of Smoke. Age-spotted hands with buffed nails curled around young, taut waists. Silver heads bent down to whisper into the ear of pretty young men who smiled and nodded or leaned up and gave lingering, pornographic kisses. Nick squirmed in his chair with unwanted arousal mixed with disgust flowing through him. He saw asses patted and squeezed. Hands sliding beneath clothes. More wet kisses. He didn't see any money exchanged—he assumed that was too crass for Smoke—but he was sure it was happening somewhere.

You'd have to be so desperate to do this. Needing money. Needing companionship. So why are we even here?

But he knew the answer to that question. Devon had to meet with some of the men who were funding his charities. Evidently, they spent their money equally in sinner and saint fashion. Though Devon was at the table now, he had drifted away several times, a cat-like smile on his lips, as he spoke to the older men there, whispering in their ears, exchanging smoky laughter, accepting brushes of lips on his cheek, even though they were aimed at his *lips*. Devon was *too old* and *too rich* to be a boy here, but he was still beautiful and alluring. He knew how to play the room. Nick had never felt so very young or naive before.

"I have to go where the money is, Bane," Devon had said to them on the street outside of the DeClare Building. Bane had started at his choice of bar, but Devon had explained, "It's for a good cause." Then with a malicious sparkle in his eye, he'd added, "Bane, you really can't object! You're a *member* there still, aren't you?"

"What?!" Nick's gaze had slid to Bane.

The billionaire had gone very still and high spots of color graced his cheeks. When his Siberian blue eyes met Nick's they were unreadable. "It's not as ... *seedy* as it sounds, Nick."

"I'm sure it's not. I mean ..." Nick's voice petered off. "I just don't know why *you* would need to be a member of a club like that. You're a catch, Bane."

Why would you need to pay for sex? Was the unasked question. But then again, he knew that Bane had been leery of real connections since Alastair. Maybe he found paying for sex appealing. Less stressful. No strings attached. No one talking about love and fate. Just a meeting of bodies.

Devon said as much when he answered for Bane, "Before you, Nick, there were times when Bane simply wanted companionship without the *complications* of feelings and courtship."

Bane flinched, but didn't contradict Devon.

"Did he meet you at Smoke, Devon?" Nick asked, eyes narrowing. Devon shouldn't get in all the barbs. But his barb ended up more like the softest of strokes.

"Me? No!" Devon laughed, seemingly delighted to be compared to a prostitute. He looked fondly at Bane. "We met somewhere completely different."

"Perhaps we should get together another time, Devon. Smoke is *not* the place for Nick and if you truly need to be there tonight ..." Bane let the sentence hang.

But Nick suddenly felt like if he couldn't "handle" Smoke while Devon could, that he would have failed in some way. He wouldn't be sophisticated enough for Bane. He wouldn't fit into Bane's world. "No, it's totally okay, Bane. I'm fine with it."

"Are you certain?" Bane's forehead furrowed.

"Totally," Nick lied.

Now he was wishing that his pride hadn't gotten in the way of his common sense. As much as he wanted to be nonchalant about what happened at Smoke, he couldn't. Part of him wondered what would have happened if he had somehow met Bane in this club instead of in his father's office. Would Bane have chosen Nick out of the crowd of young lovelies just *begging* to be picked to share his bed? Would Nick have been bold enough to meet Bane's Siberian blue eyes, take his hand and pull it around his shoulders, and kiss his cheek and then his lips?

Who am I kidding? I can't even touch Bane now and he's my lover.

But was the sex on display and for sale what was holding him back? Or was it the way that Devon and Bane were talking—about the old times, about their countless shared memories? He felt self-conscious, out of place and just wanted to go back to Moon Shadow as quickly as possible. But he had to hide all that. Otherwise, Devon would have won.

Nick took another sip of whisky and, immediately, coughed again as the fiery liquor ran down his throat. He hoped the sound was covered up by the sensual jazz that was playing, but Devon zeroed in on it immediately.

"Nick, are you all right?" Devon asked.

Nick smiled at him thinly. "I'm fine, just ... the atmosphere is a little close."

Bane frowned. "Is the smoke bothering you? It should be contained in the cigar room, but we could —"

"No, no, I'm good," Nick said even as his throat tickled. He was positive some smoke was leaking out of the cigar area. But he would *not* admit defeat.

"Oh, I'm so glad," Devon didn't seem glad at all. He took another long, sensual sip of whiskey before saying, "This is more of a *mature* person's place. I'm sure you and your college friends have never come here."

"No, *my* friends don't, but I know people who have," Nick answered.

"Looking for sugar daddies?" Devon eyes gazed at him from atop the tumbler of whisky rather like a cat might regard prey. "Wanting someone to pick up the *tab*?"

Nick had thought to get another jab in, to show he wasn't so naive, but, once more, Devon managed to turn the entire thing around on him.

"Yeah, some, I guess," Nick mumbled, red-faced.

"But *you* never did, right? Older men weren't your preference ... I mean *before* they weren't your preference?" Devon's eyes flickered to Bane meaningfully.

Nick's teeth gritted. He was trying to think of a clever comeback when Bane saved him. The billionaire put an arm around Nick's shoulders.

"I am actually quite glad that I am Nick's *first* older man. He's made an exception for me," Bane said.

Nick looked up into Bane's face gratefully. "You're one of a kind."

Bane brushed his lips against Nick's temple. Nick curled against him. He knew it made them look like the other couples here. But he wasn't with Bane for the money.

Although Dad thinks I should be.

"You said something earlier about a charity event where I could exhibit some of my work, didn't you?" Nick asked, finally drawing the conversation back to the only thing that was stopping him from leaping from the booth and flying out of Smoke. That and Bane's arm around his shoulders. "How exactly would that work?"

"Well, one of the charity's core elements I'm working on is to support rehabbing of old buildings for new uses. Cleaning up any environmental contamination and making the places habitable again often as affordable housing in formerly blighted areas," Devon explained. "We are having the event in the latest building to be rehabbed. The space has a plethora of white walls. Having artwork of the transformation of Moon Shadow would show some of what can be done."

"But Moon Shadow wasn't environmentally contaminated!" Nick protested.

"No, but it was abandoned and would have been torn down if not for Bane buying and restoring it. I admit that it isn't a perfect fit, but your photos will add interest to the walls."

Nick resisted saying that Devon could buy a few prints at the local charity shops for that. After all, Devon hadn't seen his work. But once he did, once other people did, Nick was sure his art would add to the event. Moon Shadow was gorgeous and practically sold itself.

"And so long as you are fine with all profits for the pictures going to the charity ..." Devon shrugged his muscular shoulders and took another long sip of whisky.

"Bane, are you okay with using pictures of Moon Shadow?" Nick asked. "I know how much you like your privacy."

"I actually am eager to show it and your artwork off." Bane squeezed his shoulders. "Your photographs are *excellent*. And I am not just saying that, Nick. You have true talent. Devon will see. Everyone will see."

"Well, then, I guess I'm good with it." Nick smiled. "When is this event?"

"Friday," Devon said.

"F-Friday? That's two days from now!" Nick cried.

Bane froze against him, too.

"Is that a problem?" Devon asked almost innocently.

"Getting the photographs printed and then hung and then −"

"Well, if you *cannot* do it then there will be another time ... perhaps," Devon said with another shrug.

"But I want to! I just ... there's a lot to do." Nick ran a hand through his hair. "I'd have to see the space. I'd need access to it as soon as possible."

"Of course. Whatever you need I'm sure can be arranged," Devon murmured.

"Just do what you can, Nick," Bane said, but his voice sounded strange. "We'll all help you."

"I've got to call Jade!" Nick laughed. "If I could get into the space tomorrow that would be ideal."

"Of course. What's your number? I'll text you the address. We could meet at 8 am," Devon suggested as he lifted his phone.

Nick gave his number to Devon and watched as the address of his first show was texted to him.

"Excellent. I am looking forward to seeing your work, Nick. Bane, as always, it was wonderful to see you." Devon drained his glass then and stood up. "But I must take my leave. I have more business to attend to."

Nick found himself looking at Devon with *almost* affection. Maybe he had misjudged the man. He *was* giving Nick a chance to show off his art. And now it appeared he was leaving. So maybe this jaunt to Smoke hadn't been a complete waste.

"Thanks, Devon," Nick said with a wave.

"See you tomorrow, Nick."

And then he disappeared into the crowd. Nick stared after him, still thinking on all he would have to do. Once he saw the space, he would know how many pictures he would need. He could have them printed and put on posterboard. Not ideal. But there was no way he could frame them. And then—Bane's hand was on his arm, stopping his thoughts in their tracks.

"You are a million miles away from me and I cannot bear that, Nick," Bane's voice was low and skated over his skin.

For a moment, Nick remembered his father's words about how Bane should be *first* in their relationship, that Nick's art wasn't *really* that important, and he swallowed.

"I was just thinking of all I have to do," Nick confessed, softly, uncertainly.

Bane's hands roamed over his back and sides. A tigerish grin appearing on Bane's face that had heat building between Nick's thighs. "Do we have to get home so you can start?"

"I—No. I can't do anything until I see the space," Nick admitted.

Bane's hands slid down to his waist. "Then tonight is still ours?"

Ours ... as if my art is just mine ...

"I want you to help me, you know? Moon Shadow is what will really impress people more than my pictures," Nick said, feeling his focus leave his art and turn to Bane. Bane. Bane.

The billionaire was *so close*. His lips, sculpted and plush, were right there to kiss.

"Of course, Nick. I'll help any way I can," Bane promised.

And then their lips met. A soft press of mouths. A slow slide of tongues. Heat bloomed like roses inside of him. Nick's hands fisted in the front of Bane's fine cotton shirt. The billionaire surged against him and Nick gasped. He turned his head, blushing hotly.

"What's wrong?" Bane made those words sound like the most sinful thing.

"People are looking," Nick whispered. He darted a glance into the rest of the club. Some *were* watching the two of them. Just like he had been watching *them*. And, to his shock, his erection pushed *harder* against the front of his zipper.

"They are." Bane's fingers drew along Nick's jaw, lifting his chin up so that they were eye to eye. "They're seeing that you are *mine*. They can't touch you. They can't have you. They can only *wish*."

"I'm surprised that you want to share even the *sight* of me with them, because I don't want to share *you*," Nick admitted, his voice low.

"Perhaps not." Bane's eyes *glowed* again in the dark. A preternatural light that Nick could not deny. Nick gasped. "What, my dearest one?"

"*Magic*," Nick murmured.

"*Magic?*" Bane's voice had a strange dark quality as he said that.

For a moment, the glow in Bane's eyes *shimmered* in the low light of Smoke. But between one blink and the next, it was gone and Nick blinked himself. The glow had vanished, but he'd seen it.

"Nothing. Just ... you sometimes seem so *unreal* to me. Unreal that I'm with you. Unreal that you want me. Unreal that anything like this could be true," Nick confessed awkwardly. He couldn't tell Bane he kept imagining his eyes *glowing*. That was absurd.

"Come away with me, Nick," Bane murmured against the cusp of his ear.

Nick's heart stuttered in his chest. He found he couldn't speak. All he could do was nod and let Bane lead them wherever he wanted.

CHAPTER NINETEEN

DON'T RUN

Bane stood up from the booth, drawing Nick up with him. Their bodies moved as one. He felt the other older men in the club's appraisal of Nick. He knew that with Nick's delicate features, platinum hair and lean, lithe body he was *just* the type that many of them went for. Yet they would be missing the true beauty of Nick by lusting and caring *only* about his outer shell. That Bane had counted himself among their number not all that time ago caused a shudder to go through him. His life had been so empty before Nick.

As they walked, hand in hand, through the crowd of men and boys, the beast growled low in the back of its throat. It would *not* allow any of these others near their mate. Not that any did come terribly close. Even without knowing he was a tiger shifter, the men in that room already believed he would rip them to shreds for touching what was *his*.

As soon as they left the close atmosphere of the club and emerged onto the street, Nick spun around to look at him, hand still linked with his, to ask with hooded eyes, "So where should we go? Back to Moon Shadow or –"

"Not quite yet. I thought we might go to the beach," Bane suggested.

"The beach?" Nick blinked, clearly not expecting that answer.

When they had gone into Smoke it was full-on afternoon, the sun beaming down with all its glory, but now it was the dying of the day. The club's windows were blacked out for privacy and to control the amount of light in Smoke, which was always *low*. Coming out and finding that it wasn't either bright day or complete night was almost disconcerting, but was also welcome. Sunset was his favorite time of day.

It's the shift. How ironic.

"I thought we might walk along the beach and watch the sunset," Bane said. "There's a perfect view from the private beach outside of my condo."

He knew that being out in the moonlight this close to the full moon was normally dangerous for him, but the beast seemed happy and content. Bane's notoriously bad temper around the full moon was also completely missing.

Omar had remarked upon it that morning, "Bane, you are as bright as sunshine!"

Bane had grunted. "I wouldn't go *that* far, Omar, but I do feel quite different than usual around this full moon."

He saw the hope in Omar's eyes that the Indian man didn't even attempt to hide. Omar burbled, "It is because of Nick! I really do think he is the one."

Bane was about to give his usual retort about love being an illusion, but he clamped his lips together. Nick had said he loved Bane and Bane *didn't* want to believe that was an illusion. He wanted to believe that it was the *truth*. But even if true love was real and Nick was his one and only, it didn't mean the curse would be lifted. The dream the night before indicated to him that the curse was going nowhere.

"I think even if Nick is my true love, Omar, that it doesn't really matter if he breaks the curse or not. He is a light in our lives and I am grateful enough for that," Bane answered.

That seemed to make Omar *happier* than if Bane had outright agreed with him. "Yes, Bane, I understand perfectly what you mean."

"Is this the awesome condo where you're sending Jade and I this weekend?" Nick asked, breaking him out of his thoughts.

This month for the full moon Bane had finally determined how he was going to get Nick and Jade away from Moon Shadow. He had posed the whole thing as a treat for the two of them. His condo building had a world class spa, not to mention a spectacular pool, and, of course, the ocean itself. Bane had lied and said he had business that would take him out of town and he wanted Jade and Nick to take advantage of a weekend in the city, all expenses paid for. At the mention of the spa, Jade had lit up like a firecracker so any objections to leaving Moon Shadow were washed away by her enthusiasm.

"Yes, it is." He grinned down at Nick as they strolled towards the condo tower that jutted out of the ground like a glass blade at the very outermost edge of the land before the sea swallowed everything.

"You know," Nick began, cuddling against his side, "You might just be Jade's most favorite person ever."

"She enjoys going to spas that much?"

"She's a spa junkie. I never told you about the time when she dragged me to a spa weekend?"

"You had to be *dragged*? You do not like massages?"

Nick laughed. "Actually, I *do* like them! It was the facials, which made me feel like I was being coated in slime and suffocated at the same time by moldy towels that I wasn't all that fond of. The food was also not exactly filling either. They made it all about wellness so there was a lot of juicing and small portions. Needless to say, Jade and I escaped to McDonald's a couple of times. We were like refugees as we shoveled Big Macs into our mouths in total silence. Talking would interrupt the eating, you see, which was what was all important."

"You don't need to worry about that this weekend. There is a five star restaurant in the building called Sapphire, but also, you'll have access to all of Winter Haven's eateries. You did put the credit card I got you in your wallet, didn't you?" Bane had gotten a Visa Black card for Nick to use, which drew directly off of one of Bane's accounts.

"Yeah." He saw Nick shift uncomfortably out of the corner of his eye.

"Why are you uncomfortable with the card? We discussed this. You need to concentrate on your photography. Taking on an additional job to simply make money would get in the way of that," Bane repeated the argument he'd used before. While he believed in this wholeheartedly, he also wanted to simply take care of Nick and give him everything he needed or wanted.

"Because I don't want to take advantage of you. And I don't want you thinking I *expect* or *want* your money," Nick answered with a mulish tilt of his pretty chin.

"I know you aren't," Bane assured him and he *was* certain of it. There was that faint memory of Alastair, but he didn't believe Nick would ever put money above love.

Yet a part of him was glad that he still had a hold over Nick's family. He knew that he could be difficult at times—perhaps difficult was an understatement—and with the complications of the beast ... well, giving Nick *another* reason to stay with him was likely *wise*. He immediately felt ashamed of thinking this. He knew it wasn't worthy. But he felt it nonetheless. Maybe he didn't think of love as an illusion, but he feared it wasn't as strong a motivator as most people thought it was.

"I got a letter from school saying that my next year's tuition is all paid for, too." Nick glanced over at Bane through his lashes. "We didn't talk about *that*."

Bane blushed slightly. "Yes, well, it came due and owing and I ... Nick, I—I wish to do this. You must let me."

Nick's eyebrows crawled up into his hairline. "I must *let* you, huh?"

"Yes. There are some things you must just let me do. And this is one of them. I've spent my money on good things and bad —"

"Like a Smoke membership?" Nick mumbled.

Bane sighed. "Devon *would* have told you know that!"

"I'm not mad at you about it or anything. I *get* the allure of it." There was no lie in Nick's face or voice yet it was hard for Bane to believe that Nick would ever find Smoke alluring.

"Do you?" Bane paused then added, "You put your heart into relationships. That is not how Smoke is set up."

"I imagine that it makes things less complicated though. Less messy. Because the emotions aren't there on either side." Nick shrugged. "I admit I couldn't do it. Though if Dad had gone through with kicking me out, I might have needed the money. But, knowing me, I would have fallen in love with my sugar daddy."

Bane's arm tightened around Nick. "I would have let *no one* else have you, but me."

The beast growled in agreement.

Nick let out a bright laugh. "Can you imagine if we *had* met that way? Would you have wanted me?"

"Of course."

"Enough to pay for me?" Nick's eyes widened in surprise. "I get you wanting to spend money on me *now* when you know me and care for me, but on a complete stranger?"

Bane slowed his steps and stopped, bringing Nick to a halt beside him. They were at the edge of the condo's beach. Nick looked up at him curiously. Bane knew his expression was serious, far more serious than likely Nick had intended for him to be during this conversation.

"Nick, I *did* pay for you before I knew you," Bane said quietly. "Remember? I gave your family the chance to win back their fortunes. That is far more than paying for school or a credit card."

"I ..." Nick actually blanched a little. "I guess you did ..."

"But enough of that. That is in the past. You are with me now of your own free will," Bane said quickly, realizing that this line of talk would lead Nick to think of the fact that his family was *still* in Bane's power. "The beach is nearly deserted. We are in luck."

Nick blinked and turned to look towards the water. Confusion gave way to awe as he breathed, "Oh, it's beautiful."

Bane had to agree. As the sun's rays gilded the water's surface, he found himself growing peaceful. His mind was not spinning as it usually did. He felt no need to be doing anything. Just being here with Nick was more than enough. Even the beast had settled down. It was facing outwards again, its massive head on its forepaws, its eyes halfway shut, regarding Nick and the sunset.

They took off their shoes and socks. Nick helped him roll his pants up to his knees. They left the shoes, with socks tucked inside, by the side of the condo building. The sand was still hot beneath the soles of Bane's feet. They went down to the water's edge and let the waves wash over their feet and calves. Bane dug his toes into the wet, packed sand.

"How was your lunch with your father?" Bane asked. "I didn't get a chance earlier to find out how it went."

Nick let out a choked laugh and ran a hand through his thick curls. "Oh, it *went*."

Bane felt a touch of concern. What had Charles done *now*?

"What did he say? Did he upset you?" Bane asked, his voice clipped. If Charles had made Nick unhappy he really would insist on keeping the man out of their lives.

"Let's just say that he started giving me sexual advice about how to please you," Nick's cheeks were nuclear red as he said this, but seemingly from embarrassment, not hurt.

Bane's eyebrow rose. "Now I am *terrified* about what Charles said to you."

"Oh, you might have liked it." Nick gave him a grin. "It was all about putting you first and advising me to be *adventurous* in bed."

Bane let out a sputtering laugh that was half amusement, half aggravation. "Good grief, Charles is quite *detailed* in his advice to you! I am not certain how I feel about his claimed knowledge about my sexual likes and dislikes."

Nick lowered his head and looked up at Bane through his lashes. "You don't like adventurous sex?"

The sun at that moment limned Nick's cheek and Bane could not help but follow the line of Nick's jaw with his fingers. "Oh, I *do*."

"And do you like to be serviced in bed?"

"Sometimes, but I like to *serve* as well. I would never want a lover to leave my bed unfulfilled," Bane's voice had gone low and smoky.

Nick's hand tightened on his. "I can already attest to that."

"I've hardly had a chance to show you *anything* yet." Bane gave him a tigerish grin.

That blush heightened and flowed underneath the collar of Nick's button-down shirt. "That—that sounds promising."

"I'm glad you think so." Bane flexed his toes in the damp sand again. He lowered his head and asked carefully, "Your father ... he has no problem with you being gay?"

"Oh, God, no! While my father has many faults, being homophobic is *not* one of them." Nick tilted his head and added, "You know Dad really has no problem with anyone because of their orientation, race or religion. To him people are either useful to him or they aren't and that's in the business sense."

"I suppose I should have guessed that considering he was giving you sexual advice, but I just ... worry about you," Bane admitted.

Something—understanding—flowed over Nick's face. "Bane. Oh, Bane, he's not like—like –"

"My father?" Bane's voice did not crack as he said it. He was glad Nick knew all about that now. It made things a lot easier in some ways. "No, I know that. It's strange I never worried about this with Devon or my other lovers, but with you ... with *you*, Nick, I want to be so careful. I want to *protect* you."

Nick stopped and cupped Bane's face. "I love when you say stuff like that. You make me feel *treasured*."

Love. Again that word trips off his tongue and I believe it.

Bane's eyes left Nick's and went to the horizon again. He burst out, "The sun! Nick, it is setting. Let us not miss it."

The sun was dipping behind the horizon. Nick turned and looked at it with him. Bane's hands were on the young man's shoulders and he felt as much as heard the soft sigh of pleasure Nick gave at seeing it.

The sky was painted purple, red, gold and orange. It was a traveler's sky—or that's how Bane thought of them. Traveler's skies were so heartrendingly beautiful that they made him want to travel, to go someplace where life's greater meanings could be found.

Nick turned in his arms and kissed him then. It was a sweet press of lips that lasted only a short time. Too short. Bane stood with his eyes closed for a moment after Nick pulled back though his hands remained resting on Bane's chest. Finally, Bane opened his eyes and saw Nick looking up at him, head tilted to the side and a slight, confused smile on his lips. Bane realized Nick was wondering why he kept his eyes closed.

"I kept my eyes closed, because I want to remember every second with you. Not let even one pass by without *capturing* it somehow," Bane confessed in answer to the unasked question.

Nick kissed him fiercely then and wrapped around Bane's neck. "You keep talking like that and I'm going to make you take me right here on the beach."

"Sand gets *everywhere* though," Bane said from experience.

Nick's mouth parted and his eyes widened and then with a laugh he said, "Only if we make out on land, but in the *water* ..."

"We do not have swim suits." Bane frowned.

Nick started unbuttoning his shirt. "I know. Adventurous, remember?"

"We are in *public*." Bane's heart though started to thump with excitement.

"*Really* adventurous then." Nick slipped off his suit coat and folded it gently on the sand before finishing unbuttoning his shirt.

"Skinny dipping on a public beach, Nick?" Bane let out a choked laugh, but he, too, started to undress. The beast's tail began to thump on the ground in anticipation. It liked the idea of making love to Nick out in the open.

Nick was wearing just his boxer briefs and looking at Bane expectantly. "You're too slow." Nick slipped off his underwear. "You're going to have to catch me."

Bane realized what Nick intended to do the moment before the young man pivoted and started running into the surf. "Nick, don't run!"

For I will chase.

But it was too late. Nick dashed towards the water. Bane hardly realized that he had ripped his pants and underwear off of his own body, shredding them completely in the process. The material fluttered down around him as he chased after Nick into the ocean. Nick let out a whoop as a wave rolled over his head, slicking his hair back. The water was pleasantly warm, but the first splash felt cool against Bane's overheated skin.

Nick cast a look over his shoulder to see if Bane was gaining. When he saw that Bane was, he dove into the water and tried to swim away. But Bane was not having that. Nick was *his*. He, too, dove into the water and his powerful legs and arms propelled him through the water like a scythe through wheat. He opened his eyes and could see Nick's flailing limbs. He grinned and bubbles escaped his lips. He surged forward and grasped Nick around the waist, bringing them both to the surface. Nick let out a cry of surprise and started laughing even as he splashed the water around Bane.

"You caught me!" Nick laughed against Bane's shoulders.

"Yes, and I *always* will." The beast let out a low growl that came out in Bane's voice, but Nick seemed not to notice or perhaps *mind*. "Run and I will chase."

"Just like that big tiger of yours?" Nick teased.

Bane gave him a quick flash of teeth. Nick's words were more true than he knew. The beast was no end pleased to have caught Nick. It liked that Nick was frisky and eager to play. It was how a mate should behave. Bane knew he should be concerned with all this "mate" business, but he felt the rightness of the word, too, even though it *was* animalistic. Nick was his on a deeply primal level.

They floated with their arms around each other in water a few feet deeper than Bane's height. He slid one of his thighs between Nick's, relishing the silken flesh on either side of his thigh. Nick's cock was half erect and the young man ground down on his leg with an impish smile.

Bane's hands slid from Nick's shoulders around to his spine and smoothed further down until he was cupping the young man's pert buttocks. They were perfect handfuls. He squeezed Nick's asscheeks with relish. Nick moaned even as he sought out Bane's mouth for another kiss.

As their lips came together, Bane pulled Nick's body tight against his. Their cocks were pressed between their bellies. Nick's breathing came in short, panting gasps against his mouth. They were both *trembling* with need that seemed to come out of nowhere.

Bane's fingers slipped between Nick's asscheeks and sought out that precious opening into his body. Nick hissed as his fingertips passed over it and the young man's eyes hooded in pleasure as he *pressed* against that opening. Bane knew that Nick would be happy for them to make love right then and there. He could easily stretch Nick's back passage and push his cock inside of him. The thought of doing just that had his cock pulsing with need. But then he felt his skin *prickle* and a wave of change go through him.

Panic nearly overcame him as he realized what those feelings were: the shift! The moon was already shining down upon them. Full on *him*. The moon seemed to want to *draw* the fur through his skin, change his fingernails into sharp claws, alter his bone structure completely. His stomach did a sickening flip and he swallowed the bitter, acrid taste of fear that was on his tongue.

You promised! Bane shouted at the beast. *You will not come out with Nick here!*

The beast was standing, ready to *leap* through his chest, to take over his form, to become itself.

Think about that for a moment. Think about changing in the water! Think of swallowing down ocean water! Think of having your fur wet! Bane argued with it frantically.

The beast *paused*. It did not like the thought of being in the water. It would sink. Bane sent to it images of clawing at Nick's body as it tried to stay above the surface. He showed it blood. He showed it Nick screaming as his body was shredded. A shudder went through the beast.

That's right. You can't do this. You can't be with Nick like that. You must let me be in charge and then, in two nights, I'll let you out. I promise! Please do not do this!

The beast sat back down, placing its massive head on its paws again. The prickling stopped. Bane's skin and bones settled back into fully that of a man's. The moonlight's magic on him was quelled. Bane let out a relieved sigh. This had all only taken *seconds* yet Nick had noticed.

"Bane, are you okay?" Nick's forehead was furrowed with concern.

Bane didn't answer, but instead leaned back and dunked his head into the water, washing off the slick sweat that had dotted his skin from the strain of holding back the shift. When he surfaced, he shook the water out of his eyes.

"Bane?" Nick repeated, alarm written in that word.

"Y-yes, forgive me. I had a momentary turn, but I'm all right now," Bane answered.

He saw all the questions in Nick's eyes. So many questions. The young man opened his lips to ask some of them, but then shut them. He was clearly remembering Bane's stricture from his first night back to simply *accept* that there were certain things he couldn't answer and Nick shouldn't ask.

But how long will that be enough? Nick is an inquisitive, intelligent, sensitive young man. He will not be satisfied with mysteries and silence forever.

"Are you sure you're all right?" Nick carefully asked.

Bane felt slightly weak and shaky. That was something he normally experienced around the shift, but he had hoped since things had been going so well that it wouldn't happen this time. He had been wrong.

"We should go in," Nick suggested and prepared to unwrap his arms from Bane's neck so that they could swim to shore, but Bane clutched at him.

"No! Please. I *need* you, Nick," Bane pleaded.

"You have me," Nick said gently. "But if you're getting sick, we need to go –"

"I *need* ... I *need* to be right here with *you*."

Bane's mouth descended on Nick's with sudden desperation. He knew that this would be the last time that he could touch Nick intimately until several days after the full moon. It would not be safe. But the beast would let him have this moment. It would be all right. For now ...

At first, Nick was still in his arms, not responding to him, but then the young man seemed to come alive. It was clear that he recognized that Bane needed this and would give him whatever it was he desired.

Bane's right hand slipped between their bodies and grasped both of their cocks. The feeling of Nick's shaft against his own had his whole body surging towards the young man's. His breathing stuttered. Nick shivered in his arms with the pleasure of it, too.

His left hand stayed on Nick's ass. His fingers delved between those ass cheeks and he proceeded to rub a circle around that tight, pink swirl of muscle. He started to stroke them in time with the circling and Nick's body jerked as if he had touched a live wire. Then the young man's fingers dug pleasurably into Bane's back as he gripped the billionaire as if Bane might try and escape.

Their mouths were practically fused together, breathing in each other's breaths. The water thrashed around them as they frantically moved against one another. Bane's pointer finger pressed against Nick's opening even as he slid his other hand up and down their shafts. Nick made an inarticulate cry into his mouth when Bane's finger pushed past the tight muscle of his sphincter and popped through to the other side. Bane felt Nick's cock plump, too, as he began to finger fuck him.

He delved as deep as he could into Nick's body. The young man's ass clenched around his fingers. He imagined what it would feel like when that tight ass was around his cock. His hand stuttered as he stroked their shafts.

Nick scrabbled at his back. His fingernails raking down Bane's back. He stroked Nick's cock and his prostate. He stretched Nick's back passage as if truly preparing him for penetration by his cock. Again, his stroking became jerky and not smooth. Arousal was like a live wire inside of him.

He bit Nick's lower lip and rasped his teeth over the young man's jaw, desperate to mark Nick as his in some way. Even if it was impermanent. Nick nuzzled him and moved Bane's head so that they were kissing again. Tongues stroked along one another. They shared breath.

Bane's fingers sank into Nick up to the knuckle. His other hand quickened its stroking of their shafts. His balls drew up tight against his body. The muscles of Nick's ass clamped down hard on his fingers, telling him that the young man was about to cum, too.

Bane's eyelids fluttered shut even though it was night and he was facing out to sea where no lights were. Flashes of light though passed before his closed eyes as his arousal battered him. Heat bloomed between his thighs as his cock went impossibly hard. Nick's body arched against his. Bane's fingers thrust deeper still.

There was a thrashing of water as both of them came at the same moment.

The water went blood warm with their cum. Bane's body shook as if with ague. Nick's arched three times. His hot cum streamed against Bane's belly before it was washed away by the sea. His own cock pulsed repeatedly. He felt like every drop of semen was wrung from his body.

The fingers that he had in Nick's body were trapped at first by the strength of Nick's ass muscles. He could not have removed them if he wanted to. But as Nick arched for the final time, his body spending that last precious ounce of seed, his fingers had been freed of their hot, tight prison and he was able to draw them out and rub a comforting circle around the base of Nick's spine.

Nick became boneless in his arms. His head rested against Bane's right shoulder. His breathing was slow and even. His eyelids were closed. In the moonlight, he looked like some sleeping prince.

Bane's eyelids were sliding shut, too. Shivers of pleasure, aftershocks of his orgasm, still echoed within him. All his strength had fled from him as well as all the tension. They bobbed and drifted in the sea. He knew he should swim them in. The beast kept showing him images of them curled around one another in a soft, warm bed. A den. Where they could keep their mate safe.

Perhaps they should stay at the condo or have Peter come get them in the Maybach and drive them back to Moon Shadow. But even the thought of being driven was exhausting. They should stay downtown. Nick would have to return here early tomorrow in any event. Staying at the condo sounded like the best plan.

Just as he was having that thought though he saw flashlight beams on the beach ... by their clothes. Bane's eyes fully opened. The exhaustion left him and he was completely awake and aware. The beast's nostrils flared. The beams swung out to sea and were searching for the owners of those clothes. Bane realized who it was when he heard a squawk of radios and the jangle of cuffs. Nick stirred in his arms.

"What is it?" Nick asked.

"I believe that the *police* have discovered us," he remarked dryly.

Now it was Nick's turn to come awake. The young man's eyes were wide open and a touch of alarm was in their depths. "T-the police?!"

"Yes, my sweet. It appears that we are about to be arrested for skinny dipping." Bane tipped his head back and laughed. "Adventurous sex indeed!"

CHAPTER TWENTY

ADMIRATION

Nick reluctantly left Bane in bed at the condo as he headed over to the address for the charity event. They had decided to stay in Bane's Winter Haven condo instead of going back home to Moon Shadow the night before. Even without the drive back to Moon Shadow, it had been a long night, especially with the added "fun" of having the police find them skinny dipping. But little sleep didn't completely explain how ill the billionaire had looked when they'd woken that morning. Bane's eyes had been glassy with fever and when he did move it was as if his skin *hurt* him.

"I will go to you to the space and help with the photographs." Bane had tried to sit up, but Nick had gently pressed his shoulders back down and the big man had collapsed on the bed, as weak as a kitten.

"No, you're staying *here*, in bed, resting," Nick countered.

Bane looked up at him rather helplessly. "I do not know what is wrong with me."

"Maybe it was the extra time in the water while I ran to the condo to get you clothes? Those nice police officers wouldn't let you streak pantless back there yourself," Nick suggested with a repressed smirk.

Somehow Bane had shredded his clothes when he'd taken them off before they'd gotten into the water. Nick had to quickly dress and run to the condo to get him a pair of pants while Bane remained in the water with the police officers "guarding" him.

"Perhaps, but I do not get sick," Bane protested rather like a tired child.

"Like you didn't get sick in Europe?" Nick pointed out.

Bane looked blank and then recollection had him amending his earlier statement, "I don't get sick *often*. But you need help. You only have limited time to get the photographs up."

"Jade and Omar have both agreed to help. So we've got it covered. All you need to do is rest and get better, okay?" Nick kissed Bane gently on the forehead. The billionaire's skin felt hot and clammy under his lips. Nick's belief that Bane was coming down with something, maybe a flu, grew. "Everything will be fine."

Bane frowned even as his limbs were lax and he looked quite incapable of movement. "Devon will be an ass. I know he will."

"Yeah, he probably will, but I won't care." Seeing Bane's hard look, he amended, "That much. I won't care *that much*. Because, you're right that I won against him and I'm getting to show some of my art on top of it. Can't hate the guy when I've so thoroughly beaten him."

Bane ran a hand through Nick's hair. "Do not bother hating him at all. He is nothing to me and should be nothing to you."

"I almost feel bad for him, hearing you say that. I don't think Devon's been *nothing* ever in his life." Nick caught Bane's hand, kissed his palm and tucked it back under the blankets. "If you need anything call me. I'm not going to be that far away."

Bane curled on his side, feverish eyes searching Nick's face. "I will be fine. I will not burden you."

"You're not a burden. I'd rather be with you than anywhere else."

"Even preparing for you first art show?" Bane's eyebrows lifted.

"Yes, even compared to that." Nick paused then suggested carefully, "Maybe you should move that meeting this weekend to another time. I can stay at Moon Shadow and take care of you—"

"No!" Bane's alarm shocked Nick and he was silent, at first, in response. The billionaire quickly added, "I *must* go to this meeting. I really will be fine. Do not worry about me."

Nick wasn't sure what caused Bane's panic. Was this meeting he wouldn't tell Nick about that important? Or was it that Bane really needed this weekend *away* from Nick? Not that Nick was paranoid about Bane's regard, but they did spend a lot of time together. Maybe the big man simply needed some space.

Though I wish he would just say so if that's the case. But do I really think Bane would make up an elaborate lie to be alone? No, not really. Yet whenever I mention this meeting to him or Omar, they both act really strange. I can tell Omar's lying about something. But what?

Those thoughts had raced through Nick's mind as he got ready and headed over to the charity space. It was a storefront in an area that was slowly being gentrified. There were floor to ceiling windows looking in on a space that was mostly wide open except for a divider wall with a receptionist desk in front. He caught sight of clean maple floors and fresh white walls. He also saw a large bar along the right wall. Obviously, this space wouldn't be used for low income housing. Devon had texted that he intended to use this space as one for events to support charity and art shows like Nick's.

The bar immediately inspired Nick. The base looked to be made of wedges of shale piled one on top of the other with the top being a hunk of polished onyx. Behind the bars were metal shelves filled with liquor bottles and an antique mirror. Nick thought that the sepia toned images of Moon Shadow would look spectacular near the stone, metal and glass.

He tore his eyes away to look up and down the street. Omar was driving Jade up from Moon Shadow. He didn't see any evidence of them yet, but he was early. He didn't see Devon either. Maybe the "perfect" man was inside. Nick knocked on the front door with little hope of Devon actually answering. Devon really didn't seem like an 8 am kind of guy. But to his surprise Devon rounded the divider wall. As soon as he saw Nick though, he paused in mid-stride and actually looked pained. Nick drew up straight.

He didn't forget I was coming, did he? I mean I'm a few minutes early, but so what? He's here already. I won't get in his way.

Devon came to the door and unlocked it, but only opened it about six inches.

"Nick, you're here sooner than I expected," he said, his normally cool voice sounding rushed.

"Yeah, sorry about that, but there's a ton to do so I wanted to get started as soon as possible," Nick explained. The fact that Devon was literally barring him from entering the space was jarring to him.

"Yes, well." Devon glanced over his shoulder.

"Are you with someone? I won't get in your way. I don't really need you to show me around or anything. I can look by myself," Nick offered.

"I −" Devon began, but got nothing further out as Dean rounded the same corner Devon just had.

"Devon, what ..." Dean stopped dead in his tracks as he saw Nick.

Nick took a step back from the door, but then forced himself to stay where he was. The memory of Dean's cruel hands on his body immediately flooded Nick. He remembered the gush of the man's alcohol tinted breath and the things he'd darkly promised to do to Nick. He remembered, too, Bane holding Dean up against the wall by his neck, the man's face purpling as he was slowly cut off from air.

No one spoke for long moments. This gave Nick time to see that Dean was less ruddy-faced than when he'd seen him a few months ago though the broken blood vessels around his nose were more obvious with his paler skin. Dean still had the look of former football star gone to seed, too. Nick *should* have been pleased at the nervous, sick-look on Dean's face and the contrite one on Devon's, but his heart was thudding hard in his chest and the bitter taste of fear filled his mouth.

"I'm sorry, Nick," Devon *did* sound sorry. "I didn't expect Dean to come over this morning and I thought he'd be gone before you arrived. If you'd like to wait here, I'll finish with him and—"

"No, I need to get in there and look around. I don't have time to wait," Nick found himself saying. He wasn't going to stand out on the sidewalk, afraid of Dean, as if a few inches of glass between them changed anything.

"I think —" But whatever Devon was thinking would never be said as Nick bodily pushed him out of the way by stepping towards him.

As Nick walked past Dean, he caught a whiff of the man's overwhelming aftershave and a hint of sweat. Beads of perspiration were trailing down the sides of Dean's face. His skin had flushed now to that familiar ugly red that seemed to suffuse his face the entire time he'd been at Moon Shadow.

Nick stepped around the divider wall for the receptionist desk and into the main space. He really didn't see it. He stared blankly at the walls, at the bar, at the floor. Since the attack, he'd told himself that what had happened with Dean was "no big deal". He'd been hit on by guys he hadn't liked before. He'd been even pushed into doing things sexually that he hadn't wanted to do. But now that he was in a room with Dean again, he felt like he couldn't breathe. His skin prickled as if it wanted to jump off of him and run away. But he forced himself to check out the lighting on the walls, trying to figure out many pieces would really show well in the room. He had a tape measure app on his phone and he tried to use it six times before he got it working correctly. It wasn't the app, it was him.

He heard the door to the space open and shut and then the tap of Devon's shoes as the man walked over to him. Nick swallowed down the bitter, acrid taste of fear that had bubbled up into his mouth again. Dean was gone and he could *almost* relax. He turned his head to look at the other man.

Devon was as "perfect" as ever. He was wearing tailored gray slacks, an icy white shirt with a few buttons open at the throat and a dark blue and white sweater artfully tied around his shoulders.

"I *am* sorry about that, Nick," Devon said, his lips turning down into a frown.

"Are you?"

Devon's head lifted, surprise reflecting in his dark brown eyes for a moment. "*Of course*. Whatever else you might think of me know that what Dean did at Moon Shadow was totally unforgivable."

"Yet he's still your friend. You aren't afraid to be alone with him," Nick pointed out.

"I'm not afraid of Dean. I'm—I'm not his type, I suppose, so I've never needed to protect myself in that way from him." Devon's forehead furrowed as if the concept was alien to him. "You think I should kick him out of my life, don't you? Bane does, too. Maybe I should."

"But you haven't and you don't really see a need to," Nick intuited. He went back to blindly measuring the walls and assessing the light. "I'm not your friend. Why should you care what he did to me?"

Devon leaned against the wall. His hands were loosely stuffed into his pockets. "Because you're a person and I *do* care. It's just that I deal with *damaged* people all the time. When you're interacting with the rich, you're rarely meeting people who are well adjusted. There's always the letch, the drinker, the drug-user, and the *rapist*. You just *deal* with it if you want to do some *good*."

Nick wanted to get on his high horse and tell Devon that not all people with money were creeps. Not to mention that cozying up to them couldn't be worth whatever he was getting out of it in terms of charitable donations. But then he thought of his father and brothers and their friends. There were a few good ones, but most *were* objectionable on one level or another.

"Principles are all well and good, Nickie," his father had said to him endless times. "But they're more likely to take away the roof over your head and spoil the food on your table."

"I don't know if it will make you feel better or worse, but I've never seen Dean behave that way before or since. He's given up drinking," Devon said softly. "I'm not saying that *you* were the cause of his terrible actions. I'm just saying that I've never seen the *predator* in him like that before."

"Lucky me." Nick started actually making a record of the measurements he was taking and noting down pieces he thought would work.

He felt Devon looking at him thoughtfully. "You really haven't had a good time of it, have you?"

Nick frowned and looked over at the other man. "I don't know what you mean. Yeah, the thing with Dean was bad, but that's—"

"No, I meant with *Bane*," Devon said.

Nick's back immediately stiffened. "I've had a *great* time with Bane—"

"On *one* level, certainly, but the way it all began and now how it is with your family." Devon waved a hand through the air as if there was this *mountain* of bad things to talk about.

Nick knew he shouldn't ask the question he was going to, but he did anyways, "What about my family?"

"This thing about your family and Bane. I can only imagine what a bone of contention it must be between the two of you to have their futures still uncertain." Devon's lips pressed together in a tight grimace after he spoke as if he were conflicted about what he was saying.

"There's no *problems* between Bane and me about them," Nick said, but his heart thudded heavily in his chest again. He knew that Devon was *not* his friend. He had taken Bane from the man. So anything Devon said should be listened to with a grain of salt.

Actually, a whole pile of salt.

But Devon wasn't stupid either. He wouldn't overplay his hand and what he was saying worried Nick, because it was something he, himself, had thought.

Devon raised his eyebrows and leaned towards Nick. "*Really*? You're good with him still dangling your family's feet above the fire? Or maybe you suppose he'll give them a break at the end? Just make them work for it?"

"Most probably," Nick answered as neutrally as he could.

There was a *pause*. Devon's eyes were narrowed and he suddenly nodded as if coming to some conclusion. "You're not as naïve as I thought. You understand that Bane might very well kick them out on the street at the end, too, even if you two *are* happy together."

"Bane's given them clear rules to work by. They'll figure it out and earn back the company." Nick's movements with the tape measure app stuttered, but then he went back to smoothly running it along the wall. Devon *knew* Bane. He knew what he was capable of. He wasn't lying. He believed Bane would do as he'd said.

"So you're making them earn it, too? Just like Bane? I suppose I can't blame you. The fact that they put you in a position where you had little choice other than agree to be an indentured servant or see them ruined wasn't exactly a family bonding moment, was it?" Devon gave out a soft snort. "They deserve to sweat it just like you did. After all, it was their mess. You just cleaned it up. Doesn't mean you have to fix it fully for them. Still ... some would say if you really don't want them to fail Bane's test, you should act sooner rather than later on their behalf."

"Why would *some people* say that?" Nick asked more sharply than he'd intended.

Devon's face looked rather fox-like at that moment. Sharp and all angles. "Because you're at the beginning of your relationship with Bane. It's all *fresh* and *new* and *intense*. It's at the time when you write each other poetry and believe that true love is real. He'll be more amenable to doing what you want."

"Bane doesn't believe in love," Nick found himself saying, foolishly.

Devon laughed. "Exactly! Some would say all the more reason to get what you want from him *now* before he starts seeing the cracks in the foundation—".

"Like he did with you?" Nick snapped, realizing even as he said it that it was the wrong move to make.

Devon shifted his stance. He was still smiling. He didn't look hurt or concerned by what Nick had said. "I admit I was surprised when Bane told me about you. We'd never been exclusive and I had never asked for a commitment. I didn't want to be tied down either. But then I started to realize that what Bane and I had together worked for *both* of us. Could be something good for the long term."

Nick turned fully towards him, his phone hanging loose at his side. "But he didn't think that way." It was a statement, not a question.

Devon's smile, again, didn't waver. "To be honest, I think he went a little *mad* over you."

"Excuse me?" His voice was arch.

"Think on it a minute, Nick. Think on what he did to get you into his bed. The whole deal thing. The indentured servant bit. Isn't that a little ... well, *crazy*?"

"It was a mistake. He's admitted that. Apologized. He let me out of the deal before we got together," Nick found himself explaining.

"But you're *not* out." Devon regarded him with almost sadly. "He's still got your family over a barrel and—though you might be mad at them now and happy to have them sweat a bit—I don't think you're the type in the long run to leave them hanging if you can do something about it. I mean you *sacrificed* yourself for them the first time."

"So you think I should ask Bane to let my family out of the deal now while he's all head over heels in lust with me?" Nick asked acidly.

"No, I don't think you should say a word! Bane isn't like other men and, as I said, he's a little *mad* about you. That will eventually burn itself out, but it hasn't quite yet," Devon told him slyly. "You start asking him to let them go ... well, he might start wondering if you're *only* with him for the money."

"I'm not!" He thought of how Alastair had behaved with Bane. That would be something Bane might suspect even though it wasn't true.

"Or maybe he won't want to let them out of the deal, because he likes the *deal* more than he likes *you*," Devon continued.

Nick knew his face was flushed with anger. First, seeing Dean here and now, this crap. "You must have a pretty low opinion of Bane to think he'd do that. That he'd value hurting people more than helping them."

"No, I just have a *realistic* opinion of him, and, surprisingly, so do *you*," Devon answered, his voice lowering.

Their gazes met. Gray clashed with brown and gray looked away.

"It's why you haven't asked Bane to let them out of the deal. Not out of revenge against them—though there might be a little bit of that in there—but, out of fear, *fear* that he'll say no and then what? What will you do? What are your options really?"

"I'd leave him. I wouldn't let someone treat me that way," Nick said simply, as if that was simple. The simple thought of leaving Bane made him want to hyperventilate.

"But if you leave, that would definitely ensure your family is on the streets. Not to mention you'd lose all his financial backing for school and whatnot. Yet if you ask and he says no, can you really stay with him? I think we both know the answer to that is you can't."

"You might know it, but I don't!" Nick retorted.

"Imagine that you ask and he says no then you put it into his head that you're not in it for *him*, but *them*. After that, Bane will wonder about your character. How could you stay with a man that would ruin your family is what he'll think." Devon spread his arms wide. "Completely hypocritical of him, of course, but he'll think it anyways. So you *don't* ask. You act as if you don't care about the deal. Maybe you nudge him gently, but not too much, to seeing your family's good side and the happiness you'll feel if they succeed. Maybe that will get them through to the finish line. Maybe not. But you're taking the absolute best course, Nick, with all the bad options Bane has given you. I admire you for that."

Before Nick could respond—and he wasn't sure what he wanted to say or could say—he heard the front door open and Jade's voice call to him.

"Nick? Nick! You in here? Omar's just parking the car and I—"

"Jade, I'm here! Don't have Omar park!" Nick called as he walked away from Devon without a look back. Nick rounded the wall and caught sight of Jade in a black and white polka-dotted dress and combat boots. She was carrying a black parasol against the sun.

"What? Why?" she sounded surprised.

He put an arm around her waist. He realized that he was shaking, but he forced his hand to still as he urged her out of the space, explaining in clipped tones that he was sure Devon heard, "I've got all I need here."

CHAPTER TWENTY-ONE

TRUST AND LOVE

B ane thrashed in bed all day after Nick had left. He could not sleep even though he was exhausted. Instead, he tossed and turned. When his eyelids forced themselves open, his gaze constantly swung between the door to the bedroom—wanting to see Nick entering it—and the floor to ceiling windows that gave him a fantastic view of the city and the sea.

Storm clouds passed over the sun. Sunlight streamed through a few breaks in the heavy cloud cover. Wherever the sunlight hit on the earth or sea, it seemed to sparkle. A few sunbeams actually found their way into his bedroom. One crossed the bed and he slid a hand into it, relishing the golden warmth. The sun warred with the moon. So long as he was in the sun, he was safe from the moon's power.

I know our deal, he told the beast. *I will cede control to you, but after Nick's show. You want to see his photographs being appreciated by people, don't you? You want to see them praised and for Nick to glow under that admiration? If you're in control that can't happen.*

But the beast did not like the thought of Nick seeking anyone else's admiration but theirs. It was prowling in his chest.

Tight circles. Its impressive muscles bunched and released as it moved.

It's unreasonable for you to think that he would be content just being with us! His art is important to him! I know that is difficult for you to understand, but to Nick taking photographs is as essential as hunting is for you.

The beast slowed its prowl. Its eyes were hooded, looking out at him, with emotions he couldn't decipher. They had been together for so long. They should know one another's thoughts and feelings intimately, but Bane had always shied away from truly understanding the beast.

Not just shied. Rejected. I've never wanted to really communicate with it until now. And now may be too late. He composed himself and tried to explain again, *I am not trying to cheat you or keep you in me for some selfish purpose. I want to make Nick happy. I know you want to make him happy, too.*

The beast continued to regard him out of unfathomable eyes. It did not resume pacing, but it did not sit down either. It was awake, alert, and ready to take over at a moment's notice.

That was how the whole day went with him seeking sleep and finding it elusive yet too exhausted to get up and go help Nick with the show. The beast took all his energy and left him a husk of himself.

At one point, Bane had looked up and thought he saw the old woman from India, the priestess that had cursed him, standing at the foot of the bed, looking at him with a mixture of sadness and frustration written into the lines of her wrinkled face. He'd opened his mouth to speak to her, to ask her why she still punished him, but she turned and blinked out of existence. Of course, she had never really been there at all. Though in a world of curses and tiger shifters, why couldn't there be ghosts?

Near dusk, when the sun kissed the horizon and the storm clouds were lit up as if on fire, he heard the hum of the elevator. He'd staggered out of his bed and made it to the living room when the elevator doors had opened.

"Nick!" he called and reached blindly forward.

But it was not Nick. His nose told him before his eyes confirmed it. It was Omar.

"Bane!" The Indian man rushed to his side, easing him down onto the nearest couch. "Bane, you look horrible! Sit! Sit! Do you need water? What do you require?"

He wanted to moan, "Nick." But he didn't. He swallowed the young man's name down. Nick was the *last* person he wanted here. If Nick saw him like this there would be questions. Nick would want to get a doctor. But this was not something that modern medicine could fix. It was *magic* that ailed him. And the thought of lying to Nick had him wanting to vomit.

"There can be no lasting love without trust," his mother's voice drifted through the room and, for a terrifying moment, he thought he saw her seated opposite him.

He reared back. His right hand rose up as if to ward her off. Omar saw this and looked over at the empty sofa. Because, of course, his mother was not there. She had died in an asylum over a century ago after she had seen what he was.

"Bane, please, please, tell me what you need," Omar begged.

It was clear that the Indian man was completely at a loss. Bane was rarely sick. He was ornery and agitated before the shifts normally, but never truly physically ill. Not like this. What did it mean?

"Nothing, Omar. I am ... will be ... fine after—after this weekend." Bane passed a shaking hand over his sweat drenched forehead. He passed his fingers through his lank hair. He knew he smelled of sweat from the fever.

"I have never see you like this. Is something wrong with the spirit?" Omar's big brown eyes were filled with worry.

"It wants out. It wants to be with Nick." He let out a hysterical laugh. "The one person it absolutely can have *nothing* to do with and it's obsessed with him!"

Omar went very still and Bane could almost see the man weighing his words. "Unless you *trusted* Nick to –"

"NO!" Bane was on his feet. His legs trembled beneath him, but he firmed them. He wore only a pair of pale gray silk pants and a robe. It flared open as he moved furiously. "I will *never* expose Nick to the beast! NEVER!"

"But why not, Bane? Do you not trust Nick to –"

"To what, Omar? To want to be with an *animal*? I am a *monster*. My mother lost her mind seeing me transform," he spat out and looked to the couch where he had glimpsed her for a moment. "I will not *risk* hurting Nick or losing him! Do you understand?"

"I think you underestimate him," Omar said stubbornly.

For a wild moment, Bane thought that the Indian man might go against his wishes and tell Nick the truth. He grasped Omar's shoulders and shook him. "You must promise me never to tell! Never, Omar!"

"I will not! Bane, please, stop! You are hurting me!"

Bane immediately released him and was across the room. Horror ran through him. "O-Omar, f-forgive me. I never meant to hurt –"

"I know," Omar interrupted and he came towards Bane.

The billionaire flinched away, but Omar kept coming until he put a hand on Bane's left shoulder.

"Omar, you shouldn't –"

"You are *not* a monster. You did not mean to hurt me. I know your heart," Omar said.

"But I *did* hurt you. When I am like this—when the beast is ascendant—no one is safe around me. If Nick did not have his show tomorrow I would lock myself away right now and not return until after the full moon!" Bane confessed.

"I know you think these things about yourself. And I know that words alone will not reach you, bBut I do not know what will." Omar set his shoulders back. "So I am going to say this anyways. You must find peace with the beast, Bane, and you must tell Nick about it. You will never be free if you do not."

"Then I shall never be free." Bane gave him a bloodless smile. "I shall not ever be free anyways. But, at least, this way I shall have Nick in my life. That is more than I ever hoped for."

"Do you love him?" Omar's eyes searched his face.

"You know how I feel about love –"

"Do you love him?"

Bane trembled, but he got the words out, "He is my *heart*, Omar. He is my *mate*. That is so much more than love."

Omar's lips parted and his eyes grew moist. A tremulous smile crossed his lips. "Oh, Bane, I am so *happy*. Have you told him this? Has he heard it from your lips?"

"No, not yet. I will tell him after the full moon. He will know the full extent of my regard for him then."

Bane's legs were trembling beneath him again. He had to lay down. Omar saw this and put one of Bane's large arms over his shoulders and led him back to bed. He had Bane sit on the edge of it while he fussed with the sheets, blankets and pillowcases, making the bed more comfortable.

"What are you doing here, Omar? Is Nick all prepared for the show tomorrow night?" Bane asked.

"Oh, no, there is still much more work to be done."

Bane frowned and twisted around to watch the Indian man fluff his pillows. "Then why are you *here*? You need to get back to him. Assist him in any way he needs."

Omar smiled at him. "And I will, after I get you back into bed. Nick was worried about you and I promised to check that you were all right and report to him."

Bane lightly caught the Indian man's right wrist. He raised feverish eyes. "Omar, you must not tell Nick that I am—am like *this*. He will worry. He will leave his work and come to me."

Omar looked torn for a moment. "But he will *want* to be with you!"

"He cannot help me, Omar. You know this. Only the passing of the full moon will. This is his *first* show. His first exposure to the art buying public. These are some of the people

269

that could make or break his career," Bane said. "I would not ruin this for him."

"The world is a wide and vast place, Bane. You could not ruin it for him by needing him," Omar said gently.

"I disagree. Those in Winter Haven have vast influence. I want Nick to be able to put his best foot forward."

Omar had finished fixing the bed. Bane laid down on the mattress, an audible sigh escaping from him as he stretched out. The Indian man tenderly drew the blankets over him. Bane's eyelids sank down as if weighed by anvils. This time, sleep did not escape him, but came to him on cat's paws. He barely heard Omar's whispered "good night, Bane" or the tapping of his shoes as he left to rejoin Nick.

Bane did not dream. He sank into utter blackness. His next conscious thought was when Nick laid down in the bed behind him. Bane's eyelids opened a crack. He could see it was full night out. The moon—almost full—hung bone white in the black sky.

Nick's arm slipped around his waist and the young man tucked his head against Bane's back. There was desperation in that touch. Bane though was too exhausted, too weighed down by sleep, to analyze it. If he had been aware and awake he might have thought that Nick was *clutching* onto him as if he feared that Bane would slip from his grasp.

But all he would have thought or said was consumed by the blackness of unconsciousness, sinking him down into an oblivion as dark as a jungle night.

CHAPTER TWENTY-TWO

OPEN AND CLOSED

"A re you nervous? You shouldn't be nervous, Nick. You're going to do great!" Jade enthused.

She reached up and adjusted the collar of his shirt. She'd chosen a pale blue Chinese collared shirt for him and and a simple pair of white pants. She claimed that the shirt brought out the silver in his eyes.

Nick was more worried about spilling something on the pants or sitting on something sticky. Though he doubted he would ever want to sit. He had so much nervous energy he felt like he could blast to the moon even though they had worked until the wee hours of the morning getting the photographs printed and mounted properly in the space. He couldn't have done it without Jade and Omar's help.

"Thank you again for everything you've done," he began.

"You've thanked me a hundred times," she laughed.

"Well, consider it one hundred and one. I couldn't have gotten everything done for the show without your help," he told her.

"I was happy to help. I'm so excited for other people to see your work," she said. "It's going to be so great!"

"Do you think the placement of the fountain picture opposite the bar—pride of place, so to speak—is a good idea?" he asked her.

"I think it's the one hundred and second time you've asked me that as well!" Jade laughed and patted his arm. "And, as I said the other times, *yes*, it's *perfect*."

"Oh, God, you're right." He sighed and sat on the edge of one of the plush couches in the condo's living room. "I don't know why I'm worrying though! I bet no one will even *look* at the photographs let alone buy them. They're there to sip champagne and open their pocketbooks for a good cause. If—and that's a big *if*—they buy a picture it's only because they think it's in support of a good cause. Not because they like it." Nick raked a hand through his hair. "I'll likely be standing there like an idiot, smiling nervously, hoping someone will talk to me. And then I'll say, Hi, I'm the artist! Oh, you didn't know there was art here? Yeah, I'm just crawl and die of embarrassment in the corner over there."

Jade was laughing again and shaking her head. "You know that's so not going to happen, right? You're going to be mobbed by admirers who will want you to photograph *their* homes."

But he didn't believe her. He didn't know these people other than that they were rich and went to Devon's charity events. He suddenly wished he *wasn't* exhibiting the art there. "I don't know, Jade. The pictures of Moon Shadow feel so personal to me. Far more than anything else I've done."

"And it shows in your work," she assured him. "Seriously, it's the best stuff you've ever done."

"I just don't want to let Bane down."

"How could you?"

He wasn't sure, but he said, "I mean already people are going to make assumptions about why Devon is showing my stuff."

"And what would those assumptions be?" She put her hands on her hips and cocked her head to the side.

"They're going to think I just got this job because I'm Bane's boyfriend." He rubbed his face. "Ah, fuck, it *is* true!"

"And so what? It doesn't mean the art isn't good!" She wrapped an arm around his shoulders.. "Besides everybody there will know that *Devon* was replaced by you. Why would a former boyfriend help out the current boyfriend?"

"To get back into Bane's good graces, I think," Nick said and with a mulish look, added, "I *know* he's not doing it because he likes me. He hadn't seen my work before offering me the gig."

Nick couldn't help but flash back on what Devon had said to him the day before, too, about *admiring* him for manipulating the situation with Bane so that his family would benefit.

But I'm not doing that at all!

"No, I imagine Devon doesn't like you. But the thing is that people will assume that your art must be very good for him to go out of his way like this," she theorized. "And, by the way, he *does* think your art is awesome, Nick. He might have begun all of this to please Bane, but I saw his face when he looked at your photos. He *liked* them. He *really* liked them."

"Against his will, I'm sure," Nick muttered.

"Maybe so, but he did."

Nick walked out onto the condo's living room balcony and rested his forearms on the railing. Jade joined him. He glanced over at her. The wind was blowing her hair back and there was a look of contentment on her face. In honor of his show, she had on a sepia colored baby doll dress and strappy platforms. Her makeup matched the shade of her dress.

"I can't believe that Bane is giving us this place for the whole weekend!" She grinned. "And the use of the spa!"

His sour mood lifted somewhat at her enthusiasm. The condo was incredible and it would give them a ton of time to just hang out together and do fun stuff downtown. "Don't forget the restaurants, too. He's got house accounts at a ton of them." He shifted uncomfortably as he added, "And he's given me a credit card for anything else we want or need."

"I've really never cared if you dated rich men or poor men, but I have to say ... this is great! This whole place is spectacular and I can't wait for our weekend together!" She smiled hugely and grabbed his arm, hugging him to her.

"It really is something he's doing this for us." He grinned back at her, but the grin quickly died.

She rubbed his shoulder. "What's going on? It's more than just nerves about the show or even Bane leaving this weekend, though I know you're majorly bummed by that." She cast a look back into the condo. Bane was still dressing in the bedroom. "He really needs a weekend in bed from the looks of him."

Bane did look sick. He had woken up still glassy eyed and stayed in bed all day long. Nick had noticed the billionaire shifting uncomfortably as if the light silk robe caused his skin to itch. Bane's mood had been less than stellar, too, though he'd apologized for it half a dozen times already.

"I am a bear when I do not feel well, Nick. Please forgive me for any behavior that is less than my best," Bane had said and kissed Nick gently on the temple.

"I tried telling him he should cancel whatever this business meeting is, but he won't," Nick told Jade. His lips flattened. He really wished Bane wouldn't push himself so hard, but the billionaire had almost *panicked* when Nick suggested again he stay home that weekend and rest. Nick had volunteered to take care of him once more, but that had been greeted with almost horror. Bane was intent on leaving and having Nick nowhere near him.

"Yeah, I'm not surprised. He's a workaholic," she said with a fond shake of her head. She and Bane had gone from uncomfortable strangers to friends. She focused in on him again. "So what is going on with *you*? And don't tell me it's *nothing*. I can see it's not."

He grimaced. "It's something Devon said."

Jade was already rolling her eyes. "*Devon*? Nick, you can't believe anything he says! He's got ulterior motives!"

"I know. I *know*." Nick crossed his arms over his chest. "It's just, Jade, some of what he said *you've* already said."

"Me?" She put a hand up against her chest and looked rather alarmed.

"My family … Bane still has the deal with them, but you know that. And I said I was *cool* with that, remember?" Nick asked her and a wave of misery went over him.

"Ah." Understanding flowed over her features. "I wondered when this would come up again."

"The funny thing is that it *hasn't* come up." Nick scrubbed one hand over his face. "Bane hasn't said *anything* about letting my family out of the deal. In fact, I'm pretty sure he just assumes that whatever he does with them has absolutely no effect on him or me."

She bit her lower lip and said carefully, "Have you told him that's not true? I mean if it's actually not true –"

"Of course, it's not true! I don't *like* them, but they're my family. I don't want anything bad to happen to them, especially not inflicted by someone I love." And as soon Nick said it, he realized what was *really* bothering him. He leaned against the railing. "Why doesn't Bane *know* that? Why has he *kept* me in this position?"

"You have to *tell* him, Nick." Jade looked serious. "You have to let him know that you can't deal with this."

Nick's mouth went dry. "I'm afraid of what he'll say."

"You're afraid he'll say no?" she asked.

He nodded, unable to even say the word himself. "I know he and I just started this relationship, but I've never felt *anything* like this before. It feels so *right*, Jade. But if he says *no*," he got the word out this time, but couldn't say the rest.

"Then he's not the man you believed him to be," she finished for him.

"But that's too simplistic!"

She grabbed a hold of his arm and her expression was tender. "I get it that people aren't perfect, Nick, but this is sort of a big deal, right? I mean we all have deal breakers. I'm pretty sure dating a man that would put your family out on the street is one of them for you."

She was right, of course, but he loved Bane. He loved even the bad parts of him at times, like his arrogance, his prickliness, and his quick judgment. But also, he loved the many good pars like his generosity, his genuine kindness, his tenderness, and his strength.

"Nick, I've known Bane less time than you, but I don't think he'll say no. I really don't." She squeezed his arm. "The thing is that there can't be love without trust. Well, not lasting love anyways."

"I know that in my head," he said. "I even know that I'm selling Bane short by not talking to him about this."

"Actually, I think you're selling *yourself* short," she said with a sigh. "You don't believe *you're* worth it to him to let go of his revenge against your family. *That's* what this is really about."

He swallowed. "It's just that everything is so ... *perfect*. I don't want to ruin it."

"You're not ruining it. You're making it what it *should* be," she said.

He nodded. "I'll talk to him after this weekend. He's so sick and the show and –"

"Just don't put it off too long or it will become something even bigger than it already is," she advised. "Remember love and trust go together."

"Yeah, totally. Should have figured this out before." He realized then that if he had talked to Bane about this right from the beginning it would have been easier. He could have insisted the whole deal be unwound before they started dating. "Now I'm really glad that Bane didn't go to lunch with me and Dad the other day. The last thing I need is for Bane to remember why he wanted to destroy the Fairfaxes in the first place. So keeping them apart before I ask Bane to let them out of the deal is *key*."

"You don't think your father or brothers could find out about tonight and show up, do you?" Jade asked with a worried frown.

Nick blinked. "No, I'm *sure* not. Dad does some charity stuff but not like this."

"Right and he wouldn't just show up to see Bane?" Her eyebrows crawled up into her hairline.

"He would if he knew about it. But until two days ago, we didn't even know about it," he pointed out. "And Bane's been sick in bed since then so there's no chance that Dad discovered it."

"Yeah, true. I'm sure you're right."

At that moment, Bane came out onto the balcony and Nick's heart did that little dance it did whenever he saw the billionaire. Bane looked beautiful though still unwell. The big man actually flinched a little when the moonlight hit him as if it hurt him somehow. But the smile he'd had on his face upon seeing Nick quickly returned and he stepped out to take Nick's hands in his though Nick noticed he stayed in the shadows as much as possible.

"Every time I think I've seen you in the suit I like best on you, you come out with another one on that takes my breath away," Nick told him.

Bane was wearing a pair of tailored pants in a light cream, a button down shirt in crisp pale blue and a matching suit coat to the pants.

Bane rested his forehead lightly against Nick's. "Not as beautiful as you. You could wear a bin liner and be ravishing."

"You both look gorgeous," Jade said as she clasped her hands together in front of her and rocked back and forth on her heels.

"As do you, Jade," he said gallantly as ever. "Pretty as a picture."

"Not as nice as Nick's pictures, but I suppose I'll do." She smiled. "I wanted to thank you again for this weekend. The only thing I could wish for more is if you and Omar could be with us."

Bane's expression became rigid for a moment, but then he showed true regret. Nick wondered what it was about this meeting that Bane simply couldn't miss. It seemed like the billionaire was dreading it, but yet he wouldn't give it up.

"I wish that, too," Bane finally said. "But I am certain that the two of you would like a best friends weekend together without others underfoot."

"I sort of think of us as a foursome. You, me, Jade and Omar," Nick admitted. Jade held up a hand to her mouth as giggles escaped her. Even Bane was blushing slightly. Nick reviewed what he had said and blushed. He started waving his hands through the air. "Oh, no, no, I didn't mean it like that!"

Bane put an arm around Nick's shoulders. "I think we've had enough *adventuresome* sex this week."

"Nick told me about the skinny dipping and the police!" Jade laughed.

"The police totally made more of a big deal of it than it was. But maybe if Bane hadn't *ripped* his pants off and we'd both been able to dress, it would have worked out differently," Nick elbowed Bane affectionately.

Bane scrubbed the back of his head. "Yes, yes, I suppose the ruined clothing *was* a part of their concern."

Nick kissed his cheek. "I, personally, *loved* that you were so eager to get in the water with me that you ripped your clothes off."

Bane's Siberian blue eyes glowed that sulphurous blue that had a skitter of amazement and fear trickling down Nick's spine. "I am *always* eager to be with you."

Jade started edging towards the balcony doors, saying, "I'll just leave you two alone –"

"No, no, Jade, it's okay!" Nick called. "We have to go to the show now. Can't be late." He looked up at Bane. "I hope that *you* like the photos, even if no one else does."

Bane cupped his face. His eyes were still glowing, but it was a softer, gentler light, not so wild and untamed. "It does not matter what anyone else thinks, Nick. They *are* objectively brilliant. But I am certain that the others will see that, too." He placed a soft kiss on Nick's forehead. "Now let's go do this."

He and Bane linked hands and the three of them walked off the balcony. They went down to the garage where Omar was already waiting with the sleek, black Maybach.

"I am so excited, Nick, to see others' reactions to your incredible work! I have so many favorites among them already!" the Indian man enthused as he drove them expertly down the crowded Winter Haven streets.

"See, Nick, you have three fans already," Jade said from the front seat. She chose to sit next to Omar, leaving him and Bane the back seat to themselves.

"I do see that," he assured her, feeling some of his nervousness drain away.

Nick glowed in the perfection of this moment. His friends and his lover were going to see the first public exhibition of his work. He had their complete support. It couldn't get better than this.

Bane's arm was around his shoulders. He felt the man's warm breath against his cheek. When he turned his head to look at Bane, the billionaire was smiling at him lovingly.

"Everything will work out, Nick. You will see," Bane said softly and brushed his lips against Nick's forehead.

It will. I've been stupid not to tell Bane about my feelings about the deal with my family. Jade's right. Trust and love go together. Hand in hand. I need to trust Bane.

"We are here!" Omar called gaily. "I will drop you off and then go park the car."

"There's a valet," Nick pointed out.

But Omar shook his head. "The Maybach is my special charge. I do not let anyone other than Peter drive her."

"Omar is *quite* protective of the car," Bane chuckled.

Omar pulled the Maybach up to the curb outside the event space. In the night with the lights on inside and people in evening clothes inside, the space looked very different. Very *official.*

"Nick, people are already looking at your photographs!" Jade pointed towards a crowd clustered around the fountain photograph.

Nick's chest tightened and his heart beat harder as he saw a woman gesture towards some part of the photograph and say something to her male companion who nodded and pointed something else out. He saw that other people were drifting from photograph to photograph, looking at them carefully. He swallowed hard.

"You see," Bane said with a light caress of his cheek. "They love your work. I cannot wait to look at them myself in this space."

"You need wait no longer," Omar said as he set the Maybach into park. He then quickly jumped out to open their doors. Jade had already gotten out and waved him graciously away. Omar opened the back door for Nick and Bane instead. The billionaire let Nick get out first.

As Nick eagerly stepped out onto the sidewalk, he heard his name called, "Nickie! There you are!"

Nick's heart fell into his feet as he saw who was standing just two feet away. "Dad, what are you doing here?"

CHAPTER TWENTY-THREE

BRITTLE

C harles! He would be here to ruin Nick's big night! Bane thought with a growl.

The beast's eyes narrowed and it kneaded his chest, wanting to get out and chase the elder Fairfax down the street. Bane could almost imagine the man's fear at seeing the beast and, for once, it *pleased* him. But instead of Charles Fairfax, eyes wide, coat tails flapping, and face dripping with flop sweat as he fled from a tiger, the man stood negligently just outside the door to the charity event.

Charles was dressed in a gray suit with chunky silver and diamond cufflinks that glittered at his wrists. An ostentatious show of wealth in Bane's opinion. It screamed "Look at me! I'm wealthy and powerful and better than you!" It was just so *crude*, which fit the Fairfax image. One look at Nick though, his beautiful, refined features and artistic brow, and Bane quickly amended that thought to it fit the image of *some* of the Fairfaxes.

Though the other two definitely take after their father.

Charles' two other sons flanked him. Steven was adjusting the cuffs of his shirt so that they were the exact same length. Bane had heard about his meticulousness from the people he had assigned to work with him. Steven knew where every penny was going and why. It was actually a *good* trait, but he had no moral compass to judge whether cutting waste, for example, in supplies was the same as doing so with *employees*. Everything was dollars and cents to the middle son.

Jake was the exact opposite of Steven. According to Bane's people, the man worked on pure instinct. He had *good* instincts, but they were *killer* ones. Like Steven, his good qualities were overlaid with bad. He would see promise in a new product, but if it, let's say, had a negative environmental impact designed one way versus a safe, but more expensive design, Jake would always choose the cheaper one and damn the environment. Jake's gaze shifted from Bane to Nick to Jade to Omar and then to the other people entering the space. He reminded Bane of a shark that had to be constantly moving or he would die.

In contrast to his two brothers and father, Nick looked like a deer in headlights. Faint perspiration was dotting the young man's brow. His cheeks were flushed and his gaze flickered somewhat like Jake's had, but not predatorily. It was more like Nick was trying to figure out how to keep things from exploding all around him.

"Seriously, Dad, *what* are *you* doing *here*?" Nick repeated. It was almost a bleat and Bane's heart clenched.

"I'm sure he's just here to support you. Aren't you, Mr. Fairfax?" Jade said weakly.

Nick didn't even try to act like he believed her and continued to stare at his father in disbelief. The beast lowered its head aggressively and growled low in the back of its throat. If Charles could have heard that sound he would have been pissing himself. Bane had only the slightest of worries at that moment that he was *reacting too violently*, that the beast was too forward, too much in charge and that he had to control himself. But this was only a stray thought and it quickly vanished as he watched Charles' little bonhomie act.

Charles placed a heavy hand on Nick's right shoulder and said, "Nickie, you have your *first* show and you don't tell your *family* about it?"

"It's for a charity event. All the sales from my work—if there are any—will go to the event, not to me," Nick explained stiffly. "So it's not really a show. I'm just helping out in any little way I can by offering my photographs for sale."

"So it's like pity purchases?" Jake sneered.

Nick colored hugely. There was a flicker of hurt on his face, but he quickly hid it. "Something like that."

"It's *not* like that at all!" Jade cried. She flashed a look of fury at Jake who merely gave her a cool gaze in return. He was not impressed with her support of Nick.

Let's see how he handles mine.

"Your brother is *talented*, Jake, which seems *rare* in your family," Bane said, his voice icy with disdain.

He let naked dislike show in his eyes. Jake saw it and actually took a half-step back. He glimpsed the beast, but didn't know what it was. Jade gave Bane a hidden thumbs up. Nick though still looked miserable. He, undoubtedly, thought that both of them were backing him up against Jake not because his work was worth anything, but because they cared for him.

Charles, surprisingly—or perhaps not, because Bane was sure that the elder Fairfax had seen that look, too—quickly said, "Jake, we're here to *support* Nick not tease him." He gave Bane a toothy smile. "Forgive my eldest, but you know how brothers are! Or perhaps you don't, because you're an only child, right, Bane? But let me tell you. They're constantly *needling* one another. It's all in *good fun*."

"Good fun?" Jade repeated with a raised eyebrow. "I would *hate* to see what Jake's like when he's actually *trying* to be hurtful."

Nick reached over and squeezed her arm. She sighed and turned away from the family, looking inside of the charity space instead.

"Nick knows that I'm *joking*," Jake sniffed.

"But, just in case he doesn't, why don't you apologize, Jake?" Charles didn't look at his eldest son as he said this, but Jake straightened as if the words had been barked at him instead of said almost gently.

"Yeah, sorry, Nick," Jake mumbled. "Just messing around."

"It's fine, Jake," Nick said though there was still hectic color on his cheeks, which told Bane that it *wasn't* fine. Nick turned back to his father. "I just didn't want you to make a big deal out of this, Dad. I'm nervous enough as it is. I'm not sure that people will buy my work even out of *pity*."

"Nickie! Like I said, we're here to support you and the worthy cause." Charles thumped Nick's shoulder.

Bane highly doubted that. The man had just seen his son for lunch the other day, which was the first time since the deal had been struck that Nick and Charles had physically met. On the other hand, Bane had been ducking Charles since he had come back from Europe. He could just see Charles scheming to meet him here. Charles would then be able to talk business with Bane and bask in any reflective glory from Nick's work. The meeting would then look *almost* serendipitous. Yes, that was far more likely a reason for Charles to be here. Bane's hands half curled into fists and it took all his willpower to relax them.

"Okay, Dad, just—just don't be *you* about the photos, okay?" Nick begged.

Bane knew *exactly* what Nick meant. He had seen videos of Charles working a room like it was an Olympic sport. He could, undoubtedly, sell Nick's photos, but not on their merits. Such a display would also embarrass Nick hugely.

"Can't I show my pride for my son?" When Charles saw Nick's wretched look, he quickly said, "Okay, Nickie, I promise to be low key."

"Really?" Nick didn't look convinced.

"I promise!" He threw an arm around Nick's shoulders and urged the young man through the doors. "Now show me your work!"

Nick shot a long-suffering look over his shoulder at Bane, but then dutifully led Charles towards one of the first photographs. Jade sighed, shook her head, and followed after them. Charles put his other hand on the middle of her back, including her in their threesome. That left Steven, Jake and Bane outside. Omar had had the good sense to get back in the car and go park it.

"So ..." Jake began and cleared his throat. Bane could almost imagine Charles' instructions to his sons to talk to Bane, to be friendly. Jake couldn't quite pull that off, but he was trying. "You really think Nick's stuff is good?" He scraped the bottom of his expensive leather shoe on the sidewalk. When he saw Bane's baleful look at his question he quickly added, "I'm asking because I don't know anything about art. Seems like *you* do. So it's cool that you think Nick's art is good. It's an expert's opinion. Has more weight than mine."

"Now *that* is the most intelligent thing you've said in my presence," Bane replied. "I wouldn't press it further while you're *ahead*."

Jake nodded like a bobble head doll, sealing his lips together. Bane wouldn't have been surprised if he had made the sign for locking his lips and throwing away the key. Steven kept silent, too, but he did indicate for Bane to precede them into the event. He knew the brothers shared a look behind his back, but he didn't care. As long as they were *silent* that was the best he could expect from them. The beast let out a huff of agreement. He was grateful to see that the brothers went towards the bar while he headed after Nick.

But before he had taken two steps, Devon appeared before him like a rabbit out of a hat. The man thrust a glass of whisky into his hands. Bane normally did *not* drink this close to the shift. He needed his mind as clear as possible, but he and the beast had an *agreement* this time that there would be no shifting tonight, which might make it safe for him to have a drink or two. If he was honest with himself, he *needed* those drinks.

The sounds, the smells, the colors—*everything*—was amped up about 100 notches because of the nearness of the shift. He could smell a river of perfume, cologne, sweat, alcohol and food. The scents ran like colors in the air. Every single voice was audible to him, a cacophony of sound that clawed around the inside of his skull. The red of a woman's dress was like a splash of blood. The black of a blazer reminded him of the darkness of space. Everything was just so *intense*.

He needed to quiet his senses so he drank down the two fingerfuls of amber liquid and rested the glass against his suddenly sweaty forehead. Heat whooshed down his throat and settled in his belly sending out the feel-good sensation that liquor often did. It also lessened the volume of his senses slightly.

"I could tell you needed that," Devon said with a small, breathy laugh. "When Charles and his sons showed up I worried a bit. I almost tossed them out, but –"

"Their money is as good as anyone else's and it's for a good cause," Bane finished for him. He brought the heavy cut crystal glass down from his forehead and opened his eyes.

Devon had always been willing to deal with anyone for a crisp check. Since the money was never for him, but for the needy, Bane had appreciated that fact about him. It showed that Devon wasn't above getting his hands dirty and doing hard work when needed to help others. Yet, tonight, he'd wished Devon *had* gone against his normal instincts.

But why should he? I tossed him over for Nick. He owes me no favors.

Devon was smiling at him softly though. Seeing the empty glass he reached to take it. "Want another?"

Bane already felt a little sloppy from one drink. He knew he should say no, but instead, he said, "Just one more. But I need to get some food in me after that."

"I'll send the men with the canapes your way," Devon assured him.

"Your staff looks rather busy." Bane nodded his head towards one waiter that was mobbed by the guests. He was reminded of hungry piranhas swarming prey. "I can wait."

"The party is in full swing and I have to admit that Nick's photographs are a real hit."

Devon's lips flattened just a touch at the mention of Nick, but he immediately smiled again and leaned his body against

Bane's. Bane could smell the alcohol on his breath. Devon's eyes were also slightly glassy and there was high color in his cheeks. He had been drinking more than he usually did. Bane frowned. There was this brittle gaiety about Devon that night that worried him. The beast wrinkled its nose and gave a disgusted huff. It didn't want Devon in his nose and against his skin. It wanted Nick. But Bane reminded himself that he was a *man* not a beast. Devon was his friend and had done a good thing for Nick. He couldn't just shake him off.

"I hope that they are helping the cause," Bane said awkwardly.

"He's sold five at double the asking prices. There was a bit of a bidding war going on earlier." Devon gave a startled little laugh and pointed towards where Nick, Charles and Jade were standing. "Actually, make that *six*. I see Charles is doing his best impression of a used car salesman. But it *does* work to bring in the cash. Maybe I should bring Charles to all of my events."

"God, *no*," Bane muttered.

Nick, Charles and Jade were standing in front of the photographs of the fountain. They were some of the ones Nick had taken that terrible day he'd been burned. Charles lifted his glass of whisky towards one of the photos. An elderly woman that Bane recognized from another of Devon's events was smiling and nodding at whatever he'd said. Nick's cheeks were flushed and he kept ducking his head, but there was a pleased smile on his face. Jade was rocking back and forth on her platforms, clearly happy as well. Charles was saying something *nice* about the photos and the elderly woman agreed.

"So ... has Nick asked you to release his family from the deal and give the company back to them yet?" Devon asked casually.

Bane's head shot towards him. Alarm filled him. "What do you mean? Has Nick said something about it to you?"

"We were just talking about it yesterday." Devon gave a negligent shrug and finished his own whisky. He held up the glass and reached for Bane's. "Let me get us some more –"

Before Devon could get the rest of the sentence out, Bane grasped his arm. "What did Nick say to you *exactly*?"

Devon looked down at his hand on his arm and Bane realized he was likely holding him too tightly. He released Devon and forced himself to act normally.

"He just told me how you would *never* actually throw his family out on the street," Devon explained.

"If they *succeed* in the deal then no, I won't."

"But he meant *never*. No matter *what* they did. I mean you're *dating*. So long as you're together you'll judge them as having *succeeded*, yes?" Devon gave him a knowing smile.

Bane looked over towards Nick. He and Charles were talking in low tones, heads together while Jade spoke to the elderly woman.

"... all I'm saying, Nickie, is that you keep Bane happy and we get the company back. Just do your part. You can do that, can't you? It's just a year and then we're all free," Charles voice and those words popped into full clarity as if Charles were speaking directly into Nick's ear.

Nick nodded or maybe it was just a nervous, uncomfortable movement. Bane though *feared* it was a nod and, suddenly, he was unable to hear what Nick said at all as his senses withdrew like animals expecting an attack.

Like Alastair ... just in it for what he can get. No, that's madness. That's not true. I know that's not true!

"I suppose Nick is right, really, to have such expectations," Devon suddenly said, noticing where Bane was looking. "I mean *no relationship*, not even one that began *normally* and *naturally*, could survive for long when one partner has the fate of the other's family in the palm of his hand. Well, I suppose it *could* survive if the one partner is just in it to save his family and there's no real love or affection there. What do you think, Bane?"

The beast had gone absolutely still at Devon's words, much like Bane had. Bane could suddenly only hear the blood rushing through his own veins and the frantic beating of his heart. This relationship *had* not started *normally* or *naturally*. He had *forced* it. Would it be so wrong of Nick to want to assure his family *benefited* now from their happiness? But maybe Nick wasn't happy. Maybe he was just enduring Bane's attentions. Pain lanced through Bane's head, muddling his thought processes more, as the beast's hackles were raised. It was afraid. It couldn't lose Nick. But it could not allow *falsity* from their mate either.

He found himself moving towards Nick and Charles. He wasn't sure if he said anything to Devon, not even to excuse himself. He had to know if Nick was with him because he cared for him or if it was all about saving the Fairfax fortune.

CHAPTER TWENTY-FOUR

A CHOICE

When Nick had seen his father standing at the door of the charity event, he had thought that the night was going to be awful. He imagined his father taking Bane aside to talk business, Jake making snide comments about his "art", and Steven, not so subtly, checking his watch, wanting to leave to do something *important*. And the beginning of the night had been exactly like he'd feared. But then things had changed.

His father had actually listened as he had explained his thought process behind the photographs. Charles had, incredibly, asked intelligent questions about that process. His father had taken his time examining each photo and had *appreciated* what Nick was trying to do. He'd shared his thoughts with others around them, not in his usual smarmy way but as if with fellow art lovers. Yet he'd managed to somehow *sell* one of Nick's photographs to a lovely older woman. Nick had blushed and ducked his head as the woman praised his work and said that she would love to see more of it. He had promised to get her information from Devon and call upon her at her convenience.

"Your mother would have loved these, Nickie," Charles had said and Nick couldn't help but beam in response.

There was only *one* moment when his father had reverted to form and caused Nick to want to strangle him. That was when Charles had caught Nick glowering over at Devon as the man plastered himself against Bane.

"Nickie, jealousy *isn't* attractive," Charles had said, taking a sip of his whisky. "An attractive, rich man like Bane is going to have many admirers."

Nick's head had snapped back towards his father. "I'm *not* jealous. It's just—"

"So you're *not* looking daggers at Devon Wainwright? Bane's old lover? The host of this fine shindig?" Charles raised an eyebrow.

Nick flushed, which gave lie to his words. "He's *hanging* on Bane, you know? Things are *over* between them, but Devon is still trying to get back in there."

Charles nodded, agreeing with him, but then said, "It doesn't matter if he is. You can't keep Bane by acting like a cat with him. You have to *make* Bane forget Devon and every other man every single day. Well, at least for a *year*."

"A year? What does that—Dad!" Nick's voice rose shrilly as he realized what his father was saying. He dropped his voice immediately and whispered, "Dad, I'm *not* with Bane for you to get the company back!"

Again, Charles nodded, looking for all the world completely agreeable. "I know, and that's great that your emotions are *genuine*. But all I'm saying, Nickie, is that you keep Bane happy and we get the company back. Just do your part. You can do that, can't you? It's just a year and then we're all free."

Nick's body trembled with suppressed rage at his father's words. Not wanting to cause a scene though he had merely nodded his head, but then said quite clearly, "Dad, my relationship with Bane has *nothing* to do with you. You're on your *own* in getting the company back. You need to win this yourself. Got it?"

Charles looked at him, surprisingly, with affection. "You really are just like your mother." He sighed as he added, "I just hope that it won't screw us."

"Well, it's not about *you*, remember?" Nick reminded him.

Charles patted his arm and was about to say something else when Bane appeared at Nick's elbow.

"Bane, there you are. I wondered where you got off to. Nick and I have just made Devon some money for this worthy cause." Then a concerned look crossed over Charles' face. "You're looking a little *peaked* there, Bane. Maybe you should sit down. Nickie, let's go find Bane a chair in a quiet spot—"

"No," Bane's voice was practically a growl. That sense of *wildness* was back in him and that had Nick immediately worrying. Bane looked like he was hanging onto control by his fingertips.

But control of what? He hasn't been himself for the last few days. Sometimes it seems like there's something inside of him just trying to claw its way out.

"Bane, Dad's right ... for once. You really don't look well. Seriously, we can sit down somewhere or—or maybe get some air?" Nick placed a hand on Bane's large right shoulder. He rubbed it, but Bane did not relax. If anything, he got tenser.

"Some air," Bane grunted, his voice was a low burr that normally thrilled Nick, but right now it just sounded dangerous and pained at the same time.

"Of course. Excuse us, Dad," Nick said pointedly, shooing his father further into the charity event while he led Bane towards the front doors.

He saw a flash of disappointment on his father's face. He knew that Charles had been dying to talk to Bane about business under the guise of friendly banter, but Charles nodded his head with good grace and then flashed a grin.

"I'll go sell more of your photographs, Nickie. By the end of the night, you'll be the most sought after photographer in town!" Charles lifted his drink, ignoring Nick's squawk about not doing that before he disappeared into the crowd.

Nick went back to leading Bane out of the event. The billionaire walked stiffly beside him. Nick let out a sigh of relief as they pushed through the front door and the cooler evening air wrapped around them. The interior had grown quite warm with all the bodies packed into the tight surroundings.

"Let's walk down the street. Get a little privacy," Nick suggested.

Bane simply grunted again and allowed Nick to lead him further away from the noisy, hot interior of the event. They stopped about half a block away. Nick tipped his head back and bathed his face in the night air. Bane was still stiff as a board beside him. He tried to ignore that, while he wondered what it was that Bane was upset about. He recognized this mood and stance from when they had first come to know one another. He had learned to give Bane some space to work through the initial rush of anger. But as the silence stretched on and Bane seemed no more relaxed, Nick chanced a glance over at him.

Bane was watching him out of hooded Siberian blue eyes. Those eyes were glowing. Again, Nick's breath caught. It was like being captured in the gaze of a predator. All of Bane's refinement seemed stripped away at that moment and there was this *wild* creature present.

"Bane?" he asked, and it sounded like he was asking if it was *Bane* really before him or if it was someone—or *something* – else.

"Yes, it's me."

Bane reached and brushed the very tips of his fingers down Nick's left cheek. The touch *burned*. Nick felt *marked* by that touch.

"Well, I hope it's you and not someone else," Nick laughed uncomfortably.

Bane did not. He remained silent as he continued to stroke Nick's face. Nick let out a breath and placed a hand on the center of Bane's chest. For half a second, it felt like Bane's skin *rippled* under his palm, but then the sensation was gone. Not that it could have been a *real* sensation in any event. Skin didn't *ripple*.

"Bane, what's wrong?" Nick asked. "Please, tell me. You haven't been yourself since our swim and you keep saying that everything's *fine*, but it clearly *isn't—*"

"Are you ... are you my *mate*?" Bane asked.

Nick blinked in confusion. The word "mate" was throwing him and Bane seemed to recognize this. Bane shut his eyes tightly for a moment, his jaw clenching, as he clearly tried to keep control of himself. When he opened his eyes again, they were still glowing, the wildness was still there, but it wasn't as pronounced. There was more of *Bane* there.

"Do you ... do you *l-love* me?" Bane asked.

The word "love" was even more alien on Bane's lips than "mate", but Nick understood now. A flush coated his cheeks and he nodded.

"Yes, I *do*. Is that all right?" Nick asked. He winced as he said the last. "I mean—clearly, I feel this and I have a right to feel this way, but I know how you feel about that term and—"

Bane kissed him. It was a full on, desperate, nearly animalistic kiss. There was a hot press of lips then teeth and tongue and wet and lack of oxygen. When Bane pulled back and rested their foreheads together, Nick was seeing black spots. It took a few moments before he could speak.

"Well, I guess it *is* all right that I love you!" Nick gasped out.

Bane's hands were on his biceps. The grip was so tight that it was almost painful, but Nick relished Bane's strength and the possessiveness he was showing. It definitely made clear to Nick that Bane's interest was securely on him and not on Devon.

"It is. More than all right," Bane answered, his voice gravelly. "I thought ... I heard ... I overheard your father and Devon said ... well, it does not matter."

Confusion flooded Nick for a moment, but then he realized that Bane must have heard Charles' words about Nick only having to stay with Bane and make him happy for a year until they had the company back. Nick let out a pained laugh.

"I'm sorry you heard that. Dad is really incorrigible at times, which is probably the *kindest* way of putting it." Nick ran his hands down Bane's front. "But, surely, you know that I don't feel that way? I'm sorry you didn't overhear what I said to *him* in response."

Bane's grip tightened and Nick grunted. He quickly loosened the grip. "Yes, yes, I know and I wish I had. Devon was—"

"Pouring poison in your ears? I should have guessed," Nick said glumly. "What did he say?"

He would find out what that little viper had been saying to Bane. After smoothing things over with the billionaire, he would go into the event and have it out with Devon right in the middle of the space. He didn't care if it ruined his career. Devon was *not* going to mess up the most important thing in his life, which was Bane. He just wished that Bane was acting more like himself now that he knew his fears were baseless. But there was still this barely controlled violence in the big man and, though it didn't frighten Nick exactly, it disturbed him. But he guessed that it had to do with Bane's secrets. Maybe he was ill, had some condition that made him this way and he was afraid to tell Nick about it.

"Devon wondered if you had asked me to let your family out of the deal yet," Bane explained.

Nick's heart tumbled into his feet. Bane was *upset*, rage-filled, at the idea that Nick would ask for his family's freedom?

There must be more to it than that!

"That's all Devon said?" Nick asked carefully.

Bane nodded and Nick felt a wash of cold go through him.

The billionaire added, "You would *never* ask me to do that. Your family are unworthy of you. You are above them. So much *more* than them. It will be better when the year is over and they are *gone* from our lives. Then it will just be the two of us and I can keep you safe and happy."

Nick stared at him in shock. "What do you mean 'gone from our lives'? You mean when Dad and my brothers are so wrapped up in running Fairfax International that they aren't bugging us? That definitely will get them to ignore us!"

The last was asked hopefully, but he knew that was not what Bane meant. Cold dread filled his chest.

Bane frowned. "*No*, I mean when they are *gone*. They will not *succeed* in passing my test. It is beyond them to act in a way that looks beyond money. They're already *failing* now."

Nick realized he hadn't been breathing during Bane's entire statement. He finally drew in a sharp breath and wheezed. "You sound ... sound ..."

"What?" Bane cocked his head to the side.

"*Happy* at the idea of them failing, of putting them out on the street," Nick said faintly. His hands had fallen from Bane's chest and hung loosely at his sides.

"I *am*. Aren't you? They'll be *gone*, Nick. All the things that they've done to you would be avenged. They would finally get what's coming to them." Bane gave one of those tigerish, triumphant smiles, but it was *not* endearing. It chilled Nick.

Nick was silent for a very long time. He couldn't seem to find the words he wanted to say as there was so much *wrong* with those statements. Worse, it seemed Bane didn't notice his reaction *at all*.

"If you think that having my family on the streets would make me happy, you really don't know me at all." Nick stepped away from him. He needed space to think. He needed a drink or something. He couldn't believe Bane was saying these things and, yet, he could at the same time. Because *this* was his nightmare come true.

Bane though did not let go of his shoulders. That wild light suddenly burned brighter and Bane rasped out, "Nick, where are you going? Why are you moving away from me?"

A trickle of fear ran through Nick. Bane was sweating profusely. His eyes were glowing. He hardly looked *human*. And somehow fear turned to anger.

"Didn't you hear me? Are you listening to me at all?" Nick's voice was edged. He swallowed and tried to calm himself. Bane mustn't know what he was saying! It was the sickness or whatever was causing him to act so strangely overall. He thought of Jade's advice about telling Bane his true feelings about the deal. If Bane cared for him, even a little, he would understand and let his family go. So, centering himself, he said as calmly as he could, "Bane, I want you to release my family from the deal."

Bane's eyes narrowed, glowing gas lit blue in the dark. "You mean give them Fairfax International back?"

"Yes," Nick said, meeting Bane's gaze. "I don't want my family on the street. I don't want the man I love to be the one to put them there! I don't think I could—could love a man who did that."

"You'd let them just go on with their avaricious ways?" Bane's voice held an edge of disdain.

Nick didn't want that exactly. That seemed like rewarding them for bad behavior. "Okay, then put them back in charge of the business, but you have veto power over what they do. So you can stop them from hurting people, but—"

"Nick," Bane interrupted. "The only reason they are not out on the streets *now* is because of my feelings for *you*. Because you are my mate. My ... my one. To ask more of me is—is, well, *too much*. They are not worthy of your request."

Too much?

Nick felt like he was falling. Nothing felt real. He thought of his happiness earlier in the evening in the car when they had arrived here. Everything had seemed right with the world and now ... now everything was *wrong*.

"Bane, you can't mean what you're saying!"

"I do. I look forward to seeing them hunted out of town. We will watch them slink off together! No longer will you have to deal with their snide comments about your art! No longer will you have to be hurt by them!"

He thinks he's saving me. But he's not. Not like this.

Nick tried to explain his feelings, "They're rotten in a lot of ways, but they're *my family*. Yes, they say hurtful things and are thoughtless at times, but most families have that. They love me, but we're just really different people. I thought that you ..."

"That I what?"

"That you cared about *me* more than you cared about hurting *them*."

Nick shook off Bane's hands and stepped out of reach. He was trembling.

"You are everything to me. You ... you do not understand what you mean to me, but my words are limited, because ..." Bane thumped a hand viciously against his chest. "I cannot speak or think properly!"

"You're not well. We should get Omar and –"

"I will not let your family go, Nick. I will not let *you* go. They are *mine*! You are *mine*! I will do with them as I please."

Nick stared back at him, stunned. "As you *please?*"

Bane's hands flexed at his sides and Nick knew that the big man wanted to reach for him and grab him. He had this feeling that after Bane grabbed him that the big man would run away from him.

"Yes, the Fairfaxes—the *other* Fairfaxes—will finally know what it's like to be penniless," Bane told him.

Anger mixed with absolute shock ran through Nick. He found himself shouting, "How can you stand there and tell me that you're planning on throwing my family on the streets and that I should be *glad* about it? How can you do that and still claim to *care* about me? You're *seething* at the very idea that maybe I would *want* you to let them out of an unconscionable deal! You talk about how *bad* my father and brothers are, but what about *you*? You've made mistakes and hurt people! The deal originally was a damned big mistake, right? Yet, no one is punishing you for it! But you want to judge them like some being from on high!"

Nick's voice rose up and up as the words just tumbled out of him. He was so angry! Furiously, righteously angry. Bane was letting that selfish, cruel part of himself out and Nick wasn't going to stand for it. Sick or no, what Bane was saying was utterly *wrong*. He wouldn't stand for it.

Bane stepped towards him, reaching for him again, trying to contain him. "Nick, you mustn't pull away from me now."

"Why not? You don't own me! Or—or *do you*? If we have a fight like this, if we're not together ... what will you do to my father and brothers?" Nick asked, emotions clawing up his throat.

Bane's head lowered and he watched Nick through the fall of his hair. It was literally a growl as he said, "You're *mine*."

"I'm my own!" The last shout echoed down the street.

Bane's stared at him, saying nothing. Perhaps he was too stunned to speak. Or maybe it was whatever else he was hiding that had his tongue. But either way, Nick was done with this conversation. Pain and rage lanced through him. He loved Bane, but the man had just revealed himself to be just like Nick's father, but *worse*.

Nick started to walk back towards the charity event. He had to *think*. He had to get *away*. Maybe then he could figure out how to reconcile the fact that he still loved Bane, but he couldn't be with him with this between them.

He had only taken a few steps when one of Bane's hands reached out and grabbed him, this time very painfully, around the right wrist. Nick let out a cry of surprise as well as hurt, but Bane did not release him or even lessen the grip.

"Bane, what are you—"

"Don't run from me, Nick," Bane's voice was guttural, nearly animalistic as if he were talking around fangs. "If you *run*, I will *chase*."

Nick stared up at him, the pain in his wrist still sharp and stinging. "What does that even *mean*? You're a *man*, Bane, *not* a *beast*. But you act like these things are out of your control, but they aren't! It's all *you*! Now let me go. You're hurting me."

Bane didn't let go. His eyes were like blue gas flames in the night. His lips kept writhing back from his teeth, teeth that looked abnormally white and sharp in the low light of the nearby street lamps. "You're mine. Mine. MINE!"

"Bane, stop!" Nick managed to rip himself out of Bane's grasp.

Bane *growled* like a gigantic beast. Nick stumbled back a step then another then another.

"Don't run," Bane got out, his voice not even sounding human to Nick's ears. "I'll chase."

At that moment, Jade's voice rang out from behind him, "Nick! Where did you go?" There was laughter in her tone, but that laughter soon died as she must have taken in the situation. "Nick, what's going on here?"

"It's nothing, Jade, just go inside," he said to her.

"N-no, Nick, I'm not leaving you," she said, her voice quavering a little.

"Jade—"

"Why are you all out here? All of Nick's photos have been sold! It is amazing!" Omar's cheery tones rose up and then he said, "Bane! Oh, by the gods. Bane, what—Nick, please come here. Just back away slowly and—"

"NO!" Bane bellowed. "He runs and I chase!"

"Oh, my, oh, my goodness," the Indian man whittered. "Jade, come inside. And Nick, just—"

"Just *what*, Omar? What do I do?" Nick breathed.

Nick's gaze was locked on Bane. Bane's was locked on him. The big man looked ready to *lunge*.

"He loves you. You must know this. Even this part of him," Omar said.

This part of him? What part is this?

Despite not understanding what Omar meant, Nick stopped backing away. Images of his and Bane's times together flashed before his eyes at the same moment. The way Bane smiled at him. The way Bane touched him as if he were precious and treasured. The way Bane remembered the things he liked and made sure that he always had them. The way Bane laughed at his bad jokes. The way Bane normally *was* with him: tender, caring, gentle. Whatever was going on here was not *normal*. Bane needed help. He needed *Nick's* help.

"Jade, Omar, could you go get the car? This is fine. I've got this," Nick said and he straightened.

"But, Nick, you do not know everything!" Omar cried.

Nick mentally filed this away. Omar knew what was going on here, but it didn't matter. He sensed that he and only he could calm Bane down. "I know that he needs me. That's enough. For now."

Nick didn't know if Omar and Jade did as he asked. His whole attention was on Bane. Bane's shoulders were heaving. Nick extended a hand and walked slowly towards the billionaire. He only stopped when he was six inches away from the big man. He swallowed the fear that still filled him. Bane was *huge*. He was made of muscle. He could hurt Nick easily, without even trying or meaning to. But Nick reached up and moved the hair away from Bane's forehead, tucking it gently behind Bane's ears. The handprint burn on his face looked almost *fresh*. It was crimson and so raw looking that Nick's own skin hurt just from looking at it.

"It's okay," Nick said softly, like one might to a wild animal. "It's okay, Bane. I'm right here."

He gently ran his fingers through Bane's hair as if he was petting him. Bane's eyelids almost closed completely and he moved his face into that touch like a big cat might. Nick kept on petting him for long moments. Bane kept pushing up against his hand until they had a rhythm going. The heaving had slowed to normal breaths. The scar seemed to have reduced in redness, too. Nick *thought* that things were going to be all right.

And they might have been if Omar had gotten there with the car *before* Devon stepped outside.

"Bane? Nick? Oh, there the two of you are!" Devon sounded slightly drunk and annoyed. "People are looking for you, Nick. It's your big night and you're missing it."

Nick froze at the first syllable out of Devon's mouth. Bane's eyelids, which had been, half-shut snapped open and, immediately, his upper lip writhed back from his teeth in a snarl. Ice slid through Nick's veins. He *knew*—though he wasn't sure how—that Devon was in *danger*. If the man came over to Bane something terrible would happen.

So Nick quickly flipped around to face Devon. "Devon, Bane and I are—"

"Having a fight, I see." Devon was about ten feet away and clearly, from the look on Nick's face, saw something was wrong.

Nick wanted to say "no" but they *had* been having a fight. What this was now though, was something completely different but he didn't know how to explain it without sounding vague and half crazy. So he swallowed his pride and said, "Yeah, so if you don't mind, could you give us some *privacy*?"

Go back into the event, Devon! Please, God, please, go back into the event!

Devon's steps had slowed, but not completely stopped. "Well, I would say you should argue *later* when you're not having your first show—"

"Bane's more important to me than anything else so just go away, okay?" Nick got out.

Devon's gaze slid past Nick to Bane, but then a strange look crossed his face. He blinked and Nick almost thought he was going to rub his eyes as if he didn't believe what he was seeing. Then he let out a huff of laughter.

"Well, I think Bane is done talking," Devon said.

"What?" Nick turned around to look at the big man, except Bane was not there.

As Nick frantically looked around for him, Devon added, "Seems he's left, Nick. Is this the *second* time he's disappeared on you when the goings got tough? Pity. But that's Bane for you. A selfish, secretive man."

CHAPTER TWENTY-FIVE

RUN

Thankfully, the Maybach arrived at that moment with Omar behind the wheel and Jade in the passenger seat, sparing him from having to say something to Devon in response. He was all out of cutting remarks, feeling like he was bleeding out on the ground himself. He saw the shocked looks on both of their faces when they, too, realized that Bane was *gone*.

He left. Again. Goddamn him.

Without a word to Devon, Nick got into the back seat of the Maybach and shut the door firmly in the other man's face.

"Nick, where is Bane?" Omar asked, craning his neck around, looking for the big man.

As if there is any place to hide.

"I don't know. He disappeared. What is going on with Bane, Omar?" Nick demanded to know.

"He disappeared?" Jade's eyebrows rose up into her hairline.

"Yeah, literally. I turned around to talk to Devon. I turned back and he was gone without a word, without a sound, without a trace," Nick said to her then asked again of Omar, "What is going on with Bane, Omar? What was that back there? The scar, the growling, the don't run or I'll chase stuff? I need to know *now*."

He had never seen Omar look so miserable. The Indian man said, "It is not my—"

"Secret to tell? It's Bane's. Yeah, I know, but he's not telling me. He's never going to tell me. He doesn't trust me," Nick said with a bitterness that infected every sound. "He wants everything his own way, no matter what the cost."

Omar winced. "Yes, he is selfish and short-sighted at times. Very much so."

Nick rubbed his wrist where bruises were already blooming like poisonous flowers from Bane's grip. Bane's behavior about his family was bad enough, but the secrets? He couldn't deal with those, too. Something had to change. And that change couldn't happen if he was living at Moon Shadow or in Bane's condo or using Bane's money. His heart ached at the thought of not waking up with Bane beside him, of not hearing his voice, of not feeling his kisses, but it had to be done. He had to leave with only what he had come in with. He had to reset things and restore the power balance.

And what am I hoping? That I run and Bane will chase? Not likely. But I can't stay with him. Not with things like this. Even though leaving him feels like ripping out my own heart.

"Omar, I want you to take Jade back to her place," Nick said through numb lips. He turned his gaze upon his best friend. "I'm sorry, Jade, but we can't stay at Bane's this weekend. I know how much you were looking forward to the spa—"

She waved him off. "That's totally fine. I understand." And he saw from her expression that she *did* understand. She had understood from the beginning that this would not work out between him and Bane. She didn't say, "I told you so." She didn't even look it, but he wished to God that he had listened to her. Back then his feelings for Bane had been intense, but now? Now Bane was his other half and yet he couldn't stay with him.

"And where should I take you, Nick? Back to Bane's con-do?" Omar asked hopefully, but he, too, knew that wasn't where Nick was going.

"Back to Moon Shadow," Nick said.

Alarm filled the Indian man's features and Nick knew that *something* was going on at Moon Shadow and it *wasn't* a business meeting. It was another of Bane's secrets and bitter-ness filled him again.

"Not to stay, Omar. Just to get my stuff. I've ... I've got to leave," Nick said. "Jade, I hope I can stay with you."

"It's *our* apartment, Nick," she said sadly. "Of course, you can stay."

Omar then pulled out into traffic, though it was clear that he wanted to say something, anything, but he knew there was nothing he could do to change Nick's mind. They drove in si-lence to Jade's apartment. When she got out, she looked back at him for long moments before, finally, shutting the door. Nick swallowed down the grief that filled him at her knowing, sad look.

Every moment on the way to Moon Shadow, Nick thought of Bane. He replayed every great time they'd had together. The picnic. The fountain. That first night together. He re-played the bad ones, too, like Bane's happiness at seeing the Fairfaxes on the street. But those memories didn't last. He held onto the good ones. By the time they made it to Moon Shadow, Nick felt hollowed out. He didn't want to leave. He wanted Bane desperately. But there was no choice. This couldn't go on.

What if Bane doesn't come after me? What if Bane refuses to change? What if I lose him forever by doing this? Yet I have no choice. He's made it so there's no choice.

Nick got out of the Maybach with such a heavy heart that his shoulders were pulled forward. Omar hopped out of the car, but not with his normal happy energy, but more with a frantic need to do or say something that would change things.

Nick held up a hand. "Omar, you can't fix this for Bane. This is all him."

Omar's shoulders slumped. "I know. I've always known this. But I hoped ..."

"Me, too," Nick said wearily. "I *still* hope."

Omar looked up, lips parted, about to say something, but all he did was shake his head in the end and that summed up Nick's fears perfectly. Bane wasn't going to change. This was likely the last time he was going to see Moon Shadow. Bane would probably throw his family out on the street when he found out that Nick had left him. Nick was likely dooming the Fairfaxes to a life of poverty.

I've lost my family, too. They won't want anything to do with me. Jake was right. I never should have started dating Bane. As soon as he let me out of the deal, I should have left.

If there was a way he could have made things worse, he didn't know what it was.

Nick trudged into the house and up the stairs to his bedroom. He stripped off the beautiful clothes that Mr. Fioretti had made for him and toed off the Italian leather shoes. He neatly folded the clothes and placed them on the bed. He grabbed a pair of jeans, a ripped white t-shirt, his battered leather jacket and boots. He dressed in those. He pulled his saddlebags out of the bottom of the closet and put in them *only* what he had brought with him that first night to Moon Shadow. He would ask Omar to ship the rest of his things to him, not the ones that Bane had purchased for him, but just the things his father had inexpertly packed.

He then pulled out his wallet. He took out the credit card that Bane had insisted on giving him. He placed it on the bed beside the clothes in a prominent position so that Bane wouldn't miss it. Somehow, he'd have to find a way to pay back the school loan and all the money that Bane had given him. He pulled out all the cash in the wallet and folded it beneath the credit card. A down payment.

He hoisted his saddlebags over his right shoulder and walked to the door of his bedroom. He took one last long look at the moonlight flooded room. His eyes went from the bed where Bane had once held him to the chairs where he had imagined himself and Bane sitting with Bane looking at him with love.

He was going to ride his motorcycle back the same way he had come here months ago. It felt like years. He didn't feel like the same person. He wasn't the same person. He'd changed in ways he'd never expected and not all of them were for the good.

I never thought I'd fall in love with Bane. I never thought I'd regret leaving here. I've lost everything. But I have no choice, but to go.

Nick's heart twisted, but he forced himself to turn and walk away from the only true home he'd ever known.

CHAPTER TWENTY-SIX

CHASE

L*ater that night ...*
        Bane's head was spinning as he sagged against Moon
Shadow's front doors. His vision kept *flaring* from human to
beast to human again. Nausea and weakness plucked at him
with bony fingers. He had used all his strength to control the
beast in that awful, last fight with Nick.

He'd said unforgivable things to the man he loved. He'd
known they were awful as soon as he'd said them and hated
himself the whole time, but he'd had no control to spare from
controlling the beast to control his primal thoughts. He knew
full well that Nick would *never* relish even the deserving getting their comeuppance, especially his own family. That was
part of Nick's personality, his goodness, one of the things that
drew Bane to him.

Bane could tell himself that he wished Nick free of his
family for *Nick's* sake, but that was not true. He just wanted
Nick for *himself.* Nick's family was an impediment to that—or
so he'd feared. He saw that now. Nick's arguments for why
couldn't he just put the Fairfaxes back in charge of Fairfax International and watch them, correcting their excesses, trying
to actually teach the brothers—if not the father—a better way
to do business was completely legitimate. And wouldn't that

be *better* than to simply *punish* them? Steven and Jake were smart and young enough to change. Charles, too, needed to just be shown the carrot and he'd go after it. But Bane had wanted to *destroy* them.

So Nick would have nowhere to go if he left me. Except Jade. Perhaps I would have gone after her next. He felt sick. He hated himself. He truly did not deserve Nick. *What have I done?*

Bane felt the beast's paw against his chest. He could *see* his skin stretching and the tips of the claws pushing out and dimpling his flesh. He pushed them back in and let out a helpless laugh.

"I have until midnight, you bastard beast," he muttered to it.

He could blame the beast for *some* of what had happened tonight. The beast had choked off his reason, kept him fighting for control. It had been *afraid* of losing Nick, too. It had seen him and Nick arguing, sensed Nick's pain and disbelief, known that Bane was *blowing it.* And it had tried to take control, which had just made things worse.

You scared him! Just like I told you! He shouted at the beast.

The beast snarled at him, ears back, teeth bared. He'd never seen it so angry before. But he didn't care.

If you ruined things with Nick —

The threat went unfinished. He had done the majority portion of ruining things himself. He needed to talk to Nick. He'd thought to call the young man, before he lost control completely to the beast, apologize profusely, agree to whatever terms Nick wanted. He couldn't meet Nick in person again unless he wanted the young man to see all his secrets. But he'd lost his cellphone somewhere, probably left it at the event. So he'd gone back to Moon Shadow. He intended to call Nick from there. Beg him to hold off judgment until the weekend was over—the full moon was done—and then do *anything* and *everything* to win Nick back.

I just have to call him and then the beast can take over. Just let me call Nick.

He opened the doors and staggered into the hallway. He was met by an alarmed, relieved and yet very angry Omar. The Indian man, strangely, was holding a feather duster.

Omar only cleans late at night when he is wildly upset.

"Bane! You're back! I thought—I thought you had transformed and ... well, you are back," Omar's voice fell off and the man started dusting an already dust free vase.

"Why are you cleaning?" Bane asked, holding onto the foyer's table. There was a huge bouquet of red roses there. Red as blood. His eyes blurred. He was losing it. He had to get into his office and call Nick. That was all he had the strength left to do.

"I'm—it's dusty! So I'm dusting! This is a large home, Bane! It's very hard to keep it clean by myself!" Omar snapped then he blinked back what looked like tears. "Especially since ..."

"Since what?" Bane pushed up from the table, the world spun, and he leaned back down.

"Since ... since nothing. You need to shift. We will talk ... talk *after*," Omar said and went back to dusting *furiously*.

And that was when Bane smelled *Nick*. It wasn't the old scent from Nick being there the day before or even earlier that day. No, Nick had been there *recently*.

Within the last hour.

"Is Nick here?" Bane's voice went high and tight. His senses fluctuated all over the place. He couldn't concentrate on finding Nick's heartbeat in the mansion.

Omar blanched, but then *firmed* his expression as he went primly back to dusting. "No, he is not."

Despair and relief paired in Bane. "Oh, of course, he's back at the condo with Jade."

"No, they are not there."

Dust. Dust. Dust.

"What?"

Dust. Dust. Dust.

Bane's heart beat so hard and fast that he thought it might jump out of his chest. "OMAR! What are you saying? Where is Nick? Tell me! Now!"

"He left and *you* are to blame! You are a pigheaded, foolish man! After all these years of life and you are so very stupid! You chase away the one for you!" Omar tossed down his duster. It was the first sign of real anger that Bane had ever seen the man make. The action was slightly lessened of its power as the feather duster landed lightly on the floor. Both of them looked at it settled softly onto the ground.

"He's gone?" Bane's voice sounded like a ghost's.

Omar nodded. "I do not know what you argued about –"

"His family. I said ... unforgivable things," Bane whispered. His legs felt like they were going to go out from under him. The beast was standing there utterly still.

"Well, I am certain that did not help matters." Omar wagged his finger at Bane. "But it was your *secrets* that made him go. He could see that something was *wrong*. He knew you were *lying* about what was causing you to be ill and the meeting this weekend and everything! There can be *no love without trust.*"

With every word, Bane's heart shriveled. "He has just left for the weekend. Nick will be back."

Omar stared at him with a look of ultimate sadness in his eyes. "No, Bane. Nick has left for *good.*"

Bane didn't remember if he said anything to Omar in response. He barely remembered throwing the foyer's table over in his haste to get to the stairs. There was a smash as the vase that held the huge arrangement of roses shattered on the floor. He was flying up the steps. His hands were slick with fever sweat on the banister. His vision shimmered as he hit Nick's door and slammed it open. The door handle popped through the wall from the force of it. He staggered inside.

Nick's things were all there. He could see that from the open closet doors, but then he reassessed. Everything that *he* had given Nick was still there. But Nick's things? The things that Nick had brought with him that first night? Gone ...

Bane's gaze slid to the bed. There were the clothes that Nick had worn that night. He stutter stepped over to the bed and picked up the shirt and brought it to his nose. He took in huge draughts of Nick's smell. The scent only slightly calmed the wild beating of his heart. That was when he saw the credit card and money placed just so on the bed. He slowly reached for both and brought them up to look at them like he had never seen cash and a credit card before. They fell from his suddenly numb fingers.

He's gone ...

Nick's left me ...

My mate is gone ...

Pain had him doubling over as if someone had punched him in the gut. He sank to the ground as he felt his claws scraping against the inside of his skin. He fell flat, his hands and feet beating a tattoo on the ground as he went into a fit. The shift had never been so painful. Bane wasn't fighting it. He had lost Nick. He *deserved* all the pain that was coming. He felt the beast simply *rip* out of him.

The beast arose from the floor in its magnificent form of black and white. The moonlight stroked its coat. It lifted its massive head back and roared.

And then the beast spoke, *You have failed. You have lost our mate. Now it is my turn. We do things my way. Nick has run. So I will chase.*

The Story Concludes in Cursed: Beloved Book 3 (M/M Modern Retelling of Beauty & the Beast).